FALLING IN LOVE

"You're so pretty," Ross whispered, his voice touching her heart with each word that passed his lips. "And so full of fight. I want you, Alexandra. Let me love you a little."

Alexandra stood on the same cliff that had been torturing her since she first walked into the cabin. A warm, delicious breeze was on her face, and her heart suddenly took wing. She leaned forward and tumbled off the edge as Ross pressed his lips to hers.

Falling.

Falling so fast.

Intense desire flowed through her as every thought was given up to the tender delight of being held captive by this man . . .

LAUREN KING
TENDER TEMPTATION

ZEBRA BOOKS
KENSINGTON PUBLISHING CORP.

Author's Note

The following story involves a mine called the Alexandra. Though Yavapai County, Arizona, boasts a mine of the same name, the two are completely unrelated. In addition, the events I have described as having occurred at a nonexistent place called Carver, are based loosely upon similar events that happened at Stanton. Lastly, both Sheriff Goodwin and Deputy Barnes are entirely fictitious.

—L.K.

Gold is where you find it!   — Anonymous

Chapter One

Arizona Territory, 1880.

Ross Halleck drew rein a couple of miles outside of Phoenix and watched the autumn sun ease behind the mountains to the west. He was bone weary from his trek out of Texas and paused for a few minutes to rest his horse, his aching limbs, and his mind.

Removing his hat, he wiped a film of sweat from his brow with the sleeve of his shirt, then settled the hat back down on his head. If only he could shake the unease that had been tensing up his shoulders for the past several days. He was fully aware someone was riding hard on his backtrail. He had waited two hours at the ferry before crossing the Salt River hoping the hombre would show his face, but apparently he wasn't of a mind to. Now, as he looked out over the desert, at the narrow line of buildings barely visible through the dusk gloom, he sensed that the rider wasn't far behind him.

But that wasn't all that weighed him down just now.

The fact was, his life had been turned upside down for maybe the hundredth time and he couldn't be

9

content with it. Not this time. His habit had always been to find solace in nature when his fortunes shifted. Flowers budded, bloomed to glory, then died shortly afterward. Full-grown trees could be suddenly uprooted during a heavy rain and plunged down a wash that had been dry for ten years. Life seemed to work that way, even for a man and especially in the untamed territories of the West.

Maybe it was his age. He wouldn't see his twenties again, and he wasn't quite as willing as he might have been ten years ago to simply shrug his shoulders and push on after he kicked through the burnt embers of his ranch and found nothing left to his name but his horse, his rifle, and what he carried in his saddlebags. Instead, something in him had bucked hard against the attack on his ranch. He had been robbed of a future for which he had worked nigh on eight years, and he was still angry and heavy-hearted because of it.

As he watched the gray of night spilling into the melon-colored sunset, a great feeling of sadness swept over him, burning his heart like a hot wind blowing out of the north. The sensation passed quickly enough, but left in its stead an emptiness he could no longer ignore.

He was alone again, a desolate feeling that unnerved him since he considered himself a strong man, fit for life in any rough frontier territory. He knew how to survive in a blizzard or in the unforgiving deserts of the Southwest; he had fought a Comanche to the death and lived to tell about it; he had punched beeves from drought-parched lands, across swollen floodwaters, through mile after mile of endless prairie and never faltered once. His strength and skill was equal to challenging the land, he was confident of that. But how useless he felt to waging war on something as intangible as the longings of his heart, especially when he'd done his best to find the right woman to take as wife and had made such a bad mistake.

He'd left his betrothed, Katherine Douglas, in Texas, and he knew he'd never see her again. He never wanted to see her again, which was just as it should be since she refused to stand by him when disaster struck. And now he was alone with his hopes pinned to a frayed piece of paper he carried in his saddlebags—his rightful claim to the Alexandra, a mine in which he held eighty percent ownership and which he believed would help him rebuild his life. In the distance, he saw several lights appear magically, with more to follow, as Phoenix lit up its lanterns and coal oil lamps.

Night now owned the land as a chill October breeze swept over Ross. He was about to give his horse a gentle kick and continue down the trail when the smell of tobacco smoke drifted out of the northwest. By long habit, his entire body grew quiet and attentive. He had not lived in the West for most of his life without paying heed to the subtle warnings that a slight movement of air could deliver. If he could smell the smoke, then man was not far from him, possibly even concealed purposely from view.

He remained steady as he unloosed the thong of his Colt Peacemaker. His horse, too, sensed the presence of man nearby. The dun's ears were pricked forward, his head turned toward the north and he quivered once all over as though trying to shake a bad memory.

"Easy, boy," Ross whispered. He drew his gun from his holster and held it loosely in his hand. His eyes roved the dark shadows in the distance, trying to detect movement of any kind. Stands of saguaro and ocotillo cactus obscured his view. For a fraction of a second he saw a small burst of flame, then nothing, like someone lighting a cigarette. Every inch of his body grew tense, reaching toward the place where the light had appeared, trying to intuit if he faced friend or foe. And what of the man on his trail? He hadn't caught sight of him for some time, but he could be anywhere behind him now.

Still there was no movement to the northwest. He waited, his shoulder tight as his arm supported the weight of his gun. He breathed deeply, waiting. More than once, having a little more patience than his enemy had saved his life.

Finally, the shadows spoke to him as two riders, then another, eased out of a shallow gully from the north. A tall saguaro blocked them partially from view as they drew to a halt some forty yards from him.

"Hola!" one of the men called to him in an almost jovial voice. His inflection was clearly Mexican as he spoke. "We're looking for a friend of ours. His name is Halleck, from Texas. He's supposed to be on the trail but we not seen him. You met him a ways back, maybe?"

Ross frowned, clicking the hammer of his pistol back. He didn't like the sound of the man's voice and everything about the situation felt wrong.

"What do you want with him?" Ross called out toward the men who were now inching their horses slowly forward. "You sure he's a friend of yours?"

There was a long pause and he thought he heard the riders muttering to one another. From years of sizing men up Ross knew these hombres didn't have a

12

picnic planned for him. He leveled his pistol toward the approaching band and prepared to face them off. He was about to demand they state their business with him when the dun suddenly swung his head up and down, issuing Ross a warning. The horse twisted his head back toward Ross's right shoulder, but by that time it was too late. He caught sight of a fourth man coming up behind him, the man who'd been on his trail, just as the gunman's pistol blossomed a brilliant orange and the sound of the discharge shattered the peaceful night air.

· Ross felt the bullet slam into his right side, nearly unseating him. His own pistol fired high into the air with the shock of the slug's impact and he held onto the Peacemaker only by sheer habit, guiding it instinctively back into the holster on his right hip.

At the same moment, the dun bolted forward at a dead run heading toward town. He was a fine, rugged horse and Ross had ridden him at an easy pace through the demanding desert. The dun's powerful legs pounded into the packed dirt of the road, sending dust flying behind him. Ross hunched himself into his saddle, using the strength of his knees to keep from slipping away from the onward momentum of the gelding's flight. He was overcome by a blinding pain in his side as the sounds of gunfire at his back broke over him again and again. He heard one of the men shout, "Get his saddlebags!" And the rest whooped loudly in the excitement of their chase. Every stride the dun took pulled at Ross's burning flesh and he wanted nothing more than to slide from the saddle in an effort to stop the pain. But he knew he'd be dead for certain. Whoever had laid for him intended not only to rob him, but to send him to an early grave. But why? He had no money to speak of, anyone who was familiar with him in Texas knew that much. He had only the deed to his mine.

The mine!

He spurred the gelding on, holding fast to the reins as the dun kept up his murderous pace. He heard the gunmen swear at him, violent words that rent the air harmlessly. Through his thickening mind, he heard their curses grow fainter and fainter. Apparently, they had not counted on the fortitude of his desert-bred mustang outstripping their own horses.

The cold air buffeted his face and kept him conscious. His shirt smelled burnt and stuck to his body where blood soaked the dusty blue cotton fabric.

The dun covered the first mile easily but was breathing hard as the outskirts of Phoenix wavered before Ross's unsteady vision. He had only one thought—to get as far into the city as he could before he stopped, hoping that his stormy, headlong entry would keep his assailants from pursuing him and attracting the attention of the law. Justice on the frontier was frequently a hasty and immediate affair, and more than one outlaw had met his maker shortly on the heels of committing his crime.

By the time Ross reached the first outcropping of buildings, he felt strangely cold and could no longer hear the gunmen behind him. He didn't want to stop, though. Even to take a moment to turn around and see if he was still being followed could cost him his life. He pressed on, his vision blurred, his side feeling like a knife had lodged deeply into his flesh. He was doubled over now, the dun dropping to an easy lope as the traffic of the street started to thicken. A moment more and the gelding slowed to a walk, picking his way through wagons, buggies, carts, riders on horseback, and men and women crossing the street at their leisure.

The stars faded in deference to the mounting city lights. Ross blinked frequently now, trying to clear his vision. In the distance, he saw the hotel he had stayed at the last time he'd come to Phoenix. He headed for it, the dun blowing hard from his flight across the desert.

Ross couldn't make out the faces of the people around him at all, but he could see that many curious folk stopped in their tracks and turned to stare at him as he passed by.

He heard a young boy call out, "Hey, that man's bleeding. Look here in the dust!"

Only a few feet more . . .

Chapter Two

Alexandra Wingfield was sitting in the dining parlor of her hotel in Phoenix, near a window overlooking the main thoroughfare when the boy's cry reached her ears, "Hey, that man's bleeding. Look here in the dust!"

Lifting her gaze toward the window that fronted the street, she could just see over the white lace curtain running the width of the glass panes. A second later, a rider appeared within view, slumped in his saddle. The dim, sporadic lighting from the stores lining either side of the street played unevenly on the stranger's face. Even so, she could tell that his complexion was pale, his expression drawn and tight with pain. He looked to be about thirty, with a certain rugged quality etched into the lines of his face. He was clearly a man of the West, his lean legs molded to his horse as he struggled to remain in the saddle.

Alexandra sat very still, her fork poised in midair. She was mesmerized by the sight of him as he pulled the reins in the direction of the hotel. He was badly hurt and had trouble guiding his horse. She noticed that any number of people stopped to watch his progress but didn't rush to his aid. They appeared stunned themselves as though they, too, had been injured.

She glanced about the dining parlor to see if anyone else had heard the young boy's cry or noticed the rider, but everyone seemed intent upon their plates. Remembering her own childhood, and the years her family had drifted from one mining camp to the next, Alexandra knew an urgency to help the man. Maybe it was these early experiences that had trained her to action, but sometimes speed was the only thing that saved a man's life when he was bleeding. And if nothing else, blood had flown constantly in the camps, where violent gunplay, horrible accidents, and disease ran rife.

The stranger disappeared from view and Alexandra rose to her feet abruptly. If anyone noticed her hasty departure from the dining room, she was not aware of it. The long silk skirts of her blue gown rustled as she moved quickly into the wide, carpeted lobby. Looking toward the street, she could see the rider through the glass doors at the far end of the vestibule and watched as he stopped in front of the hotel, dismounting slowly. She expected to see him fall to the ground. Instead, he supported himself by leaning heavily against his horse.

Alexandra approached the fine mahogany desk at the opposite end of the lobby. A balding clerk was half bent over a stack of ledgers when she addressed him. "Mr. Turnbull, I believe that man needs help," she said, gesturing toward the doors. "Do you see him? He can hardly stand. Would you please send someone to fetch a doctor."

The clerk, who had been busily scratching figures into one of the thick black books, looked up at her

17

and then glanced toward the door. He was a portly man, who covered his bare pate with a few strands of oily hair combed in a gentle wave across the top of his head. His spectacles sat very low on his nose and served to enhance the fact that he was clearly unimpressed with what he saw. "Do you mean that cowpoke hugging his horse?" he asked, surprised. When Alexandra nodded, he continued. "I reckon he's seen the elephant. Never you mind, ma'am, I'll send him away directly." He pushed his spectacles back up to the bridge of his nose and returned to his books.

He was about to dip his pen into the brass inkwell in front of him when Alexandra took hold of the inkwell and waved it beneath his nose. "I don't think he's drunk a'tall," she responded politely. "I believe he's been hurt. In fact, I'm sure of it. So, unless you want your shiny head dyed a real pretty black, I suggest you help that man."

The clerk backed away from the desk, his gaze fixed to the inkpot in Alexandra's hand. "Now, now, Mrs. Bradshaw," he cried. "You just settle down. I'll take care of it!" He blinked rapidly several times, then scooted quickly toward the door.

By this time, the drover had moved away from his horse and was attempting to gain his balance to the apparent fascination of several people who had begun gathering about him.

Alexandra followed the clerk outside, and before the cowboy came into view, she heard the clerk cry out, "God almighty, he's been shot!"

Alexandra moved to stand beside the clerk, her gaze drawn to the stranger's stomach and waist. His blue shirt appeared mangled and burnt beneath a wet, dark smear of blood that extended from his chest to his right hip. Dust and the faint smell of gunpowder hung about him. His hands were covered with blood where he had tried to stanch the flow from his side. He held a kerchief there, his efforts only partly successful in arresting the wound's damage.

The crowd was silent. Even Alexandra remained frozen for an instant of time.

The stranger, though pale and in great pain, smiled faintly. "If you wouldn't mind too much," he said, his voice hoarse as he addressed Mr. Turnbull, "I am in need of lodgings for the night. And a doctor, I expect."

"Someone help this man," the clerk uttered in a small, wavering voice, then turned back into the hotel, his face pasty white.

Alexandra glanced about the crowd with a quick jerk of her head. The dreadful sight of the stranger's wounds seemed to have immobilized everyone, and for this reason she grabbed the arm of a young cowboy next to her. He had his thumbs hooked over the belt of his sidearms and stared at the boardwalk beneath the man's boots. His expression dazed, he watched droplets of blood form a pool at the rider's feet. "Fetch the doctor!" she cried, giving his arm a shake. "This man will bleed to death if he's not taken care of. Do you hear me?"

"Yes'm!" he responded, looking at her with a startled expression. He turned on his heel immediately afterward, his spurs jingling wildly as he started down the street at a run.

"Was it Apaches?" A woman's panicked voice cried out. "I've got kin near Bumble Bee!"

"Never mind that!" Alexandra cried. "Someone get this man inside the hotel."

Just as the stranger's knees buckled, a tall, thin

19

man moved on a quick, firm step toward the injured rider, catching him before he toppled onto the boardwalk and supporting him about his waist. Another man rushed to hold the door open as the rider was led inside.

Alexandra turned to a strapping lad who had watched the cowboy with great interest, all the while chewing noisily on stringy strands of jerked meat. She wondered how he was able to eat at all, and pressed a hand to her own stomach, which was now churning unhappily. "How about lending me a hand with this man's saddlebags?" she asked. "You look like a strong boy! I'll bet you could wrestle a bear with one hand tied behind your back."

The boy, surprised at being addressed, choked on a bit of the leathery meat, then stuffed the remainder of it into his pocket. "Yes'm!" he exclaimed. "I'd be right proud to help, though I don't claim to be able to wrestle no bear. I did tangle with a mean hog once, and whupped him, too!" As he eagerly worked the bags off the horse, he added, "I'll take him to the stable if you like—the horse, I mean."

Alexandra nodded as a third man took the saddlebags from the boy, flipped them over his shoulder, and carried them into the hotel. Once she was sure the stranger's horse would be looked after, Alexandra returned to the lobby. The cowboy was settled on a hard bench near the stairs and she stood to one side as the men packed the wound with their kerchiefs and talked in a rattle of low voices to him. She was just far enough away that she could not make out all of what they were saying, but she heard scraps about bandits, about being attacked not far from here, and about four armed men.

The clerk approached Alexandra, a thin film of

perspiration beaded upon his lip. "Cowboys," he grunted. "Why, he don't look like he could afford a flask of whiskey nonetheless a room in this hotel. I should've sent him to the stables with his horse."

Alexandra glanced at the clerk and smiled. "Why, your Christian charity overwhelms me, Mr. Turnbull!" she responded tartly.

His cheeks, still pale from having been upset by the sight of the cowboy's wounds, now turned a dark shade of red. "I have my job to do," he retorted, straightening his spine and pinching his lips together.

Alexandra said nothing in return but merely stared at him until he cleared his throat and moved back to his desk where he began studying his ledgers again.

Left alone, Alexandra glanced at the rider, who was leaning his head against the wall. He wore the garb of a cowboy—leather shotgun chaps over rugged pants, a faded blue shirt, and a black, worn hat which now sat on the floor beside his chair. Her heart might have been softer than Mr. Turnbull's, but her opinion of the general character of cowboys wasn't so different. Drovers worked hard, earned little, and spent what they had as quickly as they made it. The clerk had reason to be skeptical.

At the same time something about the man struck Alexandra as different from the usual run of cowboys. For one thing, his steel-gray eyes, as he spoke to one of the men bending over him, were quite intense and full of purpose. His chin, too, seemed molded to some inner determination. In other ways, he looked like a cowboy—in his dress, the way his body had seemed fitted to his horse, and in the way his skin, though still quite pale from a loss of blood, was noticeably tanned—no doubt from riding herd for years on end. He possessed a firm mouth, a chin that was cleft faintly, and his cheekbones were downright arresting. A slight furrow seemed permanently fixed between thick, well-defined brows. Something about him, something intangible, spoke suddenly to her heart. Where was he from? Where was he going? Why had someone shot at him?

As though he had felt her thoughts, the cowboy turned toward her, and for a sliver of time, their eyes met. Alexandra had the strangest sensation that she had just looked deep into the future and it frightened her. How fast her heart beat! Who was this man anyway?

He blinked several times, and she knew he wasn't quite able to focus on her. To her surprise, he addressed her. "Ma'am," he said, his voice little more than a croak. "If it wouldn't be too much of a bother, would you please tell the ladies outside that I wasn't attacked by Indians. To the best I can figure, they were a band of Mexican outlaws hoping to rob me."

Alexandra was stunned by his request, as much by his politeness as by his consideration for the feelings of a stranger. "Of course I will," she responded, then hurried to the crowd who was still milling about on the boardwalk.

Alexandra delivered the cowboy's message and was about to turn back into the lobby when the doctor broke through the crowd.

"Where's my patient?" he cried. The lapel of his coat was turned under in evidence of his haste to care for the wounded stranger. He was a large man with graying hair, and had a kind look to his face. Alexandra greeted him with a quick explanation of what she had seen herself as well as what the cowboy had told her. While she spoke, he ushered her into

22

the hotel, listening carefully to her, nodding all the while.

When he spied the cowboy, he cried out, "So there you are! Well, well, you look like a strong man. I expect I didn't have to rush over here after all! Why didn't somebody tell me you were like to last out a month? I could've sat down to my supper like I'd planned to."

Alexandra smiled, liking the blunt manners of the doctor, his teasing words a sudden relief to her. She could see by his expression as he patted the cowboy on the shoulder then lifted the soaked kerchiefs to assess the damage that he was not gravely concerned by what he saw.

"Why, there's barely a scratch here," he exclaimed cheerfully. "And the bullet traveled clean through. You were very fortunate, Mr. . . ."

"Halleck," the rider responded quietly. "Ross Halleck."

Satisfied with his initial examination, the doctor begged for help in carrying Ross to a private room. Alexandra did not hesitate to direct the men to hers. They were in the process of doing so when the clerk turned on them, making a great fuss and flapping his arms. The doctor, however, would have none of it and roundly told the clerk not to make a jackass of himself. Afterward, he softened his tone and begged Mr. Turnbull to send a pot of hot water to Alexandra's room along with at least two ceramic washbowls.

The men were gone up the stairs before the clerk could protest further. Alexandra had grown tired of Mr. Turnbull and pulled a silver dollar from her netted bag, slipping it into his hand. "I hope this will make up for some of your in-

23

convenience," she said, whispering sweetly to him.

He seemed surprised and glanced nervously toward several guests who had just emerged from the dining room. He did not hesitate, however, to pocket the coins with a deft movement of his pudgy fingers. He smiled at Alexandra suddenly, and, returning to the desk, asked her if she would like another room for herself since poor Mr. Halleck now occupied hers. At the same time, he handed her his pen, suggesting she register for the brave cowboy who had so courageously survived such a vicious attack!

"And would you like Dovie to wake you up tomorrow morning?" he asked cheerfully. "She may be a bit slow, but she's always up and about, cleaning rooms and the like, before the sun's even cleared the Superstitions. I know you're heading up to Prescott tomorrow and, take my word for it—the Arizona Stage Company waits for nobody!"

Alexandra stared at Mr. Turnbull, unable to believe this was the same man who had grumbled about Mr. Halleck taking a room in his hotel. "Thank you," she said finally. "I'd appreciate that very much."

This was the West, she thought with a laugh. There were rarely soft, generous middles to people who lived on the frontier. They were all edges— rough, indifferent, or brutally sharp. And at times downright funny.

Chapter Three

The next morning Alexandra stood by the window of her room, brushing her long red hair in slow, smooth strokes, all the while staring down into the street. She felt restless, ill at ease, as though during the night she had been tormented by a dream that would not end. Only there was no dream. She had slept well, she just felt bruised in a funny way, like she'd spent the night sleeping on the floor.

Maybe Ross Halleck's gray eyes had pursued her in her dreams, she couldn't remember. But ever since she woke up, she felt like a train that had gotten side-tracked onto a spur with an unknown destination. She stopped brushing her hair in the middle of a stroke, aware suddenly that the sensation gripping her was very much like fear. But of what? she wondered.

Last night, after the doctor had finished disinfecting Mr. Halleck's wound and had wrapped his side up in a tight bandage that encircled his stomach, he had asked Alexandra if she would please clean his patient's hands, for they were caked with blood and dirt from his ordeal.

She had agreed to the task readily. Her heart went

out to the stranger whose brow was damp with perspiration from the pain-filled cleansing he had recently endured. The doctor had been merciless in his use of carbolic acid, hoping by doing so he could prevent infection from setting in.

Alexandra carried a white ceramic bowl full of hot water to the bedstand, setting it gently on a crotcheted doily. Afterward, she pulled up a chair to sit next to Ross. Using a soft cotton cloth drenched with water, she began slowly and gently rubbing his bare arms, wrists, and hands, and was not surprised to find that his skin felt warm with fever.

As she scrubbed the grime from his hands, she grew aware of how improper it was for her to be caring for him like this. She was still a maidenly young woman and had never even been married. The doctor, however, as well as the hotel clerk, believed her to be a widow, since she was traveling under the false name of Mrs. Bradshaw. She hated lying, but in order to journey easily from Independence to Prescott she had chosen to adopt the disguise. An innocent young woman of twenty, traveling alone, would cause a stir of curiosity. As it was, her supposed widowed state brought her a fair amount of respectful treatment and she hadn't once regretted her decision.

As her mind kept telling her that she ought not to be tending Mr. Halleck in this intimate way, she realized that part of the source of her discomfort was the disturbing fact that she liked the feel of his arms and hands as she cleaned them. There was something very pleasing to her about the coarseness of the black hair covering his strong, muscled arms. His shoulders were broad with strength and his muscles corded like twined rope. He had evidently seen many years of hard work and she could not restrain her admiration for the results of his labors. He was a fine-looking man.

She looked at his face, trying to determine again how old he was, and found his eyes closed. She thought that her first conclusion had been right, he could not be much above thirty years of age. At the same time, he seemed older, like he had endured many hardships.

His body bore indication of past struggles, marking him as a man destined to survive on the harsh western frontier. A long, faint scar ran along his forearm to his wrist, and her eyes were drawn to a second scar that extended across his stomach just beneath his chest. She couldn't help but wonder what manner of fight had resulted in such frightening sabrelike cuts.

She felt his hand tighten about hers suddenly. She had thought he had fallen asleep but soon discovered she was wrong. Her gaze again flew to his face and she found herself looking into a pair of eyes that seemed to slice right through her. For a long moment, she found it impossible to breathe.

"Anybody ever tell you how pretty you are?" he asked, still holding her hand. "And you've got a complexion I could almost taste, though I must say you're awful fair for the desert sun. Take pains to protect your skin out here or it'll blister like a spittle-bug." He spoke slowly, and with some difficulty, but behind each word she could hear a good humor she liked very much.

He was smiling faintly now and she felt the worst constriction of her heart as he spoke. A knot of pleasure shaped itself uncomfortably in the very pit of her stomach at being so close to the cowboy, but she didn't know why exactly. Perhaps it was his

27

strong, warm clasp as he held her hand or the direct-
ness of his gaze as he looked at her or it may have
been the fact that he was undressed from the waist
up.

But after a moment's thought she knew it was his
voice that warmed her up all over. He spoke in a
deep, rich-timbred tone that seemed to vibrate just
outside her heart, then pass quickly through, taking
a piece of her soul with it.

When she realized not only had she not responded
to what he said to her, but also that she was staring
at him, she laughed suddenly and pulled the red,
frizzy curls at the nape of her neck with her free
hand. "I'm sorry," she said. "It's very nice of you to
say so. I only hope you're feeling much better. You
were a sorry sight when you rode up to the hotel tonight. I thought the clerk was going to faint when he
saw how badly you were hurt."

The drover squeezed her hand. "I appreciate what
you've done for me, Mrs. Bradshaw," he said seriously. "I won't forget it. If there's ever anything I can
do for you, please let me know."

At this point, the doctor, who had been washing
his own hands in another bowl of water, dried them
off and then began rolling his sleeves down. "You do
have the whitest skin I've seen in ages," he said, addressing Alexandra and staring hard at her. "Mr.
Halleck is right, you know. You'd better do everything you can to keep yourself covered up. I've seen
some skin cases out here that never did heal up properly." He took his coat from off a peg on the back of
the door and began slipping it on as he continued.
"Now my wife doesn't have red hair, in fact it's a
healthy dark brown with just a sprinkling of gray,
but she has this delicate skin that I swear will burn if

28

you look at her cross-eyed. She makes this concoction for her face and hands by boiling some wool she gets from a Mexican sheepherder hereabouts. It cooks up into a fine lanolin and then she adds some cucumber to it. She's got one of the finest complexions around, and we've lived in Phoenix goin' on eight years now."

"I'm heading for Prescott tomorrow," Alexandra said hopefully, beginning to fear that if she dared step into the sun she would turn into a wrinkled fig.

"It's even worse up there," the doctor said with a firm nod of his head. "It's drier in the mountains. It may be cooler, but the air's real thin and to my way of thinking the sun's more direct and punishing because of it." He stopped suddenly, holding her gaze squarely. "Now why am I lecturing you as though you only have half a brain? You managed real fine with this cowpoke here, and if I do say so myself, I expect you know how to take care of yourself." He smiled suddenly, his face appearing like sunshine peeking through a cloud. "Good luck to you, Mrs. Bradshaw. I hope we may see you again sometime."

He finished shrugging into his coat, straightening each sleeve in turn and pulling down his vest. He shifted his affable face to his patient and said, "Well, I'd best be going. I've left you some laudanum to help you sleep if you need it. It's here in this glass all ready for you. I'll return tomorrow to check that wound. In the meantime, I want to leave you some extra bandages and some of this carbolic. Change the dressing once each day, more if you need to, until the wound has closed up tight and there's no sign of infection. I'd tell you to lie abed for about a week, but I have the distinct impression you'd laugh at me, so I'll just tell you to take it easy if you can."

29

After saying his supper was waiting, he inclined his head toward Alexandra and was gone.

She was at first embarrassed to have been left alone with a man who was very much a stranger to her. But when she saw that he was already drifting off to sleep, she ignored her discomfiture and began tidying the room. When the bowls of dirty water and Mr. Halleck's ruined clothing had been handed over to Dovie, Alexandra covered him carefully with a blanket and trimmed the lamp. By the time she closed the door to his room, he had fallen asleep.

Alexandra sighed deeply as she returned from her daydream. Pushing the white lace curtain back with her hand, noise from the street below rose to greet her in a cacophony of jingled traces, shouting masters, and groaning wagon wheels. She listened intently, the jostling movement of western life beating in symphony to the secret, unspoken, unrecognized longings of her heart. She could not even define the sweet uneasiness inside her. It was just there, beckoning her down a path that kept her nerves, at times, poised on the brink of shattering.

Letting the lace slide from her fingers, Alexandra watched the curtain dance back into place. She moved to the wood-framed mirror standing free in the corner of the room and regarded her reflection intently. She saw in her clear blue eyes not the determination she so desperately wanted to feel but rather a gnawing fear that she had made the most foolish decision of her life in coming to Arizona Territory.

Holding her silver-filigreed hairbrush tightly in hand, she continued brushing her hair as a sudden panic tied her stomach in a knot, making her feel as though she had cinched up her corset an inch too tight. She should have stayed in Missouri where she was safe and where her future was settled. She had the strongest sensation that all she was doing by coming west was chasing one of her papa's impossible dreams.

It wasn't too late, though. She still had a final leg of her journey to complete — from Phoenix to Prescott. Her father's mine, which he had described over and over in his letters, was located in a small camp some fifteen miles outside of Prescott near Bee Mountain. She didn't have to get on the stage this morning, she could just as easily purchase a ticket back to Independence — back to the life her uncle had so meticulously arranged for her, back to safety.

She laughed aloud suddenly, realizing if she returned to Missouri, she would not find independence at all, but rather her betrothed, William Bradshaw, who would make her life secure for years to come, all the while demanding implicit obedience from her as his wife. He wasn't unkind or hateful; he merely clung to his beliefs like a man who needed to be in prison in order to feel safe.

Thoughts of William strengthened Alexandra's conviction that she ought to continue on her present course. She felt at ease with herself again and was able to begin the difficult process of dressing her thick red hair. No matter whether the day was crackling dry or dripping wet, wild tendrils sought escape from the single braid she wove daily in an effort to subdue her curls. After several minutes of brushing, weaving, and stomping a frustrated foot, Alexandra finally finished dressing her hair. She had pinned her braid into a soft coil that wended its way from the crown of her head to the nape of her neck, and at long last she was pleased with the results.

She wore a light-blue traveling suit of fine silk

31

made high to the neck with a fitted bodice and a full, gathered skirt. She wished she had had time to purchase more serviceable clothing before she left Independence, but her departure had been as hasty as it was unplanned. She had not had time to consider her needs carefully.

Even her hat was a fragile, wispy straw confection topped with a white silk bow and a garland of artificial pink roses pinned along the narrow brim. It would be of little use to her in Prescott and would do even less to protect her from the harsh sun as she set it daintily on the crown of her head. The brim curved over her forehead slightly, and with a smile Alexandra realized that even though the hat was completely impractical, she loved it.

As she looked at her reflection in the mirror, she remembered how Mr. Halleck had told her she was pretty, and she felt a curious warmth wash over her. It felt very fine to have a man compliment her, to look at her face and see a little beauty residing there. For herself, she had always been content with how she looked. Her nose was straight, her brows curved over large blue eyes and her lips, though not generous, were well shaped. A funny thought struck her. Maybe if William had told her even once she was pretty, she might have stayed in Missouri. Was that what she wanted then, to have a man tell her she was pretty? That was part of it; at the same time, she knew it was far more complicated than the mere passing of compliments.

Pinning her hat to the coils of her braid with a long rapierlike pin, Alexandra took a deep breath knowing that she could not turn back now. She would go to Prescott and see what awaited her there. She picked up her heavy carpetbag and set her foot-

32

steps toward Prescott, toward her papa's mine, toward the future.

As she crossed the threshold into the hall, she wondered suddenly if she should knock on Mr. Halleck's door and find out if he needed her assistance with anything. Her mind told her that he was clearly a man capable of fending for himself and she would do well to simply pass his room by. But her heart was suddenly full of mischief, begging her to stop and say good-bye to the cowboy before she headed north. After all, she would probably never see him again.

Her heart began beating furiously and she felt silly, but why should she? Last night she had seen to his welfare and it would only be natural if she looked in on him. But the doctor intended to do as much; she wasn't needed for that reason.

Knowing she shouldn't, she walked boldly up to his door anyway. She lifted her hand to knock, but at that same moment, the door flew open and he was suddenly standing before her, his shirt open to the waist, a hand pressed to his side, his eyes narrowed with pain.

Chapter Four

He seemed as surprised as she was. "Mrs. Bradshaw," he said, frowning.

"Oh, my goodness!" she cried, taking a step backward. "I I wasn't expecting—that is, I just stopped on my way to the depot to ask how you were feeling." She felt a blush stain her cheeks as she looked at him, for his shirt was only partially buttoned and hung open to the waist. He seemed taller than she remembered and she felt overwhelmed in his presence. His eyes were red-rimmed from his ordeal of the night before, but otherwise his gaze was direct and thoughtful. Perhaps too much so, she thought, as he looked her up and down, a frown deepening between his brows. She realized in that moment that he disapproved of her somehow.

"I was just coming to ask you to help me change my bandage," he said. "But I can see that you are too finely dressed. I wouldn't think of pestering you."

Alexandra tilted her head slightly and could not keep from retorting, "Well, how do you suppose I was dressed last night, Mr. Halleck? As I recall events of the evening before, I don't think my gown stopped me from helping you then. Nor would it now. If you need my assistance, I hope you don't think I would refuse you because of my clothes. *Your* manners maybe, but not *my* clothes."

He was evidently surprised by this speech, and for a long moment did not respond. When he did, it was with a slight inclination of his head. "I've prickled your hide but good, haven't I?" he said. "Well, I'm sorry. I didn't mean to. And I do need your help. That is, I need *someone* to help me replace this bandage. Maybe that girl, what's her name? Dovie? Maybe she could lend me a hand."

"Mr. Halleck," Alexandra said, her head lowered and her hands clutching the handle of her carpetbag tightly, "if you say one more word, you'll regret it — I promise you! I will be more than happy to remove your bandage, and even happier still to swab your wound with a generous amount of the carbolic the good doctor left for you. After which, I'll apply a new bandage, but I may in the process wrap it about your neck and tie it very tight! Would that suit you?"

A slow smile spread over the cowboy's features. "Very much, I think," he responded, his eyes lighting up with laughter. Stepping aside, he permitted her to enter the room, but his gaze never left her face.

Alexandra refused to look at him, not because she was angry, but because the moment he started to smile, she got that funny feeling again, like she had last night when he looked straight into her eyes and said she was pretty. It was a sort of quivering warmth that stunned her heart and caused it to skip at least one beat.

"You've put the fear of God into me, ma'am," he added, closing the door as he spoke. "I wouldn't dare refuse you now, not with your blue

35

eyes flashing fire about as bright as your red hair!"

Alexandra tried not to smile. "That's much better," she said, amazed at the strange feelings that had begun working inside her.

As the door clicked shut, Alexandra turned to face him. She felt uneasy now that she was alone with this sturdy drover as well as by the fact that he stood between her and the door. She set her carpetbag down and moved to the bureau upon which sat the extra bandages and disinfectant the doctor had left for his patient.

Glancing over at Mr. Halleck, Alexandra saw that he was still smiling as he slowly unbuttoned the rest of his shirt. She knew a need to distract her mind from what he was doing because the warmth she had felt earlier seemed to have stayed with her and only increased at the sight of his chest covered with curly black hairs and his flat stomach ridged with muscles.

Intending to ask him about the desperadoes who attacked him, she began, "Mr. Halleck —" but he cut her off immediately.

"Please call me Ross," he said as his shirt fell open completely. "I have always made it a practice when a woman saves my life to permit her to call me by my Christian name."

"I hardly saved your life," she said. "Though I am astonished you are able to walk about this morning. You must be in some pain."

He shook his head. "It's taking this shirt on and off and other simple things that cut through my side. I find I can walk around easy enough, but I can't seem to get my clothes on without breaking the wound open and, as for the bandage, I feel like a newborn babe."

Alexandra suggested he sit on the bed while she

36

helped him take his shirt off, then asked if he knew why he had been attacked.

He shook his head. "I'm not sure," he responded, his eyes narrowing as though he was searching through his mind for an answer. "I have an idea, but it just doesn't seem right. I intend to see the sheriff today. Maybe he can make sense of it."

He didn't appear to want to talk about it further and fell silent as Alexandra took each of the sleeves of his shirt in turn and eased them gently off his arms. She began untying the bandage, and in doing so found herself bending close to his face. The brim of her hat struck his forehead and she drew back with a laugh. "I'm sorry," she said, her cheeks growing warm. She leaned away from him as she continued to work the bandage loose.

How nervous she felt. She had entered his room boldly enough once he had succeeded in raising her hackles. But now her fingers were trembling as she fumbled with the tightly wound strips of white cloth. She was very uncomfortable working so close to him.

The faint smell of soap, mingled with leather, assailed her. It was a pleasant redolence and she glanced at Ross, a little surprised. She saw a fleck of soap beside his ear and realized he had just shaved. How could he have done so much when he had been shot up the night before?

He seemed to sense her amazement and drew away from her slightly. "And I suppose that look means you are astonished to discover I use a razor," he said with a frown.

"No," she cried, startled by the spark of anger in his eyes. "Not at all. It's just that I'm having a hard enough time believing you're actually walking

37

around, nonetheless without a day's stubble on your face. What a funny opinion you seem to have of me, Mr. Halleck—that is, Ross."

He begged her pardon again, but as for offering an explanation, he said he supposed he was a touch ragged from having had a bullet chew up his side. She was not convinced this was the sum of his thoughts.

Alexandra resumed her task, her fingers clumsily working the bandages, since her hands were still quivering a little. She made one loop of the white strip of cotton when her hat bumped his forehead again. "For heaven's sake," she cried as she stepped away from him. "What a nuisance! I'll take it off." She returned to the bureau and unpinned her hat, hoping at the same time that her fingers would cease trembling. She set the hat next to the bottle of carbolic and turned around.

As she did so, she was surprised to find Ross gazing at her figure in a devastating manner. She felt frozen in place by the hunger she saw in his eyes and knew an instinct to flee from his room.

"You've got the smallest waist I've ever laid eyes on," he said, the deep timbre of his voice seeming to compress the distance between them.

"Ross, please," she responded quietly, her voice a mere whisper, her heart feeling tight within her breast. "If—if you want me to stay and help you, you can't say things like that to me."

The air in the room felt weighted and treacherous, like the sky before a thunderstorm. Alexandra couldn't move, nor could she tear her gaze from Ross's face.

He relaxed suddenly, shaking his head as though he felt confused. "I guess I've got to beg your pardon

38

again," he said. "I've been too long on the trail and my manners are in sad shape. I'll do better, I promise. I'll hold my tongue, but I won't say that my thoughts will always be as circumspect."

Alexandra let out her breath, unaware until she did so that it had been trapped in her chest. She approached him again and began unwinding his bandages, wondering why, from the moment he had opened the door, they had been near to quarreling or why, *why,* she felt so vulnerable with him?

The dressing was stained heavily with blood, some of it fresh, which brought the doctor to mind along with his belief that he would be unable to keep the drover confined to a bed for any reasonable length of time. It seemed he was right.

"You ought to be resting, Ross, not shaving and moving about," she said finally. His skin still felt warm to the touch where her fingers brushed against his stomach and back as she passed another loop around him.

"So what brings you to Arizona Territory, Mrs. Bradshaw?" he asked.

Somehow she wasn't surprised that he ignored her suggestion. Hearing him address her by her false name, however, made her wish to get rid of it as soon as she could. "I think you should know," she responded with a smile, "that I hold the conviction that when a man believes a certain woman has saved his life—even if it's not true—he has the right to address her by her Christian name. Please call me Alexandra." She was blushing faintly by the end of this speech. She had her reward, however, for he was smiling at her in a warm manner that indicated he approved of her.

"That's funny," he said. "It's an unusual name and

39

yet I know two of you. Alexandra. You have a good strong name. I think it suits you well."

She was passing the bandage behind him again and found herself close to his chest. She would have asked him about the other *Alexandra,* but she was too embarrassed by what she was doing and instead, began, "I don't mean to be practically hugging you every time I do this—"

He cut her off with a bright, "Hey! If you hear me complaining about being hugged by the likes of you, just figure I've lost my mind and fetch the doctor."

Alexandra laughed again, feeling some of her embarrassment slip away. She then responded to his first question. "As it happens, I have come to Arizona to settle a matter of business in Prescott. I don't think I'll be staying long. My home is in Missouri and I hope to return there within the month." Her throat grew tight as she considered the difficulty of the task before her. She had never received the deed to her papa's mine. She hoped the matter was simple, that it had not made the long trek through the mails from Prescott to Independence. She hadn't even known of the mine until but two weeks ago when William told her that it was his belief her father had left her a mine, and that her uncle had withheld this information from her.

He had been right. Her uncle, for all his good intentions, had even withheld a dozen letters from her father—any that had made mention of the mine. Though she had tried time and again to forgive her uncle for this officious act, her heart was still hardened against him. He had passed away some three months earlier, but even in death, it would seem, his oppressive hand reached out to her, and she resented it mightily.

40

She had come now to secure the deed to the mine: if she could, to lay claim to her rightful inheritance. Her hope, if the mine proved to be worth anything, was to sell it and return to Independence with money she could call her own. She was not sure why this was so important to her, she just knew that if there was the smallest chance she could be independent, she would pursue it.

As she continued to unwind the dressing, Alexandra was amazed at how careful the doctor had been to protect his patient's wound from possible infection. Each time she looped the bandage about Ross's waist, she was sure she was nearly finished, but another layer would appear. And each time she made a pass of the dressing behind his back, she came into such close proximity to him that she could feel his breath on her hair.

"You smell good," he said, his voice low.

She clucked at him, reminding him that he had promised to behave himself.

"I'm sorry," he said quickly. "Forgot myself. I won't say it again, but I'll think it." After a moment's pause, he asked, "Have you been widowed long?"

Alexandra stiffened slightly at his question. Seeming to sense that she was disturbed by his inquiry, Ross continued. "I don't mean to pester you, but you aren't wearing your blacks so I supposed it's been some time."

"You're not pestering me at all," Alexandra responded truthfully. She felt a prickle of guilt discussing her widowhood with Ross, or anyone, since anything she might say would have to be a lie. "My . . . husband died three years ago. He was a good man." Feeling that this was not an entirely sufficient answer, she added, "It was an arranged marriage and not an entirely happy one." She thought of William, whose surname she had borrowed for the duration of her trip, and she realized that though they had not actually gotten married, and he was still very much alive, these responses were, for the most part, accurate. Her uncle had encouraged the engagement for a good year before he passed away, and her relationship with William had been less than pleasing.

He nodded as though he understood some of her feelings. "Do you have a favorite beau back in Missouri? Though if you do, I'll tell you right now I don't think much of his intelligence. Any man who would let you out of his sight for more than a minute has got to be dumber than a mule." He placed his hand on the back of her arm in a gentle clasp as he continued. "You're as pretty as the moon at midnight."

She leaned back slightly to look at him, to reprove him for his flirtations, but this was a mistake. His eyes had grown quite dark and his hand was now sliding down the back of her arm. She found it difficult to breathe as he held her gaze.

"Do you have a beau?" he asked again.

She shook her head but found it impossible to speak.

His mouth was parted slightly, and as he began pulling her gently toward him, she had no doubt he meant to kiss her. She wanted to resist him, she intended to do so, but he held her captive by the hunger in his eyes. She felt the strength of his hand as he gripped her arm tightly now and forced her to move so close to him that his mouth was but a breath away. She should say something to him, she should rebuke him, but his eyes, clouded and gray, overcame her silent protests.

"You're feverish," she managed at last in a painful whisper, hoping to distract him. But to little effect.

"I am at that," he said, his rich voice again easing through her heart.

His mouth was on hers suddenly in the gentlest, warmest pressure she had ever known. Somewhere, in the center of her mind, she knew he was kissing her and that it was forbidden, but she couldn't stop him. She didn't want to. His lips were a sweet pleasure, a comfort as he drew back ever so slightly and let his mouth drift over hers. She reached toward him, pressing her hand against his bare chest to support herself, feeling unsteady as he assaulted her innocent lips.

She felt a tremor pass through him beneath the touch of her hand. His mouth grew more insistent and he caught his arm up about her waist, holding her tight. She returned the pressure of his lips as all the new feelings that had come to her since she had first entered the room suddenly bunched up and flooded her heart. How much his kisses pleased her. She had never felt like this before, as his hand floated lightly over her arm. His fingers touched her bare neck and a chill, exciting in a strange way, sped down her side. She parted her lips, a faint moan escaping her. As she did so, however, she felt his tongue touch her lips and she became frightened suddenly, pushing away from him. "No," she whispered. "I can't do this. I shouldn't . . ."

He released her immediately, his expression serious as he looked at her. For a long moment he held her gaze, his eyes questioning. When he spoke, his voice sounded hoarse. "It's hard to go without love, isn't it? I mean, even for a woman, once you've known a

43

man. I shouldn't have kissed you. I know that. But you have the clearest blue eyes I've ever seen. And the way you looked at me just then—" He laughed suddenly. "And now I think I've hurt myself."

Alexandra looked down at the bandage and saw that he was bleeding again. "Goodness gracious," she cried. "Well, now I'm really sorry. I know I shouldn't have let you kiss me and now look what's happened!"

Unwinding the remainder of the bandage as fast as she could, she quickly packed the wound with a thick pad of cloth. Ross held it tightly against his side as Alexandra wrapped the used dressing in a recent copy of the *Arizona Gazette*. When the bleeding had nearly stopped, Alexandra applied the carbolic to the injury first in the front and then the back. Within a few minutes, she began binding him up again. It was a slow process since she wanted to be as careful as the doctor had been. No words passed between them and she felt uncomfortable again. She had let a near-stranger kiss her in a way that she had never let anyone kiss her before! How could she have done it! But oh, merciful heavens, how wonderful his lips felt against hers!

She helped him slip on his shirt and, leaving him to finish dressing, she moved to the bureau and placed her hat back over her coiled braid. With the aid of the small mirror on top of the low chest of drawers, she worked the long pin through the crown of her hat and found that her hands were trembling again. All the while, she could see Ross's reflection behind her.

She saw only his back as she watched him carefully check his saddlebags. He wore a white cotton shirt, and after he was satisfied with his bags, he settled his worn black hat over his head. She turned around to look at him, noticing that his boots were worn, too, and for the sake of the fine wood floors and carpets of the hotel he had left off his spurs. More than ever, he looked like a cowhand, and Alexandra knew a sense of loss she could not explain — and of disappointment. She didn't disapprove of how he earned his living, far from it. She knew that a drover's lot was one of the hardest in the world. It was just that it was a wandering life, similar to the one her papa had lived. Drifters never settled, or if they did, it was always in an isolated place destined to hurt the women who loved them.

She took a deep breath, trying to forget that moments earlier, she had shared a kiss with this handsome cowboy. She promised herself that the instant she climbed aboard the stage, she would forget about Ross Halleck.

With her hat curved over her brow, she bid him farewell and offered her hopes for his continued health. Wishing him every happiness in life, she picked up her carpetbag to go.

He insisted upon opening the door for her, and as she walked through, he said, "You'll like Prescott. It's pretty country up there. I won't be but a day or two more in Phoenix myself, then I'll be heading up. Perhaps I'll see you again."

Alexandra hoped that the dismay she felt did not reach her eyes. She didn't want him to know how she felt. Looking away from him, she smiled and nodded, but her heart plummeted all the way to the toes of her laced-up boots. She didn't want to see Ross again; she didn't want one more fraction of her heart to be turned upside down by this aimless drifter." You're going to Prescott?" she queried." But whatever for? I mean, you never said a word."

He frowned slightly. "Didn't I say? I have a mining interest there. I'm hoping to take charge of the operation and maybe even make my fortune."

Chapter Five

Three days later, Alexandra sat on her bed in her hotel room in Prescott, staring down at her father's letters cradled on her lap. She pulled on the thin red silk ribbon that held the packet tightly together, but when the letters were freed from the ribbon, they remained compact, stuck in the order she had originally discovered them. The pressure of the ribbon had held the letters captive for so long a time that they didn't seem to know they were free.

Alexandra separated them carefully, as she had done several times before, and began looking for the two letters that best described her father's mine. They were the last two and she would need them both in order to prove her claim. She unfolded them carefully, afraid that she might tear the fragile sheets, and could not keep from taking a minute to read them both again.

"I had hoped to hear from you long before this," her papa's scratches and curls spoke to her from the year 1878. It's been nigh on six months since I had a letter from you. The mails are slow, especially out here. Still, a friend of mine, Crackshot Peters, has had three letters and a large package from his sister in Ohio so I know that I can't blame the U.S. Mails entirely. I only hope you'll write soon. I miss you terribly—and your ma, too, God rest her soul. I'd like you to come to Prescott soon, if you can. It's safe here, what with Fort Whipple a stone's throw away. I suppose, however, that if your uncle has his way, I won't never see you again. Don't let him ramrod you, dear. I only wish you could be with me.

"Arizona Territory grows more civilized every day, but the outlying ranches and mines are sometimes plagued with roving bands of Apaches who have not yet surrendered. We keep a watch out. Four men fought them off hereabouts not long ago by staying holed up in a cave they'd dug out of a hillside. I suppose we can do that much at the mine. So, God forbid, if one of these Injuns should take my scalp, you come to Prescott and lay claim to my mine. You've only to ask anybody whose lived here a time for directions to the Alexandra. Do you like what I named her? Crackshot liked it, too. He said if he'd ever had a little girl of his own, he would have wanted her to be named Alexandra, just like you.

"We are very fortunate that the mine is situated beside a creek. We have plenty of water and the hunting is good. We have venison whenever it pleases us, which, after having to eat Crackshot's sonofabitch stew five days out of seven, is as often as possible."

The letter ended with his hopes that she would write soon, and Alexandra felt angry all over again that her uncle had withheld her father's correspondence from her.

The last letter he wrote was dated two months before he died. She chuckled when she came to a portion of the text as familiar to her as his snoring at night. He was giving full expression to every argo-

48

naut's dream of finding a golden stope as wide as the Mississippi: "I can smell it. Oh, I know I've said it a thousand times before, but this is different. There's a fortune here. Even Lloyd Powell, who owns a claim downriver from me, offered to buy me out. If only I have time to dig deep enough in Mother Earth and capture her riches before she comes to collect her debt from me. If we find more rock like I did last week, I intend to come East. I'm hoping your ma's brother will want to put up enough investment money to build a stamp mill. We've got an arrastra going, but that's nothing to what a five-stamp mill can do.

"It's been over nine months since I heard from you and not once have you mentioned the Alexandra. I feel badly about that, thinking maybe you haven't forgiven your pa for how things turned out. I know Demarion intends to leave you his fortune—he said as much in a letter of his I got a week ago—so I don't worry anymore about you and your future. I just miss you, pet. I'd wanted you to have the mine, something to call your own, but I suppose everything has worked out for the best. I'll say good-bye now. I know I haven't been the best pa in the world, but I love you. Never forget me."

Before she could prevent it, a tear tumbled down Alexandra's cheek and dropped onto the word *forget*. The ink spread quickly, smearing her father's slanted script. When the tear had soaked into the paper and dried sufficiently, Alexandra folded the letters back up and slipped them into her netted bag. She hoped they would be enough proof to validate her claim to the Alexandra.

A painful lump remained in her throat for a long time. Sam Wingfield had meant to come to Missouri if he'd found more promising ore. He had, it seemed, maybe a month later. But on his way to Independence, he died of the influenza in Dodge City. A sheriff had found her uncle's address in her father's belongings and had sent word to him shortly after Sam's death. It always bothered her deeply to think of him dying alone, fever-ridden, without anyone to care for him in his last days.

Rising from her seat on the bed, Alexandra crossed the room to the chest of drawers where she had arranged the few belongings she had brought with her and set the rest of the letters in the top drawer. How heavy her heart sat within her breast, weighing her down. The picture of her father dying among strangers was one of the unhappiest memories she had of her family. They were all gone now — her mother and father, her brothers and sisters, her aunt and uncle. She had no kin to turn to, no blood relations who could help create a buffer between herself and the unrelenting changes of life.

And as for her father's belief that she had inherited her uncle's fortune, she could only laugh thinking how ironic it was that her papa had died believing her future was secure. She hoped now, more than anything, that she wasn't too late to file on her father's claim.

Her thoughts tumbled suddenly toward Ross Halleck, as they had frequently since she left Phoenix. Did he have kinfolk he could rely on when he needed help? Somehow she doubted it. He looked like a man who traveled the trails alone. Did he ever feel like this? she wondered. And did he ever weary of his drifting life?

More than a dozen times in the past three days, Alexandra's mind had filled with wonderings about Ross. When she thought of him, her recollections were sharp and powerful. She could smell the soap

50

with which he had used to shave. She knew in detail the feel of his calloused hands and strong arms from having washed them that night. She could see in her mind's eye the bold scars on his arm and abdomen, and when she would permit the memory to come, she could taste the sweetness of his mouth from having been kissed by him. Maybe it was the painful realization that she had lost her entire family that made her suddenly vulnerable, but the memory of his kiss came to her so vividly that she swore she could feel his lips as though he were kissing her now. She closed her eyes, her heart aching, as a strange weakness worked its way through her heart, down into her stomach, and throughout her limbs. She could not explain why she felt so uneasy when she thought about Ross, nor why she longed to feel his arms around her, nor why she knew it would be a wondrous comfort to feel his mouth pressed so gently on hers again. She should have forgotten about him entirely by now; instead, each remembrance seemed to bring him closer than before.

She pressed a fisted hand to her forehead and bid the thoughts to stop. Ross was nothing to her and could never be anything more than a chance-met acquaintance. He had spoken of a mining interest, but how long would he remain in Prescott to work it? A month, maybe. A year? Unlikely.

She would probably meet him again if he came to Prescott. But of what use would it be for her to even talk to him? No use at all.

Taking a deep breath, and straightening her shoulders, Alexandra bid the memories fly from her as she slipped the strings of her netted bag over her arm and headed for the door. It was time to find out about her father's mine.

Chapter Six

Alexandra made her way to the pine-hewn board-walk in front of her hotel and turned slowly around, her gaze sweeping the ponderosa horizon where the stately trees grew over sixty feet tall and met a sky of an intense dark blue. Prescott sat noisily in a basin of granite and pine trees, surrounded on three sides by jutting peaks that in a few months would be covered with an easy snow. Winter, according to the local inhabitants, rested lightly upon the land and Alexandra wished suddenly that she could stay through the season to see the icicles clinging to some of the log cabins and from the eaves of many of the wood-frame houses and stores. Prescott was as different from Phoenix as their spread in temperatures. Adobe buildings of the Sonoran town had blended into the desert, but Prescott had been constructed almost entirely of wood, unusual for an Arizona town.

Phoenix had been hot during the day, even in October, but a cool freshness now surrounded Alexandra in the mile-high, bustling town. The air was crackling dry, just as the doctor had warned her, but the fragrant scent of pine soothed away a lot of the discomfort of the harsher elements.

Just as she stepped off the boardwalk, a dappled gray horse pulling a shiny black carriage trotted by. The driver of the elegant conveyance caught sight of her and quickly tipped his flat-crowned black hat, a thin smile on his lips. He was not unattractive, Alexandra thought, noting the tailored fit of his black, store-bought suit. Even sitting in the carriage as he was, she could see that he was a tall man, wiry in appearance, with cool brown eyes, straight, compressed lips, and a narrow nose. He seemed at odds with the small bustling town. Prescott was warm in color and texture. The log buildings were rough with brown bark, the pine trees a dusty green, and the sun seemed to spread a golden sheen over the people of the mountain valley, over the miners, settlers, and merchants that traversed the streets. Even the soldiers, stationed at nearby Fort Whipple and riding on horseback through the town or countryside, seemed to blend with the granite terrain in their travel-worn blues.

But not this man. His face was pale, unblemished by the sun. In a sweep of her eyes, Alexandra could see that he was in many ways like William, well dressed, his side whiskers trimmed neatly, his carriage and horse well tended. He had the unmistakably soft appearance of a man who earned his living with his mind rather than with his brawn. On the surface, he looked as though he had just arrived from the East to make his fortune. Yet something about the set of his shoulders, and the narrowing of his eyes as he scrutinized every detail of her costume, told Alexandra this was no greenhorn and that he had probably been in the West for many years. She had an uneasy feeling about him as she watched him disappear down Whiskey Row.

She picked her way across the main thoroughfare

heading toward the claims office where she hoped to secure her right to her father's mine. Twice, riders whooped and shouted as they dashed down Montezuma Street. Freight wagons, heavily burdened with goods from the shipping lanes of the Colorado River, lumbered through the growing melee of traffic. Prospectors, wrinkled and wizened far beyond their years, led their familiar burros toward the Kentucky Bar, the Cobweb Hall, the Wellington and the Palace. The hour of day scarcely mattered to the denizens of the territory whose thirst was quenched from two-bit and four-bit flasks they could tuck into their hip pockets for the wearying trek into the tempting hills in a fair radius about Prescott. Alexandra glanced from one sunburnt face to the next, from miner, to merchant, to soldier, and saw within the features of each a similar passion that struck a bold chord within her own heart. Everyone was bent on wresting from this last American frontier, a future of promise. Resolve had etched itself into the deep lines of the faces about her and she knew a quickening of her step to match those of the people around her. A peculiar warmth took hold of her stomach and brought with it a sweet malaise. A feeling that she was treading on perilous ground filled her, not with fright but with sheer excitement. In this instant, she knew she was like these people, and all that remained for her to do now was to take hold of her father's mine and to exact from Arizona Territory that which belonged to those courageous enough to pursue it. Maybe there existed in her heart, as much as she rebelled against the very idea of it, the same spirit that had infested her father from his earliest years. Whatever the case, she found her spirits lifted by the very vibrancy of the people about her.

On her way, she passed by a small mercantile, not as large as Goldwater's, but smelling wondrously of coffee, apples, and bolted cloth. Finally, she reached the claims office, which was housed in a small building not far from the hotel. Once inside, she found two old-timers sitting next to a pot-bellied, cast-iron stove sipping cups of coffee they were enhancing with the contents of a shared four-bit flask of whiskey. They regarded her candidly from squinting eyes. Their faces looked like the land they inhabited, grooved with years of having lived out in the open. Toothless smiles of appreciation, along with nods and the slightest shifting in their seats, met Alexandra's own good-morning greeting.

Her heart felt joyously light as she passed the grizzled men and approached the counter. She heard an odd rasping sound followed by a snort emanating from a clerk seated on a tall wooden stool. She was not surprised to find him in a light slumber, his head leaning unsteadily against a loose stack of maps, papers, and worn brown folders. She had to clear her voice twice before the man awoke, which he did with a start followed by a series of sharp coughs. A blush rose up his cheeks as he scratched beneath the stiff, false collar of his shirt that seemed to have suddenly grown tight.

Begging to know her business, he drew forward a pen and pot of ink and appeared ready to accommodate her.

"I've come to secure a claim to my father's mine," Alexandra responded. "I don't know exactly where it's located, but I have with me several letters of my father which indicate it must be a few miles outside of Prescott. He died over a year ago, but knowledge of the mine was withheld from me for some time. I don't know quite how to proceed. I believe he meant for me to inherit his mine. Perhaps you could help me or direct me to someone who could?"

The clerk blinked several times and combed his fingers hastily through his curly brown hair. He seemed nervous in her presence. "Miss—"

"Bradshaw. Mrs. Bradshaw."

He nodded and cleared his throat before continuing. "Mrs. Bradshaw, do you have with you some manner of legal document—a written claim to the mine? Without that, as you may imagine, I will have some difficulty in even identifying your father's mining interest. I feel I ought to warn you, however, that unless the diggings have been seen to regularly, such claims often become invalid. We have very loose laws regarding the ownership of mines, but uppermost in establishing a claim is a continued operation—even working the digs twice a week has proven indisputable in court as a means of proving ownership."

Alexandra opened her netted bag and withdrew her letters. She set them on the counter in front of her, unfolded the first one, and quickly reread the portions relating to the mine.

As she tapped the letter with her gloved finger, she wondered briefly if this was where her journey would end. Without some sort of legal paper, she didn't think she had a chance of laying claim to the mine. After a moment's contemplation, she remembered that her papa had spoken of a Crackshot Peters who she believed he had hired to help work his claim. "What if my father left someone in charge?" she queried. "Someone to continue the work while he left for an extended period of time? You see, as best as I can figure from his last letter, he had intended to visit me in Missouri. He died before he reached Independence."

Alexandra watched the clerk glance down at the

56

letter. He frowned as he stared at it. He had thinning curly hair and where his pate showed through the brown tendrils, his scalp was tanned and freckled. He wore mutton-chop whiskers, possessed light-blue eyes that shifted about rapidly, and a slight paunch garnered from the easy duties of his office.

He looked back at her suddenly. "What was your father's name?" he asked, still frowning. "If he had lived any length of time hereabouts, I might have been known him. I've resided in Prescott nigh on six years now."

"Wingfield," Alexandra responded readily. "Samuel Wingfield."

"Sam Wingfield," the clerk murmured as he stared hard at Alexandra. He seemed bereft of words somehow. She saw in his gaze not the lack of recognition but rather an abundance of it. But what other thoughts accompanied his momentary hesitation she could not say.

"You knew him, then?" she asked quietly, feeling suddenly linked to her father in a way that she had not expected to. Until this moment, his adventures in the central mountains of Arizona had been cloaked with a mist of unreality. But this man had known him, and his acquaintance with her papa brought her parent close to her in a way that was surprising. Her father had been here, perhaps even standing where she was right now. He had undoubtedly been in this very office, making sure of his claim before continuing his pursuit of the argonaut's dream. Tears threatened her composure with the unexpected feeling of missing her father and she took a deep breath.

"I remember once he came in with some high-grade ore," the clerk said. "He was winking and beaming for all he was worth. Said he was sure he was close to the mother lode." The clerk laughed lightly. "But then there is scarcely a miner to be found anywhere in the country, at any season of the year, who isn't sure of the same."

Alexandra took her letters and clasped them hard in her hand. She found herself with a hundred questions she wanted to ask, yet not one would formulate itself upon her tongue.

"I knew Sam Wingfield."

A voice from behind Alexandra startled her. She whirled around to find herself staring into careful brown eyes as a matching display of even white teeth produced a smile that was both polite and properly distanced.

"He was my father," Alexandra stated, recognizing at once the man she had seen earlier tooling his carriage along the street. She wondered how long he had been standing nearby.

"That much I ascertained but a few minutes ago. You have the look of him in both your charming red hair and your handsome countenance," he responded, carefully removing his hat and bowing to her. "My name is Powell, and if I can be of any assistance I hope you will not hesitate to ask me. I am quite familiar with many of the mines about Prescott."

Alexandra blinked at him, and realized that her papa had made mention of him in one the letters. He owned a mine downstream from the Alexandra. She was going to tell Mr. Powell as much, but something in the sharpness of his gaze as he watched her clipped the words right off the end of her tongue. She was not certain she trusted him, though she was unable to explain why. Instead, she responded, "That's very kind of you, I'm sure, Mr. Powell. As it happens, I find myself in something of a quandary.

In my father's letters he made several references to his mine and to his desire that I inherit what would have been his only possession upon his death." She felt uncomfortable suddenly as Powell held her gaze, listening politely to her story. She was embarrassed and felt a need to offer an explanation, "You see, he was always a wandering man and when my mother died, he—"

She found herself unable to continue, her throat closing up tight. How many times in the course of the morning had memories of her family crept up on her and twisted her emotions in a circle.

She was grateful when Mr. Powell interjected quietly, "He was a generous man and the best of neighbors to all who knew him. I relied on his benificence myself more than once." He glanced toward the clerk and nodded to him slightly, before he continued. "But as to your claim to his mine, I'm afraid you're about a year too late. It seems a man out of Texas provided our good Mr. Vickroy here with a deed to your father's mine not more than a month after Sam Wingfield died. I dislike more than anything not only having to remind you of such a painful memory but of having to inform you as well that, according to law, you have no further right to your father's mining claim."

Alexandra reached a hand out to steady herself against the smooth wood counter. Her journey did end here. It just couldn't be possible! She felt queasy, as though a mighty fist had landed deep into the pit of her stomach, hitting her hard. Until this moment, she hadn't realized how much she had been counting on inheriting the Alexandra.

Mr. Powell moved to stand beside her. "I can see that you're mightily disappointed," he said kindly. Placing a hand under her elbow, he drew her toward the potbellied stove and told one of the old men to give up his seat to the poor lady who had just sustained a severe jolt to her nerves.

"By gawd she's white!" the old-timer cried, cocking his head to look at her. "Why, she's so white her lips are blue!"

"Git!" Mr. Powell cried in no uncertain terms. "Have you been so long from civilization you don't know how to treat a lady with respect?"

The old-timer rose from his seat at Powell's words like he'd been kicked by a mule. Scratching at his bedraggled gray head he responded, "Reckon I have, at that!"

Alexandra watched the men leave the claims office, feeling like a growing fog had taken over her mind. She felt completely stunned by the news that she didn't have the least right to her papa's mine. She lifted her gaze toward the window of the store where she watched the storekeeper sweeping the boardwalk, even as far down as the claim's office, alternately spitting chewing tobacco into the street.

"Do you know how the new owner came by my father's mine?" Alexandra asked, bemused.

"It was his explanation that he had won the deed in a game of poker."

"What?" Alexandra cried, shifting her gaze abruptly to Powell. She did not mistake the expression of cynicism in his eyes. "You don't think my father gambled the mine away, do you?"

"It's not for me to say," Powell said, glancing at his carefully groomed fingernails. "I wasn't there."

"Would you tell me, please, then," Alexandra whispered, swallowing hard, "the name of the man who showed up with the deed to my papa's mine? I think I ought to speak with him."

"If I remember correctly," he said, his eyes narrowing slightly. "He goes by the name of Halleck. Ross Halleck."

Chapter Seven

Ross joined company with several freighters in Phoenix and made a ponderous journey north to Prescott by way of the Black Canyon Highway. The wagons traveled slowly, each led by a team of six mules. Ross had decided, given the continued tenderness of his side, to travel with the heavily laden freight wagons instead of accompanying the faster stagecoach. Riding alone would have made him an easy mark for marauding Indians or for the desperadoes who failed to kill him six days earlier. He was still convinced these men had been hired to attack him, but by whom he hadn't the least idea. He had spoken with the sheriff the next day, but it was generally agreed there was little anyone could do since Ross couldn't offer the lawman a single description. Three deputies had backtrailed the bandits but lost them in the rocky terrain of a winding creekbed five miles east of Phoenix. Common sense dictated that Ross cloak himself with the safety of the company of other men, and the easy pace of the wagons suited the wound that still kept his activities at a hateful minimum.

Surprisingly, the long journey up into Prescott had

renewed much of his strength. The cooler mountain air was a relief from the heat of the desert and his bandages were no longer soaked with perspiration. He found himself, during the last stage of the journey, drawn particularly to the land outside of Prescott. Gentle hills rolled down to a grassy valley dotted with beeves. It might not be the endless plains or the open rangeland of Texas, but it was good ranchland.

The sight of the cattle grazing peacefully brought to mind his own love of the land as well as his desire, if he could glean enough money from old Wingfield's mine, to purchase a sizable spread in Wyoming. There, he wanted to build a ranch he could pour his life's sweat into. He could never belong to another man's dreams. He must have his own, regardless of the cost.

He had lost everything in Texas when he was burned out, but something deep inside him refused to be quenched by the thunderous, painful hand of Providence that had, in one evening, brought his fledgling ranch buildings to a heap of smoking, charred wood. Instead, he had found himself more determined than ever to pursue his desire of creating a fine ranch that he hoped would one day rival even the XIT. There was plenty of land to be had in Wyoming, and once he had some money with which to purchase a couple thousand head of shorthorn stock from Idaho or Oregon and some Thoroughbred bulls from the East, he meant to forge his way into the rough northern territory and take his future in hand.

As the cavalcade of wagons approached Prescott, Ross found his spirits weighed down with a bitter memory he wished he could find some way of forgetting. All his recent ruminations upon his hopes for the future reminded him that he had lost not only his budding ranch but the woman he had hoped to make his wife as well.

Katherine had driven out to see him just a few hours after the disaster. She was a beautiful, intelligent young woman whose father was the owner of a strong, vital ranch that he had built up in Texas over the space of twenty-five years. He was a hard man, a good man, and had approved of Ross. Once he had even told him that he saw himself in Ross, his younger days, of course, and expressed his hope that his plans would prosper.

As any doting father would, he had provided amply for his daughters, of which he had three. The young women enjoyed a mode of life that was the envy of every female within a three-hundred-mile radius and were sought by every unattached male south of the Red River.

But from the first, Katherine, with her large, flirtatious brown eyes and light, rippling laughter, had shown a clear preference for Ross. He had been equally as taken with her. In all his scores of travels, throughout the West and even to distant Chicago, he had never met so captivating a female.

She found him, that day, kicking at the smoldering timber of his barn where a foal had been burnt to death in the attack on his ranch. The air was still thick with the smell of scorched hide and roasted flesh.

"Ross!" her horrified voice had called to him. "I came as soon as I heard what had happened. Who did this to you? Why? If we'd all been in the midst of a range war I could understand, but there isn't a man hereabouts who would harm you like this!"

He had turned to look at her. She sat upright in her carriage, wearing a pretty, pink-and-white flowered dress adorned with a starched lace collar. He

64

could still see her holding a dainty parasol in one hand, the reins in the other. In her eyes, however, he saw a stricken look that went far beyond the shock of seeing his ranch destroyed.

"You might as well go, Katherine," he had said quietly, turning back to view the remnants of his half-built home.

"I don't want to go, Ross," she answered, her voice breaking slightly. "I don't. I *want* to stay here and help you, help *us!*"

"Help *us* do what!" he had snapped, wheeling on her, his throat constricted. "Trail a band of thieves into Mexico and fight them for a thousand head that have no doubt been long since broken up and sold off? I've been cut off here before I'd even begun. Eight years' savings gone in a blink! My God!"

She had just stared at him, all tense and closed up, her brown eyes glinting with pain as she watched him. He could see she was torn right into two parts and he hated her for that. The truth was, she didn't even deliberate. The words she had spoken had been only the smallest expression of regret.

In his finest daydreams he had seen Katherine walking steadfastly beside him, enduring graciously every travail and heartache that could afflict a man during the course of his life. The fact that she did not even step down from her tidy, glossy little buggy told him all he needed to know. She was not a woman who could stand with him.

The bustling sounds of the vigorous mountain town broke Ross's reverie. He breathed deeply and let his gaze drift over the collection of wood-frame and log buildings, upward to the tall pines, and higher still to a deep blue sky that seemed as if a man would just stretch a little, he could touch it. Taking another breath, his side rebelling slightly as he filled his lungs with fragrant air, he felt alive suddenly. The past was just that—the past. Time moved relentlessly forward, bringing its own peculiar healing with it. In his experience, he understood that life had a way of changing from day to day, week to week, and what was critical in this hour would become fodder for quiet amusement in the next.

As he parted company with the wagons, he found himself guiding his horse along Montezuma Street where a dozen saloons beckoned to his dry throat. Ordinarily, he would have drawn rein and satisfied his thirst. Instead, he continued beyond Whiskey Row to the hotel. He had long since decided he would do well to attend to his wound before doing anything else.

Tying his horse to the hitching rail, he remembered suddenly that he would probably see Alexandra again. This thought, coming so hard on the heels of his memories of Katherine, affected him powerfully. Like skipping stones across a pond, one vision after another piled up in his mind—of Alexandra gently scrubbing the blood and dirt from his hands and arms, of her readiness the next day to help him, of the sight of her small waist when she had stepped away from the bed to remove her hat, and of the kiss they shared. He had slipped his arm about her inviting waist as her tender, well-shaped lips parted beneath his own and her sweet breath floated over his mouth. It had been some time since he had kissed a woman, but never had he known such a quick fire to sweep over him as it had when he had held her for that brief moment tucked within the circle of his arms. He had forgotten entirely the pain of his wound as he kissed her hard, enjoying the feel of her so close to him and having her respond. Maybe that was what had affected him strongly—she had taken

66

to his kissing like wind to fire, and he wondered what it would be like to take her to bed.

Of course she had become frightened, a reaction he could easily understand. She might be a widow, but she was clearly a lady with good, strong values who wasn't likely to give anybody a tumble in the hay, nonetheless a stranger. Still, the thought of it was pleasing, especially since she had such a spirited disposition. She also appeared to be a woman of some means, if her gown was any indication. She was, in some ways, like Katherine.

This last thought, as he stepped onto the board-walk, brought him up short. *Like Katherine.* He hadn't considered the matter before, but Alexandra wore clothes similar to Katherine's and carried herself in the same proud way. He wondered if Alexandra, too, given the same circumstances, would have remained seated in her buggy and ultimately driven away.

These unhappy reflections gave him no pleasure at all, and he decided, as he began brushing the traveling dust off his clothes with his black hat, that he would immediately dismiss his cogitations. They didn't add to his happiness, and whether his conjectures were true or not it hardly mattered. Alexandra had made it clear she meant to return to Missouri as soon as she was able to conclude her own business in Prescott, and he had no reason to involve himself with her — except maybe in the lightest of flirtations, and to see, if possible, whether or not he could steal another kiss from her.

With his thoughts now directed into a far more agreeable vein, Ross crossed the threshold of the hotel, the door closing with a snap behind him, and he stopped dead in his tracks.

Before him, Alexandra stood in front of a tall

pinewood desk, her head bent slightly as she dipped her pen into an inkwell. He was stunned by her appearance. Gone were the delicate blue rustling silks, the pert bonnet, and neatly arranged hair. In their stead were a long dark-blue skirt of a plain fabric, a white blouse made high to the neck, a round, plainsman hat that a boy might wear, heavy leather riding gloves tucked into her waistband, and a pair of rugged boots encasing her feet. She was outfitted for a trip through harsh terrain, and for the life of him he couldn't imagine where she meant to go.

He knew his mouth was at half-cock as he watched her. Even her red hair hung down her back in a long braid, with tendrils escaping their imprisonment. She looked so different that his mind kept whirling about in a circle. At the same time, he could not keep from staring at her. She was so damn pretty! He was struck, too, that in her bearing, as she set to scribbling out something on a sheet of paper, was an unease he knew had not existed when he first met her in Phoenix. Her mouth was fixed in a grim line and he wondered what had occurred both to disrupt her peace as well as to strip her so quickly of her silks?

He realized much to his astonishment that aside from his desire to kiss her again, he was genuinely glad to see her.

He approached her, thankful that the vestibule was empty of people at the moment, and moved close to the desk. She was lost in her letter-writing and she did not appear to see him. He leaned against the edge of the desk, lowered his head so that when she looked up he might see directly into her eyes, and said, "I wouldn't have recognized you at all, Alexandra, had your red hair not started shouting at me." He smiled at her, and found himself staring into her

68

blue eyes. His heart seemed to stop for a moment as she blinked twice. She was even prettier close up and something within the depth of her gaze pulled hard at his heart as though he was looking at someone he'd known and loved for years.

To his surprise, however, her cheeks turned a dull red as she backed away from him. If he didn't know better, he would think she was angry with him.

"What is it?" he asked, startled. "Why do you look at me like you wish you had a whip in one hand and a pistol in the other?"

"Tell me, Ross," she whispered, a wild look on her face. "How did you come by Sam Wingfield's mine? Did you rob him while he lay dying in his bed? Or did you wait till after the funeral?"

Chapter Eight

Alexandra found blood rushing to her ears and her breath grew painfully compressed within her chest. She had not intended, when she met Ross again, to accuse him of anything so wicked as robbing her father. Not yet, at least. But ever since she learned that not a month after Sam's death, Ross had arrived in Prescott to lay claim to her papa's mine, she had been possessed by the thought that he had come by the Alexandra unlawfully.

Every time she reread her papa's letters, she became more convinced that Sam Wingfield wouldn't have gambled his mine away unless something was terribly wrong. None of it made sense. Why, for instance, would he have been journeying east, supposedly to raise money in order to develop the Alexandra, then suddenly lose the mine in a poker game to Ross Halleck?

Terrifying suspicions had begun running around in her mind, and though she suppressed the thought, she had even begun to wonder if her father had really died of the influenza. Her uncle had told her as much. What if Sam had been murdered? What if her uncle had merely been trying to protect her and told her a lie? It would be just like him if he had.

She had been in the process of writing a letter to William, asking him to inquire into the details of her father's death, when Ross appeared. Maybe if he had not come upon her so suddenly, she could have restrained herself until she had more facts at her command. As it was, when his voice hit her, so many emotions had been running near the surface of her skin that she fired off in rapid succession the first words that leapt to her mind.

She regretted them now, pressing a hand to her face and shutting her eyes tight. She knew only one thing, that she must get away from Ross, to think, to figure out how to proceed. She ought to talk to the sheriff, to lay the matter before him. As a lawman, he would know a lot about what had been going on at the Alexandra and he might even know more details about her father's death.

Taking a step away from Ross, she jerked her letter off the desk, then headed toward the door.

She didn't get very far. Ross's hand shot out and gripped her arm, bringing her progress to an unceremonious halt. He kept hold of her, staring fiercely into her eyes, his brows drawn together. "I don't know what the hell you mean by such an accusation," he said, his low-timbred voice painfully quiet as his words rolled over her. "But if you were a man, you'd be lying on the floor spitting teeth between bloody lips."

Alexandra couldn't breathe nor could she look away from him as she desperately longed to do. In her confusion and in her anger toward Ross she found herself unable to speak as she returned his glare. When she finally did give utterance to her thoughts, her voice shook. "Have you ever been to Dodge City?" she asked in a whisper.

71

He nodded. "Several times. Why?"

"Sam Wingfield was in Dodge City once. He died there, supposedly of the Spanish influenza, but not before you relieved him of the deed to his mine, or so it would seem."

Ross shook his head, an expression of bewilderment chasing the anger from his face as he asked, "Is that the kind of man you think I am? Do you honestly believe I would've stolen from Sam, from any man, on his deathbed?"

"Didn't you?" she asked. "You have his mine now."

Alexandra could see the fight go out of Ross as he released her arm. "I see," he responded quietly. "I think if you have anything more to say, you should tell it to the sheriff. I'll be at the blacksmith's if he should want to speak to me afterward. It's been a real pleasure knowing you." These last words were spoken bitterly as he turned to leave, heading toward the door.

"Ross, wait," she called after him. She knew in her heart that he would no more have committed such a crime than she would have. He turned back to look at her, his face solemn. "Don't leave just yet," she said. "I feel very confused and upset. I hadn't meant to say these things to you. I don't know why I did. I suppose it was the way Mr. Powell looked when he said you had arrived here only a month after Sam's death to file on his claim, like he suspected you of claim-jumping."

For a moment Ross seemed torn, pausing by the door and batting his hat against his chaps. Slowly, he retraced his steps to stand in front of her. She could see that he was very unhappy about all that she had said to him. "I only met Wingfield once," he said quietly. "We played a game of poker, that's all.

72

He wandered into my camp where we were bedded down some thirty miles outside of Dodge City. He seemed nervous and pretty tense, but—" He stopped in midsentence, looking hard at her. Awareness dawned on him suddenly. "Alexandra," he whispered. "Are you his daughter? Is this the business you had to take care of here in Prescott?"

Alexandra nodded, sinking into a chair opposite the desk. She laughed slightly, her gaze falling blindly to the floor. "I came here to claim the mine as my inheritance." After saying as much, she felt as though she had just fallen into a deep hole. She could not remember a time when her spirits had been lower than they were now.

Ross pulled up a chair to sit beside her. "I should have realized who you were before this, what with your red hair and all," he said. "Wingfield sure had a headful. And I can understand how things must look, but I didn't steal the mine from him. It happened just like I said. There were others in the camp that night who would tell you as much, but they're all down in Texas right now."

Alexandra dropped her forehead in her hand and let out a heavy sigh. "I believe you; I do. It's just that I can't make sense of what happened? I have several of papa's letters that indicate he had only one intention with the Alexandra, to develop it. He was headed for Missouri to ask my uncle for a loan. He wanted to build a stamp mill. I was told you had boasted of winning the mine in a card game. I just couldn't believe my father would have gambled it away."

"I don't know," Ross responded. "I remember he said he was sure the mine was sittin' on the mother lode, but I didn't pay much heed to that, especially since he didn't seem hesitant about staking the Alexandra in a card game. He was gone by morning. I never saw him again. Thinking it was the provident thing to do, I saw to the ownership of the mine right away, just in case it might one day prove to be worth something. But I didn't learn of his death until I got here like you say, a month later. Deputy Barnes told me about it, though I don't remember him saying anything about the Spanish influenza, only that he was dead. I remember he was real shook up at the time. I guess he and Sam were pretty good friends. I just wish you had tried to contact me about your father's mine sooner. Why didn't you?"

Alexandra explained about her uncle, that he had kept the letters from her. "I didn't even know about the mine until a few weeks ago," she added. "I suppose Uncle Demarion was a good man at heart, but I have sure resented his keeping me and my father apart like he did." Not wanting to dwell on her uncle, she changed the subject abruptly and asked Ross who had been tending the mine for him, since it was obvious he hadn't been back to Prescott since he first filed on the claim.

"A man your father hired to work the diggings with him, and who I made my partner as soon as I had a chance to size him up. His name is Peters, Crackshot Peters. He's an honest man, hard-working and good-natured; with a skill that leaves you in little doubt about how he garnered his nickname."

Alexandra nodded. "Papa spoke of him in one of the letters."

At that moment, two men descended the stairs at the far end of the vestibule. Glancing at them briefly, Alexandra turned back to Ross and lowered her voice. "The more I turn everything over in my mind," she continued, "the more I have grown afraid that something is very wrong. Ross, do you suppose the men who attacked you outside of Phoenix did so because of the Alexandra?"

"I have been thinking as much for some time now. It leaves me both hopeful and worried. If someone wants the mine, it's possible your father had told one man too many that he'd struck it rich, in which case his claim must be worth something. At the same time, even Crackshot isn't safe."

The men passed by, both tipping their hats politely to Alexandra and Ross. Once again, the entry hall to the hotel was empty. Ross lifted his hand toward her to cradle her elbow with a gentle grasp as he looked at her intently. "I'm not certain I can say for sure why," he said, his voice low. "But it's become real important to me that you trust my word, that you believe what I've told you is true."

Alexandra swallowed with some difficulty as she met his gaze. "I do," she responded. "And I'm sorry that when you first spoke to me, I hit you with my suspicions like that. I was just so upset."

"It's all right," he said, stroking her arm gently. "I understand. I'm sure I would have felt the same way."

It's his voice, Alexandra thought as her heart began to fail her. Once again it seemed those rich tones drove straight through her chest. His face was full of concern as he watched her, and she resisted the strongest impulse to place her fingers lightly on his face and smooth away the furrow between his brows. What was this man to her that simply being near him brought her such a warm sensation. She wanted something from him, but what? She felt she had a question, as yet to surface within her mind, that was imperative for him alone to answer.

Growing uncomfortable with all the mounting disquietude of her heart, Alexandra shifted her gaze away from him and slowly withdrew her elbow from his hand. She inquired politely about the wound in his side, her heart growing warm at being so close to him.

He told her he was healing up just fine then thanked her again for her assistance in Phoenix. She made the truly grave mistake of smiling at the memory of the kiss they had shared and she felt her cheeks grow hot.

With a quick movement, he caught her chin with his hand and forced her to look at him. "You're blushing!" he said with a smile. "Are you remembering something . . . pleasant?"

"No!" she retorted. "And if you say anything about—about *anything,* I'll return to my room this very instant."

"Then I'll keep quiet because I don't want you to leave just yet." His voice dropped suddenly as he leaned closer to her and whispered, "I missed you. I didn't realize how much until just now. I love to see you fire up when I tease you."

Alexandra liked the way he talked to her. "You're flirting with me," she said, her heart whispering urgent warnings to her.

"Maybe I am," he responded. "Do you mind?"

"I suppose not, so long as you behave yourself."

"Well, I won't promise that much," he retorted.

Alexandra decided it would be wise to ignore this last remark and instead addressed a different matter entirely. "I've made arrangements to have a prospector who is familiar with the area take me out to my father's—that is, to *your* mine. He should be here anytime, that is, if you don't mind my paying the Alexandra a visit."

"Of course not."

"I know it must seem funny to you, but I want to

see the place my father spoke so much about in his letters. We weren't very close, you see. I hadn't seen him for eight years. His life was lived in all the places he wanted to be next, never in the place where he was. "She laughed lightly. "He was truly an Argonaut, and in my way I loved him. But he couldn't grow roots if his life depended on it. When my mother died, I went to live with my aunt and uncle in Independence."

Ross glanced toward the window. "There's only one problem," he said, frowning. "It's too late in the day to be heading out to the camp."

"Why's that?" she asked.

"I don't know what this old-timer told you, but it's a pretty rough ride through hilly terrain to get to the mine — six hours by horseback or mule and you'd better be prepared for a shift in the land. Prescott's a pretty place, but the farther out you travel, the trees soon give way to chaparral and rocky, granite hillsides, and the mine itself is up high — Bee Mountain tops Prescott by almost two thousand feet. I'd be more than happy to take you out there in the morning if you like."

Alexandra's mind nudged her to refuse him, reminding her that little good could come of spending an entire day with Ross, but her heart spoke for her instead as she responded, "I'd like that very much."

Chapter Nine

Deputy Barnes looked at the two men solemnly. He felt sweat beading up on his upper lip even though the day was cool. He didn't want either man to know he was nervous and quickly shifted his glance to a stack of papers on his desk. It would be a lot simpler if Sheriff Goodwin would return from Carver. He was the right lawman to deal with Halleck. They'd received word from the sheriff of Dodge City two days ago that he knew for a fact Sam Wingfield had been murdered. Barnes was afraid he'd bungle it if he asked the wrong questions and got things stirred up. Besides, it was Goodwin who wanted to look into Sam's death.

"When did Halleck get here?" Barnes finally asked, as he began randomly reordering the sheets in front of him and trying not to keep from wiping his face with his kerchief.

Fred Spangler, the taller of the two, responded, "I don't rightly know. We come down the stairs and there he was talkin' to Mrs. Bradshaw. I think he'd just rode up. I recognized him from a year ago. He ain't changed much. Mrs. Bradshaw dropped her voice real low when she saw us. I expect they was talkin' about the mine. Does she know her pa was killed and that Halleck may have done it?"

Louis Barnes felt his skin jump. He didn't like it at all that Sam's daughter had shown up. She was bound to get hurt if things got rough. There was nothing for her here, after all, since Halleck had a legal right to Wingfield's mine. "How the hell should I know," he answered Spangler. "I haven't even met her yet. Don't want to, neither. Sheriff's the one to see to this, not me. Besides, Ross Halleck don't look like no murderer to me, so if you have anything more to say, just wait till Goodwin gets back from Carver."

Both men looked at him as though he'd thrown a bucket of cold water on them.

"Git, now!" he cried.

The shorter of the two by six inches responded with his hapless stutter. "J-j-just want to see ju-justice done, Deputy."

"So do I," Barnes responded irritably. "We were good friends, Sam and I. But I ain't movin' a hair until Goodwin gets back. They've got a mess down there in Carver. A mother and her two young kids was burnt up trying to leave that hell-bent place and no one saw who did it."

"Cherry cows," Spangler said darkly.

"Wasn't the Apaches," Barnes retorted, glad to be off the subject. "No one saw a single sign of Indian. Now, just rest easy the pair of you and don't do nothin' foolish. Leave Halleck to Goodwin."

There was nothing more for the men to do than leave the jailhouse. Barnes felt ill suddenly as he untied his red handkerchief from about his throat and mopped his face. He was too heavy and too old to be a deputy sheriff, especially in a busy town like Prescott. He wasn't even fifty yet, but, gawd, he felt like a hundred. Sam's death had sat hard on his mind. But the worst of it was, there wasn't a thing he could do about it. He just had to wait, and if there was one thing he was mighty poor at, it was waiting!

On the following morning, Alexandra mounted a sturdy black horse, settled her round tan hat forward on her brow, and nodded to Ross indicating she was prepared for their trek to his mine. Within minutes, they left the town proper and loped easily along the main northern road toward Granite Creek and the gnarled vista of huge granite boulders known as Point of Rocks. Alexandra rode behind Ross, lost a little in her own thoughts. She grew increasingly aware that a faint sensation of emptiness had settled deep within her heart, robbing her minute by minute of her peace. Since yesterday she had been preparing herself to return to Independence after her visit to the mine. But everything within her spirit rebelled against the idea of leaving Prescott so soon.

As she glanced at Ross, his fine, broad back straight in the saddle, she knew he was part of the reason she was so unhappy about going. They had spent a comfortable evening together, sharing a meal at the hotel and chatting easily, as though they had been friends for months instead of days. Only once had she stumbled into difficult territory. She had learned of the loss of his ranch in Texas and when she expressed her surprise that he had owned such a good-size spread, he bristled immediately.

His deep voice dropping very low, he looked at her with a hard expression and said, "You know how you can tell a storm's coming? The air starts crackling and the wind blows in fitful gusts. Afterward the rain comes. When you spoke just then, I felt like the air was snapping all around me. It wasn't what you said, either. It was your look of amazement, like you couldn't believe I could accomplish such a thing. So tell me, how long have you thought so poorly of drovers and the like?"

"I don't think badly of any of them," Alexandra had responded truthfully, feeling stunned by the strength of his reaction to her question. "But I do think it rare that a man can transform a drover's wages into a ranch, or even want to. I had always supposed that cowboys liked moving around a lot. Am I wrong?"

He stared at her for a time, as though searching for the right words to answer her. "Maybe you have a point in what you say. Maybe most men, most drovers, don't aspire to owning a spread. I don't know. I can't speak for them, only for myself. All I know is that ever since I was a boy, I've hankered for a place to call my own. And I still aim to build one, only I intend to head north this time, to Wyoming, where there's land aplenty. If I am offended, it's by something you aren't saying to me, but which I can read in your eyes as clearly as if you shouted at me."

Alexandra had turned away from him. The lighting was poor in the dining parlor, but obviously not bad enough to protect her from Ross's ability to divine her thoughts. She wanted to explain some of her feelings to hìm, but she didn't think she knew him well enough to try to tell him what it had been like for her as a child. Instead, she responded, "I didn't mean to offend you and I do admire your ambitions and hope for a better life. I do."

"Look at me," he commanded softly. She swung her gaze back to him and found a crooked smile on his lips. "It isn't all your fault," he said. "I pressed you hard just now because of things that have happened to me. Maybe we've both been hurt in ways it's difficult for the other to understand. You said your father was a drifter, never sticking in one place. That's a hard life for a woman, especially when she starts bearing her young. I can understand that you might not look kindly upon men who choose an adventurous life over a tidy one." He looked like he wanted to say more, but asked instead what her life in Missouri had been like.

Conversation eased up after that and Alexandra breathed a sigh of relief. She didn't like wrangling with Ross, and the more they talked the more she wanted to be with him, a desire that would surely bring her to grief if she pursued it. Something about him, however, appealed strongly to her, and before she could explain when it had begun, pretty soon all she could think about was whether or not he would kiss her again, like he had in Phoenix.

As Ross walked her back to her room, she was quiet the entire way. When they reached her door, he leaned down to her, but to her intense disappointment he placed the smallest, most innocent kiss to the side of her mouth. She knew an almost overwhelming desire to protest, to grab hold of him and beg for more. She was about to reach out to him when he took a step backward, tipped his hat, and strode away.

Alexandra stared after him, her nerves prickling over the entire surface of her skin. How could he have just walked away?

She entered her room and closed the door with movements that felt empty and dreamlike. She leaned against the door and in the darkness of the room squeezed her eyes shut. She felt enormously dissatisfied and, at the same time, confused. How could not being kissed by Ross, really kissed, leave her feeling so miserable?

As she looked at Ross now, taking in his graceful, fluid appearance in the saddle, she came to a stunning awareness that she was drawn to him in a way she had never experienced before in her entire life. The thought frightened her and the corresponding movements of her knees and heels caused her horse to lengthen his stride.

What would life with Ross be like? Memories flooded her — of her mother, gaunt and pale from a lack of proper nourishment and sleep, tending twin boys, who were dying of pneumonia, in a drafty cabin in Colorado. Pain drove through Alexandra's heart as she kicked her horse hard and galloped past Ross toward the Dells. Fear rode her as surely as she rode the black horse beneath her.

Chapter Ten

As the cool October air rushed over Alexandra's face, she breathed in deeply and pretended that her unsettled feelings drifted away in the wind behind her as her mount sped over the dirt road. Riding hard helped, and her thoughts soon turned sweet as she concentrated on the trail before her. For a full mile she sailed on, the sunlight chasing her through the shadows of the pine trees about Prescott into the winding road leading toward the northern valleys. Before long, Alexandra brought her horse to a trot and only then did she realize Ross trailed behind her quite a ways. She pulled her horse to a walk, waiting for him to catch up with her.

"I wish I could've joined you!" He grinned as he came within talking distance. "I don't dare, though. Not with my side still as tender as it is."

Alexandra grimaced. "I'm sorry," she said, drawing her horse alongside Ross. "I forgot all about it. Of course it's your own fault. Nobody would ever guess you'd been hurt only a week ago by the way you look. And how can you hold yourself so straight in the saddle? I'd be slumped over and crying by now!"

"That I don't believe," he responded with a smile.

They fell into conversation after that, talking about the land and the route they were traveling. The Dells, as the Point of Rocks was sometimes called, was the first landmark they would pass on their way to the mine and was located only a few miles northeast of Prescott. In the distance, Alexandra could see the rounded, jutting granite outcrops.

"This has always been a place of treachery," Ross said, his eyes narrowing as he scanned the horizon before him. "The Apaches used to attack the mail riders here regularly, though you don't hear of it much anymore since Geronimo surrendered. Every once in a while, however, a renegade stirs up the countryside—and sometimes a white man or two will lay for the Wells Fargo stage. Because the post is not far away, there isn't much trouble nowadays to speak of."

"The post?" Alexandra queried.

"Fort Whipple."

Alexandra nodded, liking the idea that the Army was close by. The passageway through the Dells was bordered on both sides by gullied walls of granite rock. Deep shadows kept the trail cool in the shade and the spacing of light and shadow played tricks on Alexandra's vision. To the left, from the corner of her eye, Alexandra thought she saw a flicker of light, but she wasn't sure. The sun burned white on the rocks and it would be easy to start seeing images that simply weren't there.

"I thought I saw something," she said, glancing over at Ross. "Like the sun reflecting off metal. Did you see anything?"

Ross shook his head. "No, but I have an uneasy feeling about this place. I think we ought to get through here as quick as we can."

Alexandra felt her mouth grow dry. Maybe it was Ross's sudden sense of unease that unnerved her, or it might have been the way the granite shapes loomed over them both that set her skin to jumping, but whatever the case, she was happy to follow Ross's lead as he eased his horse into a trot. She tried not to think about the pressure each jolt brought to Ross's side. At the same time, she was confident he could bear up under the strain.

As she worked to stay close to Ross, keeping her horse at a steady trot next to his, Alexandra felt her heart rapping out a loud cadence. Glancing at him, she could see that he was tense, one hand holding his reins at a rigid angle and the other hand hovering just over his pistol. Her body grew quiet, as though every inch of her was trying to reach forward into the silence of the rocks, trying to listen for a hidden enemy.

Ross turned toward her slightly and looked her directly in the eye. With the smallest, taut lift of his hand, he motioned for her to stop. She pulled her mount up hard, every muscle in her body tight with fear, as he did the same.

The wind tumbled through the peculiar shapes and whistled every now and again. Then silence, until a skid of dust and pebbles fell down a wall some twenty yards ahead. Ross's gaze was fixed upward toward the source of the slide.

In the distance, to the right, came the quivering sounds of a rattler. Alexandra leaned toward the sound, her lids blinking rapidly to keep her sight clear. She could sense, as she was sure Ross could, that someone was there, waiting.

Again, out of the corner of her eye, Alexandra saw a flash of light, and as she turned to look in that direction, she saw the dark hat of a man appear just over a rim of granite. Light flickered off the barrel of his rifle. "Ross!" she screamed in warning as she dug her heels into the flanks of her horse. A mo-

86

ment later, a gun bellowed within the passageway.

Alexandra careened along the winding trail through the Point of Rocks. The sound of gunplay smashed time and again against her ears. A bulky object rolled down the cliff in front and to the left of her, and as she tore past it, she realized it was a dark-haired man now curled up in a heap at the base of the rocks, leather straps of ammunition crisscrossed down his back. She found her throat closing up and her stomach rolling uneasily as she leaned into the neck of her horse and sped on. She felt a bullet brush the crown of her hat, tipping it awkwardly on her forehead. She could hear the pounding of horses' hooves behind her as the gun battle continued. She was certain she was being pursued and kicked her horse again. Finally, she reached the end of the granite pathway and emerged on the other side onto open road.

She dared not pause for even a moment to risk looking back. She believed in her heart Ross was lying dead in the Dells and her own fate resided in her ability to keep her horse moving at a breakneck speed. At a distance of what appeared to be two miles, Alexandra could see a faint plume of smoke rising from the chimney of a house. She set her horse in the direction of the smoke and kept her pace steady. She could feel the horse breathing mightily with each intake of air, but she pushed him on, encouraging him with a raspy word spoken in his ear as often as she could manage it.

Her legs ached with the effort of sustaining the maddening pace. She could hear the man behind her calling to her, shouting at her to pull up. But not until he had barked out his command three times did Alexandra realize that her pursuer was Ross. She looked back at him, disbelieving that she was actually hearing his voice. When she recognized him, she quickly began drawing rein. Her horse, however, did not respond at

87

once. The heat of flight was fully upon the black gelding, and only after much coaxing was Alexandra finally able to bring him to an easy lope.

By then Ross had rejoined her and motioned for them both to head toward the ranch house. He was doubled over himself, clutching his side.

"Are you all right?" she cried. He was gulping in air as he nodded, working carefully to sustain the lope along with her.

Within a few minutes they had reached the large log house. Chickens scratched all about the yard, roses bloomed in a garden before a long window at the front of the house, a hoe rested against the pump by the narrow watering trough. No one seemed to be around.

As Alexandra dismounted before the trough, she found that her legs were shaking. Ross stepped around his horse and looked Alexandra over carefully. "Are you all right?" he asked. When she nodded in response, he let out a breath and leaned a hand against the saddle on her horse and checked his wound.

"How is it?" she asked, noting that his shirt wasn't stained with blood.

"It's all right," he said, still breathing hard. "I think it broke open a little, but not much. Are you sure you're not hurt? I'm almost deaf from so many guns firing all around us."

When she assured him again that she had escaped uninjured, he shook his head. "If you hadn't seen that man up there, we'd both have been dead. Your warning alone gave us the second or two we needed. I shot one of them, but there must have been at least two, maybe three more."

Alexandra straightened her hat and pushed loose tendrils away from her face. "I thought you were dead," she whispered hoarsely. "I didn't see what happened back there. I just kicked my horse and here I am." She looked at Ross, her knees feeling weak, her heart loose within her chest. She turned away from him slightly and buried her face in her hands, trying to forget the image of the man lying sprawled in the dust. The horses smelled strongly, their coats lathered heavily. The odor seemed to weaken her legs further. She stumbled slightly and felt Ross's arm about her waist.

"Whoa, there," he said, his voice low and gentle. "Shaking a little?" Alexandra nodded and let her hands drop to her sides.

With his other hand, Ross took her chin in hand and turned her face so that she was forced to look at him. "You did just fine, Alexandra. We're both alive and I expect we'll see many more days ahead."

Alexandra looked into concerned gray eyes and felt all the danger of the moment sweep over her again. Her legs were still trembling. "Ross," she whispered. "I'm so scared."

"It's all right now," he said quietly. Because it seemed a natural thing to do, he leaned down to kiss her, still holding her chin lightly in his hand.

He meant only to comfort her a little by kissing her, to dispel some of her fright. But the moment his lips touched hers, he was overcome by powerful, unexpected emotions. Uppermost in his mind was the realization that he could have lost her back there in the Dells, and the thought shook him up badly. Instead of releasing her as he had intended doing, he pulled her tightly against him, his lips seeking from hers an assurance that she wasn't hurt. A strange languor, charged with tension, overcame him as he kissed her hard. He let go of her chin, slipping his arm around her shoulders, drawing her closer still.

Alexandra let the feel of his warm mouth soothe away the fear coiled tightly in her chest. His lips were bold and demanding. She felt a wondrous heat spread

89

over her like she had just sunk down into a hot bath. His body was pressed the entire length of hers, the muscles of his legs firm and strong. She knew a sense of safety in his arms that she had never known before. A yearning rose within her heart to hold him close, at the same time she knew it was impossible and even undesirable for her to do so. She had to leave Arizona soon to return to Independence, to the greater security of a large town, to gather the remnants of her life, to find a better future for herself. But the thought of leaving Ross now served only to increase her sudden, intense longing for the man who was bruising her lips.

She leaned into him, taking great pleasure in the closeness of his body. She felt his tongue touch her lips and this time, she permitted him to violate her mouth. She heard him moan slightly as he thrust his tongue against hers. A surrendering weakness invaded her limbs as a blinding passion filled her. She should not be kissing Ross, she told herself a hundred times over, but the pleasure she found in his embrace was beyond anything she had ever imagined. If only it could continue forever . . .

After a moment, Ross drew back from her slightly and looked down into her eyes. "I wish we were in a secluded place right now," he whispered, drifting feathery kisses over her face. "I'd take you to bed. Alexandra, I want you!"

She heard his words and was stunned by their meaning. She knew her cheeks had begun to burn a bright red and she hid her embarrassment by dropping her forehead to his chest. *I'd take you.* He'd said the words so easily. How could he think she would . . .

Oh, Lord, Alexandra thought, remembering that she had lied about herself. *He thinks I'm a widow, a woman of experience.* She had to tell him the truth. Lifting her head to look at him, she opened her mouth

90

to speak, but realized as she did so that his whole body had grown stiff with tension, that something was wrong. His eyes were shifting quickly, back and forth, searching—for what?

The horses quivered slightly, snorting into a breeze that brought the scent of freshly harvested hay from across the fields.

Alexandra looked at the horses, noting how their ears had picked up and were twitching. She was about to make mention of it to Ross when a large Mexican hombre suddenly moved from around her black horse and leveled a Sharps buffalo rifle at them both. He had the same coloring as the man lying dead in the Dells.

"I will kill you if you dare to move!" he cried, his accent heavy. He was a big-chested man with thick black hair parted down the middle. His nose was hooked and ominous and his eyes were black chunks of coal. "Now, slowly, to the house! *Andele!*"

Chapter Eleven

Alexandra stared down the muzzle of a rifle that could drop a buffalo at four hundred feet. Even if she had wanted to, she didn't intend to argue with a man so mightily armed. With Ross following closely behind her, she walked quickly toward the front of the house. What they would find there she couldn't imagine, but her worst fear was that this isolated dwelling housed the same unconscionable men who had fired on them at the Dells.

Noting a faint movement by the window, Alexandra knew the Mexican wasn't alone and her legs began trembling again. She looked back at Ross with a pleading expression, but was surprised to find he appeared quite calm. He seemed to understand her distress and, with a brief nod of his head, stepped forward quickly to slip an arm about her waist.

"Don't worry," he whispered, holding her tight. "I know the widow who lives here, at least I spoke with her briefly a couple of times when I was in Prescott a year ago. She was a good friend of your father."

"Anything could have happened in a year," Alexandra replied, unwilling to believe they were safe. "Maybe she doesn't live here anymore."

As they neared the front of the house, the sweet scent of roses growing beneath the window met Alexandra just as the door flew open. A woman of some forty years stood staring at Ross, a Winchester tucked under her arm and slung toward the ground and a grin on her pretty face. "Is that you, Halleck?" she called out. "I heard you were in town. When did you ride in?"

Alexandra let out a sigh of relief so heavy that the woman turned her attention to her. "What's happened here?" she cried, reaching forward to take Alexandra's hand. "Good Lord, you're white. You feelin' faint? We heard guns popping at the Dells! If you were attacked out there and then accosted by Manuel, I'd be nigh to swooning myself. "She then addressed the Mexican. "I know these folks. This is Ross Halleck who owns the Alexandra — most of it anyway. Crackshot's his partner. And you can put that cannon of yours away! Oh, and would you get Windy to see to the horses?"

The large brown man looked Ross over carefully, finally giving a nod of approval before he turned to walk away.

"Come inside," the woman cried, pulling Alexandra along by the hand. "Don't pay any heed to Manuel. He's very protective of me. Lupe!" she called out over her shoulder. "Lupe, come here!" She rattled off a few words in Spanish, until a round-faced Mexican woman, heavy with child, waddled into the hallway. She was clearly frightened, her brown eyes wide, as she asked in halting English if Apaches were coming to kill them all.

"Not today," the widow returned with a smile. "As you can see, we have guests. Would you please bring some tea to the parlor." She paused to glance back at Ross with a quirky smile on her lips, then added, "And a little redeye, too?"

"*Sí, señora.*"

Alexandra watched her disappear down the hall and was struck at the same time, as she glanced left and right, by how carefully tended the house was. Not a speck of dust clung to the polished wood floors or to the furniture. Handmade doilies adorned a lifetime's collection of fine tables, chairs, a sideboard, a piano, and several cupboards. Even a contented clock ticked over the mantel in the dining room to her left. Peace owned these rooms and Alexandra realized this was the kind of home she'd dreamed of living in as a child.

Alexandra and Ross followed the widow into a large, well-appointed parlor to the right of the hallway. She introduced herself to Alexandra in her brisk manner. "I don't even know if Ross here remembers me. It's been so long since he first came to Prescott to lay claim to the Alexandra. I'm Mrs. McCormick, but please sit down. I won't be content until I see color in your cheeks."

"Thank you, ma'am," Alexandra said as she seated herself on a dark, navy-blue velvet sofa decorated with three white crocheted antimacassars. Her legs were still trembling as Ross introduced her to Mrs. McCormick as Sam's daughter.

The widow's cheeks paled rapidly, and for a long moment she didn't speak. When she did, her voice had grown considerably subdued. "I never expected in a hundred years to meet you," she said. "I thought for certain you were fixed in Missouri. You see, I knew your pa pretty well." Did Alexandra see tears dot her lashes, or was it just the sunlight from the window sparkling on her hazel eyes? "He came to call on me quite a bit the last year he worked his mine. So you're his daughter? Well, of course you are! You've the same red hair and blue eyes. Sam was such a fine-looking man! What a day full of surprises this has turned out to be!" She then seated herself in a rocking chair near

94

Alexandra, searching her face over and over as though trying to find more of Sam reflected there. "Good gracious, such manners!" she cried at last. "You must forgive me, but looking at you is like looking into the past and I can't quite accustom myself to it."

She pressed a hand to her bosom as though she was pained a little, then turned back to Ross who had drawn up a chair next to Alexandra. "So tell me, what happened back there at the Dells? Was somebody shooting at you or—or Alexandra?"

"Both of us, I think," Ross said, holding his black hat in hand and narrowing his eyes. "This wasn't the first time, either. Four men caught me outside of Phoenix and cut my side up pretty good with a .38." He held Mrs. McCormick's gaze, the perpetual serious frown between his brows deepening as he queried, "It's the mine, isn't it? Sam must have told you something and I sure would like to know what's going on."

Mrs. McCormick was a bright, energetic woman with just a few gray hairs marring her thick dark-brown hair. Alexandra had the impression that she could outlast anyone on a dance floor, so strong and vivacious did she look. But just now she looked strained and tired.

When Mrs. McCormick answered Ross, she leaned back heavily into the rocking chair and stated, "Sam found some ore like none he'd ever seen before. I think that's why he died. Somebody found out about it, wanted his claim, and just up and killed him. I never did learn how he died, not that it matters much now, but since you folks seem to be up to your ears in trouble, maybe you ought to find out. I know he thought someone was after him and if he was killed you'd be one step closer to puzzling out who attacked you both."

Ross was thoughtful for a time, his hands clasped

loosely together thinking about what Mrs. McCormick had said. "What neither of us understand, though, is why Sam staked his mine in a poker game with me. It just doesn't make sense, especially if he knew the mine was worth something."

Mrs. McCormick nodded, sprang from her chair, leaving it rocking in her wake, and crossed the room to a lowboy by the door. From one of the drawers, she withdrew several letters and began flipping through them until she found the one she sought.

"Ross," she said, returning to her chair with the letter in hand. "You've been on the frontier for many years now. I've lived in the West twenty myself. You learn things about people, and I think your instincts become real sharp. How long would it take you anymore to know the cut of a man's cloth if you happened to meet him in a saloon or say if you wandered into his camp one night?" She smiled softly. "Sam had you figured out before he sat down to poker and cheated his way to losing that mine to you." She handed the letter to him.

"What?" Ross cried as he took the letter from the widow's hand. He opened it quickly and began reading.

Alexandra did not wait for an invitation, but moved close to Ross, feeling hungry to find out what her father had written to Mrs. McCormick. She read along with him, silently.

"I'm doin' everything I can to stay alive Sarah, but sometimes when the flood waters rise a man knows his time has come. I've been shot at so many times since I left Prescott, that I've lost track. And I've been riding my poor horse so hard, hoping to stay one step ahead of the outlaws on my trail, that he's about done in. You'll probably think I've gone plumb crazy when I tell you that I gambled the Alexandra away to the first decent man I met, a drover named Halleck out of Texas. He seemed mighty proud of his skill at cards, and I still laugh when I think about it. I only hope he can profit from the mine. He said he wanted to build a big spread of his own. Maybe that will help. Now he's the kind of man I would've wanted for my Alexandra. I think he'll do right by Crackshot, too. I write these words and I shake my head. What has my life added up too? I had hoped more than anything that things would turn out different this time — only look at me, holed up in a hotel room in Dodge City. Waiting.

"I've sent a letter on to my daughter but I haven't heard from her in so long that I don't know whether she's alive or dead. She's well cared for by my brother-in-law and she'll be a rich woman some day, so I don't regret too much her not getting her namesake.

"If I get to Independence, I aim to send word to Halleck about the men on my backtrail. I don't worry too much about him — he looked about fit for anything.

"I've gone over everything in my mind a hundred times, and I still don't know who would be after my mine. I wish Barnes had come with me, like he wanted to. But maybe it's for the best since I would have hated for him to get hurt just because of the Alexandra. He's sure been a good friend to me. I aim to see the sheriff here in Dodge City, much good that will do. Unless you're dead, they don't pay too much heed to suspicions and will just as soon set down the attacks to Indians as to anything else. The only thing I know for certain is that whoever is after me, is downright determined."

The rest of the letter Mrs. McCormick held back, saying it was just a few fond farewells and if they wouldn't mind, she'd prefer to keep them to herself.

Alexandra found so many thoughts tearing around

in her mind and bumping into each other that she hardly knew which one to look at first. One thing she knew for certain, her father didn't die of the Spanish influenza. He must've been killed. She could hardly breathe with the thinking of it.

She felt Ross touch her arm lightly. When she looked up at him, he asked, "Did you ever receive word from your father, a last letter from Dodge City?" Alexandra shook her head.

He nodded slowly. "Neither did I," he said, handing the letter back to the widow. "Not a word."

Mrs. McCormick took it from Ross. "I don't think it's to be wondered at too much," she said, chuckling softly. "When I first came out here as a young bride, I remember seeing somewhere on a long stretch of prairie, several U. S. mail bags rotting away under the hot sun. Whenever I don't hear from a friend or relative for a long time, I always think of those bags. "Besides . . ." she added, her eyes welling up with tears. "Sam may simply have run out of time."

At that moment, Lupe arrived carrying a polished silver tray bearing tea, fresh warm cookies, and a decanter of whiskey.

Ross took a glass of whiskey Mrs. McCormick poured out for him and, with an ironic smile said, "And I thought I was playing such a skillful game that night. I suppose that'll teach me."

"Well, you had no one to warn you now, did you? Boy, could Sam play a wicked game of poker." She handed Alexandra a cup of tea and laced it with some whiskey. She laughed at Alexandra's surprise, then winked at her. "That oughta bring some color back to your complexion."

Alexandra found the more she was with the widow, the more she liked her. She was reminded of the doctor in Phoenix and his open, bluff ways. Mrs. McCormick was a lot like him and she could see why her pa had no doubt taken a shine to this lively woman.

Glancing at Ross, Alexandra saw to her surprise that he was looking at her with a funny expression in his eyes, one she remembered from Phoenix, an expression of disapproval. She wondered what he could possibly be thinking. He didn't even smile as he looked away from her and took another sip of his whiskey.

For several minutes they discussed all the possibilities surrounding Sam's death, the mine, and what ought to be done next. The matter was settled quickly when Manuel appeared suggesting that he take several of the hands to the Point and hunt for the desperadoes who had attacked Alexandra and Ross.

Mrs. McCormick agreed to it right away. But when Ross insisted on going with them, asking only for a fresh mount, Alexandra protested. "What if they're still there?" she cried. "All of you could be killed?"

"I doubt that there will be a single sign of these bandits," Ross said. "Including the one who died. If the men who attacked us have even a grain of sense among them, they will have already hightailed it out of the Dells. And if Mrs. McCormick's hands intend to ride over, I must go with them."

Alexandra realized he was right and nodded to him as he set his glass down on the silver tray and followed Manuel toward the back of the house, heading for the stables.

When their footsteps disappeared down the hall, Mrs. McCormick walked briskly back to the rocking chair and assured Alexandra that Ross and her hands would be just fine. "All they hope to do now is find some clue to the identity of the men who shot at you. Ross is right. They won't even find the body of the bandit who died."

Alexandra did not want to think about it anymore.

Every time she pictured that man lying in heap at the base of the rocks, her stomach turned over.

Fortunately, Mrs. McCormick had many questions to ask of her, not least of which was why she rarely answered Sam's letters.

"Papa didn't know my uncle very well," Alexandra responded quietly, sipping her tea. "I didn't even learn of the Alexandra until a few weeks ago. Uncle Demarion kept back about a score of my father's letters from me, in particular those that made mention of his mine."

"I knew it!" Mrs. McCormick cried. "Bless your pa, he was awful buffleheaded about some things, in particular the worth of those people he sent you to live with. I knew there had to be reason why he hardly ever heard from you. So, tell me, are you rich now like Sam thought you'd be?"

Alexandra felt her throat constrict tightly. "My uncle died a wealthy man, that much is true. But he left me his inheritance on a — a certain condition which I have found quite difficult to meet. The only way I will see his money is if I marry a lawyer by the name of William Bradshaw."

"Another Bradshaw?" she asked, startled since Ross had introduced her as Mrs. Bradshaw.

"There wasn't a first one," Alexandra responded. She felt her cheeks grow warm beneath the other woman's surprised stare. She had not known Mrs. McCormick long, but everything about her demanded trust. "I've been pretending to be a widow by the name of Bradshaw. It's been a lot easier to travel as such than if I were a — an innocent young lady, but I can't tell you how many times my conscience has lit a fire in my mind. The truth is I've never been married and, as for William, I broke my engagement with him when I headed west. He said he'd wait for me, believing I was

100

just chasing a silly notion I'd soon come to regret by leaving Independence. But the fact is, I just don't love him. He's not a very warm, loving man, not unlike my uncle in many ways, which is why I'm sure he chose William for me."

"Ross thinks you're a widow, doesn't he?"

"How'd you know?"

"By the way he kissed you outside a few minutes ago, like he sees you as a woman who's had a little experience of life."

The blush on Alexandra's cheeks started to burn. "I was just so scared after the attack at the Dells. I — I — "

"*I* understand perfectly," Mrs. McCormick said, laughing at the younger woman. "You don't have to explain anything to me. I took one look at those fine, strong shoulders of his and I said to myself if I were you I'd have done the same thing."

Alexandra shook her head at Mrs. McCormick, denying that she had deliberately taken advantage of the situation in order to get a hug and a kiss from Ross.

"I'm just teasing you a little," Mrs. McCormick responded with a warm smile. "I've got two grown daughters of my own who are both married, thank the Lord, and being a woman myself, I know very well how much a little manly consolation can go to easing a woman's heart. I don't blame you one bit. The way you are feeling about that man is perfectly natural. Now, tell me how on earth you met up with Ross in the first place."

When Alexandra told her about seeing Ross ride up to her hotel in Phoenix, with his side shot up, Mrs. McCormick cried enigmatically, "Why, I don't think I've never known Providence to be so bold before. All I ask is that you invite me to your wedding!"

"I — I don't know what you mean," Alexandra responded. "Ross and I aren't getting married. We hardly know each other. After I visit Papa's mine, I'll be boarding the stage back to Missouri."

Mrs. McCormick was quiet for a full minute, leaning back into her chair and setting it to rocking. Her gaze never left Alexandra's face, but it was clear to her that the older woman had something of import to say to her.

After a couple of minutes, Mrs. McCormick said, "You remind me a little of myself about twenty years ago. I can tell that you're very uncertain about what to do next. "She paused, looking away from Alexandra, her hazel eyes taking on a thoughtful expression, as though she were trying to find exactly the right words to frame her thoughts. "Be very careful about letting Ross go," she said at last. "A man like that doesn't come down the trail but once in a lifetime. You only have to look at him, to know that much. Those shoulders were meant to carry a heavy load, and if I were ten years younger — and maybe had a headful of red hair — I'd tie my handkerchief about his wrist and lead him home."

"I can't stay here!" Alexandra cried, holding out her hands as though she was imploring Mrs. McCormick to believe her. "I like Ross very much, but he's not the man who can give me what I want."

Mrs. McCormick held her gaze steadfastly and with a twinkle in her eye, responded, "Then you're as big a fool as I ever was, Sam Wingfield's daughter!"

Chapter Twelve

Ross was right about the trip out to the Alexandra and then some. The farther they got from Prescott, the more rugged and demanding the trail grew until Alexandra felt every joint in her body had been jerked apart at least a dozen times. She was not used to riding through such rough country, and though it was only a little past one o'clock, she ached in places she had not known existed.

They had left Mrs. McCormick's house an hour and half after Ross, Manuel, and the other ranch hands returned with nothing to show for their efforts. Mrs. McCormick had wanted Ross to go back to Prescott and let the sheriff know what happened. "You've got to get the law involved," she said. "If nothing else, the sheriff's interest could discourage any more attacks."

"I'm pretty anxious by now to get out to the mine," Ross said. "Crackshot has been out there by himself for some time and I'd like to make sure he's all right. Besides, as much as I might want to speak with Sheriff Goodwin, I understand he's still down in Carver and I don't have a great opinion of his deputy, Barnes, even if he was a good friend of Sam's. I took a minute yesterday to let him know I'd had some trouble in Phoenix, but he didn't do anything more than wipe his forehead with his red kerchief and mutter that he'd send word to the sheriff there and see what he could find out. Needless to say, I didn't sit down and have a long chat with him."

Mrs. McCormick agreed that Louis Barnes was not precisely the most effective peacemaker Sheriff Goodwin had ever hired, but he was trusted by many of the more refined folks in Prescott, especially since he played a lively fiddle. "And that puts me in mind of something," she continued, her eyes brightening. "I always give a New Year's Eve party and I'd like it very much if you and Alexandra would plan on attending."

"I can't speak for her," Ross answered. "But you can count on me." He then looked at Alexandra with a direct, questioning stare.

Alexandra had felt challenged by the expression in his gray eyes just then, but couldn't understand what he meant by it. She remembered how, after reading the letter her papa had written to Mrs. McCormick, Ross had gotten a strange look on his face, almost as if he was angry with her.

Not certain what she ought to say, especially since Mrs. McCormick had teased her about marrying Ross, she answered finally, "I don't know if I'll still be in Prescott at that time, but if I am, of course I'd love to come to your party."

"Good!" Mrs. McCormick exclaimed, flashing her quirky smile. "Then I'll see both of you on New Year's Eve, if not before!"

Alexandra started to protest, but Mrs. McCormick merely slipped her arm about her waist. "You're here in Arizona to stay," she had whispered. "And Ross Halleck is your man. You'll just have to get used to the idea, that's all."

As Alexandra worked hard to keep pace with Ross,

her thighs and knees aching, she felt her cheeks burning from the memory of Mrs. McCormick's parting remark. Glancing toward Ross, she saw that he had pulled his mount to a stop and was staring down over a ridge into what she supposed was a gully. Was he her man? Somehow this thought, as she watched Ross slip his hat off and touch the back of his sleeve to his face, brought an unexpected thrill rushing through her. He was skylined against a dark-blue expanse, sitting straight in the saddle. She felt her heart weaken at the mere looking at him. Why did she feel this way about him? *A man like this doesn't come down the trail but once in a lifetime.*

As she drew near, her black horse picking his way carefully to a place just behind the wiry mustang, Ross turned back and said with a smile, "I forgot how pretty it was here."

As her horse crested the rise, she looked down into a shallow, grassy valley with a gentle stream flowing through it. A weathered cabin, appearing cold and abandoned, sat at the northern end of the valley where the forest of pines trees began. Alexandra was as much startled by the trees as she was by the beauty of the well-watered land.

"We're at the edge of Bee Mountain," Ross said, answering her unspoken question, "which rises to over seven thousand feet. That's why you see these pines. I have the nicest feeling, though, like I've just come home!"

Alexandra glanced up at him, surprised. "I was thinking the same thing," she said. "I guess because my father spoke about his mine so much. Still, I didn't expect anything so lovely. Look at all the yellow flowers! They're everywhere. Is that Crackshot's tent? I wonder why he doesn't use the cabin?"

Against the cabin leaned a small shed surrounded by

a fenced corral, and about a hundred yards below the cabin sat a tent not far from the creek. There was no sign of Crackshot, but in front of the tent, a rock-ringed fire, mounted with a tripod and kettle, was burning steadily, steam rising from the blackened caul-dron. To the west of the creek, a gaping hole, situated on the side of the ravine wall which rose steadily up-ward for several hundred feet, proclaimed the location of the mine. A wood chute led from the entrance of the mine down to a round pit in the ground which Alexan-dra realized from her father's descriptions must be the arrastra which they used to break up the ore. Near the stream, a sway-backed, sturdy-looking horse, proba-bly used to working the grinding pit, nibbled on the fresh grass. Had Alexandra or Ross been in doubt upon which mine they had stumbled, the large, bold letters THE ALEXANDRA had been burnt into a thick board that was nailed to the top of a support beam fronting the mine.

Alexandra read her name and found her throat clos-ing up as tears misted over her eyes. Her father had made the sign and this one display of his love for her brought him closer than ever before. Had she only known of his letters and his mine, she would have come west sooner to be with him. Maybe he would still be alive if she had come to live here in this little valley. As her gaze swept over the wind-tossed grassy land, to the pines, the cabin, the tent, and back to the mine, an overwhelming sensation of loss filled Alexandra's heart until it felt tight with pain.

"What is it?" she heard Ross ask gently.

Alexandra blinked her tears away. "I should've come sooner," she said quietly. "When Papa was alive."

"Why didn't you?" he asked. "Were you afraid?"

"No. Not exactly. I didn't like traveling to one lonely spot after another, that much is true. But I believe if I'd

106

known about this place, I would have set aside my feelings and stayed here with him. You have to understand, too, that because my uncle didn't give me so many of my father's letters, I didn't think he really wanted me around."

Ross nodded. "I see," he said, his expression solemn. "It's hard to understand why your uncle would have done such a thing. Well, let's take a look at this place and see if we can find Crackshot. He's probably in the mine, but for the life of me I can't figure out why he's got a fire burning. Do you smell that? He's got something cooking!"

"Sonofabitch stew!" Alexandra cried happily. When Ross turned to look at her in surprise, she laughed aloud and explained that her father had made mention of Crackshot's stew in his letters, that he had applied this unhandsome nickname to his friend's efforts at cooking. She sniffed the air then added, "Why, it doesn't smell bad at all, does it! Papa said he didn't like it much, but I can't imagine why not!"

"Neither can I!" Ross cried, giving the reins a slap and clicking his tongue at the mustang. "I didn't know how hungry I was until just now." He began leading his mount down the crest, heading toward a path to the northwest that led into the valley. Just as Alexandra gave her horse a gentle kick, the sound of a woman's frightened scream rose high in the air.

Chapter Thirteen

Alexandra's horse shied sideways at the sound of the woman's cry and half slid, half ran down the slant of the rise, away from the mine. "Whoa!" she called sharply to the gelding. The horse threw its head up and down to each jerk of her reins as she called to him several times and it was a full minute before she brought the horse to a stop down the trail from which she had just come.

Turning the horse around, she saw Ross had had an easier time keeping his mount under control. He, too, was on the near side of the hill, protected from the camp's view. His face was taut in appearance, his eyes intense, as he patted his horse's neck and talked to his mustang in a low voice. He looked back toward Alexandra and motioned for her to stay where she was. He slipped from his saddle and, pulling his horse behind him, eased his way down the side of the crest, heading toward the path where Alexandra waited, motionless.

She watched him, aware that her heart had begun drumming in her chest. What was a woman doing out here anyway? And what was wrong with her? The scream that rent the air had held an eerie, unsettling quality, as if her mind wasn't right.

Ross beckoned Alexandra to ride over to him. She

crossed the thirty feet that separated them and took the reins he held out to her. He then ran nearly to the top of the crest, dropped to his knees, and finally to his stomach, where he crawled forward until he could see just over the rim and down into the valley. He waited there for several minutes, finally backing up in the same manner in which he had approached the crest.

Gathering his reins back from Alexandra, he said, "There's a squaw down there, folded up and rocking herself on the ground. Crackshot's kneeling beside her. I'm going down, but I think you should wait just in case one of them has gone loco and starts shooting. If Crackshot does, we're both likely to end up six feet under!"

Alexandra nodded, her mouth feeling cottony as she tried unsuccessfully to take in a deep breath.

She watched Ross lead his horse on foot down to the trail that opened up into the valley. Even before he could be visible to Crackshot or to the woman, he called out, "Ho there, comin' in!" He repeated this greeting several times, including his name, but Alexandra didn't hear anyone respond.

For a long time she listened intently, but from her position she was unable to hear much of anything. Her curiosity about the woman began to grow until she was no longer willing to remain hidden and wait. She dismounted quickly and tied her reins securely to a small shrub nearby and repeated what she had seen Ross do earlier. She scrambled over to the edge of the crest, dropped on her knees, then crawled to the rim. Her dark-blue skirt was a serious encumbrance and her knees kept catching in the fabric. But by the time she could see down into the valley, Ross had crossed half the distance to the camp and Crackshot was standing beside a bundle of tan leather that was still rocking in the sunshine. He waved a hand to Ross and shouted out a greeting that Alexandra could not quite make out.

She didn't wait for an invitation, but returned to her mount and led the black gelding down to the path that entered the valley. Following Ross's example again, she called out, "Ho, there, Alexandra! Comin' in!"

Sitting by the fire on a large overturned wood crate, Alexandra smelled with great pleasure the stew steaming on her spoon. The slices of meat had a pungent smell of sage, with a rich brown gravy, and chunks of potatos. She was hungry from the long ride to the mine. Sliding the spoon slowly into her mouth, she closed her eyes, enjoying the bright flavor of the meat. It tasted familiar, but she wasn't sure exactly what it was. Based on her father's letters, she thought it might be venison. When she opened her eyes, she saw that everyone was watching her expectantly. She glanced at Crackshot and was about to ask him what kind of meat was in the stew when his squaw, a white woman who had been held captive since a child by the Apaches, stated simply, "Rattlesnake. You like?"

Alexandra kept from choking only by the strongest of efforts as she shifted her gaze toward the tent and saw two dead snakes hanging on a pole inside. Earlier, she had wondered why Crackshot and his woman kept them there, but now she knew why. Her stomach jolted hard against her ribs as she smiled and nodded, returning her gaze to her tin pan. She scraped her spoon around and around the pan, pushing aside bits of potato and meat as she tried to figure out how she was going to keep eating when her stomach was flying end over end. She didn't want to offend her hostess, but, good Lord in heaven! Rattlesnake?

"I no think she like it much, Mr. Peters," the squaw said, shaking her head at Alexandra, but smiling. "She turn paler than before, white like flour."

110

The men burst out laughing and Crackshot took pity on Alexandra. "That ain't rattler," he said kindly. "Venison. We've got a lot of mule deer in the forest hereabouts. I'd never let Cecilia cook up a snake."

Alexandra let out a soft sigh of relief, which set all three of them to laughing hard. She then smiled at Cecilia, telling her it was a good joke, and had the pleasure of seeing the woman grin back her.

In Alexandra's opinion, Cecilia Tharsing was one of the homeliest creatures she had ever seen, with a long, narrow face, a pinched nose, and teeth that crossed and recrossed each other at least a dozen times. She was in her thirties, by best account, but her hair was already streaked with stiff gray hairs that stood out atop the softer black ones underneath. Her large eyes were handsome, however, being a soft blue interwoven with steel-gray flicks. When she smiled, even though her teeth looked like they'd just had a war, her expression was warm and friendly. According to Crackshot, however, she was given to fits of insanity. That she had cooked the stew was the reason it tasted of heaven. Cecilia had already informed them that she would die before she would eat any of Crackshot's stew. "Not fit for a mad dog!" she had cried.

When Alexandra had first walked up to the camp, Cecilia had run into the tent and started wailing. Crackshot greeted Alexandra quickly, then went inside the tent himself, closing the flap behind him. While he was tending the poor woman, Alexandra and Ross gathered handfuls of grass and rubbed down the horses before leading them to drink in the clearwater creek. By then Cecilia was calmer and actually emerged from the tent, smiling nervously to them both.

Crackshot had explained that his squaw, as he called her, had seen them both on the hill and had gone crazy, which she always did when she was scared. "She ain't

111

been right since she was took back from the 'Paches. I think maybe she oughta stayed with 'em. I found her a few months ago walkin' outside of Prescott, maybe six miles or so, heading south. She was talkin' about going to San Carlos where her people were. She's got a brother at the post, but he's drunk half the time and don't seem to care about her much." After a moment's pause, a concerned look passed briefly across his face and he added quietly, "I think she's better off with me." He shrugged then, his expression a little sheepish as he turned to smile at Alexandra and said he had just taken to her for some reason.

Cecilia had listened to him speak and, when he was done, she nodded several times, saying, "Mr. Peters good man. I stay with him. He good husband, even if he need more baths. Not so clean like Apaches. But he good man. Good man."

Crackshot shifted on his feet and cleared his throat, a blush starting to creep up his neck. Alexandra could find no fault in the arrangement, seeing within these two people, the strange turnings of the West, its harshness at times as well as its desire to make right its wrongs. She turned away from Crackshot's embarrassment to exclaim over the fine-smelling stew!

Alexandra began eating the stew again, her gaze drifting several times to the rattlers inside the tent. She wondered if it was some kind of Indian charm, to keep snakes around like that. Crackshot noticed her interest and explained, "I save 'em for the Chinee. I pickle 'em in alcohol and when I make my monthly treks to Prescott, they'll buy every one I've got. They say it cures rheumatism. All I know is that the money I get keeps me in good rye. Say, you remind me of someone I know. Do I know you? Bradshaw, huh?"

He fell to studying her face, and Alexandra thought that since he'd teased her about the stew, she would let his mind fuss a bit as to why she looked familiar to him. "I know for a fact we've never met," she answered truthfully.

By the time Alexandra finished her stew, and a dark, heavy coffee was passed around, Ross told Crackshot about the attacks on his life. Crackshot in turn related a brief history to them both, from the time he had joined up with Sam and helped him work his diggings until today. In the telling, he would occasionally glance at Alexandra and remark on how she had the look of someone he knew, but for the life of him, he just couldn't remember who! Alexandra was still of a mind to keep her identity secret and Ross made no effort to enlighten him, either.

As for the Alexandra, according to Crackshot, her father had come across some rich ore a couple of months before he left Prescott. But by the time Crackshot received word that Sam was dead, the vein had played out. From the time Ross had come to claim ownership of the mine, Crackshot had done a little dynamiting, working the diggings carefully but finding only enough gold to pay for timber beams to shore up each hole afterward and to keep the camp in supplies. "I wouldn't even call the dig promising right now," he said, with a serious expression on his face. "Which makes me wonder why anyone would try to kill you for it, unless they know something I don't. And I've been all over this stake, drilling and blasting in every direction possible, and I ain't found nothing that looked even close to Sam's ore." He shook his head and dropped his gaze to the dust at his feet. His boots were thick with dirt, as were his pants and shirt. Even the skin of his fingers were embedded with the earth. A weight seemed to settle on his shoulders as a frown ridged his forehead. He appeared to be about fifty, his brown hair streaked with gray, his small blue eyes crinkling when he smiled. He was not a tall man, standing about three inches over Alexandra. He was lean in appearance, but she did not for a minute mistake the slimness of his build for a lack of strength. Pounding steel bits into solid rock, drilling holes for dynamite sticks, and doing it six days out of seven was not the work of a milk-fed greenhorn!

After a long pause, Crackshot continued. "The only thing that keeps me here is that Sam was convinced he'd hit the mother lode. I know what you're thinkin'—the dream of the argonaut!" He laughed, shrugging slightly, something Alexandra noted he did quite often. "Maybe it's just a dream, but I've been real happy here, especially since I have a stake in the Alexandra now, and I'm of a mind to keep on going a while longer. If nothin' comes of the claim in another six months, Cecilia and me, well, we'll just push on."

Ross sipped his coffee, his elbows on his knees. He had listened carefully to all that Crackshot had told him. "Two men can do a sight more than one," he said at last. "I've come here to see if this mine holds anything for me." He glanced at Alexandra and said, "I think Mrs. Bradshaw here has something similar in mind."

Crackshot glanced at her and asked, "How's that?"

"Why, Mr. Peters, haven't you figured it out yet?" she asked, smiling.

He shook his head, pinching his lips together as he stared at her. "Very familiar! But I ain't got a clue!"

She tilted her head and said simply, "I'm Sam's daughter."

He jumped up like he'd just been stung by a bee and spilled coffee on his boots. "By Gawd," he cried. "The joke's on me! Here you been sittin' by my fire and me keepin' on saying how you look familiar, and me teasin' you about rattlesnakes! Alexandra! Cecilia, the mine's named after this lady here! Maybe we'll have a little luck now and strike it rich. You gonna stay out here with us and keep Cecilia company? Why, it'd be like havin' Sam around all over again."

Alexandra felt uncomfortable by the question, especially since she knew Ross was watching her intently. She couldn't understand what he wanted from her. Avoiding giving an answer, she asked Crackshot about the cabin.

He shrugged, and rocked his head. "That was Sam's place. When he died, I didn't have the heart to touch anything. I still don't, and as fer movin' in there, Cecilia couldn't have done it, if she wanted to. She thinks the ghosts of the Hualapais live in there."

When Alexandra asked who they were, he explained that years ago a fierce battle had taken place between two Indian tribes at Mescal Gulch, the Hualapais and the Yavapais. "The Yavapais call this place Bee Mountain, and to this day they won't come near the gulch, nor anywhere else around here. It seems that the ghosts from that battle have taken up residence here, but I ain't seen a one and I've been here nigh on four years now!"

Alexandra glanced at Cecilia, then back at Crackshot, and asked, "But what does the cabin have to do with Mescal Gulch?"

Crackshot shrugged. "The gulch ain't far from here and as for Cecilia and the cabin, darlin', if I knew the answer to that, I'd know where to find the next strike! Cecilia just gits an idea fixed in her brain and there it stays. But it don't matter much, tent-livin' is fine fer me. Besides, if you stay, you can live in the cabin. Everything's right where your pa left it. You might want to go take a look if you've a mind to."

Alexandra said she was most surely "of a mind to" and shortly afterward made her way to the cabin alone. She was grateful that none of the others came with her. She mounted the three steps to the shallow porch, and peeked in through the smoke-stained window off to the

115

right. She couldn't see very much because the interior was dark and the window was dirty, but dimly outlined were a table and three chairs which sat near the window.

Her heart began sounding in her ears as she approached the door. Her papa had lived here the last years of his life. What would she find? she wondered. Ghosts, maybe? Giving the door a shove, she walked inside.

Chapter Fourteen

The small house smelled musty from rain, time, and dust. Were there ghosts here? Probably, but not the kind Cecilia feared, only relics of the past that could set about haunting the unsuspecting.

Alexandra stood on the threshold, aware that there were memories alive in these rooms, ready to pounce. She felt like she was poised on the edge of a cliff, in serious danger of falling. How could a room, a house, make her feel like that? As though to break up the strong feelings that surrounded her, she took a firm step forward, then another, until she was standing flat-footed on the boot-worn boards of the cabin floor.

Strangely enough, instead of dispelling the bold impressions of the cabin, Alexandra had a profound sense that love had been born in this house. She looked quickly around as though trying to determine just what had given her that idea. In most ways the small house was like any number of frontier dwellings, built in a square and divided by one wall that separated a bedroom from the rest of the house. But nowhere could she find a source for that brief moment of intuition until her gaze settled on a vase of withered, web-draped flowers that sat on the mantel of the fireplace. Living alone, her papa wouldn't have had reason to buy a vase and bring it back to his cabin, nonetheless fill it with water and afterward settle a dozen or more flowers into it. Had a woman come here, someone her father had loved? How strange to think of him that way, as a man needing love.

Her thoughts naturally turned to Ross and her growing feelings for him. What was bothering him that he kept looking at her in that particular way of his, like he was daring her to do something he believed she didn't have the courage to do? She was at a loss to understand him she only wished right now that she hadn't come to the mine. The sensation returned to her of being on the edge of a cliff. Her heart quickened and she pressed a hand to her stomach where she could feel the ridges of her corset against her fingers. Why was she so unsettled? Why was she even here? What did she hope to find? What was it she was looking for? And why did Ross confuse her so mightily, pulling her first this way then that?

She lifted a hand, striking it quickly through the air, trying to cut off her thoughts. She breathed in deeply, smelling the dank quality of the cabin, reminding herself that she ought to look quickly around, then demand Ross take her back to Prescott. They would have to be starting their return trek anyway or they would find themselves stuck on the trail in the dark and that wouldn't be wise, not after the attack at the Dells.

Alexandra took another deep breath and cleared her mind. She would give herself five minutes to look around the cabin, then she would leave.

As she scanned the first room in its entirety she was surprised by how well equipped it was for a man living on his own. To the right of her stood a rough, splintery table and three weary-looking chairs that she had seen through the window. As she turned back toward her right shoulder, she saw that the window overlooked Crackshot's tent and the mine. She could see Ross and Crackshot talking and looking in the direction of the horses which, as she approached the window and looked to the southwest, were now grazing at the bottom of the meadow. If the sight of Ross standing tall in the sunshine, running a hand through his thick black hair, caused her heart to jump, she ignored it and turned back to examine the rest of the house.

Alexandra walked quickly to the kitchen area where the large stone fireplace, black from use, made up a large portion of the outer wall to her right. On its mantel, in addition to what she could now see was a hand-painted vase, sat an open tin of matches rendered useless by damp weather, a glass lamp containing about an inch of oil, and, to her surprise, a photograph of herself she'd had taken in Missouri almost four years ago. She laughed aloud at the solemn expression she wore. She looked so young, but then she had been only sixteen at the time.

Alexandra touched the picture. Was it real? Was she here? How strange to think of her father living in this cabin, keeping her portrait on the mantel and the place going untouched for a year. It caught one of the last moments of his life, trapping it in time.

To the left of the fireplace, sat a cast-iron stove, caked with dust and grime. Opposite the fireplace, a long, high worktable ran half the length of the whole wall. It was flounced with a blue calico print and tacked on with small nails. She realized with a start that her father wouldn't have put a skirt on a table. Who then? Mrs. McCormick? *A man like that only comes down the trail once in a lifetime*. Had she been speaking about her father?

Moving to the door that linked the two rooms of the house, Alexandra pushed it open and was astonished to

119

find her mother's finely carved wood bed sitting against the wall opposite the door. Her father still had it with him, and Alexandra understood suddenly that she was seeing things about him she had never seen before. He hadn't needed to keep this bed. Why had he, then? In a sharp moment of insight, Alexandra realized that she was looking at her father through different eyes now. She was no longer the girl of twelve, she was when she first went to live with her aunt and uncle, but a young woman of twenty. The difference in perception was what was startling her, surprising her with each memory the cabin evoked. She was changing, and maybe that was one reason she felt so confused about Ross.

She resumed the task at hand. The bed still had a mattress and was covered with a thick quilt that looked like it would be warm in the winter. She couldn't resist lifting the quilt to see what was beneath it, but all she found was a lumpy mattress made of cornhusks.

That will have to go, she thought.

Alexandra jumped back from the bed as though it had just reached out and bit her. She stared at it, horrified. She wasn't staying. She wasn't. She had no reason to. Then why had such a thought come to her, *That will have to go?*

She took another deep breath and she glanced around the rest of the room. Several hooks adorned the wall near the door making her aware that the cabin lacked a cupboard in which to hang clothes. A chest of drawers, however, sat on the same wall as the bed and was probably all that her papa needed. On the other side of the bed a small window to the southeast overlooked the valley. She walked to it, and looked through the several small panes to see both horses lounging in the sun, their long necks bent toward the rich grass. She could see Cecilia walking the far length of the valley, gathering a bouquet of the tall yellow flowers in her arms.

Crackshot was with the horses now, patting them and checking their hooves. She agreed with Cecilia; he was a good man, everything about him spoke of honesty and trust. She liked him very much and saw readily why her papa would have taken him on. She wondered how much of the claim Ross had given to him and was struck suddenly by the fact that Ross had done right by Crackshot, just as her father hoped he would. She felt pleased somehow.

She couldn't see Ross at all, but since the tent and the mine were not within the scope of the window, she wasn't surprised. No doubt he was looking down the throat of the main mineshaft, investigating for himself the state of his claim.

But upon hearing the creak of a board, she turned around suddenly, and was startled to find Ross leaning against the doorjamb, looking at her with eyes that had grown quite black in the dim shadows of the dark cabin. She had no idea what he was thinking or why he'd come here. All she knew was that he filled that doorway, and her heart seemed to leap toward him, beating hard in her chest, a constant measure of her increasing desire for him, for she could call it nothing less.

For a long moment he didn't say a word, but Alexandra could swear he was talking to her. Even the air in the room seemed charged with his thoughts as he held her gaze. When he spoke, his voice moved like an arrow across the distance between them, piercing her heart. "I want you stay with me," he said, his gaze never wavering once from her face.

Chapter Fifteen

Alexandra pressed her hand to her stomach as she had done earlier, trying to hold back the feelings that had begun to roll over her. Why did Ross affect her this way? She felt like a stand of wheat being blown in rippling waves by a steady prairie wind. As much as she might be powerless to stop the wind, however, she knew she could at least try to escape it!

"I'm going back to Missouri," she said finally. The expression that flitted across Ross's face, of iron will, brought fear suddenly flooding her heart.

"You're not going anywhere," he said, his voice low.

"I don't know what you mean," Alexandra retorted in a frightened whisper. "I told you I only came out here to see Papa's mine. I never said I'd stay. I don't want stay. I want to go back to Independence."

Gathering her courage about her, Alexandra settled her tan hat more firmly on her head. "And right now, it's time to head back to Prescott," she said, crossing the small room in a few quick strides. She stopped in front of Ross and, not daring to look at him, asked politely, "Will you please let me by? It'll be dark in a few hours. We should be leaving right away."

He didn't say anything for a long time and she refused

to lift her head to look at him. Finally, when he continued to remain silent, she said in a softer voice, "Ross, please stop this. I — I don't think I can give you what you want."

Ross touched her arm lightly. "Maybe not," he responded, his voice husky. "But I think I can give you what *you* want. One way or the other, however, I won't let you pass until you let me see that pretty face of yours."

Alexandra swallowed hard, wondering what he could possibly mean by saying he could give her what she wanted. One thing she did know was that she was in big trouble with this man. And she knew exactly what would happen if she met his gaze, even once fleetingly.

"Let me pass," she whispered, then on impulse tried to dart by him. He quickly barred her way, and now she was standing right next to him, his strong shoulder nearly brushing her cheek.

His voice sparkled with faint amusement as he whispered, "I won't let you go until you look at me. I just want to see if your eyes are still as blue as the sky out there. Is that asking so much?"

She felt his hand just beneath her chin as he encouraged her to lift her gaze to meet his.

"You know darn well just how much you are asking!" she retorted.

He chuckled at that, the pressure on her chin increasing. "I suppose you're right," he responded. "But you still have to look at me."

There was nothing for it, Alexandra realized at last. She'd have to do as he bid. Even the thought of gazing into his gray eyes took some of the fight out of her, her legs weakening at the thought of what was sure to follow.

Slowly, Alexandra lifted her head. In slow stages, his face came into view beyond the brim of her hat, first his cleft, resolute chin, which she had come to believe housed a certain degree of mulishness, then his lips that held just the hint of a truly rakish smile, to a straight nose

123

and well-defined cheeks that made him such a handsome man, to those damning eyes that hooked her right into his thoughts and desires.

He caught his breath as he met her gaze, his eyes full of longing suddenly, his lips parting as if to speak. But words didn't come, only a faint sigh of deep satisfaction. He leaned toward her slightly. "You're so pretty," he breathed at last, his deep, resonant voice touching her heart with each word that passed his lips. "And so full of fight. I want you, Alexandra. Let me love you a little."

Alexandra stood on the same cliff that had been torturing her since she first walked into the cabin. A warm, delicious breeze was on her face, and her heart suddenly took wing. She leaned forward and tumbled off the edge as Ross pressed his lips to hers.

Falling.

Falling so fast.

Intense desire flowed through Alexandra, her heart plunging mightily within her as every thought was given up to the tender delight of being held captive by Ross.

He slipped his arm quickly about her waist, pulling her tightly against him and kissing her hard. Alexandra lifted her hand to touch his face. Her fingers drifted lightly down his cheek as his lips sought hers again and again, growing more insistent with each touch of her hand to his skin.

To her surprise, Ross moved slightly and began kissing her fingers. She felt torn, wanting to feel his mouth on hers at the same time she reveled in the sensation of his lips seeking out each finger in turn. She watched this assault on her hand with growing anticipation, and when his tongue began flicking against the palm of her hand, she felt a flush of desire spread over her body in a roll of pleasure so intense that she caught her breath, a moan escaping her lips.

Ross heard a soft sound issue from Alexandra's throat

and his own longings for her sharpened suddenly, her evident pleasure increasing his own. He could not keep from letting go of her hand and returning to her lips where he kissed her again, this time thrusting his tongue deeply between her parted lips.

He felt her arm encircle his neck, her body arching and pressing against his own, her fingers lacing through his hair and tugging hard as he drove his tongue into her mouth, tasting wildly of its moist depths. How exquisitely her body fit against his, how much he longed to be inside her, to feel her respond to his loving. He thrust harder, then pulled back to feather his kisses across her mouth. She trembled in his arms at this light, seductive movement, and he heard her whisper his name, as though beseeching him for more, her hand again seeking his mouth. He returned to her fingers, but only for a moment as he moved swiftly to again invade her mouth.

How hard she held him as though she was afraid he would disappear if she let go. For an instant of time, the thought seared his mind that maybe he had found the right woman to walk beside him, the right woman with whom to build his ranch. How quickly he banished the thought, fearing that by the mere thinking of such a prospect, he had ruined his chance of obtaining it. How fragile hope was these days. All he knew was what he had said to her while she stood at the window, her red hair alive with the afternoon sun — he wanted her with him. Beyond that, he refused to look, to speculate, to hope.

Alexandra was overcome with passionate feelings that moved relentlessly within her. They swarmed up to her mind, honey-sweet, and drifted over her entire body with each thrust of Ross's tongue, bringing goosebumps to her neck that traveled like lightning down her spine. In all her dreams of being married to a man and having him love her, she had never imagined that her body or her heart could crave something as much as this man's touch.

125

She wanted more from him—to be joined to him as a man is to his wife. She felt him take the hat off her head, tossing it away from her. With the same strong hand, he stroked her in a long, smooth movement that ran from the tendrils on her forehead, down her thick braid, to the base of her back, then encircling her waist again, to hold her tight. With his other hand, he stroked her side for a moment with his fingers, which caused more goose-bumps to rise up the length of her body. He shifted away from her slightly and, before she knew what he was going to do, his hand covered her breast, touching, circling, kneading.

Alexandra was at first startled by the sensation of her breast being touched, but she was so caught up in the powerful sensation of his kisses that she soon found that his caress increased the desire mounting within her. His palm moved gently over the soft round curve of her breast in a slow, smooth rhythm, and every time his hand pulled across her nipple, she felt her body arch into him, her hips leaning harder against his. His tongue slowed to match the movement of his hand, and Alexandra found her breath growing uneven as a forbidden ache moved from her stomach in a downward motion to the soft warmth of her womanhood. She understood completely then what she wanted of him as his palm began hovering over just the tip of her nipple and his tongue barely flicked her lips. Never had such pleasure consumed her entire body. But where would it lead?

He pulled away from her suddenly and turned her half into his shoulder as he began fumbling with the buttons of her blouse that ran down her back. She should stop him now, but she didn't want to. He had aroused a fierce passion in her, and she wanted more.

He pulled the blouse from the confines of her skirt, then drew it toward him, away from her breasts, exposing a chemise held in place by her corset. Her wrists were

126

bound by tightly buttoned sleeves, but he seemed impatient, and rather than take the time to unbutton the sleeves, he let the blouse fall in front of her. Alexandra found her hands and arms restrained by the blouse, but right now she she didn't care at all. Ross moved with a sense of urgency as he dropped quickly to his knees before her and slipped the chemise below her breasts. She couldn't imagine what he meant to do. She supposed he intended to caress her again as he had done before, and how strange she felt seeing herself bared to a man in this intimate way. He gazed at her breasts for a long moment, and Alexandra could not resist raising her hands to touch his thick black hair. Before she realized what he meant to do, his tongue was on her breast, and then he took the peaked nipple into his mouth.

She could have screamed for the intensity of the pleasure this brought her as Ross began suckling her breast, gently at first, then harder. Each pull brought the ache between her legs to a rise that would fall away, only to climb higher. His hands stroked her back, sliding down to caress her hips and buttocks, afterward circling in front to run the length of her body, from her shoulders, across her breasts, down her pelvis and thighs. Again her mind cried, *Where would this lead!* She couldn't let him continue, but she didn't want to stop.

When he lifted her skirts, however, and his hand felt the softness of her thighs and moved to touch her womanhood through the thin fabric of her undergarment, Alexandra jerked back from him suddenly with a startled cry of *no!* She tottered sideways from this clumsy movement, her arms imprisoned awkwardly, and fell on her backside.

Chapter Sixteen

Because Ross was already on his knees he was on top of her at once, forcing her backward onto the floor, kissing her again, all the while not realizing she was distressed. She felt the hardness of him as he thrust his hips against hers and her fears mounted rapidly, replacing all her former pleasure as she tried to push him away. She understood, as his hips moved into hers again and again, that he was caught up in his own passion and tears of frustration began tumbling down her cheeks. What had she done? She knew enough as a woman of twenty to know that to protest now would be horribly unfair to him, but she didn't want it to happen like this.

Ross did not become aware that something had changed until, after at least a minute had passed, he realized that the body beneath him no longer melded to him, that the mouth beneath his had grown quiet. He drew back with a start, and seeing Alexandra's face, he cried, "Oh, my God! What's wrong? Have I hurt you?"

Alexandra looked at him through a blur of tears. "No," she whispered hoarsely. "I just didn't—I couldn't! Ross, I'm so sorry!"

Realizing that for some reason Alexandra was unable to continue, he rolled off her and stayed flat on his back for a long time, staring up at the ceiling and feeling like a hundred little knives were flying through his blood and cutting him up but good. He breathed deeply several times, thinking he'd made a jackass of himself. He'd moved too fast for her, widow or not. He didn't even know if her experience with her husband had been a good one, though he couldn't imagine it otherwise. He remembered, however, that she had told him her marriage had been arranged, and how had she put it . . . ? *Not an entirely happy one.* Maybe her husband had been a brute. He sighed. Whatever the case, he shouldn't have been so damn anxious. He looked over at her and saw that she had replaced her blouse and was now struggling with the buttons. She was such a wonderful woman to kiss and to touch. No matter how he had caressed her, she had been like a flower opening to the sun, basking in its warmth.

She still wasn't looking at him, but another tear rolled down her cheek as she finished buttoning her blouse. He could sense that she blamed herself for what had happened, that she felt badly. He loved her for that. She could just as easily have accused him of trying to hurt her.

When she looked as if she meant to rise to her feet, he caught her wrist and kept her from getting up. "Don't go yet," he said. "I want to say something to you." He rolled on his side, still holding her arm. Leaning up on one elbow, he looked at her and saw that tears still drenched her cheeks. He began wiping them away with his fingers. "I was too hasty," he said, shaking his head. "I'm sorry. I'm so sorry."

Alexandra looked down at Ross, at the sweet sincerity on his face, and everything in her heart shifted then and there. If she were to fix a name to it, the sensation

129

that rose from deep within her chest felt very much like love.

She reached down to touch his face with her hand and he immediately kissed her fingers, holding them to his lips in a tender way. He would never know how much she appreciated his concern for her at a time when he would have been justified to have been enraged. She leaned over to him and placed a lingering kiss on his mouth. "Thank you," she said, fresh tears spilling onto her skirt as she sat back on her heels.

He rose to a sitting position himself after that, wearing a boyish smile and shrugging in a way that reminded her of Crackshot. "You know, there's really only one thing wrong with where we are right now, don't you?"

Alexandra blushed, glancing at the bed, and wondering if he meant to try to get her there in hopes that she might be more willing to oblige him. "And what's that?" she queried, feeling nervous.

With a playfully serious expression on his face, he said, "This floor is dirtier than hell!"

Alexandra twisted around and looked down her back. Thick lines of dust clung to her clothes. She burst out laughing and, after jumping to her feet, she began swiping at the dust and pretty soon she was practically running in circles as she chased the back of her skirt. Ross caught her arm and, pretending to help her out, started brushing the dust away with a series of hard slaps that bruised her backside a couple of times and made her about ready to spit fire.

She gave him a dose of his own medicine and, with a stinging whap that made her own hand hurt, she struck him hard just like he'd slapped her.

"Hey!" he shouted, and when she tried to do it again, dashing behind him, he whirled around, caught her up quickly in his arms, and kissed her.

Alexandra was so happy in this moment, as he again

drove his tongue deep into her mouth, that she threw her arms about his neck and returned his kiss as hard as she could. After a long moment, he pulled away from her and said, "You gotta stop doing this if you want me to be good."

Alexandra wanted to tell him that she hoped he wouldn't be good, but she knew if she did, maybe next time he wouldn't be able to show so much restraint. Instead, she released her arms from about his neck and tried to pull away. But he held her close and said, "Tell me you want to stay here with me. I meant what I said before, I wasn't just trying to tease you or upset you. I want you here."

Alexandra was stunned. She hadn't really thought he was serious before, but now she knew for certain he was. Her first reaction was a strong desire to throw her arms around him a second time and say, *Yes, oh, yes!* But would that be wise?

Shifting her gaze to the top button of his shirt, Alexandra's mind began working quickly, feeling like a roulette wheel, where each slot held a different number, and in this case, a different path. One path said, "Return to Missouri, marry William. Live the safest life you can." Another flashed with each spin of her mind, "Stay here with Ross and let him 'love you a little.' " A third suggested she stay in Prescott and have Ross court her—but what would she do then? What did she want right now, for herself or from Ross? How confused she was.

"I don't know what to say," she responded, shaking her head, her gaze still fixed to the button. "My heart tells me to stay with you. I think I could be very happy here. At the same time, Ross, there's a strong part of me that feels compelled to return to Missouri."

She looked up at him and saw that he was watching her with that now familiar stare of his. "What?" she

131

cried. "Why do you look at me like that? Ever since you read Mrs. McCormick's letter from my father, you've been casting a mean eye toward me and I don't like it. I don't even know what it means. What are you thinking right now?"

He let go of her and stepped toward the tall chest of drawers where he rested his elbow. He was lost in his thoughts for a minute, his hand pressed to his mouth, until finally he said, "I'm sorry if I've caused you any distress. The truth is, there *is* something on my mind. In your father's letter, he seemed to believe you would be a wealthy woman when your uncle died. Naturally, from everything I've seen of you, I've had no reason to think otherwise. Why then would you have come to claim his mine?" Shaking his head, he looked straight at her and said, "Things don't add up with you."

Alexandra watched him, noting the way his body grew tense as he spoke about her supposed riches. She suspected more lay behind his unease than just her father's letter — but what? As for his apparent concern that he didn't understand her, she responded, "The fact is that I'm not at all a woman of property. My uncle left me an inheritance, conditionally, and as yet I have not been able to fulfill the stipulation written into his will. I don't know if I can."

"What is it?" he asked, a little surprised. "How hard could it be?"

Alexandra let out a long breath. She thought of William and a particular memory came rushing back to her. She had been engaged to him for three months and the most extravagant display of affection he had ever shown her was to press her hand upon leaving her uncle's house after dinner one night. She had fussed over that for nearly a week, feeling unsettled and bruised in her heart. She wanted William to love her, to cuddle with her like she'd seen her papa do with her mama. Was it asking so much? Was he afraid of her? But two weeks after that incident, when he still hadn't so much as held her hand, Alexandra decided she would talk to him about it. How stiff and disapproving he had been. Even now, the same feelings of disappointment weighed her heart down. William was a pious man, he didn't want to offend her, or in any way sully her honorable name by being so bold as to kiss her before they were joined in matrimony. Alexandra had done the only sensible thing, she had thrown her arms about his neck and placed a firm kiss on his mouth. In her girlish daydreams, she was sure he would respond, kissing her in return, unable to control his desire for her. Instead, he had pulled her arms from about his neck, and told her if she ever did anything like that again, he would be forced to speak with her uncle. He expected his bride to be circumspect in all things. "I don't want to be circumspect," she had cried, imploring him. "I want to be loved!"

He had laughed the incident off lightly and said once she had grown up a little more she would put such silly ideas behind her.

Alexandra thought now about Ross's question, How hard could it be to meet her uncle's stipulation. So far, it had been impossible. The thought of marriage to William put a chill over her heart she couldn't shake off. On the other hand, a day didn't go by when she didn't long for the safety of the life she had known in Missouri.

Ross was still waiting for her to tell him what the strangling condition to the will was. If she told him that much, she would have to reveal to him that she had lied about being married. Since she was still so unsure of what she was doing, of what she wanted here in Arizona now that she no longer had a claim to her father's mine, she was reluctant to say anything to Ross. Finally she said, "I don't feel right about telling you what it is."

To her surprise, the lines of his face seemed to deepen and his eyes grew black again in the shadowed light of the cabin. "What you're saying," he said with an effort at controlling his temper, "is that you don't trust me enough to confide in me."

Alexandra shook her head, moving toward her mother's bed where her hat rested upside down. "That isn't it," she responded quietly. Picking up the hat, she settled it over her tousled red hair and stuffed as many loose curls up into the crown of the hat as she could. She would have to wash her hair once she returned to Prescott, for even her braid had tufts of dust clinging to it.

When Ross remained silent, his eyes narrowed as he watched her, she felt obliged to add, "It isn't that I don't trust you. Not exactly. At least — well, maybe I don't!" She looked straight at him as she brushed the dust from her braid and said, "You haven't exactly offered to marry me, though you seem willing enough to take me to bed!" She couldn't believe she'd actually said such a thing to him.

"I hear the air snapping all around me again," Ross said. He slid his elbow off the chest of drawers and, standing upright, he asked, "Do you want to get married? I'll take you to Prescott this very minute and tie the knot if that's what you want! But I don't think that's what you want at all!"

There it was again, Alexandra thought, flipping her braid behind her, that ornery stare of his. She was all bristly as she glared back at him. Sure, she'd riled him up good by throwing that punch about marriage at his stubborn chin, but why did he stand there now almost daring her to marry him? Didn't he think she would? The moment this thought streaked through her brain, she knew she had hit a startling truth. Catching her breath, her anger turned upside down suddenly and transformed into utter amazement. He was right. She wouldn't marry him, but what astonished her most was that he knew it!

Turning around, she started walking toward the door, feeling slightly dazed. "How did you know as much when I didn't even know myself?" she asked, not expecting an answer. "You were right. I don't want to marry you." She stopped and looked at him over her shoulder. "I guess we'd better head out now. I'll be taking the stage back to Independence tomorrow."

"So that's all you're going to say to me? 'I'll be taking the stage . . .'? I guess I had you figured all wrong, Alexandra. I thought I'd found a woman with a fighting spirit, someone strong enough to bear the trials of life, especially out here on the frontier, but I was wrong, wasn't I? I suppose one day I'll feel grateful, but right now I feel like you just blew the boots off my feet." With that, he brushed by her and walked quickly out of the cabin.

Chapter Seventeen

Later that night, Alexandra soaked in a warm tub of soapy water, her hair clean, her face and hands scrubbed, the ache in her legs easing up a little. She should have felt a lot better than she did. But no matter how much she was able to wash away the dust from her clothes and body, she could not get rid of the dull pain that seemed to have settled over her heart. How easy it had been to tell Ross she wouldn't marry him, that she meant to return to Missouri. But here she was, alone in her hotel room, the oil lamp turned down low, experiencing feelings so desolate that it was all she could do to keep from crying. She refused to shed a single tear, however. She needed to think, to do some hard reckoning like she'd never done before, to figure out why the sight of Ross leaving the cabin had become stuck in her mind.

The trip back to Prescott from the Alexandra had seemed to go on forever. Weariness of heart and body made each climb of the land, each rocky descent, each turn of the road, hard to manage for her. Conversation had lagged. Though it was a reflection of their unhappy parting, Alexandra didn't think she could have done much about it anyway, even if he had been Moses, ready to impart to her news from the mountain.

She was bone-tired.

When Ross left her at the door to her room, she noticed that he didn't seem angry anymore, though a troubled frown had deepened the creases along his forehead. She remembered mumbling an apology along with an expressed hope for his future happiness. But when she offered her hand to him, he said, "Not a handshake, Alexandra, not for you." Then he shocked her by taking her quickly into his arms and placing a warm kiss on her mouth. He released her just as fast, whispering a serious good-bye, his voice trapping her heart firmly in a place of despair.

By the time she had fitted her key into the lock, he was gone.

And she was left here, sighing heavily as each memory of Ross sent her confused thoughts spinning harder still. When at last she climbed into bed, however, fatigue chased her into a deep slumber where her dreams must have been sweet because when she awoke the next morning, with the sun on her face, she couldn't remember a one of them.

Alexandra lay quietly on her side, the fresh smell of a laundered pillowcase beneath her cheek, the warm sun a delight on her skin. If only she could stay. She liked the way Prescott smelled pine-sweet. Her thoughts were loose in the morning, on first awakening and she let them drift randomly, thinking a little about Cecilia and Crackshot, about Mrs. McCormick and her fierce Manuel, about the feel of Ross's lips on her fingers, about the pungent taste of the venison stew, the grassy valley, and the horses grazing contentedly. She rolled on her back and stretched. Today she would make plans to leave.

Like a summer storm flooding across a desert plain,

137

this last thought brought an agonizing pain washing over her heart. She remembered one of her dreams suddenly. Her aunt Henrietta, whom she had loved dearly and pitied even more, had taken her hands tightly within her own, and spoken to her emphatically, but about what she couldn't seem to recall. How insistent her aunt had been, the sad lines about her mouth deep, her eyes intense. She was wearing a small black veil draped over a black hat. *Aunt Hetty,* Alexandra thought, *what do you think I ought to do?*

With a start, Alexandra sat straight up in bed. She had been so overwhelmed by visiting the mine and her papa's cabin, as well as by trying desperately to figure out what to do about Ross and whether or not to stay or go, that she had completely forgotten why she had come in the first place. She leaped from the warm bed, the wood floor cold on her bare feet. In a number of separate places, she hunted for the money she had brought with her from Independence. It was an inheritance she had received from her aunt Hetty just before she died, which Uncle Demarion had not known about — two thousand dollars, not a fortune, but maybe enough to purchase half-ownership in a mine!

She had hidden the money in several spots — her carpetbag, a secret pocket she had stitched on the inside of her corset, the hem of her silk traveling gown, her netted purse, and the lining of her straw hat with its pretty white bow. When she had the inheritance money amassed, the stack of bills was thick and unwieldy. She had been afraid of being robbed and had hoped that by keeping her aunt's money in several places, she could protect it better. Fortunately, she had been spared the horror of having to undergo a robbery. She laughed, thinking that while she may not have been robbed, she *had* been attacked and almost killed.

She rolled the money up tight and tucked it into her

netted bag, wondering if Ross would be willing to take her on as a partner. He'd told her he had been burned out in Texas and that his funds were low. She also knew that the mine was barely producing enough cash to keep itself going. She thought hers a reasonable offer as she pulled the strings of her purse tightly together. But would he understand?

An hour later, she hunted him down at the blacksmith's, where he was having his horse reshod. When he saw her, he wore such an expression of astonishment that she finally said, "Close your mouth, Mr. Halleck. Maybe you haven't noticed, but there are at least a dozen pesky flies buzzing around here."

He walked toward her, his head cocked at a funny angle, as though he was trying to convince himself she wasn't a spectre. "I thought you'd pulled out on the stage this morning. What the hell—I mean why are you still here? Tell me you've changed your mind!"

He had reached her by then and taken hold of her arm. He was smiling for all he was worth, the satisfaction on his face having a strong effect on her. Her heart began thumping against her ribs and her cheeks grew flushed, so much so that for just a moment she forgot why she was even talking to him.

"Don't look at me that way, Ross," she whispered at last, full of so many confusing feelings she could hardly walk straight. "I'm staying, but not for the reasons you're thinking."

"I don't care why," he cried forcefully. "Just so long as you're here." He guided her away from the curious stare of the blacksmith.

The sound of a red-hot horseshoe hissed suddenly in the water, and Alexandra wished she could cool her burning cheeks in the same way. They walked toward a stand of pine trees, her boots crunching on a thick carpet of dry pine needles. When they were out of earshot of the smithy, Ross stopped and asked her what had changed her mind about leaving.

"Now don't go getting mad at me for what I'm about to say," she responded, touching her fingers absently to the kerchief about his neck, then letting her hand drop away. "I have something for you, if you'll take it. But in exchange I need something from you." She swallowed hard, and opened her netted bag. Pulling out the thick roll of bills, she took his hand and slapped it firmly against his palm. "I want to buy into the Alexandra. Is this enough to build a five-stamp mill like my papa wanted to? And hire a few miners along with it?"

Ross stared down at the wad of bills, shock having stolen over him at the feel of the money in his hand. "How much is here?" he asked.

"It's only two thousand dollars. My aunt's money. It's all I've got that I can call mine. But will you sell me a percentage of the Alexandra—say, forty?" She found her heart was beating hard. What was he thinking? Would he laugh at her? Would he be angry?

Ross lifted his gaze to meet hers as he pushed his black hat away from his face. "Is that what you want?" His eyes searched hers, his expression questioning.

Alexandra knew by the way he spoke that he was addressing something bigger than just her interest in owning a part of his mine. She nodded slowly. "Yes, this is what I want, what I've come here for. You told me when we first met that you had a mining operation to take over, that you hoped to make your fortune. Well, after we quarreled yesterday afternoon, I couldn't make sense of what I was doing. Even last night, I went over everything in my mind about a thousand times and still I couldn't think of a reason to either stay or go. But this morning I remembered my aunt's money," she laughed slightly, and swatted at a fly that was pestering her. "Why, I even had a dream about her and she was lectur-

140

ing me strongly about something. At any rate, I knew then that what I wanted was not so very different from what you said you wanted from Papa's mine. A fortune. At least enough to give me independence; maybe I'm as foolish as my father to even consider buying into the Alexandra, but it's what I want to do."

Ross stepped toward her, bringing his body close to hers, but not touching. He spoke in a low voice, as he leaned down to look tenderly into her eyes. "You know, if you'd marry me, you wouldn't have to spend a penny on purchasing a share of the mine. You'd own it right along with me."

Alexandra looked into his warm gray eyes and felt his gaze reaching deep into her soul, grabbing her heart and holding her tight. One part of her wanted to say yes, but the other refused as fearsome memories rose suddenly to fill her mind.

When she didn't answer, he leaned away from her. He sounded hurt as he said, "Forget it. I can see it written all over your face. You're not of a mind to."

Alexandra felt like her heart was being twisted by a pair of strong hands and wrung tightly. Tears burned her eyes, and just as Ross turned away from her, she took his arm near the elbow and pulled him back to her until he was again standing right next to her. Her voice trembled as she whispered, "By the time I was twelve years old, I had lived in seven dirty, disease-infested mining camps, seven that I can remember. My mother gave birth to a child each year, three of them were born dead. We never had a doctor near enough to help. Being the oldest, I helped Mama care for each of the babies and grew to feel like a mother myself by the time I was eight. But that year we lost five of the children to scarlet fever. The next year twin boys died of pneumonia, and when I was twelve, my mother, my favorite sister, Isabelle, and the newest baby all died of the cholera. I don't know why I survived. You don't know how many times I wished I hadn't. The camps were often a scourge, where the women and children were left to fend for themselves. Missouri was clean, and safe, compared to the camps, with plenty of doctors around." She stopped for a minute, glancing down at the ground where unbidden tears dropped onto pine needles and splashed onto one of Ross's boots. She continued. "If I could follow only my heart right now, I'd become your wife without blinking an eye. But I can't. Whatever happens with the Alexandra, whether you accept my offer or not, I'm heading east afterward. I want children someday, but I won't rear them out here on the frontier. I won't. I just can't."

Ross had listened quietly to the history of her family. He caught her elbow and gently caressed her arm. He smiled at her in a sweet way and said jokingly, "And for a minute there I thought you were leaving because you didn't take to me."

"Didn't take to you?" Alexandra cried. "Why, I let you take my blouse off!" The words were out before she could stop them, and she clamped a hand to her mouth, her netted bag dangling from the same wrist and striking her chest.

He laughed aloud and then teased her by saying he would give her thirty percent, *and only thirty!*

"Forty," she responded, folding her arms across her chest and eyeing him in what she intended to be a stubborn way. "And I intend to live out at the camp."

"Darlin'," he cried, "I'd've given you seventy had I known that before."

Chapter Eighteen

Ross sealed their agreement with a handshake, but thrust two hundred dollars back into her hand and told her to head for Goldwater's and purchase whatever she needed to make the cabin comfortable for herself. "In the coming months we'll see some snow," he said. "And when it isn't snowing, the air is chilly and the nights are cold with frost. Right now, I'm going over to the sheriff's office. I learned from the blacksmith that Goodwin is back from Carver. We'll see what he knows about your father's death and I especially wanted to let him know about the attack at Point of Rocks."

Alexandra bid him good-bye, demanding Ross tell her everything the minute he returned from speaking with the sheriff. She watched him retrace his steps to where the blacksmith stood hammering out a shoe, and for a few seconds remained beneath the pines, just looking at Ross. He was nicely tall and handsome, carrying himself with pride, speaking in a direct way to anyone who addressed him. She felt her heart warm to him as she took a deep breath and finally set her feet in motion toward the store. To be his wife, that would be a wonderful thing. If only she could.

A few minutes later, Alexandra found herself inside Goldwater's, standing before a brand-new, cast-iron, potbellied stove. The fireplace would do little to warm up the cabin, but a stove like this one, kept crammed with wood! She just had to have this stove! She stared at it hard as though she hoped it would suddenly sprout feet and walk away to the camp with her. Lord, she'd need an axe, too, and a hatchet for slicing up kindling. There were so many details to take care of that several times, as she had made her way around the store, she felt overwhelmed.

She had already picked up a scrubboard and a large tin tub for washing her clothes, doing up the dishes and for bathing. What about a bucket for hauling water? She'd need soap, eating utensils, and what about food? How much would she need for a month, maybe two? She realized she'd never set up a house before. She would need medicine, and toiletries, and a pillow! As she glanced about the store, feeling battered by all the necessities crying out to her, she saw a rocking chair and some ready-made dresses. She sighed suddenly as the things she needed began vying with the things she wanted. The problem was, two hundred dollars may have been more than adequate in Missouri, but everything in the store was so expensive! She knew it was the cost of freighting all the merchandise to Arizona that made the goods so dear. It took months for supplies to reach Prescott, whether they came entirely overland through Phoenix or up from Ehrenburg by way of the steamboats on the Colorado River. Still, when she saw that candy was a dollar a pound, she felt like swooning.

She was about to throw up her hands and walk out for a spell when she felt a woman's arm around her waist. She nearly jumped out of her skin when Mrs. McCormick gave her a hug, her spritely voice striking her ear. "Alexandra!" she cried. "How nice! But what are you doing here? I thought you'd be heading back to Missouri by now!"

Alexandra spun around and greeted the older woman with a sheepish smile, returning her hug with a feeling of affection that took her a little by surprise. She could see Mrs. McCormick was teasing her and she confessed her change of plans. "I'm staying on at Papa's mine," she said. "I've bought into the Alexandra."

Mrs. McCormick looked at her with a playfully severe frown creasing her brow. "Why, Ross should've given you part of that mine," she responded immediately. "It was as good as yours anyway."

Alexandra shook her head. "That's not true at all. Papa gambled his mine away, whatever his reasons. Besides, I think it's better this way. I want Ross to look on me as a partner, not someone he did a favor for."

"Well, I think you're bein' foolish," she returned with a brisk nod of her head. Lowering her voice, she continued. "I saw the way Ross looked at you when the pair of you were at my place. If ever I saw a man in love! All he needed was the smallest push! I wish you'd have come to me before you decided to give your money away. Together, we could have brought that man to heel."

Alexandra would have explained that Ross had already proposed to her and that she had refused him, but at that moment, she noticed that Lupe was standing on the boardwalk trying to catch Mrs. McCormick's eye. In her arms, she held a crying infant. "Did Lupe have her baby already?" Alexandra asked. She then shook her head with a laugh. "But that can't be hers. It's too big."

Mrs. McCormick turned around and saw Lupe. Without offering a word of explanation to Alexandra, she went to the Mexican woman and began quietly arguing with her. When Mrs. McCormick reentered the store, Alexandra watched Lupe give her employer a disapproving shake of her head. She then crossed the street and mounted a buggy, where she rocked and soothed the baby as best she could.

As Alexandra shifted her gaze back to Mrs. McCormick, she saw that though she was smiling, a certain tension was now etched into the lines of her face. For the first time, she noticed that the older woman's complexion was pale and that she had dark circles under her eyes, as if she wasn't getting all the rest she needed. She remembered seeing her mother in a similar condition almost constantly, but especially after a baby was born and she was in milk. Was that Mrs. McCormick's baby? But she was a widow of some five years, so Ross had told her.

When Mrs. McCormick returned to stand by her and didn't make mention of the baby, Alexandra did not feel it was proper to ask about the child. The older woman immediately began questioning Alexandra concerning the state of the cabin and what she needed to provision her place. Before long, the widow had taken her in tow, not only helping her decide everything she would need from Goldwater's, but dismissing any article of which she had more than one at her own house.

"My daughters are both gone!" she cried when Alexandra started exclaiming that she couldn't accept so much from her. "I've more things in storage, including a feather mattress you are welcome to take with you, than I'll ever be able to use. I'll warn you right now, though, if you don't accept my generosity,

146

I intend to take everything I've offered you and set up a nice big bonfire. And that includes a spare dining table and chairs I have, along with a rocker. Of course it's not so fine as the one you keep admiring over there—" She laughed when Alexandra asked if her interest in the chair had been that obvious, then continued. "But I think you're right. Most of your money ought to go for buying this potbellied stove and as much food as you can stock."

"So you don't think I had anything to do with Sam Wingfield's death," Ross stated.

Sheriff Goodwin shook his head. "I think whoever shot at you outside of Phoenix, probably murdered Sam. I know there are some folks who suspect you of having jumped his claim, but the wound in your side is all the evidence you'll need to the contrary. Barnes and Fred Spangler have both been pretty hotheaded about your ownership of the Alexandra, but I think once they learn about this latest attack . . ." He paused abruptly, slapping his thigh with his open hand. "I wish I could take a box of dynamite and blow up Point of Rocks. I've had more trouble out there . . . ! Anyway, I'll see that my deputy in particular has his suspicions laid to rest."

"I'd appreciate that. I got a frosty reception here the other day when I told Barnes about being chased by four desperadoes."

Goodwin laughed. "Between you and me, he's fit for retirement, but not much else. He's a good man, though."

Ross liked Sheriff Goodwin. He was a tall man, with no nonsense about him. He stood pouring two cups of coffee from a blackened pot, and handed one to Ross. "I could've used a man like you, Halleck. What a mess we have down there in Carver. I won't deny I was sickened by the sight of that wagon and the charred bodies of two young children and their mother, a widow by the name of Ferguson. They'd been there a full week, before anyone found them, and all horse sign had been washed away by then." He sipped his coffee, turning around to sit on the edge of his pitted desk as he stretched his long legs out in front of him. He had a full black mustache, peppered slightly with gray, and looked to be almost forty. His eyes were a clear blue and his black hair was thinning at the temples. He continued. "As it was, nobody in that town, if such you could call it, knew a thing about it. I strongly suspect a man by the name of Black was behind the murders."

"Why?" Ross asked.

The sheriff glanced at him, his expression ironic. "Black owns the mercantile now, which belonged to the widow. Mrs. Ferguson sold her business to him, took his cash payment, headed north toward Prescott, and died the same day."

"And no proof of anything."

The sheriff nodded. "The only thing I can hope for is that someone saw what happened, or maybe heard Black bragging about it, then I'll have a shot at bringing him to justice. That's one reason I visit all the bars along Whiskey Row quite regularly—besides partaking of a little refreshment myself once in a while. You can learn a whole lot by just listening."

Ross was sitting in a hard-backed chair and thought about his own difficulties. Proof. Now where would he be able to learn the identities of the men who had attacked him?

"But I imagine you didn't come here to listen to my woes," the sheriff said. "Looks like you've got trouble on your hands. It would seem that someone wants that mine real bad."

"That's about how I have it figured," Ross said.

Goodwin took his seat at that point and made himself a few notes. After pondering over them for a minute, his jaw cupped in his hand, he asked if Alexandra had been hurt.

Ross shook his head and added, "The moment the shooting started, she was riding fast out of the Dells. I don't know that she could tell you anything more than I could, but if you want to talk to her, she's staying at the hotel, probably at least until tomorrow. After that, she's moving out to the camp."

If the sheriff seemed a little surprised by this last statement, he remained politely silent, and for that Ross was grateful. Goodwin then attended to the business at hand, asking questions about how many men Ross thought had been laying for him and if he was sure the man who fell was dead.

"If he wasn't," Ross said quietly, "he would've been busted up pretty bad. I'd say he fell almost thirty feet, facedown. There was a hole out his back, where I shot him, and blood everywhere."

"Good Lord," the sheriff cried, disgusted, rubbing his forehead with his fist. "I'll tell you right now, there hasn't been a funeral here in the last week, which makes me think 'your friend' was probably dumped in some gully and left to the coyotes. I'll tell you straight out, it doesn't look hopeful. We've got more drifters blowing through this place then there are flies on a buffalo chip. And most of 'em will hire out a gun for a two-bit flask. Then they're gone. What I will do is take a posse to search out some of the ravines hereabouts and start my rounds along Montezuma Street. When I know something, I'll send Barnes out to the Alexandra. He knows his way there. He and Sam often played poker together."

Ross rose to leave, and as he was settling his hat on

149

his head, Goodwin offered his hand. "By the way," the sheriff said, "Lloyd Powell owns a stake about two miles downstream from you. He's a bit of a tinhorn, but you might want to introduce yourself. He's been around a while. He might know something I don't."

Chapter Nineteen

It wasn't that Ross didn't like Lloyd Powell. He just didn't trust him. He was a tinhorn, all right, smelling of fine cologne and wearing a fancy suit, with a small black silk tie and boots that gleamed.

Ross had found him in the Cobweb, apparently at ease as he leaned back into his chair and shifted a card in his hand. He was playing poker, his black, flat-crowned hat sitting at a slight angle over carefully brushed hair.

Ross stood at the bar, listening to him talk in his friendly way to the four other men at his table. He played out his hand appearing unhurried and relaxed, but Ross sensed that here was a man who thought out everything in advance. Even his laughter sounded measured and careful.

No, he wouldn't trust this man as far as he could throw him.

What Sheriff Goodwin's opinion of Powell was, he didn't really know. All that the lawman had suggested to Ross was that he acquaint himself with the man. He meant to do at least that much.

When the hand was played out, Ross strolled up to

the table and introduced himself as Powell's neighbor. "I own the Alexandra," he said simply. "Goodwin suggested I talk to you."

Powell looked up at Ross, tilting his head and glancing sideways at him. His expression was cloaked, as though his mind was busy weighing a dozen details all at once. After a few seconds, he smiled and said, "The sheriff's a good man. If he thought we oughta talk, then I suppose we should."

When he gathered up the large stack of greenbacks and coins in front of him, a general groan of disappointment went round the table.

Ross bought himself and Powell a drink at the bar. The whiskey was a fine burn on his throat. He looked the tinhorn over carefully, watching the pale-skinned man sip his drink, wondering what had brought a man like him out west.

"So you own the Alexandra," Powell said at last, curling his lips inward, tasting the whiskey on his teeth.

"That's right," Ross said quietly. "But it would seem someone else wants it, too."

Powell smiled, a silent chuckle making his chest dip suddenly. "I knew Wingfield for several years before he died. The minute he found a little ore that had some real shine to it, he came running down the creek to show me. He could act just like a kid, that man." He paused, then added slowly, "But he may have been a bit foolish for this territory." Only then did he look at Ross, holding his gaze for a long moment, afterward returning it to his glass.

Ross didn't like the smooth way Powell spoke, nor his insinuations that Wingfield was at fault for somebody else's greed. "You don't strike me as much of a miner," he said, irritated.

Powell's easy smile broadened a little as he shifted

152

his eyes to scan Ross's clothes. "Neither do you," he responded.

The man spoke and acted like he had grease running the length of him. He was as slippery as a bar of soap in a tub of water. Right now he didn't care what Goodwin thought of Powell, he wasn't saying a word to him. He leaned close to the tinhorn and said, "So, tell me. How did you kill Sam Wingfield? Did you shoot him outright or stick a knife through his heart?"

To his surprise, Ross watched Powell's face harden and he found himself doubting his initial impression of the man.

"I don't know what you're talking about, Halleck," Powell said. "But the fact is, I never use a knife to settle my disputes. I've always favored a Smith & Wesson .45."

He leaned back slightly and pulled his black coat behind his pistol. Ross glanced down at it. There was no way he could know how fast Powell was with his sidearm, but it wouldn't do a lick of good to try to find out now. He still didn't like the way Powell talked. "You don't look like much of a gunman, neither," Ross said.

Powell frowned, but let his coat fall back in place as he responded, "And neither do you."

At this, Ross took quick stock of a situation that could turn bloody if he didn't tread lightly. Taking a sip of his drink, he said, "I suppose you're right. Fact is, I'm only a drover who happened to meet up with Sam Wingfield a few days before he was killed. That I won his claim in a game of poker at first seemed like a stroke of luck. Now, I'm not so sure."

After he saw that Powell had laid his feathers, at least for the time being, he decided to see how the tinhorn would react to telling him about Sam's death and the attacks on his own life. "I'll put it to you straight," he said, his gaze fixed to Powell's face. "I've been shot at a couple of times and Wingfield was murdered. Someone wants the Alexandra. Goodwin thought you might have an idea who." If Ross expected the gambler to reveal anything to him by a look or a twitch of his eye, he was mistaken.

Powell finished off his drink, twisting around to scan the barroom. "The way Sam let loose with his mouth," he said, "it could've been anyone. Unfortunately, for what he possessed in charm, he lacked in discretion. You can ask Sarah McCormick about that."

Ross thought he sounded bitter and wondered what he meant by it, but didn't think it was any of his business. "I'd take it kindly of you," he said, draining his glass and setting it on the counter, "if you'd let me or the sheriff know anything that happens to come your way concerning Sam or his mine."

Powell gave Ross one of his most friendly smiles. "I'm always happy to oblige Sheriff Goodwin," he said cheerfully.

Ross might not have been completely satisfied with the tinhorn's response, but he said good-bye anyway and headed toward Goldwater's. It didn't take long to reach the store. Prescott was a young town and still mighty small by eastern standards.

Once there, he stood outside one of the windows, looking in. He was surprised to see Mrs. McCormick and Alexandra together. They were bending over a potbellied stove and examining the interior, though he couldn't imagine why. The cabin had a nice big fireplace.

He would have joined them right away, but he stayed where he was, taking a moment to admire Alexandra without her being aware of it. A strong feeling took hold of his chest at the sight of the thick red braid trailing down her back, the tan hat, and the blue skirt fitting snugly around her wonderfully small waist. How had it begun? he wondered. When had he started feeling like his world began and ended with the pretty, red-haired lady now standing up straight, her hand on her hip? He held his own hands up in front of him and tried to shape them into what he figured must be the size of her waist. He realized he could probably fit his hands right around her and promised himself at the first opportunity to see if he was right. Would her waist still be as small if she wasn't wearing a corset? This question brought a sudden desire coursing through him and he decided to set aside such disconcerting thoughts until he was alone with her again. Then, he promised himself, he'd get at the truth.

He only wished she'd marry him.

Time, he thought. That's all she needs. Time to come to know him, to trust him. He wanted her with him in Wyoming, to build his ranch, to rear his young. But would she ever be able to forget enough of her childhood to agree to go with him?

He entered the store and called out a greeting to both ladies and had the pleasure of seeing their faces light up at his approach. Mrs. McCormick immediately told him to come look at the stove Alexandra had purchased.

He didn't know what to make of it or why Alexandra thought she needed it.

When Mrs. McCormick saw his somewhat stricken look, she took him to task. "Now, what were you thinking, Ross?" she cried. "That Alexandra would go out there and live in that goddawful cabin with a fireplace that couldn't keep an outhouse warm? It gets mighty cold up there by Bee Mountain. No use having her die of pneumonia and all for want of a little warmth!"

Ross looked at Alexandra and knew that this last reference to pneumonia had caught her on the chin. He stepped toward her and wished they were alone so he could put his arm around her and ease the look of pain from her face. "A stove it is, then," he said, trying to catch her eye. "I hope you've bought up about a hundred wool blankets as well."

At that, Alexandra looked up at him. "As a matter of fact," she said, her expression lightening, "Mrs. McCormick is prepared to load me down with just about everything else I'm going to need." She looked suddenly self-conscious and said, "Ross, may I speak to you for just a moment. There's something I've got to ask you!"

She then begged Mrs. McCormick to excuse them as she drew Ross aside. She started to say something, but Ross couldn't keep from interrupting her. "You're so pretty," he whispered. "Once we get on our way, I want to kiss you, like I did yesterday. Besides, we've formed a partnership, you and I, and I think the only way to seal it is with a kiss, don't you?"

Alexandra felt a blush steal over her face knowing that Mrs. McCormick was watching them. She turned away from her, and found herself looking at bolt after bolt of cloth. "Will you stop with your nonsense?" she muttered under her breath. "I don't know what you're thinking about, but I'm not going to kiss you anymore!"

"You're not?" he asked innocently. "But I thought you enjoyed my kissing, and," he paused, lowering his voice further, "other things."

"Oh, hush! Why are you being so ornery when I'm trying to be serious?" Fingering a bolt of blue-and-pink calico left on the counter from a previous customer's inspection, she mused absently, "I'm going to need some clothes, too."

"You're not being serious," he said, addressing her original question, "You're being silly!"

"I am not!" she exclaimed aloud, and looked back to find that Mrs. McCormick was watching them with a smile on her face. She resumed her whispering. "She's looking at us now like she thinks we're in love."

"We are, aren't we?" he queried.

Alexandra was startled by the question and looked up at him in surprise. "Are you in love with me?" she responded, her heart starting to beat very fast. If only he wasn't so handsome, she thought. She liked his looks so much, and those eyes of his! They were so warm and intense all at the same time. She wanted to touch his face and then told herself she had to put away such dangerous ideas or else she'd soon be in trouble with Ross all over again.

His smile grew mischievous and she lifted a finger, trying to prevent him from saying anything too horrible, but without effect since he whispered, "Of course I love you. I took your blouse off, didn't I?"

This reference to her earlier remark, along with the naughty look on his face, caused her to reach out and give his arm a slap. "What am I going to do with you?" she asked, not expecting an answer.

He gave her one anyway. "Marry me," he said simply.

Her heart sank and she cast her gaze down, feeling the color drain from her face.

"I'm sorry," he whispered. "Just forget what I said. I didn't mean it. Well, maybe I did, but forget it anyway. Now tell me what you wanted to ask me when you first brought me over here."

Alexandra pulled her braid from behind her and draped it over her shoulder. She absently flipped the

157

end of the braid up and down. "Where are you going to sleep?" she asked at last, unable to look at him.

He couldn't keep from laughing. "Is that what's got you so worried?" he asked, watching her flip the braid, the blue bow on the end bouncing with each jerk of her hand.

"Yes," she breathed. "I don't feel right about having you stay in the cabin, but if not here, where else would you go?"

"I've already bought a tent," he responded. "Along with everything else I'll need, except I was hoping I could persuade you to permit me to share meals with you."

Alexandra breathed a sigh of relief and looked up at him. "I'd like that very much. My cooking isn't great, like Cecilia's, but I can make pretty good soups and stews and I know how to make biscuits, pies, bread, and the like."

"Do you know how to make doughnuts?" he asked suddenly. When Alexandra nodded, he exclaimed, "Good! Then it's settled. The only thing I need to figure out now is how we're going to get that stove out to the mine."

Alexandra cleared her throat and rocked on her heels slightly. "Ross, I think you'd better hire a wagon. A *big* wagon."

"Why?"

"When I said Mrs. McCormick was giving me just about everything I could need, that meant some rather large essentials like a decent dining table and chairs, linens, blankets, medicines, dishes, a cupboard for dishes, a *large* cupboard, a rocking chair, and—and . . ." She felt the blush again creep up her cheeks. "And a very fine feather mattress."

An expression Alexandra could only think was composed entirely of a truly unconscionable satisfac-

158

tion twisted Ross's lips. "By all means," he said. "Why didn't you say so in the first place. I'd hire a wagon for the mattress alone!"

Alexandra had had just about enough of his teasing and indelicate hints. Setting her hands on her hips, she said, "Just make sure that wagon's big enough. I don't aim to make a second trip! And as for the rest of it, you can just forget all about it! No more kissing!"

Ross tore the hat from his head and nodded obsequiously. "Yes'm!" he answered emphatically, a devilishly warm light glinting from his gray eyes.

Chapter Twenty

Early the next morning, Alexandra worked outside the McCormick ranch house helping load onto a large freight wagon the several dozen crates, boxes, and tins the widow had lavished upon her. Six mules waited patiently in harness, the day was cool and lovely under a sky of dark blue, and everything was as it should be except for the freighter.

He was proving to be an obnoxious man, smelling horribly to Alexandra of whiskey and sweat. Every time he passed by her, she held her breath and turned away from him. What was worse, he seemed to have developed a leering interest in her and went out of his way to brush against her twice. She had thought the first incident was an accident, but the second time she realized he was purposely bumping into her, his hand running a long stroke across her buttocks. He begged her pardon, but the leering light in his red-rimmed blue eyes led her to believe he somehow felt free to take liberties with her.

Mrs. McCormick was still searching through every room of her house, including the attic, in hopes of discovering one more utensil, one more tin of spice, one more piece of linen or bottle of medicine to bestow upon Alexandra. Ross was working with Manuel to figure out how best to protect the several large pieces of furniture that were making the trek out to the mine. For that reason, Alexandra had been left alone with the freighter for almost half an hour.

He was a burly man with a protruding stomach and fleshy arms. His hat was worn and sweat-stained, covering a straggly head of reddish-brown hair. His face was stubbled with the same color hair, though peppered with gray, and his teeth were a dreary shade of brown. As he spit a thick wad of chewing tobacco onto the dirt near his wagon and smiled at her, she knew the source of the repulsive color. She only hoped now that she didn't step in it.

She was about to go back into the house when she felt one of his thick paws on her arm. "Mrs. Bradshaw . . ." he said in a low, hoarse voice, his words drawled together. "You look mighty tempting with that purdy white skin of yours and them rosy lips. How long you been a widow lady? Been a long time without a man? I can fix you up good, if you'll let me."

Alexandra jerked her arm from his touch and said, "Just tend to your work, you hear!"

He laughed, stepping back toward his mules and slapping one of them on the flank. Addressing Alexandra, he said, "You don't cotton much to my society, do you, Mrs. Bradshaw. I ain't such a bad fellow once you get to know me, and I could tell you things some would be plain shocked to know. Take that poor widow lady down in Carver. I got me a notion who killed her, but you don't believe me, do you?"

Alexandra was doing her best to ignore him, sorting through two boxes and condensing the contents of both into one. She hoped he would take the hint and leave her alone; instead, he was next to her suddenly,

161

grabbing both arms this time and drawing her toward him. She was so startled she didn't at first do or say anything, responding only to the thick stench of whiskey on his breath by groaning out loud, her stomach turning over a half dozen times.

"You're just plain drunk!" she cried at last.

She started struggling against him, kicking him hard on the shins with her tough boots, but he didn't even flinch. Pressing his lips to her cheek, he said, "Come on, Mrs. Bradshaw! Give me a kiss! You sure are a wild one to fight me like this! I been lookin' at you all morning wantin' a poke so bad, I could kill fer it!"

By this time, Alexandra was screaming for help, calling out Ross's name until the freighter silenced her with a sweaty hand over her mouth. As he fumbled clumsily at her breast, he lumbered into her, his legs sprawling apart. She didn't hesitate, just as she collapsed backward beneath his awkward weight, to place her knee solidly in his groin. He fell on top of her in a heap, crying out in pain. In the process, however, he knocked the air out of her.

She attempted to push him off, but he was too heavy, and no matter how hard she tried, she couldn't drag a bit of air into her lungs. Pinpricks of light bounced over her eyes and she wondered how long it would be before she lost consciousness. As her vision began to fade, she felt his body move away from her.

Looking straight up and working steadfastly to bring the image into focus, she realized Ross had plucked the freighter off her as if the heavy man had been a small boy.

She could hear Ross's voice now. He was shouting, but the words were lost to her. She felt confused and sick and still wasn't breathing as she rolled on her side, her mouth open, her hand pressed to her stomach. She could see Ross holding the man up by the front of his shirt and backhanding his face over and over. Blood spurted from the man's nose, his body still arched inward from the blow Alexandra had inflicted on his body. Dust flew everywhere as Ross kept backing him away and hitting him.

She tried to speak, to tell Ross the man was out of his senses, that he had been nipping too long at his four-bit flask, but she could see that a rage was on him. She thought he might kill the freighter, but wasn't able to cry for help. She struggled to bring air in, and when the first tiny pocket entered her lungs, she croaked, "Manuel!" But a dog with sharp hearing couldn't have heard her.

A deeper breath, and she fought to stand up, but failed, calling to Ross, then to Manuel. A third breath, and she was screaming at the top of her lungs.

Manuel came charging out of the house. He took in the sight at once, running toward Ross and clasping him firmly around the chest from behind. He was a fearfully strong man himself, his arms thick and muscled. Even then, he had difficulty restraining Ross, all the while talking calmly to him in Spanish. He forced Ross to release the freighter, and the heavy drunk fell backward into the dirt.

Ross appeared to calm down in stages, the dust around him flying as he reached out to kick at the freighter, who was now lying unconscious at his feet. Manuel dragged him backward a step or two, still pinning his arms to his sides.

At the same time, Mrs. McCormick came out of the house. Taking one look at Alexandra, she was beside her quickly, slipping an arm around her waist and helping her rise to her feet.

Alexandra felt weak as she leaned into the widow. "That man kissed me, or tried to," she said, her voice

163

hoarse. "He's dead drunk. I tried to tell Ross, but he was so angry and I'd had the wind knocked out of me. I've never seen Ross in such a rage."

"He had good reason, though!" Mrs. McCormick cried, watching Manuel hold Ross back. She shook her head at the sight of the freighter stretched out in her yard. "Lord have mercy!" she cried. "I haven't seen such a stupid man in ages. He isn't long for this earth if he means to attack women when the fancy strikes him. Not out here, anyway."

"I was thinking the same thing."

When Ross had convinced Manuel that he had himself under control, the big Mexican released him and Ross went to the horse trough where he filled up a bucket with water. Returning to stand over the freighter, he dumped the contents over the man's head.

The freighter moved slightly, then awoke. He leaned up on his elbows and, touching his jaw, mumbled, "I need a doctor. Someone's been plowing up my chin."

Alexandra could see that it took a great deal of effort for Ross to turn away from the man. By then, several hands had come running, having heard her screams. Manuel related to them what had happened, then instructed them to take the freighter to the barn and tie him up until he was sober.

Ross crossed the yard to stand next to Alexandra. His eyes were still bright with anger as he asked her gently if she was all right. "Did he hurt you, or anything?"

"I only had the wind knocked out of me," she responded. "Thank you for coming when you did. I tried to tell you he was drunk, but I wasn't breathing by then. For the past hour he's been taking swigs from his flask. I just didn't realize how far gone he was until he grabbed me." Not wanting to stay fixed on what had happened, since she could see that it would take very little to get Ross hotter than a branding iron again, she queried, "Who's going to take us out to the Alexandra?"

It was a good diversion, that much she could see at once as Ross relaxed a little, taking his kerchief from about his neck and mopping his face. "I don't know. We'll figure something out."

Mrs. McCormick said she was sure one of the hands could drive the team out for them, then bring it back. She'd take care of the rest.

"But you've done so much for us already," Alexandra protested, glancing at the growing pile of household supplies. The wagon was a third full, and it hardly seemed like they'd loaded anything at all, from the pile still left in the hallway. And that didn't even include the large pieces of furniture. "I can't ask you to do any more than—than all this!" She waved a hand, encompassing the wagon.

Mrs. McCormick shook her head with an expression that indicated she thought Alexandra was being sheepheaded. She wouldn't listen to another protest, merely saying that she had had a great fondness for Sam Wingfield and anything she could do for his daughter was little enough for all he'd done for her.

Within another hour, with the sun rising in the sky, the wagon was loaded and creaking down the road toward the mine. Ross rode his mustang and Alexandra sat astride another horse hired from the blacksmith's stock. The freighter was to have returned the horse to him, but it had been agreed that one of Mrs. McCormick's hands would see that the paint gelding was restored to its owner. As for the freighter himself, it was generally thought to be a wise idea to have him taken to Sheriff Goodwin's office and given a good talking to—after he sobered up, of course, along with maybe a few days in jail. Alexandra wondered if he would even remember what he had done. With a smile, as the small caravan headed down the trail, Alexandra thought that the freighter's smashed lips, undoubtedly broken nose, and bruised jaw would be an excellent reminder.

Watching Ross as he again sat tall and straight in his saddle, his legs fitted to his horse like they were one creature, she was overcome with a swell of pride in him. How quickly he had rushed to her defense, how enraged he had become that another man had tried to take advantage of her. Was this a man to step between herself and the trials of life, to soften her way as she in turn eased the way for her children?

If only it was possible! her heart cried out. At the same time, she was convinced it was hopeless.

Despair almost took hold of her, but she refused to give it sanction in her heart. She couldn't change Ross, she couldn't even alter the strong feelings for him that seemed to grow daily in breadth and heighth. She would continue on her own course, seeking what the Alexandra had in store for her. Time enough to see what might come of her ripening love for Ross Halleck.

Chapter Twenty-one

As they traveled along the stretch of road that formed the eastern boundary of Mrs. McCormick's ranchlands, Alexandra could see that Ross's interest was held securely by the vista before him. Several hundred beeves grazed on wheat-colored grass, the rolling valley meeting a sky of blue dotted with puffy white clouds. She watched Ross lose himself in thought, his gaze traversing the land in long, appreciative sweeps. Was he thinking about the ranch he'd left behind in Texas or the one he hoped to build in Wyoming? She felt saddened, knowing that their lives would only be entwined for this short time as they shared ownership of the mine.

Still, it was a very fine thing to simply know Ross, and she was determined to take pleasure in his company despite her belief they would eventually travel different paths into the future.

The ride out to the Alexandra did not seem nearly as long as the previous trip, partly because they whiled away a lot of the time discussing the mine and what each of them hoped to do if they struck a vein of good-quality ore. And when they had thoroughly worn out the subject, Alexandra remembered

Ross hadn't as yet told her of his conversation with the sheriff.

Ross remained silent for a moment, as though trying to fix his thoughts in order, and finally related to her several details of his encounter with Goodwin. He explained carefully that the sheriff had finally received word from Dodge City to the effect that her father hadn't died of the Spanish influenza after all, but had been murdered, just as they both suspected, in his hotel room. "Goodwin is persuaded I am innocent of any wrongdoing," he added. "Mainly because of the attack outside of Phoenix and the later one at the Dells. However, Barnes will be a little harder to convince. He isn't happy about my owning a mine that belonged to his friend."

"If you remember, I thought you were guilty too, before I realized you couldn't have done anything so cruel. Barnes has only to get to know you a little and he'll come around. There's just one thing I'm not clear on. Was—was my father shot?" Alexandra asked, her gaze traveling along the ridges of dust mounded up on the side of the trail. She wasn't sure she wanted to know the answer.

Ross told her he didn't know. "I don't think the sheriff knows, either, but he seems to be a pretty thorough lawman. He's not finished with any of this just yet." He then went on to relate to her his talk with Lloyd Powell.

"I don't know what it is about that man," Alexandra said. "But I just don't trust him. He's very nice, well mannered and all, but when I spoke with him last, I felt as if he was looking at me like a snake, with a film covering his eyes."

Ross expressed a similar reaction to the tinhorn.

168

After that, they talked of everything and nothing, about some of Ross's experiences punching cows and Alexandra's childhood in Colorado as a child. When she'd told him practically her whole history of growing up in rough mining camps, she in turn asked him about his own boyhood. She wasn't surprised, though very much saddened, to learn that he had grown up with only a father, no siblings, and his mother had died when he was young.

By the time they reached the mine, however, the sun was well advanced as their provisions and furniture were unloaded outside Sam's cabin. Mrs. McCormick's ranch hand swung the lightened wagon back up the trail and disappeared quickly from the narrow valley. Crackshot had offered him a bed for the night, but the hand, a salty fellow who'd been on the frontier most of his life, returned a polite "thank you kindly," but knew for a fact the moon would be high and he preferred his own bunk.

After Ross tended to his horse, he and Alexandra shared some of Cecilia's flavorful stew, along with a portion of Crackshot's saltless hardtack that only seemed palatable to Alexandra if it sat in the stew for about five minutes. After that, Cecilia retired to their tent, refusing to go near the cabin, while Crackshot and Ross began carting the crates, tins, and bulky pieces of furniture into the front room.

Alexandra didn't know where to begin, partly because the cabin was so dirty. She thought, however, that making up her bed might be the first task of importance as well as seeing to some firewood. The moment the sun disappeared behind the hills, the early November air bespoke the onset of the cooler months. Unearthing one of Mrs. McCormick's shawls — she had given her three! — and wrapping it

169

about her shoulders, she went in search of some wood while the men were moving in the heavy furniture. She didn't have to go far. Crackshot had laid in a supply of logs behind the shed and, after a few minutes, she had a fire blazing on the hearth.

Satisfied that the fire would last, Alexandra went into the bedroom where she removed the dusty quilt from the bed and folded it up. Tomorrow she would hang it over a line and beat it briskly until it started smelling sweet again. She then asked the men to remove the lumpy cornhusk mattress.

When they did, she took a rag from one of the wooden crates and set about rubbing down the old carved bed. Memories floated all around her as she traced every crook of the carvings—of her papa chasing her mama around the bed, with a baby babbling in a cradle nearby and three young ones asleep on the floor in the kitchen. It was a happy memory, one Alexandra had forgotten until this very moment. How strange that she would think of it now, after so many years! She couldn't have been more than five or six at the time. Had her mother been wildly in love with her papa?

It wasn't long until the new feather mattress was in place, the sheets, blankets, and pillows comfortably arranged, and her clothes cupboard standing against the far wall.

When Ross asked where she would like the rest of the furniture that was jammed into the front room, night had almost completely cloaked the camp and she was just now lighting the oil lamp. She didn't hesitate to tell him to see to his own tent and belongings, that she would be quite comfortable until tomorrow.

When he said he'd be happy to help her now if

she wanted, she reassured him, and Crackshot, that she wanted to scrub the house down before she did anything. Both men seemed relieved by her response. It had been a long day, especially for Crackshot, who had spent the better part of ten arduous hours drilling holes for dynamite. He was properly exhausted and headed back down the creek to his tent, and to Cecilia.

Ross, on the other hand, made no move to leave, but instead shut the door quietly. When he turned back to Alexandra, she saw that he wore a familiar mischievous expression in his eyes as he said, "I've been waiting all day for this."

Alexandra felt a sudden warmth pass through her, rushing all the way to her feet. "I don't know what you mean," she cried, finding that any fatigue she had been feeling herself from the exertions of the day had suddenly deserted her. "I already told you I wasn't going to kiss you again. And I meant what I said."

He sauntered toward her, wending his way through the maze of crates and furniture. "I'm sure you did," he responded with a smile twitching his lips. "But this kiss is meant only as a formal seal to our partnership, if you'll remember. Nothing more."

"Why is it!" Alexandra asked, with an irritated jerk of her head, "you always seem to have an answer? I suppose now I'll have to oblige you or I'll lose my fifty percent of the mine."

"Fifty?" he queried with a gleam in his eye. "We agreed to forty."

The closer he moved toward her, the weaker her legs seemed to grow, and she found herself instinctively backing away from him. She would have gone farther, but the worktable stopped her progress. She

171

thought about trying to reason with him, but she knew that wouldn't work. Besides, she could hardly control the quick pulsings in her heart that occurred with every step he took. Even her breathing grew difficult. She sure liked this man. She remembered again how hard he had gone after the freighter, how he had almost killed him for having come so near her. Was he her man? She teased him as he drew close, "But you said you'd give me seventy percent if I came to live at the cabin. I thought I'd settle for fifty."

He was standing in front of her now, and began stroking her arm lightly. "What I said was," he retorted, his voice low and resonant, "that you could have bargained for a bigger percentage. It's too late for that. You're here now and we already agreed to forty." He slipped a gentle arm about her waist and pulled her next to him.

"I want more than that," she said, looking deep into his gray eyes as he leaned down to her.

"I'll give you more," he said. "But it won't have a thing to do with your interest in the mine." And then his lips were on hers in a painfully hard kiss that buckled Alexandra's knees and made her feel like she was going to tumble to the floor. She couldn't have done so, though, since Ross was holding her tight.

His tongue sought entrance right away, driving quickly into her mouth. How exhilarating the sensation was, as a sudden desire raged through her, reminding her of the last time she had been with him. She was startled by the powerful feelings that swept over her body, by how immediate her response was to his kisses, by how much she longed for more from him.

172

Tentatively, she touched her own tongue against his. To her surprise, this small movement brought a whisper of pleasure traveling the length of her. Ross responded in kind, his tongue moving against hers. She could hardly breathe. Her body felt tight, all coiled up inside, as she wrapped her arm about his neck and pressed her mouth firmly against his. When he tried to withdraw his tongue, she resisted by taking it deep into her mouth, pulling on it in a sucking motion that brought a groan dying in his throat. She hadn't meant to do it, she didn't even realize what she had done until she had done it, but Ross's response shocked her as he leaned his body hard over hers, bending her backward slightly, all the while pressing into her hips with his own.

Passion flowed over her in a hot wave. She wanted Ross so much, wanted to be possessed by him. She was in complete awe of how his kisses brought such a sweet madness riding her body. At the same time, where could such intimacies lead? It wasn't just that they weren't married, it was that she knew in her heart she couldn't belong to Ross, not completely, and certainly not forever. The tensions in her mind traveled to her heart, which in turn rebelled mightily. She kissed Ross harder still, holding his tongue captive within her mouth, hugging him tightly, her fingernails digging into his neck until she again heard him moan.

She felt his hand slide from her arm to caress her breast. She didn't realize until this moment how much she wanted him to touch her. His palm moved slowly in a circle, tracing the fullness of her breast, then stopping to remain poised over the nipple, as though he wanted something from her. But what? She waited, her mouth releasing his tongue, her body intensely desiring to have his hand caress her. She felt a tight spring of tension rise from deep within her. His lips became feathery soft on her mouth, desire for his touch increasing as each second slipped by.

"Ross," she whispered, or did she? Her mind cried out for him to caress her. Still, he paused. When she could wait no longer, she laced her fingers through his and forced his hand down on her breast.

She gave a cry as he again thrust his tongue into her mouth and rolled his palm across her breast in a rough kneading motion that brought a tremendous flame of pleasure burning inside her.

She heard him speak as though from a place so far away that had he not been next to her she would have supposed he was shouting into the wind. How strange it sounded in her ears. "Tell me it's all right. I won't do anything unless you want me to."

For a long time, as his hand magically caressed her, she could make no sense of what he was saying. Of course it was all right. What was all right?

"I want to love you — now, tonight, here. Tell me it's all right, Alexandra."

Slowly, understanding pervaded her mind. He was asking for permission to take her to bed. She couldn't. Drawing in shallow breaths, desire still raging in her blood, she gently, slowly began pushing him away, feeling as though the act of separating from him was like ripping a piece of fabric apart. She hurt physically. Did he feel the same? She didn't want to know.

"I can't, I can't," she said in a hoarse whisper. "Please go. Please. I'll fix breakfast tomorrow for you, only go now. Please."

Not once had she looked at him. She was suffering too much to do more than catch a glimpse of his back as he slipped from the cabin.

Ross was grateful that he could release some of his frustration by setting up his own camp. Sheer physical exertion, or an ice-cold bath, was the only thing he knew that could help displace the strong feelings that had his body tied up in a knot. He didn't blame Alexandra at all. At the same time, he was unable to explain why her touch, or the feel of her hands in his hair, or the way she had held his tongue captive in her mouth, had affected him so powerfully. He was almost beyond control with her. She drove him to a place of passion that stunned him since he had never experienced the likes of it before. All he could think, as he rolled the tough canvas out on the ground not far from Alexandra's cabin was that when he held her in his arms, it was as though he was embracing not just a woman, but everything he wanted from life. It was as though he knew she could be the source of all good things for his future. For this reason alone, he was able to tear himself away from her. He feared hurting that which his heart told him was infinitely precious. He was astounded by the fact that he could let her go, especially when what he really wanted to do was throw her back on the worktable and force himself on her, into her. Did she suffer as he did? She certainly appeared to. Her face had been unbelievably pale, her blue eyes hazy, not with desire, but with pain. He didn't understand entirely why she withheld herself from him, but that it required every ounce of strength for her to do so. he knew full well.

What would be the end to this? What should he do now? If only she would marry him. But that seemed to be the problem anyway, that she simply didn't trust him enough to commit her life into his safekeeping. Would she ever? This thought struck a chord of fear running straight through Ross's heart. He had lost so much already, what if he lost Alexandra, too.

By the time his tent and cot were set up and he had stretched himself out under a warm wool blanket, Ross knew one thing for certain: he would do everything he could in the coming weeks to convince her that her own happiness rested with him.

Chapter Twenty-two

The next week was one of the sweetest Alexandra had ever known. November was upon them, the temperatures dropping rapidly every day, the crispness of the autumn days a welcome change from summer. Ross had been nothing less than a gentleman, at least in terms of not pressing her. As for his kisses and caresses, however, he seemed to take advantage of every moment they were alone together, to touch her, to hug her, to remind her of the past, to promise wondrous things if she would only give her heart to him.

When she had first cleaned up the cabin, he had found her with a kerchief tied round her hair and her skirt soiled from scrubbing the floor. He hadn't hesitated to draw her swiftly to her feet, catch her in his arms, and plant a kiss on her lips, as though he was greeting the prettiest lady he'd seen in a long time. She had felt flushed with pleasure, as much by his kiss as by the fact that even though she looked a sight, he had still wanted to kiss her.

Later, when she had greeted him at the table with fresh biscuits, beans, and apple turnovers, the latter of which Mrs. McCormick had slipped into one of the tins, he'd praised her for a plate of beans that she knew tasted watery and flat. He was a good man, she realized yet again, especially when she sat down to eat her own supper and found she couldn't.

Another time he had come upon her by the stream while she was filling a pail with water. He had pinned her arms while standing behind her and held her close to him. She had protested his hugging her in plain view of the camp, but he kissed her neck and ear, explaining that Cecilia and Crackshot had gone hunting. Then he'd whirled her around in his arms and kissed her until she felt as if she was floating. On another occasion she had been chopping kindling for her fire when he approached her with a huge smile, took her hatchet out of her hand and set it aside, slipped his arms about her waist and swung her in a circle. He told her she was as pretty as the flowers that bloomed in the meadow and twice as sweet. Then he'd kissed her hard. Always, when in his arms, desire rose sharply within her. Always, she longed for more, and always, he stopped after a few minutes to start up a conversation about what she was doing, how the cabin was progressing, and whether or not she was happy.

Was she happy? More than she wanted to admit, even to herself.

It had taken the entire week to get the cabin the way she wanted it. She had scrubbed her hands almost raw bringing a shine to both rooms of her little house. But by the time she was finished, she was very satisfied with the results. The old table and chairs now belonged to Crackshot and Cecilia and she adorned the new set every day with fresh yellow flowers mixed with pine boughs which she gathered from the woods and the meadow nearby.

Opposite the table stood a narrow oak cupboard that housed a set of white dishes, a few glasses and serving bowls, and a variety of odd-shaped linens. She had gathered a pungent bouquet of weedlike plants, tying up the stalks with a pink ribbon and hanging the bouquet over the cupboard. The strong fragrance softened the smoky smell of the cabin walls and ceiling which all her scrubbing seemed unable to get rid of.

Ross had set up the potbellied stove to the right of the oak cupboard, and Alexandra was pleased with how much warmth the stove emitted. The kitchen remained the same, except that now it gleamed and the fabric which draped in a skirt about the worktable had been both washed and ironed. She found she rarely made use of the fireplace, except when she bathed. Then she would build a blazing fire, fill up her tin tub with the hottest water she could bear, and let her legs dangle over the side that faced the fire. She supported her head by resting it on the seat of one of the chairs, and she could almost say she was comfortable. She would sit there, enjoying the fire as it leapt up the chimney in bright dancing flames, until the water in the tub grew cold. Then she'd dry off and put on a thick flannel nightgown. With a large rock warmed by the fire and wrapped in a towel, tucked between her sheets, she would crawl into bed, exhausted but satisfied, in a way she had never experienced during all her years with her aunt and uncle in Missouri.

Only one aspect of her life in the camp bothered her, as it did the others—the ever-present awareness that someone wanted the mine and had killed trying to get it. There was no reason to believe they wouldn't one day have to face whoever it was who was after the Alexandra. For this reason, hardly an hour passed by that Alexandra didn't scan the meadow and the wooded ridges surrounding the camp for sign of the desperadoes who had perpetrated the attack at the

Dells. Only one thing brought reassurance—the mine was located in a rough area, difficult to find without help. The terrain might be just enough of a deterrent to hold the claim jumpers at bay.

Other than worrying off and on about the safety of the camp, Alexandra found that her life settled quickly into a comforting routine. During the days, she tended to her house or chopped firewood from logs Crackshot and Ross had hauled in from the forest and split, or she took turns with Cecilia each washing the other's hair. She got to know the strange woman better during these times. Cecilia's life had been hard, thus far, until she met Crackshot.

"He kind to me," she had said recently in her broken English. "And all I do is cook food. Not much. My brother not good man. I make clothes for him, I polish boots, I feed horses, I wash, I clean. Then he beat me. I feel ugly inside. I miss my home with Apaches." She hit her fist to her breast several times. "Mr. Peters make me pretty, inside. I happy now."

Mr. Peters make me pretty.

From then on, when Alexandra would look at Ross, she would frequently think, *Mr. Halleck, he make me pretty,* and she would touch her fist to her breast and smile.

The evenings took on a familiar pattern as well, and one that generally left Alexandra tingling. Ross would come in for supper, after washing up in a tin tub he kept in his tent. They would sit down to dinner and chat easily about their respective days, particularly how the ore was looking in the mine. When they were done eating, Ross would build up a strong fire in the potbellied stove while she cleaned up. But always, before she had a chance to sit down, but just about a second after the last plate was put away in the cupboard, he'd pull her into his arms and kiss her.

By the second week, Alexandra had come to expect him to do so, but this time he drew her onto his lap while he sat in one of the chairs. She knew right away this wouldn't be like the other nights, especially because he had that peculiar glint in his eye. He spoke to her of his love, of his desire to marry her. He asked her again if he could take her to bed. Alexandra felt weak all over, sitting on his lap, feeling his muscular legs beneath her, his strong arm around her shoulder, his warm fingers as he took her chin in his hand and held her face tenderly as he placed a gentle kiss on her lips.

"I want you," he whispered in a low voice. "I don't know how long I can keep being around you so much, having you so close, and not loving you the way I want to."

She felt herself slipping away as his tongue played against hers, his mouth warm and seductive. She wanted him so much. Maybe she should marry him. But she couldn't. She just couldn't!

Her mind again warred with her heart, with her desires for him. His fingers began drifting away from her chin, teasing the sensitive skin behind her ear, traveling in slow circles down her shoulder, down the length of her arm, to return to her neck. His mouth grew more insistent, he kept whispering, "I want you." Shivers seemed to trade places on her body, snaking down her neck and spine, shooting across her arms, suddenly appearing then disappearing from her legs. His fingers were again swirling over her, this time across her neck from one shoulder to the other. Desire began growing in her as each pass he made dipped lower and lower until his fingers eased along the fullness of her breasts. Alexandra felt her breathing shorten as she lifted a hand to caress his face. She wanted him to touch her, hoping he wouldn't stop, praying he would. He kissed her fiercely, his fingers traveling in feathery strokes over her breasts. She moaned as he caressed each breast fully now, his palm and fingers exploring the curves, kneading the soft skin, until Alexandra was calling his name with each pressure on her breast, with each kiss he placed on her mouth.

His hand moved lower, beyond her breasts, caressing her stomach, pulling at her waist. Slowly she felt his fingers descending toward her womanhood. A fire raged within her, beckoning him, the skin of her abdomen where he touched her sending shivers in fiery darts down her legs. She wanted him to keep descending, but at the same time a fierce panic rose within her and she stood up suddenly, pulling out of the circle of his arm. She couldn't do this. She couldn't.

She turned away from him to stand in front of the potbellied stove, her hands on her face. She felt frightened and embarrassed. She didn't know what he was thinking, but whatever it was, she was sure he hated her. Why wouldn't he, when she knew she must be causing him intense frustration.

To her surprise, she felt gentle hands clasp her arms, and, crossing her own, she reached back to cover her hands with his. Tears tumbled down her cheeks. "I'm sorry," she said. "Ross, this can't go on."

"I know that," he whispered, his breath warm in her hair.

She leaned her head back deep into the hollow of his shoulder as he held her tight. She loved him.

Her mind stopped. Her feelings thinned out to nothing.

She loved him.

She loved him!

There! She had admitted the truth to herself. She loved him, and she always would. She wanted to marry him, she wanted to give herself to him. But she couldn't. More tears welled up in her eyes and flowed down her cheeks. What was she going to do?

At that moment, Crackshot knocked on the door, calling to Ross in a distressed voice, "Halleck! Get out here quick! Someone's in the mine!"

Chapter Twenty-three

Ross left the cabin immediately. Alexandra ran into the bedroom and jerked a knit shawl off one of the hooks on the wall. Flinging it over her shoulders, she raced out of the cabin, slamming the door shut behind her.

Outside, the air was cold and the night sky full of a thick band of stars that lit the meadow in a cool white layer of light. As Alexandra ran hard after the men, she saw the glow from Crackshot's campfire and Cecilia outlined through the canvas of her tent. She sat huddled and rocking, and silent. Alexandra headed toward her as the men, carrying rifles, moved stealthily toward the opening of the mine.

When she reached Cecilia, she knelt beside her and put her arm around the woman's shoulders. Cecilia turned her face into Alexandra's shoulder, not whimpering, as she half expected her to, nor did she say anything. She just continued comforting herself by rocking back and forth.

"Crackshot told us someone was in the mine," Alexandra said, keeping her voice low and trying to sound calm. "What did he mean? Did he hear someone?"

"We both hear," Cecilia said, her voice ragged. "Mr. Peters die. He die."

Alexandra heard the frantic sound in Cecilia's voice and hugged her close. She knew any farther questions would only upset the woman, whose mind had long since lost all flexibility. Without realizing she had done so, she began moving along with Cecilia in a rocking motion that suddenly seemed very ancient.

How weighted her heart felt, burdened as it was with fear. Who could be in the mine? she wondered. The bustling activity of setting up her house and all the comfortable evenings with Ross had served well to distract her mind from the fact that someone was intent on stealing the Alexandra. Now the truth was facing her again, and she didn't want to look at it.

With these thoughts, Alexandra was suddenly overcome by panic, a paralyzing drag to her mind that pulled fiercely on her ability to reason and keep calm.

Mr. Peters die. Cecilia's words repeated themselves several times in her mind. *Mr. Peters die.*

Ross could die if someone armed was waiting for him to enter the mine where it was darker than night. How long would it take for Ross's eyes to adjust to the blackness of the main shaft, with only starlight at the opening to light the way. He would be vulnerable the moment he stepped into the mouth of the mine.

She watched him now, with Crackshot at his side, their rifles both held at a tight angle to their bodies. She wanted to call out to Ross, warning him to stay back, to keep away from the mine. But if she did, she could easily distract him the very moment he would need full use of his wits and instincts.

Around the entrance to the mine, tailings from the several mine shafts that wove their way through the Alexandra had piled up year after year forming an earthen ramp that led both to the creek as well as to the arrastra.

185

Ross and Crackshot climbed on the loose slide of dirt that mounted at an easy grade to the opening. A stand of yellow flowers had sprouted nearby in stark contrast to the disemboweled earth.

Alexandra's heart pounded out a warning the men could not hear. Cecilia was whispering softly to herself, rocking and rocking. She hoped the woman would not break into a wail, like she had the day of their arrival.

Ross climbed up the last few feet with Crackshot now behind him and lay on the dirt listening. He stayed there for a long time. Alexandra felt dizzy from the tension, as she kept her gaze pinned to his back. What if he got shot? Blood pounded in her head. She realized that kneeling as she was had cut some of the blood flow to her legs and her feet were growing numb. She shifted to seat herself, still holding Cecilia tightly about her shoulder.

Ross started to move. Like a sleek cat he lifted himself up, sprinted into the mine, and was inside within the blink of an eye. Alexandra held her breath. She waited for the sound of a gun retort, but none came. She let out her breath. The next second, Crackshot did the same. Alexandra took another deep breath, holding it, but again nothing happened.

Time became her enemy. Every second seemed like a minute. Every minute that passed felt like an hour. She felt sick with dread.

Suddenly Cecilia lifted her head and looked straight into Alexandra's eyes. The pupils of Cecilia's eyes were fully open, giving her a wild, strange appearance. She opened her mouth as if to say something, but nothing came out. Alexandra felt the woman's fright creep between them until she felt ready to scream.

Everything began happening fast. She saw a blur from the side of her eye. She looked back at the mine and just as she was trying figure out what had happened, a loud roar filled the little valley, fire and smoke burst from the opening of the mine, as dirt shot straight out. She turned instinctively into Cecilia, who did likewise, as both women threw themselves back into the tent. A smattering of debris struck the top of the tent, rolling off the slant of the canvas to the ground, sounding as if a heavy rain had started up then quit as quickly as it had begun.

When the shock of the moment passed, terror filled Alexandra. Where were Ross and Crackshot?

She was on her feet, dragging her shawl against the tent flap as she ran through the opening and headed straight for the creek. She saw both men right away, lying prone in the dirt, their hands folded over their heads.

Alexandra's boots hit the boards that formed a bridge across the creek. Each thump sounded loud in the silent aftermath of the explosion. *Ross.* Her throat became clogged with pain and fright. He was moving now, he wasn't dead. Would he die later?

Crackshot was sitting up staring at her, and Ross had his head down, shaking it in an effort to clear his mind.

"Ross!" she cried, stumbling twice as she scrambled up the earthen ramp. "Ross. Are you all right? What happened?"

Ross lifted his head to look at her, his face drawing up into a scowl as he cried, "Get back!"

Both men gained their feet at the same time, picking up their steps quickly into a run as they headed toward Alexandra. She didn't wait for instructions, but whirled around and half slid, half ran down the ramp, onto the boards crossing the creek, back to the tent. Ross commanded her to get inside with Cecilia and to lie flat. He and Crackshot flung themselves behind overturned crates, stretching themselves out on the grass of the meadow, rifles poised next to the crates at ground level and pointed toward the mine.

"Someone has got to come out of there," Ross said.

Alexandra buried her face in her arms. She could hear the men talking, discussing possibilities. How long would they stay like this, waiting. Who did they expect to emerge from the mine? Why would anyone be so foolish as to attack the men with dynamite and seal themselves in or risk being shot at when they tried to leave? It didn't make sense.

She heard Ross ask Crackshot if there was another opening to the mine, another shaft, forgotten maybe. Silence fell between the men, and Alexandra imagined that they were looking intently at each other, trying to figure out if this was what had happened.

She leaned up on her elbows, her mind fixed on the same idea. It was the only explanation that seemed logical. Another opening to the mine!

"I don't know of one," Crackshot responded slowly. "But that's gotta be it. Cecilia and I were just sittin' here and I was whittlin' away on that piece of wood over there when we heard a crash, like timbers breaking. Knowing the mine like I do, and checking the wedges every day, I knew that none of my timbers coulda collapsed. Do you suppose someone was in there trying to wreck some of our equipment and force us out?"

"I don't know," Ross responded. "But it figures that whoever was in there couldn't've been dumb enough to throw a stick of dynamite at us without having a way out for himself."

"Y'er right."

As if to prove their reasonings were sound, the pounding of hoofbeats echoed up the valley from the gulley below, an eerie sound in the night like bats flapping their wings in a cave.

Both Ross and Crackshot stood up, staring into the shadows of the night at the far end of the meadow. Whoever the horseman was, he was heading toward Lloyd Powell's mine.

188

Chapter Twenty-four

Both Ross and Crackshot decided to wait until morning to begin searching through the various shafts of the Alexandra to find out where the intruder had entered. Maybe the location of the second opening to the mine would provide a reason for the continued attacks. If there was another entrance, it could very well be that a deposit of gold had been found near there.

What concerned Ross more, however, as he walked Alexandra back to her cabin, was the direction the horseman headed. "I have no basis for suspecting Powell," he said to her. "On the other hand, it seems awfully convenient. Maybe I oughtta ride out there tomorrow."

Alexandra listened to Ross with increased difficulty. Her concerns right now were so different from his that she had no opinion to offer him. In addition, her limbs weren't behaving themselves. She had started shaking and couldn't stop. Fear had taken hold of her and every word Ross spoke only made her sense of panic grow stronger.

Ross could've died.

Over and over in her mind the same horrible

thought presented itself, laughing at her newly discovered love for him. When she stumbled slightly just before mounting the steps to the porch, he slipped his arm about her waist, and found that she was trembling all over.

"Good Lord!" he cried. "Why didn't you say something. You're shivering!"

Her teeth chattered as she spoke. "I-it's not the temperature. I'm about h-half scared out of my mind. Ross, you almost died back there."

He held her firmly, helping her into the house and settling her in a chair by the stove. He said he'd be right back as he walked quickly back to the door and passed through.

Alexandra held her hands to the warmth radiating from the potbellied stove, but her fingers jiggled so badly she finally just clasped them hard in her lap and kept them there. Her knees were trembling, too. This had never happened to her before. She couldn't understand it.

When Ross returned, not quite a minute later, he had a pint of whiskey in his hand. He took two glasses from the oak cupboard next to the potbellied stove and poured out a small measure in each. Handing one to Alexandra, she took it gratefully and began sipping the liquid that soon burned her throat. She wasn't used to it, having never cared for the taste of strong alcohol. Ross, on the other hand, downed his quickly.

"You'll feel better in a minute," he said quietly, trying to reassure her. "I've had this happen to me before. I had a fight with a Comanche once, a long time ago. That's where I got these scars you've seen on my arm and stomach. Afterward, I couldn't have held a gun in my hand if I'd wanted to, I was shaking like a leaf in a strong wind."

190

Alexandra looked up at him, barely hearing what he said. The whiskey did seem to warm up her veins, and before long the trembling stopped. Ross was so tall as he stood before the stove. She wished he'd kiss her again. She reached out her hand to him. He seemed a little surprised as he surrounded her hand in a warm clasp.

"Feeling better?" he asked, holding her hand tightly. "You're not trembling like you were."

Alexandra shook her head slowly, and pressed his hand in response to his question. She didn't shift her gaze from his, but stared directly at him, willing him to read her thoughts. She didn't want to say what was in her heart. She wanted him to know how she felt, how frightened she had been by the thought that he could have died, how much she loved him, how desperately she wanted him. Now.

He understood right away what she was asking. "I'd be taking advantage of you," he said in his deep voice, answering the silent cries of her heart.

"No you wouldn't," she responded in a whisper, again shaking her head. She felt her eyes fill with unexpected tears.

Ross gazed into luminous blue eyes that mirrored his own growing desire. He felt utterly lost in the warmth that resided there and drew her to her feet. In answer to her plea, he slipped an arm about her waist, placing a full, warm kiss on her lips as he had done so many times before. He could sense that all resistance was gone, and the mere thought of what was ahead brought a sudden passion rolling over him.

Alexandra parted her lips and felt his tongue invade her mouth. How much she had grown to love this intimate touch of his, she thought, as a sweet rush of pleasure rose from deep within her to envelop her

191

heart. A haze of desire tingled all over her that softened the edges of the fright still gripping her mind. Slowly, he began gliding his tongue into the secret recesses of her mouth, moving rhythmically, languidly.

She felt joined to him, as she never had before, to his thoughts and to all that he wanted from life. An inexplicable desire for his fulfillment in everything moved within her, a sign of her growing love for him. She returned his kiss, enjoying the feel of his mouth as she slid her tongue against his in a similar, easy movement. She heard him groan as he pulled her tightly to him, his tongue moving harder against hers, driving fiercely now as though some part of him relived an ancient rite, man striving with woman.

Alexandra felt a familiar weakness work its way up through the pit of her stomach, through her heart and into her senses. She both leaned into him and drifted away from him, her back arching of its own volition. A moan escaped her as he cradled the back of her head, forcing his tongue deeply into her mouth. An ache swept over her and her breath grew short and labored. Her hand found its way into his thick black hair as she worked her fingers through the strands, pulling, kneading, and tugging in symphony with the seductive thrusts of his tongue. She felt dizzy and weak, yet feared above all things that he would stop plundering her mouth.

Ross began easing back, knowing that he was near to losing control with the mere kissing of Alexandra. He heard her protest as he distanced himself slightly from the passion mounting within her. The feel of her hands in his hair had filled his body with an urgent need for release. He had never known a woman's passion to surround him as hers did. It was a tangible

MORE PASSION AND ADVENTURE AWAIT... YOUR TRIP TO A BIG ADVENTUROUS WORLD BEGINS WHEN YOU ACCEPT YOUR FIRST 4 NOVELS ABSOLUTELY *FREE* (AN $18.00 VALUE)

Accept your Free gift and start to experience more of the passion and adventure you like in a historical romance novel. Each Zebra novel is filled with proud men, spirited women and tempestuous love that you'll remember long after you turn the last page.

Zebra Historical Romances are the finest novels of their kind. They are written by authors who really know how to weave tales of romance and adventure in the historical settings you love. You'll feel like you've actually gone back in time with the thrilling stories that each Zebra novel offers.

GET YOUR FREE GIFT WITH THE START OF YOUR HOME SUBSCRIPTION

Our readers tell us that these books sell out very fast in book stores and often they miss the newest titles. So Zebra has made arrangements for you to receive the four newest novels published each month.

You'll be guaranteed that you'll never miss a title, and home delivery is so convenient. And to show you just how easy it is to get Zebra Historical Romances, we'll send you your first 4 books absolutely FREE! Our gift to you just for trying our home subscription service.

BIG SAVINGS AND FREE HOME DELIVERY

Each month, you'll receive the four newest titles as soon as they are published. You'll probably receive them even before the bookstores do. What's more, you may preview these exciting novels free for 10 days. If you like them as much as we think you will, just pay the low preferred subscriber's price of just $3.75 each. *You'll save $3.00 each month off the publisher's price.* AND, your savings are even greater because there are never any shipping, handling or other hidden charges—FREE Home Delivery. Of course you can return any shipment within 10 days for full credit, no questions asked. There is no minimum number of books you must buy.

4 FREE BOOKS

TO GET YOUR 4 FREE BOOKS WORTH $18.00 — MAIL IN THE FREE BOOK CERTIFICATE T O D A Y

Fill in the Free Book Certificate below, and we'll send your FREE BOOKS to you as soon as we receive it.

If the certificate is missing below, write to: Zebra Home Subscription Service, Inc., P.O. Box 5214, 120 Brighton Road, Clifton, New Jersey 07015-5214.

FREE BOOK CERTIFICATE

4 FREE BOOKS

ZEBRA HOME SUBSCRIPTION SERVICE, INC.

YES! Please start my subscription to Zebra Historical Romances and send me my first 4 books absolutely FREE. I understand that each month I may preview four new Zebra Historical Romances free for 10 days. If I'm not satisfied with them, I may return the four books within 10 days and owe nothing. Otherwise, I will pay the low preferred subscriber's price of just $3.75 each; a total of $15.00, *a savings off the publisher's price of $3.00.* I may return any shipment and I may cancel this subscription at any time. There is no obligation to buy any shipment and there are no shipping, handling or other hidden charges. Regardless of what I decide, the four free books are mine to keep.

NAME

ADDRESS _____ APT

CITY _____ STATE ____ ZIP

TELEPHONE ( )

SIGNATURE _____ (if under 18, parent or guardian must sign)

Terms, offer and prices subject to change without notice. Subscription subject to acceptance by Zebra Books. Zebra Books reserves the right to reject any order or cancel any subscription. 039102

GET
FOUR
FREE
BOOKS
(AN $18.00 VALUE)

ZEBRA HOME SUBSCRIPTION
SERVICE, INC.
P.O. Box 5214
120 BRIGHTON ROAD
CLIFTON, NEW JERSEY 07015-5214

thing, dancing all over him, driving him to the point of madness.

Kissing her face gently, his lips traveled the line of her cheek to her ear. "I have a fire nipping at me from your caresses," he whispered. "You'll have to be patient with me or I won't be able to pleasure you as I want to."

She leaned her cheek into his own, as his tongue sought out the shivering hollows and ridges of her ear. Alexandra grasped his shirtsleeve, knotting it in her hand, clinging to it as pleasure rippled through her body with each thrust of his tongue. His hand sought out her breasts and he stroked each with a feathery movement, touching her through the finely woven cotton fabric of her blouse, and again her body drifted and arched as his fingers repeatedly fluttered over her taut nipples in cadence to his pleasuring tongue. She felt lost in the sensation as he touched her lightly over and over again.

He pushed the shawl from her shoulders and set it on the chair by the fire. Turning her around, he began undoing her blouse. This time he took it off completely and she was left standing with her back to him wearing a lace-edged camisole held in place by her corset and skirt.

She started to remove her camisole, but he stopped her suddenly, moving to stand behind her, the length of his body pressed against her. Slipping his arms around her, he held her close. "I love you," he whispered in her ear.

To Alexandra's surprise, he bid her sit down and afterward dropped to his knees beside her. His gray eyes were warm with affection as he looked at her and smiled. "I've loved you," he whispered, "since I first saw you in Phoenix." And before she understood

193

what he meant to do, he leaned down and took a soft, peaked breast in his mouth.

Alexandra caught her breath, feeling dazed by the abrupt pleasure that darted through her as his tongue swept over her nipple through the thin white cotton of her camisole. She was catapulted back to her former state, filled with joy and wonder at the sublime uneasiness building within her. Her breathing came in little gasps as he sucked ravenously, dampening the cloth covering her breast and drawing from deep within her a sense of urgency she had come to expect from being with him. Slipping her hands and arms around him, she began rubbing the corded muscles of his shoulders, neck, and back, holding him close, wanting him closer still.

Ross felt the tense, uneven movements of her hands up and down his back, and knew that she was as much enslaved by desire as he was. Her hips moved uneasily, restlessly, demanding more from him. The hardness of his own flesh forced him again to draw back, and when he did, she held fiercely on to his neck, refusing to let him go.

"I feel as though I will break inside," she said, her breath hot on his neck. "I've never known such an ache as this in all my life. And yet I don't ache at all."

Ross laughed as he took her arms from about his neck and pulled her to her feet. "I know exactly what you mean." He drew her gently in his arms and, embracing her fully, planted a firm, loving kiss on her mouth. "Come, sweet one," he said, leading her into the small bedroom that smelled sweetly of pine.

The moon shone in a square patch on the pastel quilt of blues, pinks, yellows, and greens. The chamber was redolent of sagebrush, pine, and herbs that hung in ribboned clumps on the walls.

Ross brought her to the window so that the moonlight drenched her pretty face and smooth white shoulders. He took delight in helping her unweave her braid and drawing her soft, curly red hair over her milky skin. He eased the camisole beneath her breasts and fondled the delicate fullness with his fingers and again sought her mouth, plunging his tongue deep within. He groaned as she took his tongue, sucking it lightly, then harder still as he pulled her close.

Alexandra felt the hardness of his flesh against her and felt another weakening in the bottom of her stomach. She was frightened yet at the same time she longed to give herself fully to him, to feel him deep inside her.

After a moment, Ross released her to remove his shirt.

Alexandra took pleasure in the sight of his broad shoulders and strong, muscled arms. She lifted a hand and tentatively touched the curly black hairs matted over his chest, then slid her fingers through the coarse tangle of hair. As she did so, she lifted her face to him and brushed her parted lips against his in a dozen whispery kisses until his tongue again took possession of her. Smoothing her hands across his chest, she slipped her arms about his shoulders and reveled in the warm heat of his body as she eased her breasts against him. When his arms melted around her, holding her fast, she laid her head upon his shoulder, peace enveloping her. Tears, unbidden, flooded her eyes.

Ross felt Alexandra's tears touch his shoulder. "What is it, my love?" he asked. "Why are you crying?"

"I don't know," she whispered. "I just feel so safe in

195

your arms. You're a strong man, Ross, and I do love you. I do."

"Alexandra," he breathed into her hair, overcome by her words and the heady sensation of her soft breasts pressed against him. He moved his hands slowly down her velvety back and began untying the strings of her corset. At the same time, he undid her skirt, letting it drop in a circle about her feet. When he removed the corset, tossing it on the bed, he gripped her waist, gently at first, then harder, rolling his thumbs downward, at the same time seeking her lips again with his own. She was wearing only her camisole and undergarment, and the thin cotton teased his flesh as he took pleasure in the smallness of her waist.

Alexandra felt a heat rushing from her waist in a hot descent to her femininity. She gasped, rocking her hips against his in a movement that brought him connecting with her soft flesh. He groaned, holding her waist more firmly still.

"I remember that first day, after I was shot," he said, his deep-timbred voice low and husky in her ear. "I remember looking at you and thinking you had the smallest waist I'd ever seen. I can put my hands all the way around you. Can you feel that?"

Alexandra drew in her breath sharply at the shards of pleasure cutting through her hips and abdomen as his strong hands kneaded the delicate skin at her waist. The pressure of his fingers sent a fiery blaze burning into the depths of her womanhood. After a moment, he released her waist to slide his hands over her buttocks. Easing his groin into her hips, he moved into her with a series of strong circles. His hard flesh fed the fire building within her, desire mounting like flames that licked unceasingly at burning logs. Alex-

196

andra clasped her hands about his neck. He invaded her mouth again, his tongue pulsing with the enticing movement of his hips until Alexandra began crying his name over and over. His lips brushed hers with each whimper until he slowly eased back and finished removing the rest of her clothes.

She realized with a start that she was standing before Ross without a stitch of clothes on. She felt embarrassed suddenly. He kissed her and seemed to sense her discomfort. "Why don't you climb into bed and get nice and warm under the quilt," he suggested. "I have these boots to take off, and they're always a bear." He crossed the room to sit in a small chair by the door.

Alexandra was stunned by his consideration for her and looked at Ross with deepening appreciation. He continually surprised and pleased her, especially in his gentle understanding of her feelings.

Her initial modesty dissipated and she followed him to sit on the edge of the bed, kicking her feet, her gaze fixed to Ross's large frame as he balanced himself on the small chair and worked fiercely to remove his tough leather boots. When he looked up to find that she had not hidden herself beneath the safety of the quilt, a smile of satisfaction spread over his tanned, handsome face.

He tugged on the first boot and, with some reluctance, it finally burst off his foot. But the second one, after a short battle, sent him rocking backward in the chair so that he struck his head on the wall and came up laughing.

Alexandra laughed, too, asking whether he had damaged her wall. "I worked hard cleaning and sprucing up this little shack," she cried indignantly. "And I won't have you busting through my

197

walls and destroying the fine home I've built here."

He returned quickly to her. "Did I tell you how nice this place looks?" he asked, his expression summery as he drew her to her feet. "Yeah, I know it's little more than a jumble of dried-out planks, but every inch of it seems warm and friendly now, just like you. We could build a house together and make ourselves a family to be proud of; a fine, healthy brood of handsome, red-haired girls and a dozen or so ornery boys."

His rich voice, as always, struck a sweet chord in her heart. "I'd like that," Alexandra responded.

She laced her hands through the dark curls on his chest, spreading her fingers outward to feel the muscles of his shoulders and across his arms. His hands caressed the rounded curves of her buttocks as he eased and rocked his swollen flesh against her. His tongue penetrated deeply into her mouth again, thrusting with the steady pulse of his hips. When she began sucking his tongue, he groaned, holding her fiercely to him.

"My darling," he cried as he shifted her slightly to unbutton his pants, removing the final barrier to their joining.

Alexandra trembled at the feel of his naked body and of his manhood, so rigid against her. The awareness of her virginity surfaced slightly in her mind, and a brief shudder of fear convulsed her, but receded quickly. Nothing could stem the tide of desire rising within her as he again enticed her with a pulsing of his groin. He asked her in a hoarse whisper to part her legs for him just a little, and when she did, he positioned himself between her so that she felt his manhood melding with the throbbing ache of her womanhood. The pleasure of this touch forced her back to arch suddenly as he began sliding against her,

198

though not yet inside her, his tongue at the same time still driving relentlessly against her own.

When his movements became fitful and rapid, Alexandra wanted to scream out an impassioned plea for him to just take her. She dug her fingers deeply into his hair, his neck, his taut, muscled back. She drew his tongue to the farthest recess of her mouth. He moaned with these gestures, then withdrew from her to gently lay her down on the bed.

"Ross," Alexandra said, a shiver of panic rippling through her. "There's something I need to say, to tell you—"

"You don't have to tell me," he cried warmly, stretching out on top of her. "I know it's been a long time for you. I'll be gentle, I promise."

Alexandra wanted to say more, but she was suddenly afraid that if he knew the truth, that she had never known a man before, he would refuse to love her. She wrapped her arms closely about his neck and received him as he began penetrating her womanhood. He eased into her slowly, thrusting himself a little deeper each time, all the while placing tender kisses on her cheeks and lips.

"Tell me if I hurt you," he breathed, placing a full, moist kiss on her mouth.

Each pulse of his hips against her soft mound was a torture so exquisite that she could not even form words within her mind with which to answer him. She could only hug him close and kiss his hair, moving in unison with him, rocking in sweetly painful movements until he struck too deeply and she cried out in pain.

"My God!" Ross cried, lifting himself off her chest slightly, though remaining deep within her. He stared at her in bewildered shock. "You can't be . . . Alexandra, why? Why didn't you tell me? Don't you know that I can't, I won't—"

Alexandra clung to his neck and rose swiftly up to him, silencing him with a kiss. "Love me," she whispered against his mouth, as she drew him back down to her. "Love me. Love me."

For a brief moment, Ross struggled with his conscience. He didn't understand how she could be a virgin; at the same time, the warmth of her femininity surrounded him with a pleasure that destroyed his ability to reason. As he gazed into eyes that were heavy with desire, he returned to her, passion gripping him at the wonder that he was the first to possess her. Instead of subduing his desire, this knowledge increased it. He ravaged her lips, glorying in the moans of pleasure that bubbled in her throat. After a moment, he told her to hold him fast and with a quick thrust broke through her maidenhead.

Alexandra writhed with the searing pain that robbed her for a moment of her pleasure. Tears trickled down her cheek with the sudden awareness that in this split, frightening second she had become a woman. She felt Ross begin kissing her cheek, taking her tears on his lips, then whispering into her ear. Words of love flowed from him, each syllable smoothing the pain away.

Ross did not move within her for several minutes, waiting for her body to relax. He began stroking her breast with his hand, his fingers floating down her ribs and stomach. She spoke his name softly and he began teasing her mouth with the tip of his tongue until he felt the hidden part of her moisten and grip him. Only then did he carefully move within her.

Alexandra expected pain, instead, a sudden streak of pleasure brought all former passion rippling

200

through her. She heard Ross speak to her, but his words were indistinct. She felt caught up in a whorl of light, pleasure, and sensation that dimmed her sight and hearing. With each thrust came a need for release that sent her back arching and her hips rushing to meet his as he connected more and more deeply within her. She clung to his back, holding him fiercely, digging her fingers into his skin, her breathing fitful and wild. Again and again he drove into her body, feeding the mounting tension within her, receding and mounting. Ross breathed hot kisses over her face and moved his hand in circles against her breasts as he called her name. The whorl caught her up, spun her dizzily, as he moved against her, faster and faster until a dam of piercing sensations broke deep within her, breaking like a violent storm over her as she cried out, her womanhood aflame with ecstasy. He plunged harder within her, prolonging the intense, needlelike bursts of pleasure that streaked through her. She cried out his name, again and again, desire satisfied pulsing within her, flooding and spreading to every part of her body.

Ross felt her surround his manhood with hot, rolling waves that burned his flesh. His own breathing grew ragged and hoarse; passion flowed through him, an intense bolt of agonizing pleasure that tore all thoughts from his mind. Frenzied euphoria swept him down a violent path as he drove deeply into her body and gave of his essence—his seed—to the woman he loved.

After a long moment, Alexandra realized they were both breathing in heavy, labored gasps. She could not restrain a chuckle as she hugged Ross close, stroking his thick hair at the nape of his neck. He nuzzled her ear, whispering again his love for her. She felt full of life and every good thing. Her eyes misted over, as she watched the barest sliver of a cloud drift across the bright autumn moon. For this moment in time, her path was sweet and good. A drowsiness took hold of her and she felt herself drifting into a peaceful slumber, her heart and mind at ease with the world.

Chapter Twenty-five

"I don't want you to go," Alexandra whispered into Ross's ear. An hour had passed, perhaps two, she wasn't sure. She had drifted off to sleep, snuggled against Ross, the warmth of his body a comfort like none she had ever known. She awoke, however, to a cold draft of air as Ross drew himself out of her bed.

"I won't sleep here," Ross said, crossing the room to slip his clothes back on. "Not until we're married."

Alexandra pulled the covers tightly beneath her chin, watching him dress in the darkened room, the shadows shifting about as he pulled on his pants, his shirt, and, with great effort, his boots. She didn't know what to say. She had expected him to stay, only because she wanted more than anything to wake up in his arms. But now that he had stated the truth so flatly, that they weren't man and wife, she had to agree. It was one thing for Crackshot to have a squaw in his tent, it was quite another for Mrs. Bradshaw to have a *man* living in her cabin.

Once Ross had his boots on, he retraced his steps

and leaned over to place a tender kiss on her mouth. "Come Saturday, why don't we ride to Prescott and get married." It was more a statement than a request or even a proposal.

"All right," she whispered. Had she spoken these words? Had she said she would marry him?

She reached out to him in hopes of taking hold of his arm, but the quilt, blankets, and sheets seemed to grab hold of her hand. Before she could untangle herself and flip the covers back, he was already across the room. Within a few seconds she heard him shut the cabin door.

Alexandra rolled onto her back, the sheet cold and uncomfortable against her skin. She slipped from bed quickly and donned her warm flannel nightgown, along with a thick pair of socks, and quickly crawled beneath the covers. She lay for a long time, thinking about what had happened, about the wonderful pleasure Ross had brought to her. It all seemed so impossible. Yet it had happened. And now they would be married.

Married.

She had agreed to marry him, without even a bit of hesitation. She sighed deeply, contentment resting lightly on her heart. She wanted to marry Ross Halleck. She wanted more than anything to become his wife.

Feeling drowsy again, Alexandra's mind slipped from one pleasant image to the next, of Ross kissing her and touching her and loving her. She was almost asleep when her thoughts rolled back to the past and inevitably toward the future as though, even more than the present, the two were bonded together.

Sleep deserted her. She knew that the Alexandra was only a diversion from the true course of his life. He longed for a ranch, even if he had never told her so. She had seen as much on the trip out to the mine when he had gazed longingly at Mrs. McCormick's rolling, stocked ranchland. Where would his dreams take him once his sojourn at the mine was over? Could she follow him? Would she want to?

Alexandra covered her head with her pillow. She didn't want to think about these things right now. She had fallen in love with a wonderful man and he loved her. They were going to be married. The future would have to take care of itself.

The next morning, Alexandra rose early and prepared a breakfast for herself and Ross of biscuits, bacon, and apple pie. She wished she had some laying hens. She could think of nothing finer for breakfast than a few eggs, fried up in a little bacon grease, served with potatoes and coffee. If it looked like they were going to stay any length of time, she thought it might be a good idea to build a henhouse and see if Mrs. McCormick could part with some of her hens and a couple of roosters. The only problem would be the forest predators who would be only too happy to break into the coop and steal her chickens.

These were her domestic thoughts as Ross entered the cabin, his eyes a little sleepy-looking as he sat down at the table. Alexandra brought him a cup of coffee, smiling at him, her cheeks feeling warm with affection as well as embarrassment. "Good morning," she said quietly." Did you sleep well?"

He actually grinned, which made the blush on her cheeks deepen. "Best night I've ever had," he teased her, taking a sip of his coffee. "I mean sleeping-wise, that is."

She turned away from him, her face on fire. She meant to return to the stove where the bacon was sizzling in the skillet, but he caught her wrist, and before she could protest — even if she had wanted to — he had pulled her onto his lap and was kissing her. Thoughts of the night before, and every intimate touch, drifted through Alexandra's mind as Ross assaulted her lips with his own. She felt curls of desire begin wrapping themselves about her legs and arms, the feel of his tongue sliding into her mouth reminding her that intense pleasure awaited her at the end of this road.

But it was daylight!

She pushed away from Ross, her hands on his chest.

"What is it?" he asked, his eyes heavy with desire.

Alexandra glanced toward the window. "Ross," she said, startled. "We can't — I mean, the sun's up!"

"What does that have to do with it?" he queried softly, smiling at her and touching her cheek with the back of his hand. "I'd like to look at you, deep into your eyes, when I'm lovin' you."

Alexandra felt that familiar weakness flow straight through her. She wondered what it would be like, to see his face, to look into his eyes, to touch skin awash with the light of day. She was about to succumb to his way of thinking when the smell of burning bacon hit her.

"Oh, no!" she cried, leaping off his lap before he

had time to do anything about it. She ran to the kitchen and quickly removed the skillet from the stove. She stood looking at it, her hands on her hips, and felt thoroughly disgusted. "Now what am I going to feed you?" she cried over her shoulder.

"Come back here," he said softly. "I'm not very hungry anyway. Leastways, not for food."

Somehow the disruption of the burning bacon had returned some of her former embarrassment and Alexandra found she couldn't move. Instead, she responded, "you're being silly. You've got to eat and I know Crackshot wants to talk to you about last night."

She glanced at him nervously, not knowing what to do next. Ross, however, seemed in little doubt of what they ought to do and rose from his chair, crossing the room to join her in front of the cooking stove.

"You're awfully pretty," he said, not even trying to argue with her. He pulled at her carefully woven braid, untying the blue silk ribbon that held it secure, and began drawing apart the thick plait. Her red hair was curly and frizzy and, delighting in it, he fluffed it around her face, pulling it forward across her shoulders. He dug his hands into her hair and drew her face toward his. His mouth was firm on her lips, his tongue plunging deeply, sliding against hers, reminding Alexandra again of the night before. The feel of his hands in her hair robbed her of any resistance, as desire for him began to mount in quick stages. Her knees again felt weak as she leaned into him. He encircled her waist with his arm, pulling her so tight against him that she could hardly breathe. His tongue drove deeper still, his hand gliding through her hair. How much she loved him.

Ross felt his passion for Alexandra rise sharply within him. He didn't want to frighten her, but how easy it would be to take her fast and hard. He pulled away from her slightly and led her into the bedroom. Closing the door, he kissed her again, wildly, his desire hot within him. He didn't take her immediately to the bed, but instead pinned her to the wall, his hips locked against hers. He stroked her arms with his hands and when he reached her fingers, he entwined his with hers, his lips brushing her own with quick strokes.

Alexandra was surprised by how different Ross was this morning. The urgency of his movements excited her, the sweep of his mouth over hers becoming a fire that burned down through her limbs. She wanted him now, clasping his hands hard in return. As his tongue drove into her mouth, plunging against her own, his hips moved into her. She realized with a start that she felt almost as hungry for him right this minute as she had last night. It had all happened so quickly. She was astonished by the sudden passion that held sway over her. She had not expected to feel this way and knew a desperate need to have him inside her. She moved with him, against him, and heard a moan issue from his throat.

He stopped kissing her, and, releasing one of her hands, slipped his fingers into the hair at the nape of her neck. He kissed her once quickly, then looked into her eyes, as he had said he wanted to. "I love you," he whispered, his gray eyes intense with his desire for her.

Merely looking at him brought a heady sensation

of passion enveloping Alexandra's body as his hips thrust into hers. She needed him closer and longed for release. "Ross, take me," she breathed, imploring him not to wait.

To her surprise as he held her tightly about the waist, he lifted her skirts and slipped her undergarment from about her hips. His hand caressed her buttocks for a moment and then she felt him struggle with his pants. Before she could guess what he would do next, she felt the bare skin of his legs against hers and his manhood, swollen with desire, sliding between the flesh of her thighs.

She felt overcome by the sensation, an intense pleasure rising within her that at the same time felt compressed to the point of pain. He thrust against her, but not in her, his hips rocking into hers as he kept her pressed to the wall. His mouth was again on hers, his hand caressing her breast through the fabric of her blouse.

He stopped suddenly, leaning his head against hers. His breathing was labored as she in turn stroked his hair. She remembered from last night that he had needed to stop more than once.

"Come here," he said at last, his voice low. Drawing her to the bed, he didn't bother with clothing, but laid her gently down and stretched himself on top of her. He didn't do anything right away but stroked her face with his fingers and kissed her several times, expressing his love for her again and again.

Alexandra felt caught up as much by his passion and love for her as by her own desperate desire for him. She ached to be possessed by him, and felt relieved when at last he sought entrance, thrusting slowly into her, each time more deeply, until they were one. As he began moving faster, the bulk of her skirt seemed strange yet exciting fixed between them as it was. He didn't kiss her, either, but gazed into her eyes. His thoughts became her thoughts, his passion belonged to her, just as she gave her love to him. Time stopped, then moved at lightning speed with each thrust, each climb toward ecstasy, only to repeat itself. Alexandra felt the tension mount within her, driven by the gray eyes that held her gaze steadily, the passion mounting on his face a wind to the blaze of her own fiery desires. She moved beyond the earth, caught up in his eyes, in his love. Intense pleasure swept over her until she arched backward, his hips driving deeply into hers. He called her name, over and over, as the final wave of ecstasy broke in a feeling so piercing that she cried out, his mouth covering hers finally, his own pleasure bursting forth inside her at the same time.

Alexandra held Ross close to her, his head now buried in her hair. He was breathing heavily, still calling her name, still professing his love for her. She felt sated and full. Whole. Nothing mattered to her except Ross and keeping him close. She felt stunned by the sheer wonder of what was happening to her, what was growing between them, how ripe the love was that had given birth to their passion. She felt humbled, somehow, that this was her lot. She knew it was not everyone's, but it was hers, sweetly, powerfully, wonderfully, hers. And Ross had given it to her.

She wondered suddenly if it had been her mother's lot.

Tears again welled up in her eyes, as they seemed

to so often lately. She knew only a heartfelt gratitude for this love that had magically taken hold in her heart. She loved Ross, even if the bunched-up skirt between them now seemed a little absurd.

With a laugh, and feeling very much like a wife, she asked, "Are you ready for breakfast yet?"

The rumbling chuckle that sounded into her hair from deep within Ross's throat told her he had taken her joke just as it was meant.

How very much she loved him.

After a minute, Ross again kissed her and touched her face with his fingers. "I didn't feel right about asking you last night, Alexandra," he began. "And I don't mean to make you uncomfortable by doing so now, but I can't figure out how it is you're still a maiden. Unless your husband—" He left off completing his thought.

Alexandra looked away from Ross, wondering how he would respond to the truth. "I was never married, that's all." She then explained about her betrothed and taking on William's name for her own sake while she journeyed west. "I just wanted to be left alone and most men are very respectful to widows. Besides, I had only meant to be here a couple of weeks, then return to Missouri. And I certainly never thought I'd meet the likes of you. I hope you're not angry. The truth is, I've gotten so used to being Mrs. Bradshaw that I just never think about it. I hope you don't mind, or think badly of me."

Ross chuckled, drifting his hand over her breast as he snuggled his head into her hair. "How could I mind when nothing could have pleased so much as finding you'd never been touched before."

Chapter Twenty-six

Ross could not remember feeling this light, this easy with his thoughts, with the world. He was loping his horse across the meadow, heading down the trail that led toward Powell's mine. The air was cool on his face, his body felt loose and relaxed from having been with Alexandra, and he realized that if a man could ever feel that life was good, it was at a time like this, when he had been with the woman he loved, when he was living each day in full pursuit of his dreams, when he was ready to do battle with anything or anyone that gave evidence of wanting to stop him.

Today, life was very good.

The trail ran down to a riverbed where a shallow stream flowed over rocks, around tough chapparal shrubs, and through tangled clumps of pine needles and drifting deadwood. Crossing the stream, according to Crackshot's directions, Ross followed a narrow trail along the edge of the streambed. He was heading steadily downhill. Crackshot had told him that Powell's mine was near the streambed where he had hired a couple of men, down on their luck, to do some placer-mining for him.

After he'd traveled about a mile and a half, he slipped his rifle from his scabbard, and eased his horse into a slow walk. Whoever had been at the Alexandra last night could just as easily try to take a shot at him now. He began to wonder, though, how serious his assailant was about wanting him dead. It seemed to Ross that if a man was intent on his purpose, there was always a way to get a job done. The small camp at the Alexandra was isolated out here near Bee Mountain, and how hard would it be for an armed band of hired guns to simply ride in, start shooting, then ride out. Who would be left to give descriptions? He was reminded of Mrs. Ferguson and her children, killed on the road, no witnesses, and no strong evidence to lead Sheriff Goodwin to the killer. On the other hand, the only reason he and Crackshot had survived the dynamite explosion was because of their quick reflexes — nothing more. As much as he didn't want to admit it to himself, the fact was, someone or maybe even a band of outlaws, wanted him dead.

Even Alexandra wasn't safe, and it occurred to him he ought to move both the ladies back to town until the Alexandra was safe.

As Ross drew close, he saw that Powell's camp was not much more impressive than his own. One large tent sat a couple of hundred yards from the river on a rise, against a windbreak of trees and shrubs. The pines didn't reach down to this level, and the camp was more exposed than his own. A collection of rockers, pans, and water barrels were scattered haphazardly about the claim. The

213

streambed itself—notched, gouged, and torn up—
had suffered the effects of the mining, and it was
not a pretty sight, any more than the earthen
ramp flowing out of the mouth of the Alexandra
was. Both mines, for all the hope of a quick fortune they offered their owners, were something of
a blight to the land.

Unlike cattle, Ross thought with satisfaction,
which were never unsightly to his way of thinking.
Beeves looked handsome spread out on a vast tract
of rangeland, a soft contrast to the green or yellow grasses they grazed. He might spend a year or
so working the mine, but after that he would
build his ranch.

As he approached Powell's camp, he saw to his
surprise that there were several men clustered
about the fire, drinking coffee. When the sun
glinted off something metallic on one of the men's
shirts, he realized by the height of the same man
that Sheriff Goodwin was here, along with his
deputy, Barnes. Lloyd sat in the middle of them,
wearing his black suit and looking like a crow
among sparrows. The two other men present appeared to be the miners Powell had hired to work
his claim. Their clothes were dirty and worn, their
faces stubbled with several days' growth, their skin
tanned from working the bed out in the open.

Ross was greeted affably by the sheriff and
Powell and, a little less so, by Barnes. The miners
nodded, but otherwise appeared indifferent to his
arrival.

Ross replaced his rifle and, after dismounting,
joined the men. Sheriff Goodwin offered him a

cup of coffee, and as he handed it to him, queried, "Blasting kind of late last night, weren't you?"

"You might say that," Ross answered. He glanced easily from one man to the next. "Seems we had some unexpected company after supper, someone who thought we needed to heat the place up a little."

The sheriff frowned as he watched Ross, narrowing his eyes over the rim of his cup. He remained silent, though, and it was Barnes who asked, "What do you mean? Didn't you set off that charge? We were sittin' here last night, scraping up the last bite of beans when a roar came down the mountain. The ground shook a little, too. Didn't make sense. Sounded like it went off outside the mine."

"Just at the opening," Ross said. "Fact is, Crackshot and I were almost killed, but as you can see, the good Lord isn't finished with me yet, nor Crackshot, neither, I suppose."

One of the miners, strong in the shoulder and wiry from long hours of labor, added his mite. "You gotta be careful with dynamite. The tips have a trigger-happy fuse. Why, a good solid blow in the right spot can set one off."

"Maybe that's what happened," Ross returned with a smile. "But if it did, it also had wings, because it came flying at us real fast. We had about one second to get out of the mine before all hell broke loose."

By this time, all the men were staring at him, full awareness of his story dawning upon each one. Sheriff Goodwin in particular wore a serious expression. "Strangely enough," he said, "Barnes and I came out here to see what we could do about the trouble you've been having. It would seem this time we brought it with us. Tell me what all happened."

Ross looked straight at Powell and held his gaze for a moment. The tinhorn had no expression on his face, staring back at him with an unconcerned, blank look, like the one he had used during his poker game at the Cobweb. The same feeling came over Ross of just not being able to trust this man. "After the explosion," he said, finally, shifting his gaze back to Goodwin, "we waited by the tent, our rifles drawing a bead on the opening to the mine. We expected someone to appear any minute, until it occurred to both of us that the only way anyone would have thrown dynamite like that was if there was another way out of the mine. Crackshot's looking for it now, combing through every tunnel carefully. The reason I'm here is to find out if any of you heard a rider come through here last night. Someone tore off down the streambed just a few minutes after the explosion."

Claim-jumping was as old as probably the first man to strike it rich. Ross knew there were at least a dozen ways to accomplish it. A good lawyer could help a lot. A bad one, even more. Keep a man drunk and happy for a week or two and he could lose all his rights to a stake, simply because he hadn't been working it. But a dead man had the least claim of all.

The men looked at Ross now as though he were

the latter, all staked out by someone who had an eye to taking his mine.

Goodwin shook his head. "If the man rode by," he said, "he was awful quiet. I know I didn't hear anyone, and we were all up playing poker till the moon crossed the sky."

"And everyone stayed in camp?" Ross asked, taking a sip of his coffee.

"Everyone," Goodwin stated with finality, nodding his head.

Ross turned to Powell and asked, "Did Sam ever say anything to you about another entrance to the mine?"

"Never" was Powell's flat response.

Ross dumped the remains of his coffee on the fire, the hiss and spiral of smoke that followed a precise reflection of how he felt inside. That's all he'd done by coming out here, hissing a little and smoking and not doing a damn bit of good. The only thing he could think to do now was see if he could find the rider's trail and discover where it led. Even if he suspected Powell was the man who was trying to take the Alexandra, he couldn't prove it. The truth was, he couldn't figure Powell. When he had last spoken with him, he had nearly gained a sense he was all right. At the same time, there was something about him that didn't set right with his bones.

Ross said his farewells and headed back toward the trail. Halfway to the Alexandra, he found the rider's sign and, working steadily for an hour, picked his way to a spot half a mile from Powell's camp. The rider had apparently slept the night there, then ridden on.

Ross was about to leave, when he noticed another set of prints. He dismounted and, after searching the area, found a set of clear bootprints that led in the direction of Powell's camp.

So that was it, Ross thought with little satisfaction. Someone had met the rider, but not right away. Maybe in the middle of the night when everyone else was asleep. Why did that sound so much like Lloyd Powell? But he had no proof.

When Ross returned to the Alexandra, Crackshot had already located the second entrance to the mine. "It opens up down by the streambed. It looks like it had been all boarded up and overgrown with grass and roots. You could never have seen it from the outside, that's for sure. I think it might have been the original mine shaft. Now, as fer inside the mine, the opening is off to the side of a shaft that had been almost completely blocked by a dynamite explosion. I never bothered my head about that section of the mine. Sam said it was worthless, that no matter which way he'd picked, dug, and dynamited, there weren't a single sign of gold."

Ross listened to him intently, wondering what he ought to do next. He told Crackshot that he was in a fair way to suspecting Powell of trying to jump their claim.

Crackshot nodded, a frown on his face. When Ross asked for his opinion, he said, "I never could decide whether Powell was a snake or just a harmless lizard dressed up to look like one. I don't think, though, that I ever figured him for anything like this. Do you think he had Sam killed?"

Ross sighed. "I don't know. I don't even know what to think. None of it fits exactly, if you know what I mean."

Crackshot said he could rightly understand Ross's confusion. "If it is true," he said, chuckling, "then it's one of the darndest things that ever happened. You see, Sam kind of took to him. Powell used to come over all the time, especially when Mrs. McCormick was out here. We'd play poker, the four of us, until dawn sometimes, in the summer."

Ross felt like Crackshot had picked up a thin sapling branch and had set to whipping him with it. He was surprised to learn that Powell had been a guest at the Alexandra, but he was particularly shocked to find that Mrs. McCormick had been a frequent visitor. "She'd come out to the Alexandra? All this way? To see Sam?"

"That's right," Crackshot said, scratching at his chin. "She'd fallen in love with him. Used to stay in his cabin. The good folks in Prescott was pretty upset. Sam wanted to marry her, but she wouldn't have it. Said he had sails on his feet and was sure that the smallest whiff of a breeze was likely to fill up those sails and carry him away. Me, I couldn't figure it. She could as like to go with him as not. What difference did it make where he went? She was his woman, wasn't she? It was her place to go where he wanted to go. And boy, how she loved him! I never seen a woman light up the way she did when he walked in a room." His face was all scrunched up now, his blue eyes clouded

219

with his effort at trying to understand women.

Ross watched him, feeling like each word the miner spoke was another stinging whap of his switch. He wasn't even sure why he felt his words like blows, except that his mind had become filled with the sight of Alexandra's unhappy face and the tight, distressed quality to her voice when she had spoken of her childhood. Did she want something from him she already knew he couldn't give her? Is that why she had resisted until now even the thought of becoming his wife?

He rose to his feet, not yet sure why he had done so. All he knew was that he was filled with an urgency to speak with Alexandra. She already said she would marry him; they were as good as engaged. But did she understand exactly what that meant, at least to him?

"I have something I've got to take care of right now," Ross said.

He half turned away, glancing back at the cabin, when Crackshot stopped him by saying, "Oh, and there's something more . . . You know how Sam got this mine?"

Ross shook his head. He could easily imagine old Wingfield leading a burro loaded with tin pans, a pickax, and supplies, trudging up into the mountains. But by the look on Crackshot's face he had the feeling that wasn't the case at all.

Crackshot slapped his knees. "I don't know how he done it, but by Gawd he won the Alexandra from Lloyd Powell in a game of poker four years ago."

Chapter Twenty-seven

Ross only got halfway to the cabin when he heard the sheriff's voice call to him. He turned around and saw that both Goodwin and Barnes had ridden up from Powell's camp. There was nothing he could do but set aside his intention of talking to Alexandra and meet with the sheriff.

Goodwin and Barnes stayed for nearly an hour, examining for themselves the second entrance to the mine and discussing several possibilities with both Ross and Crackshot about who could be after the Alexandra. The whole exchange frustrated Ross since the only conclusion anyone could draw was that Sam had told too many people that he was sure he was sitting on the mother lode.

Goodwin did have some news to communicate. He was nearly certain that he had found the body of the desperado Ross had killed during the attack at the Dells. "One of my men found him at the base of Granite Mountain. The coyotes had got to him already, just like I thought. There wasn't much of him left, not enough for anyone to recognize except that he had black hair and wore clothes that a Mexican outlaw might. Sorry, Ross. As for Whiskey Row, I haven't learned a thing of use as to who might be tryin' to jump your claim."

After drinking some of Cecilia's coffee, the sheriff said they ought to be heading out since the day was quickly dwindling away. "But first I'd like to meet Mrs. Bradshaw if I might."

Alexandra was seated at the dining table, preparing to record all of her personal receipts in a black ledger book she had purchased at Goldwater's. In addition, Ross had asked her to see to the accounting of her investment in the Alexandra, to keep and record all the receipts that related to the mine, as well as the balance of the money. Thus far, he had purchased only a few new rock-drilling bits, a sharp knife for cutting dynamite fuses, and several dozen candles. He had already told her that though he was inclined to build a stamp mill, not only was he unsure of the cost, he also didn't know as yet whether the mine would actually make this kind of expenditure worthwhile. She agreed wholeheartedly, wondering for the hundredth time if perhaps she and Ross weren't suffering from the same disease that had plagued her father, gold fever, and whether or not they were foolish to throw Aunt Hetty's inheritance into the belly of the mine. Crackshot certainly had not discovered ore worth hauling to a mill, not yet at least.

The cabin smelled of honey and rising bread and the day thus far had been full of tasks that left Alexandra feeling satisfied. Even though it was only a little after the noon hour, she lit the oil lamp to see her ledger and receipts better. The house, for lack of large windows, was very dark all day long, especially since the pines ran almost up to the back wall and left the cabin in shade from dawn until dusk.

As she picked up her pen and dipped it in the ink-well, she found that her thoughts were restless, jumping from sweet reveries of Ross, to the perpetual questions about the value of the mine, to wondering how she would survive the winter when the snow started piling up, to the most enchanting daydreams about what she ought to wear to Mrs. Mc-Cormick's New Year's Eve party.

She'd be married by then, she thought with pleasure, leaning her chin on her hand with a sigh. She would dress up in a beautiful gown of emerald silk and she would wear her red hair piled high atop her head, arranged in the manner of some of her fashionable friends in Missouri. Her uncle had never permitted her to do more than wear her braid coiled at the back of her head, with a slight fluff of curls on her forehead. But to this party she wanted her curls everywhere, laced with a few artificial flowers. She could take the ones from her hat . . .

What idleness! she chided herself. She had a lot of work to do, and she couldn't afford to waste too much of her time pursuing even the most charming of daydreams. Turning back to the chore at hand, she again dipped her pen into the shiny brass ink-well and headed the page with two columns—one for her receipts and one for Ross's. She had more tasks to do after this, not the least of which was going into the forest in search of firewood. After that, she needed to take stock of her food supplies and

223

make a list of things she knew she would require for the coming months. A second trip to Prescott would be in order pretty soon and she wanted to be well prepared. She scratched the items listed on each receipt into the ledger but couldn't help but wonder how long it would take for her to make up a dress for Mrs. McCormick's party.

When she was almost finished adding up each column, she was startled by a knock on the door, accompanied by the sound of Ross's greeting.

What a rush of tender feelings swept over her, even at the mere sound of his voice. She was so happy to be here, at her father's mine, to be with Ross, to be preparing to become his wife. Not even the constant apprehension about who was after their claim could dim the breathless feelings of wonder that rose within her at just being near him.

She rose quickly, bidding him enter. But her hasty movements had caused a runnel of ink to drip from her pen, and as she stood up, she smeared the ink across her finely headed page. How disappointed she felt. She had wanted Ross to see that she was tending to business, but now the smudge made her efforts look childish.

Even so, she left the table and her books, and, as the door opened, was about to throw her arms wide about Ross's shoulders when, fortunately, she caught sight of two men on horseback just beyond the porch.

Ross opened the door, standing aside so that she could pass by. He introduced the sheriff, as well as Deputy Barnes, to her, explaining that Goodwin had asked to meet her.

"How d'ya do, Mrs. Bradshaw," he said, tipping

224

his hat to her. Louis Barnes did the same, but remained silent.

"Very well, thank you, Sheriff," Alexandra said, touching her hand to the support beam of the porch. "I've heard many good things about you and I sure do appreciate your riding all the way out here. I suppose Ross told you of our trouble last night?"

"Yes'm," he replied. "I'm awful sorry you've had to endure so much since arriving here. I just want you to know that we're doing all we can to assist you folks. If you need anything, just let me know, or Barnes here. We're always glad to help any way we can, especially a daughter of Sam's. He was a good man, an honest man, and we were all sorry to hear of his death."

Alexandra thanked him for his consideration, and after he refused her invitation to have a cup of coffee, the sheriff expressed his need to be returning to Prescott.

"What a nice man!" Alexandra exclaimed, waving good-bye as the men turned their mounts toward the trail. "Mrs. McCormick said I would like him, and I do!" She turned to Ross and taking him by the arm, drew him into the cabin saying, "Not as much as you, though!"

Ross went with her willingly, and once the door was shut she pursued her original impulse, throwing her arms about his neck and hugging him. He held her tight, but after a moment Alexandra grew aware, by the tension knotting up his shoulders, that something was wrong.

"What is it?" she asked, pulling back from him and looking into his eyes. "What's wrong? Did you learn something from the sheriff, or from the visit

225

to Powell's mine, that you're afraid to tell me?"

Ross took her arms from about his neck and led her back to the table where he asked her to sit down. "There are a couple of things that I think we need to talk about, but first, no, I haven't uncovered anything I would feel necessary to withhold from you. Goodwin and Barnes had spent the night at Powell's camp, and though they heard the explosion last night, unfortunately they didn't see anyone—nor did Powell, who was also there, nor the two miners who work for him. It made for a cosy campfire, but nobody knew or saw a thing." He then told her about discovering that a man had been camped about half a mile from Powell's mine and that someone from his camp—maybe even Powell—had paid him a nocturnal visit. Ross seemed to lose himself in his thoughts after that, dropping into a chair across the table from Alexandra, his expression concerned. "I've never been in a situation like this before, where I don't know who I'm fighting."

Alexandra stretched her hand out to him, placing it on his sleeve and stroking his arm. "Goodwin's a capable lawman," she said. "If anyone can get at the truth, it'll be him."

Ross covered her hand with his own, pressing it hard. "I'm sure you're right," he said. After a moment's pause, he told her about the second entrance to the mine.

Alexandra's gaze never left his face as he related to her all that Crackshot had told him. The light from the oil lamp lit her features with a warm glow. Ross felt transported to a peaceful place of contentment as he watched her eyes glimmering with affec-

226

tion for him, her rosy lips upturned in an encouraging smile. He was overcome suddenly with his love for her and lifted her hand to his lips, placing a gentle kiss on her fingers. He wondered if she would be happy in Wyoming, and the thought pulled him sharply back to earth.

For a minute he had forgotten all about his reason for wanting to speak with Alexandra, but a heaviness had returned to weigh down his heart and he knew he had to find out whether or not she was a woman who would stand with him.

"Alexandra . . ." he began, his voice little more than a whisper. He felt shaky inside, as though he had suddenly walked onto a frozen pond believing it was safe only to find the ice crackling beneath each step. "You know we haven't talked much about the future, about what I want for myself in the coming years, about what you want." He pressed her hand tightly, hoping he would say the right things and that Alexandra would rise from her seat when he was done, slip her arms about his shoulders, and tell him she wanted nothing more than to walk by his side the rest of her life, to go wherever he wanted to go.

Alexandra watched his concern shadow and deepen across his face. Her initial joy at seeing him, hugging him, having him kiss her hand, faded abruptly. Fear possessed her again. She didn't want to talk about the future, not now, not ever. Her mind grew numb, and her heart felt like it was turning quickly to stone. "You don't have to say anything, Ross," she said, trying to end the conversation before it had begun. "I'm satisfied now with becoming your wife, with working the mine,

227

with finding out whether or not Papa's belief in the Alexandra had merit. I don't want more than that." She shook her head several times as he pressed her hand harder still.

"We must talk about this," he responded firmly, his gray eyes growing dark even in the glow from the oil lamp. "We must."

Realizing he would not be moved, Alexandra nodded to him finally, her gaze dropping away to the ledger in front of her.

"I want a ranch," he said quietly, his low voice surrounding her, reaching deep into her heart, easing her fears away. "I want it to be mine, I want to raise my sons on it and pass it on to them when I die. Or to my daughters, if they're of a mind to be ranchers. I want to spend my life chasing beeves over hundreds of thousands of acres, hiring young men who are as I once was, without a hope and a promise to live on, but with determination to make something of themselves. And I want you with me, that much you know already. I've never felt like this about any woman. Sometimes, when I'm away from you, I try to imagine what my life was like before I met you and I can't remember, except that it seemed duller, like the land under a cloudy sky. Do you know what I mean? Everything looks muddy-colored and slow. But when the sun comes out, even the leaves on the trees sparkle. That's what my life with you is like now, golden and summery."

Alexandra looked up at him. "Golden?" she queried, her heart softening up a little. When he talked, she felt safe, his rich voice wrapping her up tight. But the moment he stopped speaking, she knew that her fears waited, like a wall of floodwaters, ready to pour over her, to drown her, to destroy the love that had blossomed between herself and Ross.

He reached out to touch her red hair, and said, "We should be mining copper, not gold. Copper would be a much better way to express what I'm feeling about you, but then I'm no poet. Just a cowpoke, wanting to have a wife and build a ranch." His heart grew suddenly full of the dreams he had been lacing up in his mind and in his heart for so many years. "My ranch in Texas was a good start, but to go to Wyoming, that would be something fine and wonderful. Winters can be harsh up in Wyoming, but the land is just right for ranching. I know there won't be many women about, and that is one of my concerns for you. I guess what it comes down to, though, by my way of thinking is this: If you're my wife, I'll expect you to go where I go."

Alexandra didn't have a clear idea of where Wyoming was. Winters being harsh, however, was all the description she needed of the nature of the land to know that it was north, rugged and isolated.

She sat very still, her gaze fixed on his face. Her eyes took in his strong cheekbones and faintly cleft chin, the thin nose, the way a frown seemed permanently etched between marked brows. She realized he was quite a serious man for all the playfulness he exhibited when he was with her. He thought about life, about what he wanted, and he did not seem to leave a lot to chance. He could have remained silent about his future, especially since he already knew that her fears traveled along this line. He could have avoided saying anything to her, but he didn't. He wanted everything right out front. She valued his

229

honesty, his forthrightness. But how could she explain to him that telling her straight out that he expected her to go where he wanted to go was like opening a sluice gate in her mind. Fear began shooting throughout her body, traveling down her mind, her limbs, her heart. A terrible sickness took hold of her stomach. She was certain had she been standing, she would have fainted. Would Ross ever be able to understand what it had been like for her to watch her mother's life, to watch her siblings die, to be left with so little when she was but a child of twelve? She knew, as she looked into the anxious gray eyes of the man she loved, that for whatever reason, he just wasn't able to comprehend at all.

She also felt, as he began stroking her hand, that whatever his past had been, it had become very important to him that his wife take on his dreams as her own. "I desire more than anything," she said at last, her throat pinched, her heart beating fast in her chest, "that you have what you want most for your life. But Ross, I can't go to Wyoming with you. I'm not even sure if you still owned your ranch in Texas that I could live there. You've got to understand me a little. There's nothing more for a woman and her children in one of the northern territories than the constant dread of disease and isolation. I know there are women who would go with you, who wouldn't even blink at it, and who would think mighty poorly of me right now. I can't blame Wyoming entirely. It's me, and the fears that batter my mind. I want children, too, as many as God will give me. But when Mama died I made a promise to myself that I would live in a place where they could be safe, at least as safe as I could make it for them, and for myself, too. That means neighbors close by and doctors, more than one in the town if possible. Isn't there somewhere else in the country you'd be willing to settle?"

Having put forward the idea, Alexandra looked at Ross hopefully, the panic in her heart easing back a little. It was a reasonable notion. Maybe he would even consider staying here in Prescott. But when the light in his eyes seemed to disappear, a coldness stealing over his face, all of Alexandra's anxieties crashed down on her as he slid his hands away from her.

Leaning back in his chair, Ross shifted his hands to his legs and stared back at Alexandra. He felt stunned by all that she had just said, his heart growing heavier with every second that passed. Her face seemed to change before him, becoming liquid and taking on the features of another woman who had once sat so upright and proud in her little buggy, her parasol in hand. In his mind's eye, he saw Katherine give the reins a neat slap against the horse's flank and in a few minutes disappear down the lane between grass-covered fields lining each side of the road.

"Ross, talk to me," Alexandra pleaded. She had said these same words three times now, but she couldn't reach him. He seemed so distant, so removed from her. What was he thinking? Did he hate her for speaking her mind? Was he so unmovable that he wouldn't even consider her suggestion?

Finally, he said, "Maybe you ought to return to Missouri and make good the condition of your uncle's will. You'd probably have everything you needed then to be safe. You'd at least have all the money you could desire. If we strike it rich here, I can always forward your share."

How cold he sounded, almost indifferent. It seemed strange to her that he would mention her uncle's will. She laughed to herself at the thought of marrying William. Ross didn't know it, but she could never be the wife of a man like William Bradshaw now that she had known what love could be like.

"I won't pretend even for a minute that I have the smallest idea of returning to Independence now. I aim to see our venture here at the Alexandra through to the end. After that, we'll see." She lowered her gaze to the ledger in front of her, the smudged heading now seeming appropriate. "I suppose there's nothing left to discuss then," she added quietly.

"I guess not," he said.

She moved to the end of the table and started to walk behind him, but he caught her wrist suddenly. "Tell me you'll go with me," he whispered, his voice tense. "Don't do this to me, Alexandra. Tell me you'll go wherever I aim to go. I need you, more than anything, to trust me in this."

His hand felt hot against the skin of her wrist. She didn't dare look at him. He had turned in his chair and was watching her. If she met his gaze, even for the smallest fraction of a second, she might do something foolish, like tell him she'd jump off a cliff if he wanted her to. Shaking her head, she responded, "I can't. I just can't. I'm sorry."

She moved quickly into the kitchen where her bread dough had risen so high it was almost overflowing the sides of the bowl. She was frustrated be-

yond words and hit the dough with a hard fist. She
watched the dough sink down below the rim. Tears
stung her eyes, and she blinked them away. She had
been prepared to wait out the future, to give it days,
weeks, even months to creep up on her if it wanted
to. Never had she expected to meet it headlong so
soon. It wasn't fair. She had just discovered her love
for Ross, she had taken pleasure in his love for her,
and now it was all gone. Just like that.

Just like that! her mind cried as she punched at
the dough again and again with her fist until it was
a solid lump.

In the distance, she heard Crackshot give a long
cry and then a series of whoops. What was the matter now? she wondered, though he didn't sound upset. In fact, he sounded excited.

She heard Crackshot give another long cry, his
voice closer than it was before. Maybe he'd found
gold. She turned toward the door and saw that Ross
had thrown it wide. A sliver of anticipation sped
through her mind as yet another whoop and a shout
echoed up the creek toward the cabin. Had Crackshot found gold?

She took a step toward the door, her heart starting to beat fast, then she stopped. But what if he
had? Of what use would it be to her now? Ross
would take his portion, move to Wyoming, and she
would never see him again. What would her life be
worth then?

She wasn't surprised to hear fast, pounding footsteps on the porch one second and Crackshot holler
out his greeting the next as he burst across the
threshold, his hair flying. Alexandra looked at the
wild expression on his face and her heart began to

sound in her ears. She hadn't really thought he'd struck a vein, but now, what else could it be?

"It was that dynamite!' he cried. "Opened up a rift to the left of the entrance, and there she was! A foot wide and tapering at an angle to the north, gold ribbons so pretty you could cry, sloping down toward a tunnel I'd been working on for some time. I wouldn't call it the mother lode, not yet anyway, but Halleck, I think it's time to build that mill, hire us some hardrock Cornish miners and see what the Alexandra is made of."

Ross glanced back at Alexandra, his expression pained. "Seems to me," he said, "I already found out."

"What's that?" Crackshot cried. "Don't you believe me? I'm tellin' you, we've got us the prettiest stretch of gold slicing right through that rock like you've never seen!"

Ross looked back at Crackshot and took him by the arm. His features had taken on a warm expression again as he shifted his attention away from Alexandra. Pulling Crackshot toward the doorway, he cried, "Come on then! I'd better see this for myself before you explode!"

Chapter Twenty-eight

Two weeks later, Alexandra stood on the porch of her cabin, a shawl wrapped tightly about her shoulders, as she let her gaze drift slowly over the meadow. It was hard to believe this was the same place she had come to only three weeks earlier. November was hard upon the land, presaging winter, a frost already having blackened the yellow flowers, leaving not a single blossom with which to adorn her table. Half a dozen tents now lined the narrow valley to the south of the creek in a tidy row, lending a military appearance to the camp. Ross had hired a dozen Cornish miners, called the Cousin Jacks for their strict clannishness, who came willingly to take on the Alexandra. They were a bruising lot, tough in body, hard-drinking, but respectful to women. They worked long, twelve-hour shifts, drilling holes with steel shafts of varying lengths into the rock until they reached a seven-foot mark. The holes were then tamped full with capped sticks of dynamite, the fuses interconnected and lit, bringing about a five-by-seven area of rock crashing in on itself and blowing outward back into the tunnel. Done right, it was a miracle, neat and perfect, causing just the right quantity of rock to shatter and spill out into the tunnel to be shoveled into gravity-fed shutes. Done wrong, there would be at least one grave to be dug, sometimes more. But Ross had brought in, along with the miners, an engineer to supervise the placement of the holes and to see that the square-set beams were properly installed and maintained with wedges. Any time a wedge became displaced and fell to the floor of the tunnel, the engineer and Crackshot would check all the beams in the immediate vicinity for the smallest shifting of the square-sets in an effort to determine if a cave-in was impending. Every precaution was taken to see that the men were kept safe.

Alexandra had seen little of Ross over the last two weeks. Shortly after the discovery of the promising vein of gold, he had tried to persuade both her and Cecilia to move to town where they would be kept safe from any possible attacks by the men who he felt certain would be even more determined to jump their claim. Cecilia stubbornly refused, saying that she wouldn't be safe from her brother if she stayed in Prescott. As for Alexandra, she pointed out that since the camp would soon be full of strong hardrock miners, she thought it unlikely anyone would be so foolish as to try to take the Alexandra now. Besides, she had no intention of leaving no matter what Ross said. He didn't try to dissuade her further, but kept a respectful distance which left her feeling more alone than she had felt in years.

Alexandra and Cecilia had taken on the duty of feeding everyone in the camp. Meals were served in a long tent that had been set up just for dining. The women worked side by side, cooking up enormous quantities of food — big pots of beans, or stew if Crackshot brought in some rabbit or deer; thick slabs

of fresh-baked bread, biscuits or muffins; pie, doughnuts, or cookies, and always several gallons of coffee — or at least it seemed like that much to Alexandra.
They charged fifteen cents a meal, and even with the
most conservative accounting, Alexandra knew by the
amount consumed, they would do little more than
break even. But every time one of these men, so far
away from their native home on the western coast of
England, would smile at her and express his thanks
for such a delicious hot meal, she felt amply re-
warded. Next to what each of the men endured as they
began a shift, cooking seemed an easy task indeed. Of
course, it became easier when Cecilia overcame her
fear of the cabin and joined in. Then baking up several loaves of bread or six dozen doughnuts was an
enjoyable task, especially with someone to talk to.

Besides, Alexandra had her own investment in the
mine to think of.

Much she cared for that anymore, she thought with
a sigh, her chest feeling as though her heart had disappeared entirely, leaving behind a large hole she
couldn't fill. Without Ross, or even the prospect of
belonging to him, she wondered why she bothered
staying on at the mine. He had broken with her completely the day Crackshot discovered the ribbon of
gold. He was polite and considerate, but when he
looked at her she could see that the light had gone
from his eyes. What he was thinking or feeling she
didn't know. He went about his business in his matter-
of-fact way, seeing to the progress of the mine and to
the building of the stamp mill beyond the creek, on
the other side of the hill close to the streambed. If he
felt anything for her, he concealed it well.

As she gazed out at the meadow, a cold, northerly
wind whistled through the trees for a moment, disap-

pearing down the hill. The only other sound she could hear was the ringing of several distant hammers on the site of the stamp mill. Winter hovered over the silent camp, the air biting cold, dark clouds sitting heavily on the forested hills above her. Snow would be coming soon.

As she prepared to turn back into the cabin, she noticed a mule and then another appear at the crest of the ridge to the south of the camp. The laboring beasts strained forward pulling a covered wagon driven by a man who called to the mules in a cheerful voice. He clicked his tongue and slapped the reins as though enjoying himself. But beside him sat a woman who held a hand gripped tightly about the back of her seat as the wagon rocked its way over the ridge. Once the mules topped the crest and headed down, they began descending the easy grade into the meadow at a fast, stumbling pace. The man pulled back on the reins and kept the team in check as he followed old wagon marks and guided his team toward Alexandra. He wore a wide smile the entire time. It was easy to see he was a man who loved travel and adventure.

Shivering slightly and making sure the door was closed securely behind her to prevent more heat from escaping the cabin, Alexandra moved to the end of the porch nearest the approaching couple. She wondered who they were and why they had driven all the way out to the Alexandra. But one look at the thick, muscled arms of the man, and the ease with which he jumped down from the wagon to approach her with his hand outstretched convinced Alexandra she was looking at a miner in search of work.

"Howdy!" he called to her, taking her hand in his and pumping it warmly. "I been hearin' about this place in town. This is the Alexandra, isn't it?" When

238

she nodded, he jerked a thumb back toward the wagon and said, "As you can see by the missus here, I sure need work. Is the foreman around?"

"We don't have a foreman as such," Alexandra replied. "One of the owners, Ross Halleck, manages the mine. He would be the one to speak to. I believe he's downstream right now where he is overseeing the building of a stamp mill."

The stranger's blue eyes lit up. He was a young man of medium height with auburn hair and a laughing expression to his face. "Why, I worked in a mill only last year," he exclaimed, as though the news was some of the finest in the world. "Just point the way and I'll speak to, er . . . Mr. Halleck, did ya say?"

"That's right," Alexandra responded, smiling in spite of herself. The young man's enthusiasm was infectious. "Ross Halleck. He's a good man and he'll treat you fair. I just don't know whether he's ready to hire anyone yet. Follow the creek not more than quarter of a mile. The hammers will lead the way, they haven't stopped but once or twice all morning." She glanced over at the stranger's wife, who was watching her husband with a soft glow of love on her face. She could not have been more than seventeen. When she shifted uncomfortably on the hardwood seat of the wagon, Alexandra realized she was several months pregnant.

The sight of the miner's wife, the bulge of her stomach barely concealed behind a brown shawl, tore at her heart. How familiar it seemed, a young couple beginning their life together, setting their shoulders against the future, believing that all good things would surely come to them just because they were in love. Maybe that's the way it was for most people, she thought, wondering why she couldn't be as free in her spirit to follow her heart as these people seemed to be. The strongest sensation of envy rushed through her. How much she would have liked to be like this young woman — very much in love and following her man, probably without question.

They introduced themselves as John and Miriam Horn, who had been traveling West almost from the day of their marriage not eight months ago. "I had to come!" he cried, his freckled face beaming for all it was worth. "It's 1880, and by the time the railroads spread their lines throughout the territories, why there won't be a western frontier to speak of." He glanced over at his wife, who remained sitting in the wagon. Nodding to her, he added in a softer voice, "Miriam here wasn't quite as delighted with the prospect. All of her family's in Pennsylvania and that's not easy for a woman. But I hope to make my fortune, see a little of the country, then we'll head back, unless, of course, we find some land that suits us. Then maybe we'll build us a farm, maybe even take on a few head of cattle. Wouldn't that be something?"

Alexandra found it difficult to listen to him talk, coming so hard as it did upon her break with Ross. She could do little more than offer him a polite well-wish that he would one day have his heart's desires. She then invited Miriam to join her in the cabin where it was warm. Miriam agreed right away, an expression of relief flooding her face. Now it was her turn to smile broadly as she asked her husband to help her get down. John supported her about the waist as she climbed carefully down the tall wagon. Afterward, he unhitched the mules, giving them each a slap on the flank, encouraging them to graze on the wintry grass of the meadow.

When John trailed off down the creek, Alexandra

soon had Miriam sitting in the comfortable rocking chair, a cup of coffee in one hand and a fresh doughnut in the other. By now she realized the mother-to-be was completely exhausted by her trip out to the mine, leaning her head back against the rocker and sighing rather than speaking. She sipped occasionally at her coffee but didn't seem to have even enough energy to bring the doughnut to her mouth.

Alexandra tried twice to engage her in conversation, but it was clear to her that what Miriam needed was a nap. Refusing to listen to the young woman's protests, Alexandra led her to the bedroom where she was soon tucked beneath the quilt. It seemed to her that before five minutes had passed, Miriam was sound asleep, snoring lightly.

Ross was mad, plain and simple. Slamming the hammer hard on the nail, he at least had the pleasure of seeing the nail drive a full inch into the pine board. He wasn't sure exactly what had fired him up, whether it was the affable smile on the young man's face or the fact that building the stamp mill would take a full week longer than expected or that he was damn sure, as he glanced back at John Horn, that in Alexandra's mind he was just like him.

Wham! The sound of steel against steel ricocheted down the gully toward the riverbed.

The mill was being constructed on the other side of the cliff wall closer to the river than the camp, in order to permit gravity to have an effect in the process. The more frequently they could feed the ore into chutes that led downhill, rather than hauling it, the easier it was all around to get the job done. With the mill on this side of the cliff, a chute could be constructed that would run the ore from inside the mine, straight down into the trough where the five stamps would set about breaking it up. The stamping machine, made up of five heavy weights dropped from a height of about fifteen feet, would be enclosed in a wood house. It was this structure he and two other men were in the process of building.

Ross continued to hammer the nail in quick, hard whacks, the smell of the pine wood strong in the air. When the nail was flush with the board, he ran his finger over it, feeling the smooth wood and addressing the hopeful miner. "Now whatever prompted you," he said, "to bring your wife along on such a trip when she is going to have a baby?"

John seemed surprised at the question, his auburn eyebrows arched, his blue eyes wide. "I suppose because I know she's a real strong woman," he responded with pride. "That's one reason I decided to marry her in the first place. If anyone is fit to bear children with ease, it's my Miriam. Her mother was that way. She gave birth to a dozen of 'em and didn't lose a one, at least not right away. Scarlet fever took one of the girls off but not till she was almost thirteen. Miriam comes from good stock, I don't fear for her. Besides, she's my wife, her place is with me."

Good Lord, Ross thought, as he glanced back at the boy who was asking for a job working the mill. *Is that how I seemed to Alexandra?* He remembered his precise words of two weeks ago and felt a shudder of regret travel right down his spine. *If you're my wife, I'll expect you to go where I go.* But he hadn't meant it quite the way it sounded when John said it. Or had he? What was it about this auburn-haired greenhorn that felt like a burr in his hide? One thing he knew for certain, he would never have asked Alexandra to make

242

a trek like this out to a mine, not unless they meant to settle there permanently.

For a brief moment, his thoughts grew full of Alexandra. The past two weeks had been a torture to him. The loneliness he had felt upon leaving Texas was nothing to the fire of hopelessness that seemed to burn in his chest around the clock since he ended his romance with Alexandra. Every time he saw her, morning and night for meals, he ached to reach out and pull her onto his lap as he had done so many times before. When her back was turned away from him, he would look at her, drinking in the sight of her glorious red hair, her tidy figure that always beckoned to him, the way she walked with her head high. He loved to listen to her talk to the miners, as she asked them about families left behind in England, or other parts of the country. One night he had retired to bed and heard her singing. The notes weren't perfect and the words seemed jumbled at times, she had even laughed at herself when she couldn't get the melody right. How hard it had been for him to remain in his tent. He had wanted to go to her so badly. He saw himself walking boldly into the cabin, taking her in his arms and kissing her as hard as he could until she begged him to stay and love her. He wanted to feel her arms about his neck, her hands in his hair, her lips warm and passionate beneath his own.

But how futile these thoughts were, then and now. Maybe he was so mad because John Horn, for all of his inconsiderate treatment of his wife, had still been able to accomplish the one thing *he* couldn't — to persuade the woman he loved to walk by his side.

Setting his hammer aside, he turned fully to the man and assessed his character as best he could. He seemed eager to work and had a quality of honesty

243

about him Ross trusted. He would be an asset to the Alexandra, and whatever his objections were to the young man's notions about caring for his wife, he set them aside in favor of John's general trustworthiness. "I will be needing someone to operate the mill," he said at last. "And since you've had some experience, I've no objection to giving you a try and seeing how you work out. But it will be another week or so before we're ready to process ore. The stamps won't be here until then, anyway, though I'm hoping to have the housing finished before that. Until the mill's ready we'll be working the arrastra. If you want to set up camp in the meadow alongside the other tents, I'm agreeable, as long as you have supplies with which to make your wife comfortable and can do some hunting and wood-gathering for the ladies. Mrs. Bradshaw and Mrs. Tharsing do the cooking for all of us. I would hope you would join us, though I hasten to tell you that all the miners, except Crackshot and myself, are Cornish. Do you understand about them?"

John frowned slightly, nodding his head. "Mighty clannish. I doubt I'd be welcome below ground, but I expect they'd accept me if they know I'll be shoveling ore at the mill."

"Those were my thoughts, too," Ross said. He then clapped John on the shoulder, shook his hand, and on impulse said he wanted to meet his wife, if that was all right with him.

Chapter Twenty-nine

Alexandra heard Ross and John Horn set heavy footsteps on the porch, then knock on the door. They were talking loudly, or at least so it seemed to her since she had been walking about on tiptoe trying not to awaken Mrs. Horn. She was already scooting quickly to the front door, hoping to open it before they pounded on it again in greeting, but she wasn't quick enough. She grimaced at the loud thumping that ensued and flung the door open, holding her flour-covered hands on her hips as she whispered hotly, "Quiet! For heaven's sake, you sound like a couple of bears lumbering up here and trying to break in."

She saw their startled, almost frightened, looks as they each took a small step backward. John pulled his hat from his head and begged pardon, while Ross immediately asked, "What's wrong?"

"Just lower your voices, please," she responded.

As she stepped aside, begging both men to come in and not let all the warm air out of the house, she meant to explain that Mr. Horn's wife was asleep, but Ross interrupted her. He had lifted the corner of her apron — without even asking if he could! — and began wiping something from her cheek.

"I'll bet," he said, "that you've got more flour on your face than in your bread, or whatever it is you're baking this time."

Alexandra felt confused by him, by his presence, standing as he was so near to her, by the feel of his fingers brushing against her skin, by the teasing quality of his words. He was so different from even the morning meal. She didn't know what to think! She tried to push his hand away, but he wouldn't let her, slapping her hand down and holding her wrist tightly in case she attempted to disrupt his efforts a second time. She wouldn't have, of course, but he didn't know that. She very much liked having his fingers hold her arm captive, but for the life of her she couldn't figure out what had happened to bring about such a change in his attitude toward her.

Ross knew the flour on her cheek was a pretty poor excuse, but being next to her was something he wanted so badly that he would have made something up if he had needed to. As it was, a white, dusty cheek would do just fine. On the other hand, standing right next to her was almost worse than staying away, when it meant he could smell her freshly washed hair but couldn't touch it, when he could see her slightly parted lips but couldn't kiss her, when he was but inches from her small waist but couldn't slip his arms around her and hold her tight. Of course, if Mr. Horn hadn't been watching him, he would have kissed her anyway, and to hell with his notions of what a wife ought to be!

Alexandra knew if she didn't say something quick, she'd lose her resolve to protect her heart from further injury. Ross's views of what he needed from a wife were pretty harsh and there didn't seem to be any possibility of reconciling her fears with his requirements. Tearing her eyes from his face, she nodded toward the young man and said, "I see you met Mr. Horn."

There was nothing for it, Ross thought. He'd have to give her up now. Releasing the apron as well as the wrist, he let her escape to the kitchen. "Yes, I have," he responded, closing the door. "I've hired him on to work the mill. I came up here to meet his wife."

Alexandra glanced sharply at Ross, wondering why he had quit work to come and meet Mrs. Horn. He smiled at her and she realized that some of the light had returned to his eyes. Why, he'd told a fib! He'd come here to see her, but why now? Oh how her heart jumped in her breast. What on earth had happened?

"You can't see her just yet," she said. "Mrs. Horn is curled up in my quilt, sound asleep. I wouldn't think of disturbing her. That's why I wanted the pair of you to keep your voices low."

"Miriam?" Mr. Horn cried. "Asleep? Why, I've never known her to do that before."

Alexandra looked at the young husband, and debated saying anything to him. But after having seen Mrs. Horn's exhausted state, she wanted Mr. Horn to know that his wife had suffered in coming out to the mine. In a gentle voice, she stepped toward him and, gesturing with her hands in an imploring manner, said, "I've never seen anyone so tired in all my life as your wife. I don't mean to be too officious when I say this, Mr. Horn, but it's awful tough work carrying a child, no matter what anyone tells you. I told her to lie down and she's been snoring ever since!"

Mr. Horn did not seem to know what to say as he glanced from Ross to Alexandra. He still held his hat in his hand and had begun twisting it between nervous fingers like a schoolboy caught in mischief. "She never said a word to me!" he cried. "Honest! I suppose I just didn't think a thing about it. Mr. Halleck said I'd been kind of careless in bringing Miriam out here, at least not in so many words, but truly I didn't mean no harm."

Alexandra again looked at Ross, this time with surprise. "You did?" she queried.

He scowled at her, in what she understood to be a half-playful, half-serious manner. "Of course I did," he answered. "It's a long trek for a woman in her condition."

Alexandra was stunned. "It is?" she asked again, not expecting an answer, just full of amazement that he actually held such an opinion. "I mean, of course it is."

He fixed his gaze on her, but not in an angry or mean way. It was as though he was trying to say something to her. He had wanted her to put his trust in him where her future was concerned. She found her cheeks growing warm, and a feeling like pleasure stole over her heart. He wanted her to know what he was made of. Had she misjudged him completely, or misunderstood their last conversation?

Still, *Wyoming!* For a woman like her it would be like living in a desert with no water.

When she glanced at Mr. Horn, she could see that his cheeks had grown pink underneath his freckles. Seeing his embarrassment, she said, "Well, never you mind. Enough said, I'm sure. Would you like some coffee? I've some cookies in the oven! Oh, my goodness! They're either done right now, or black! Just sit down and make yourself comfortable. You, too, Ross. If you can stay, that is." She was feeling very nervous and hoped more than anything that he

248

wouldn't leave right away. When he nodded and took a seat at the table, Mr. Horn drew up a chair as well. She turned quickly to the stove and was grateful she had caught the cookies in time. They were golden brown on the bottom, just as they ought to be.

Ross continued to sip his coffee, watching Alexandra over the rim of his cup. She was busy baking the cookies she would serve to the miners when they finished their shift. In two large pots, sitting atop the stove, bubbled a stew she kept tasting and adding a pinch of salt to—or pepper, and sometimes sage. Frequently, she would glance at him and smile. They weren't able to talk because Mr. Horn was still with them, fidgeting in his seat, unsure of what he ought to do next.

Conversation with Mr. Horn had not lasted long. He was a very young man in experience compared to either himself or Alexandra and there wasn't a lot to be said. The boy, as Ross thought of him, had a great deal to learn. When another ten minutes passed and not a word had been said, he suggested to him that he see to his mules before they wandered into the streambed below. "You'll be lucky to find 'em if they start wandering through this country!"

Mr. Horn seemed relieved by the suggestion and rose to his feet. Thanking Alexandra for her hospitality, he fitted his hat firmly back on his head, tipped it to her, and left.

Alexandra could not bring herself to look at Ross. She felt loose inside, and unsteady. As she drew another tray of cookies from the oven, she saw to her dismay that her hands were trembling. What was it about this man that could cause her to feel frightened yet excited all at the same time?

When the cookies were arranged on a plate and covered with a thin cloth, Ross called to her. "Come here for a minute, will you, Alexandra? There's something I want to say to you." He then laughed lightly and, keeping his voice low so as not to disturb Mrs. Horn, he said, "I didn't think he'd ever leave, poor fella."

Alexandra wiped her hands on her apron, and with knees that felt like they would crumble beneath her, she crossed the short distance between them. When she was standing before him, he took her hand in his and pressed a kiss on her palm.

"I've missed you so much," he whispered, looking up at her, cradling her hand between both of his.

Trying to take a deep breath, Alexandra found her heart beating in a strange, scattered way. She pressed a hand against her breast. "I have felt so empty inside," she returned quietly. "I've missed talking with you and being with you. Every time I see you at one of the meals . . ." She was unable to finish her thought.

"What?" he queried softly." What were you going to say? Have you wanted to, touch me and kiss me, to have my arms holding you tight? That's what I feel whenever I'm within a mile of you."

He covered the hand resting against her heart with his own, stroking her fingers lightly. The tips of his fingers barely touched her breast through the fabric of her calico gown. It was a small, innocent movement but brought a shiver of desire rushing through her. He rose slowly, not saying a word, his gaze fixed to hers. He sought her mouth with a tender, warm kiss.

With each touch of his lips upon hers Alexandra felt as though she was floating, drifting away from the floor of the cabin. How much she had missed him. She ran the tip of her tongue over the edge of his lips very lightly and was greeted with an answering touch. His kiss was so gentle, his tongue exciting as it barely moved against hers as his fingers slid off her hand, exploring the fullness of her breast. She felt her breath disappear into her lungs, not to return. Passionate feelings surged quickly within her as he suddenly released her hand, slipped an arm about her waist, and held her close.

"Alexandra," he whispered hoarsely, plunging his tongue deeply into her mouth.

She felt lost again, as she always did in his arms. Time disappeared, along with all her fears. If only she could feel like this when he wasn't with her. But it seemed the moment he would let go of her, terrifying thoughts cascaded through her mind, freezing her feet to the path she had set for herself.

He stopped kissing her for a moment, holding her tightly in his arms, his lips on her ear. "Come with me, Alexandra," he whispered, the breath on her ear sending chills coursing down her spine. She wanted him to kiss her again. "I can keep you safe, and our babies, too. I want you to trust me. I'd never ask you to do what Mr. Horn has so ignorantly asked his wife to do. I'd have things settled for you, we'd have neighbors to rely on, if not next door then close enough to be with you when you needed them. We can figure this out, I know we can."

Alexandra listened to him, her head pressed against his shoulder. She wanted to believe him, she longed to place her life in his hands. "I know you believe what you say," she responded, her heart feeling heavy. "But what happens when you're not there, or get injured branding an ornery calf, or, God forbid, if you die?"

251

He pulled back from her and gripped her arms firmly, holding her gaze. "If you let so many worries take hold of you," he said, kissing her forehead, his expression serious, "life will walk right by you and leave you behind. I think you know that's true. I think that's why you're here at the Alexandra, why you haven't returned to Mr. Bradshaw. He can give you all the safety and assurances your heart seems to be crying for. But somewhere deeper still, you know that it wouldn't be enough, not for a woman like you. I won't say that I have known hundreds of women in my life, because it just isn't true. I've been riding the trails since I was a lad, and believe me, especially twenty years ago, there weren't all that many females in the wilder territories. But I do know that most women wouldn't have had either the desire or the fortitude to make a trek alone from Missouri to Arizona just to see if *maybe* there was a rich mine waiting for them."

He released her after this speech, but with a smile. "You're here because you've got the inner strength and need to demand more from life than a safe marriage to a man who sounds like the greatest dullard ever born. It's the same reason you've fallen in love with a man like me. The only thing you have to realize now is that you can't have it both ways, not completely."

Alexandra couldn't find words right away to argue with him. She cast him a dark look to express some of the inner turmoil she was feeling. "You're confusing me, Ross," she said at last. "I know what I feel. Maybe William is a—a little dull, and his piety does wear on me, but if you think I'll change my mind just because your kisses are better than honey and you have an exciting way of talking, well, you're wrong. I

252

won't go to Wyoming. I won't." Even to herself, her words sounded childishly stubborn.

One thing she knew for certain, however—she didn't like the smile he wore. "And you can stop looking so smug," she cried.

"I won't leave you alone," he responded with a shake of his head, his gray eyes laughing. "In the end, I'll persuade you, see if I won't!"

He left shortly afterward, stepping lightly off the porch, a strong swing to his arms. She heard him let out a triumphant whoop when he'd gotten past Crackshot's tent, heading back to the mill. She could see that he was pleased with himself, with whatever idea had gotten fixed in his brain. But what did he mean, in particular, by insisting he would *persuade* her?

Chapter Thirty

You can't have it both ways!

Ross's words had gotten stuck in Alexandra's brain and she couldn't get them out. She was sitting in the kitchen, peeling two dozen potatoes one of the miners had brought her from Prescott the Saturday before and trying for the hundredth time to sort out her thoughts. But it was an impossible task because Ross was proving to be an impossible man.

For the past week, his short lecture to her about the kind of woman she was had rattled around in her mind until she'd grown dizzy. Was she so different from other women? Would most have agreed to marry William Bradshaw without batting an eyelash? Ross sure seemed to think so and taunted her with his opinion of her forbidding character by saying that were she to marry Mr. Bradshaw, or the likes of him, there'd soon be a murder in the house. He added, however, that he would be happy to attend her funeral.

Alexandra protested strongly against his opinion that she would make William, or any man, such a horrible wife. But he only responded that the bit would start ripping up her mouth the moment the vows were spoken and then there'd be the devil to pay.

"Now as for me," he added with an increasingly familiar self-satisfied smile, "I know how to handle a mettlesome filly."

"And how's that?" she'd asked, feeling both irritated yet intrigued. "With a whip?"

He shook his head firmly. "Not even close," he responded. The rich timbre of his voice encircled her heart as he spoke. Slipping his hand about her neck, he continued. "There's only one way. With a touch as light as a warm, lazy summer breeze that blows across the meadow late in the season when even the bees have grown fat." With a languid movement, his fingers drifting through her hair, he leaned down and kissed her full on the mouth.

She couldn't have prevented it, even if she'd wanted to, not when he looked at her with those eyes of his tearing her soul apart. Not when it was all she could think about anymore, being in his arms, being loved by him. His kisses had been light, his touch easy, his manner gentle, just as he had said. Was she mettlesome? She certainly felt fidgety in his presence until he started kissing her. Then she turned to mush, plain and simple.

That's how he had been pestering her every day, kissing her until she was ready to give him her soul if he asked for it. He never seemed to go farther than that, either, which was a mystery to her. Instead, he would release her, tell her he loved her, tell her he wanted her with him the rest of his life, and sometimes he would talk about the ranch he hoped to build in Wyoming. In short, he was seducing her with his fine talk, with his kisses, with his dreams.

Just as she finished peeling the last of the potatoes, she heard Cecilia's laughter, and rose from her seat to look out the window. She could see the tan fringe at her elbows and ankles bouncing as she ran toward the cabin. Crackshot was chasing her and teasing her as he frequently did, and only left off when she ran up onto the porch.

A second later, Cecilia burst into the cabin, her face alive with laughter, the lines about her eyes crinkled, her crooked teeth happily displayed in a wide grin. She was breathing hard as she shut the door behind her and leaned against it. "Mr. Peters!" she cried, breathless. "Sometimes he scare me silly!"

"He loves you an awful lot," Alexandra responded with an answering smile as she began cutting up the potatoes and dropping them into a pot of water.

"I almost forget," Cecilia cried, as she joined her by the stove. "Mr. Horn go to town for Mr. Halleck. He go now. Maybe you go, too. Good time. Weather good."

"I should go," Alexandra murmured to herself, then glanced at her friend. "But that would leave you with all this cooking and baking! No, it'll have to wait until Saturday."

"Snows come soon, too late by then maybe. You go. You need fabric now. Take many days to make dress."

Alexandra realized Cecilia was right. It was already early December and if she didn't start making her dress pretty soon, she wouldn't have time to finish it before the New Year's party. And she couldn't get the material until she went into Prescott. She continued cutting up the potatoes, weighing everything in her mind. There were other supplies she needed as well. Still, she hesitated.

Finally, Cecilia took the paring knife out of her hand, turned her around and gave her a shove toward the door. "Mr. Horn no wait. You go!"

It felt good to Alexandra to be in town, among so many people ambling down the boardwalks. The air was crisp, the sun nicely warm on her shoulders, and she felt deeply content as she headed for Goldwater's. She had only an hour in which to purchase her fabric and supplies. If she and Mr. Horn did not head back right away, they could be caught in darkness before they were able to reach the mine.

In addition, she had to speak to the sheriff. Two days earlier, Ross had happened to tell Alexandra about the Widow Ferguson and her children. She had been horrified, asking the very question no one seemed able to answer—who had done it. Only this morning, however, as Mr. Horn's wagon rolled past the McCormick ranch house and Alexandra remembered vividly being attacked by the freighter did she recall his curious words about knowing something concerning the events that had transpired in Carver. The sheriff ought to be informed, she thought, and for that reason, after she spent a quick half hour in Goldwater's, purchasing the most beautiful length of emerald-green silk she had ever seen, she crossed the threshold of Goodwin's office.

She could see right away that the sheriff was in a bad humor. He sat at his desk, scowling at her as she made her way to stand in front of him. "If you've come for news about any progress I've made on the Alexandra, you'll be mighty disappointed!"

Had Alexandra had the luxury of time, she would have excused herself politely and returned to speak with him on another day. She could see he was in a testy frame of mind, but she didn't see what else she could do but pull up a chair and tell him about the freighter.

He listened intently, the scowl deepening on his face, his fingers drumming out a frustrated cadence on his desk. By the strange workings of his mouth, Alexandra could tell he was trying with all his might to hold back a whole string of curses as he slapped his hand on his desk and rose to his feet to pace the width of the room near the door. "If that don't beat all!" he cried at last.

"What is it?" Alexandra queried, turning in her chair, her netted bag held tightly on her lap as she watched him march across the floor.

Since she was a female, the sheriff expressed a dislike for telling her what had happened, but Alexandra pressed him saying that because she had been so closely involved with the freighter's crime, she had a right to know what had happened to him.

Goodwin paused in his tracks, looking at her beneath a furrowed brow, apparently taking stock of her. "A couple of days ago . . ." he said finally, measuring his words with care as though he was afraid he'd hurt her if he spoke too fast, "the freighter was broke out of jail, taken to the Dells, and killed. But by who, I just don't know. Barnes was the only man watching him at the time. He said that when his back was turned, someone stole into the jail, pulled an old flour sack over his head, and clubbed him senseless. I found him a half hour later, just struggling to sit up, his head split open. But if what you tell me is true, then whoever sprung him probably had something to do with the killings in Carver."

"The Widow Ferguson, you mean?" Alexandra asked, wanting to make certain she got her facts straight.

258

"That's right," he said, nodding. "There's just one more thing. I finally heard from Dodge City and I want you to tell Halleck that the freighter's throat was slit, just like—" He broke off, a look of horror coming over his face. "Just never you mind about this," he amended hastily. "I shouldn't have—"

"Like who?" Alexandra cried, her hands gripping the arms of her chair. She didn't like the look on his face. "Who were you going to say? You mean, *like my father,* don't you? Don't you?" Her chest seemed to pull in on itself as her heart began sounding in her ears. When he nodded, she found that the room had turned a strange yellow color, her stomach dancing wildly as she leaned her head forward and tried to keep from being sick.

She heard the sheriff begin moving around the room in a fitful way along with the sound of splashing water. The next thing she knew, he had lifted her braid and placed a cool, damp kerchief across the back of her neck. Until that moment Alexandra hadn't realized how hot her skin had become.

"I could kick myself," he said, bending down beside her and taking one of her hands in his. He began patting it gently and apologizing all over again for giving her such a shock. "I didn't mean to shove it at you like that. I learned only yesterday about—about your father, from inquiries I'd made over a month ago. My wife has told me a dozen times I'm about as tactful as a mule. I hope you'll forgive me."

"Of course I will," Alexandra responded. "Anyway, I was the one who asked you to tell me. It wasn't your fault."

"Are you all right? Do you need a doctor? You're awful pale."

She shook her head. "No, I'll be fine in a minute.

259

Honest. It's just that even though I knew Papa had been murdered, I didn't know *how* until you told me just now. In fact, I was waiting for word from a—a friend of mine in Missouri. I had asked him to see what he could find out about my father's death in Dodge City, but I haven't heard from him yet." Alexandra was quiet for a moment, thinking about all they had just discussed, when she glanced sharply at the sheriff and said, "Do you think there's a connection between the men who killed Mrs. Ferguson and the men who are trying to take the Alexandra?"

He nodded slowly. "I know I'm taking a leap, but I think it's possible the same man that killed the freighter also killed your father, a man, an hombre, who prefers knives to guns."

By the time Alexandra returned to camp, night had fallen and Ross was waiting for her on the porch. He helped Mr. Horn unload the supplies, including Alexandra's, and afterward joined her in the cabin. When she emerged from the bedroom, having removed her hat and shawl and brushed out her hair, he told her to sit in the rocking chair, informing her that he had been keeping some stew warm for her on the back of the stove, if she was hungry, that is.

"How nice," she said, feeling very grateful. "Ross, you're such a fine man."

"Don't I know it," he responded cheerfully. "Shall I dish you up a plate."

"A very small one. I feel a little lightheaded so I know I should eat, but after that long trip today, I'm not real hungry."

He sat across from her, chatting easily while she ate. His conversation drifted along the usual lines; the

260

mine, something or other one of the Cousin Jacks said to him that struck him funny, what their house in Wyoming would look like.

All the while he talked, however, Alexandra felt uneasy. Not with him, but with her visit to the sheriff's. She took small bites of the stew, half listening to Ross as the vision of her father, lying dead in a hotel room with his throat slit, suddenly crashed in on her mind. The plate dropped to her lap with a thud as she covered her face with her hands.

"What's the matter?" Ross asked, sliding from his chair to kneel beside her.

Alexandra couldn't answer him right away, because her throat had closed up completely. After a moment, she explained about her father's death.

"Papa," she whispered, the horror of his death hitting her all at once as sadness and tears overcame her.

She felt Ross's arms around her, and she buried her face in his shoulder. The rocking chair hit the wall behind her with this movement and Ross took the plate of stew from her lap setting it on the potbellied stove. He then pulled her from the chair, drawing her onto his lap, cradling her as he sat on the floor.

How long she cried Alexandra didn't know, but it seemed forever. She cried for losing her father twice. Once because her uncle had kept his letters from her when he was alive and the second time, in his death. After a while she grew quiet, blowing her nose into Ross's kerchief, taking comfort in the strength of his arms around her.

Chapter Thirty-one

Within the next several days, Alexandra became more and more reconciled to the way her father had died. Ross had been a comfort, especially that first night, and it wasn't long before her heart didn't hurt nearly as much as it had the day she came back from Prescott. The busy routine of the camp also helped to keep her thoughts occupied. It seemed the miners grew hungrier every day—they certainly ate everything, *everything*, put in front of them. Alexandra began to think it was good thing they didn't have a pet dog around, for the poor thing would starve to death before a scrap would fall from that table!

As for Ross, it seemed once he saw that her spirits were lighter, he started after her again in earnest, kissing her when no one was looking, touching her, making her laugh. She felt herself slipping again, as she had before.

Every morning she'd wake up, resolving to do better, to fend off his assaults on her vulnerable heart with greater skill, but by evening, somehow she found herself enjoying her bath with only one thought in mind—a deep longing that Ross would break the door down and spend the night with her!

She was down at the creek now, filling two buckets with water in preparation for her bath later that evening, when Ross was suddenly beside her.

She looked up at him and pushed back a strand of hair from her face. "Where'd you come from?" she cried.

"Didn't you hear me?" he asked. "I was only moving on my tiptoes and as slow as a 'possum."

She cast him a mildly disgusted look and returned to her task. He tried to take one of the buckets from her, but she refused saying she would fill up her own pails, thank you kindly! And when he asked if he could carry the buckets back to the house for her, she flatly refused, since she knew exactly what he meant to do. He'd take the buckets all right, and then he'd follow her into the cabin and then he'd kiss her! Well, not today!

But he laughed at her, taking the buckets quickly out of her hands before she could so much as protest, and walked them up to the porch.

Alexandra refused to follow him and waited down by the creek, her arms folded across her chest. When he got to the front door, he looked back at her, that same wicked gleam in his gray eyes, and asked her, oh so innocently, "Won't you please open the door for me?"

"No," Alexandra responded, lifting her chin. "You may leave my water on the porch, thank you very much. Then you may go about your business. I won't have you in my house today, and you know very well why."

He frowned slightly, but even in his frowning Alexandra knew he was up to no good. "Well, that puts me in a fix, doesn't it? Because I'm not leavin' this porch till I help you with these buckets."

Alexandra knew that his voice carried all over the camp. And even though most of the miners, as well as Crackshot, were down in the mine, there was one poor soul stretched out on his cot with dysentery and both Miriam and Cecilia were in their respective tents. Any of them could hear every word if they were of a mind to.

Alexandra didn't know what to do, but she was growing weary of fending Ross off, especially when her own heart was by far her worst enemy in the situation. If she stayed by the creek, she wondered how long he would remain standing where he was, a bucket hanging heavily from each hand.

"You can stand there all day, much I care," she retorted. She was so irritated by then, that, on impulse, she turned her back on him, and headed north into the forest. Ross could do whatever he pleased with the buckets, she thought, though it would be particularly nice if he would stick his head in one of them. For herself, she intended to walk off her frustration.

She didn't look back, but picked up the skirts of her warm wool gown, slipping occasionally on the slick pine needles that covered the trail by the stream. A light snow had fallen a week earlier, but most of it had disappeared into the ground when warmer weather struck. The day was fast departing, and the walk among the trees was quiet and pleasant, with only the sound of her breathing to keep her company along with an occasional chattering squirrel or the whoosh of the wind as it eddied through the pine boughs.

She was happy, she realized as she made her way up the creek, heading higher and higher. The cool air nipped at her nose and cheeks, but moving as she did kept her nicely warm. When she was sure Ross wasn't

264

following her, she was pleased with how she had handled him. He would think twice next time about teasing her so much. She would just start walking away and leave him to regret his misdeeds.

The forest grew darker, the trees thicker, the higher she climbed. She felt at peace being away from the mine and the camp and Ross's taunting eyes. She paused and looked about her, noting small things like the rugged brown bark of the trees and the small rabbit tracks across a patch of snow and the pine needles clustered around rocks in the stream.

She turned back to look down the creek. She couldn't even see the camp from where she stood. But what was she going to do about Ross? She had to talk to him, before she started raving like a madwoman. Couldn't he see how he had her all twisted up inside? Or maybe that's what he wanted.

That's when she'd heard the snapping of twigs behind her.

"Pretty country, isn't it?"

Alexandra whirled around to find herself staring at Ross. If she hadn't known his voice so well, she would have let out a startled scream. Why hadn't she heard him? How was it possible he could have snuck up on her? She'd listened so carefully. As it was, she cried out, "You black-hearted coyote! What are you doing up here? Why did you follow me? I know what you're up to, but it won't work. Now you stop it. Don't you come near me. Ross, stop it —" She broke off suddenly, catching sight of his wet socks. "Why, you don't even have your boots on! So that's how you did it! Like an Injun, you scoundrel! I wish you'd go away and leave me alone!"

He smiled the same teasing smile he'd been exhibiting for two weeks now. She felt her heart sink. If only

265

he weren't such an appealing man, she thought, with his thick black hair and laughing eyes, and that faint cleft in his chin.

It was more than that, though, Alexandra realized, shaking her head as he began stepping toward her. She liked his determination, not just in his pursuit of her but in everything he did. She knew enough about him by now to know that he possessed a rock of iron will in his spirit. Nothing would ever keep this man down, not for long, anyway. She liked so many things about him, just about everything, in fact, except the road he wanted to travel.

"If it's any consolation," he said with a grin, wiggling his toes. "My feet are almost half frozen. If we stay here much longer, I'll be frost-bit."

"Well, it's nothing less than you deserve," Alexandra retorted sharply. She turned away only to have him take her gently by the arm and pull her toward him.

"Why are you running away from me?" he whispered, drawing her close. "You afraid of me?"

Alexandra shook her head. "You know I'm not," she responded. "What's there to be afraid of? I know you're a good man." She touched the blue plaid flannel shirt he wore, running her finger back and forth across one of the lines. She couldn't bring herself to look at him. "It's just that when you start kissing me and hugging me, I can't think straight. My mind feels like a whirlwind is racing through it, around and around. Why are you doing this? What do you want from me?"

He lifted her chin and looked deeply into her eyes. "You know what I want," he whispered, leaning toward her with each word he spoke. "Come to Wyoming with me. I'll keep you safe, I promise."

Alexandra knew she was losing the battle as his lips met hers again. "I can't," she breathed, feeling his mouth hovering just above hers. He was teasing her now, kissing her but not kissing her, his tongue flicking lightly over her lips. "Ross, stop it," she breathed again. "Why are you torturing me?"

Only then did he kiss her hard, pulling her tightly against him, driving his tongue into her mouth until she moaned faintly. She felt his hand caress her breast, her desire for him rising hotly as his fingers explored the delicate peak of her nipple. She ached for him, longing to know him again as before.

"Alexandra," he whispered. "I want you so much."

To her surprise, he pulled her behind a tree, protecting her from being seen by anyone who might be wandering from camp. His lips returned to hers immediately, his tongue driving into her mouth in a rough way that caught her up in a sweep of desire. The forest cloaked them, the fragrance of pine swirling about them, the cold air buffeting their warm bodies. His hand moved restlessly over her breast, to her waist, down the length of her thigh. He pressed himself hard against her, his hips moving into her, until passion flowed throughout her limbs. She wanted him to take her. He had teased her so much over the past couple of weeks. She ached for him.

Ross heard the hoarseness of her voice as she called his name, begging him to touch her, to take her. Desire spiked hard in him, and he wanted nothing more than to oblige her, but he also wanted to wait until she promised to come with him to Wyoming. He knew they were right together, perfect in love as a man and woman ought to be and he wouldn't leave Arizona without her. Once she actually said she would go, he'd kidnap her if she dared change her mind afterward.

He wondered, however, how long he could keep going like this.

Her breath was hot on his neck as she continued pleading with him. He felt her leg wrap itself about his thigh. He leaned into her, his hips catching her low and pressing her against the tree. The bark must be hurting her a little, but she said nothing, cleaving to him. He wanted her so much, he felt ready to break into two parts as he felt her hips respond to him, a moan issuing from her throat. But he had to stop.

Pulling her slightly away from the tree, he enfolded her within his arms, hugging her close. "I love you, Alexandra. The sun rises with thoughts of you and sets with a longing that overtakes my heart until I feel it will burst. I want you to come to Wyoming. Say you'll come."

Alexandra felt the urgency of her passion slowly drifting away, like a leaf down a lazy stream. She watched it disappear in stages, her breath growing even, the tensions in her body unwinding but leaving in their place an uneasiness hard to define. She felt an ache in her muscles as if she was getting sick, even though she knew she wasn't. She shook her head, and he released her, tipping up her chin with his finger.

"You can't live without me," he said with a taunting smile, gazing deeply into her eyes. "And I'm going north as soon as I have a few greenbacks tucked into my pocket. You only have to think about the kisses I'll give you to know what answer you ought to give me in return."

He didn't wait for her to argue, but started back down the hill on a brisk tread, avoiding patches of snow. Every once in a while, he'd step on a pinecone or a sharp twig and give a cry.

She knew he was doing all that for her benefit. And

all Alexandra could do was smile as she watched his comical, bootless figure skate on the pine needles, heading toward the camp. She sighed, thinking he would be a lot of fun to be married to. But, Wyoming!

Chapter Thirty-two

Later that evening, Alexandra took her two buckets of water, now sitting by the hearth, and poured the entire contents into a large black kettle atop the stove. While she waited for the water to get steaming hot, she set about preparing for her bath, taking her red hair out of the braid and building a big fire in the fireplace. When she felt certain the blaze would last for an hour or two, she went to the front porch to retrieve her tub. She had begun storing the unwieldy article outside after she found herself stumbling over it in the kitchen every time she turned around.

As she stepped onto the porch, she noticed that Ross was standing by the opening to his tent, gazing up at the stars. Earlier, they had shared a quiet dinner together, since the miners had gone to Prescott for the night, but shortly afterward, Ross had retired to his tent for the night.

She smiled at him now, though, feeling a sudden impulse to ask him to visit with her for a while. At the same time, she knew it was hopeless. They were both resolved on the paths they'd chosen — what more could they say to each other?

What his thoughts were, she couldn't guess, but he

waved to her with a lift of his hand. "Good night again," he said, sounding distant and cool.

She remained fixed in one spot, searching in her mind for something more to offer. Even her feet seemed reluctant to move. She didn't want the day to end like this, with a quiet politeness hanging heavily between them.

"I'm taking my bath now," she said finally, with a gesture to the tub. She found a blush rising on her cheeks since the moment the words were out, she knew it wouldn't take much for Ross to picture her without a stitch of clothes on. "Well, good night," she added hastily and slipped back into the cabin.

Before she shut the door, however, she heard him call to her. "When you're dreamin' tonight," he said. "Look over your shoulder. I'll be there."

Now what did he mean by that? she wondered. It was bad enough she had to look over her shoulder all day long just waiting for him to pounce on her. She didn't want to have to start protecting herself from him in her dreams as well.

How much she wanted this bath! Even her shoulders felt like they were riding up about her ears, so tense was she. The hot water would soothe her muscles and hopefully some of the disquiet ever present in her mind these days. Most of the time, once she had gotten settled in the tub, she could forget entirely about Ross. But at others, she found herself thinking only about him, about the times they had come together, about how gentle his kisses were. Tonight, could she set aside her thoughts of him? She doubted it, but she'd try anyway.

Alexandra arranged the chair behind the tub, along with a thick pad of cloth to serve as her pillow. Pouring most of the hot water into the tub, she added just enough cold to make it bearable. She had already strung a curtain of blue-and-white calico between the fireplace and the dining table for privacy and she set about quickly removing her clothes, draping her gown, corset, and undergarments over the back of the chair. She sat down carefully into the tin tub, the water almost painful as it inched up her hips. The round tub was just big enough to hold her, as long as she dangled her legs over the side. She knew she looked silly, but she hardly cared since it was unlikely anyone would ever see her.

The fire was wonderfully hot on her feet and the warm, soothing water loosened her tight muscles. She leaned her head back onto the pillow and closed her eyes. Her mind became liquid as it skipped easily from one thought to another. She was almost ready to sigh with pleasure at feeling so relaxed when her thoughts turned abruptly to Ross. The memory that hit her, however, was totally unexpected. She swore she could feel the weight of Ross's body as he pinned her against the tree and how, when he had caught her hips with his own, she thought she would cry out at the pleasure of it. Why was her mind so ready to betray her? She found herself squirming in the tub, her memories making her uneasy.

Ross paced the side of the cabin, knowing that Alexandra was taking her bath. He wished more than anything that she hadn't actually spoken the words aloud. Around him, the camp was peaceful and quiet, in tough contrast to the passion climbing steadily within him. She'd be sitting in her tub, without anything on. He felt like a wolf as he retraced his steps for the tenth time, walking the distance from the porch to the back of the cabin and back again. Pine needles crunched beneath his boots and the cold air bit at his cheeks.

He stopped pacing and wondered what it could possibly hurt if, after her bath, he asked to speak with her.

His feet were in motion instantly.

Not a thing, of course, if *speaking* was all he had in mind. But it wasn't. If he crossed the threshold of the cabin, he knew there'd be no turning back. As he made a twelfth pass at the house, all he could think about was what her clear, perfect white skin must look like, aglow from the flames of the fire as she sat in the tub.

To hell with it! his mind cried as he stepped on the porch. With just a few strides, he was standing in front of the door, his hand paused tensely on the leather thong that served as a doorknob.

Alexandra heard his footsteps, and she swore her heart stopped beating.

Ross.

If only he would walk through the door. She wanted to call out to him, but her mind warned her against it. Only confusion could possibly come of it.

She heard more footsteps, her heart still silent in her breast, but the steps grew faint, finally to disappear.

He had walked away.

She took a deep breath, her hand falling into the water and splashing her knees. If only he would come back. She kept thinking about the afternoon, and how it had felt to be crushed against the tree.

She felt tears of real frustration burn her eyes. It wasn't just how she felt physically, either. Whenever he took her in his arms, it was as though she had found part of herself that had been missing all her life. As she sat in the tub with the water starting to

273

cool, Wyoming suddenly began looking good to her.

She rose from the tin tub and added several ladles of steaming water from the kettle on top of the stove. She was about to get back into the tub, when, on impulse, she ran into the bedroom and pulled one of the wool blankets off her bed. Wrapping it securely around her, she left the cabin and stood on the end of the porch, near Ross's tent.

"Ross," she whispered, calling to him. But there was no answer. "Are you there? Do you—do you want to come in for a while?" Her bare feet started tingling in the cold air. She felt so strange doing this, wondering what she was doing, why she was inviting him as she was.

Still, he didn't respond.

A minute later, when her knees started to shake, she decided she was making a fool of herself and returned to the cabin and, to her warm bath. It was just as well, she told herself. Ross was wise to ignore her, and yet how much she wanted him with her!

Ross had been standing no more than three feet from her when she appeared at the end of the porch. He was cloaked in the shadows by the side of the house and wasn't able to see her nor was she far enough forward to catch sight of him. But he saw the bulky outline of her figure, cast by the light from the window on the ground near him. He had wanted to reach out to her, to hold her, to take her. What good would it do? He wanted all of her, not just a momentary joining. He realized she was as vulnerable to him tonight as he was to her. It was up to him to be sensible.

He stood frozen in the same place, striving with himself, trying to find some excuse for going, or for staying. He felt caught in a strong vise of conflicting desires, and he knew he was ready to explode inside.

274

Thank goodness the miners were gone, otherwise he would have been spoiling for a fight, something he hadn't done in years, just to get rid of the frustration that was building up in him.

Alexandra leaned forward, hugging her knees. The water was warm again, and the fire heated up her feet right away. Tears that had burned her eyes earlier, now trickled onto her legs. Why couldn't life be simple for her like it was for Miriam or Cecilia? Why hadn't Ross come to her?

Ross went back to his tent and slowly took off each boot. He sat down heavily on his cot, and stuffed another log into his own stove. The tent may not have been warm, but neither was it ice-cold. It was just right for sleeping, only he didn't feel like sleeping. Slowly, he removed his flannel shirt. Underneath he wore long johns and wool pants, but couldn't bring himself to take them off yet. He remained on his cot, thinking about Alexandra, not knowing what to do. He looked toward the cabin, his thoughts turning back to the afternoon and how quickly she had responded to his kisses, as she always did. He wanted to talk to her again, to make her understand she could trust him to care for her, that he wasn't a wandering man like her father, bent on carting her from one disease-ridden mining camp to the next. He was a man who knew how to save money and purchase a ranch. He'd done it once and he'd do it again. He found his ire rising within him, angry all over again that she stubbornly refused to see what he was made of.

He jumped from the cot quickly, his mind suddenly made up. He knew exactly what he wanted to do as

275

his legs and feet made quick tracks to the cabin, sprinting all the way.

Throwing the door wide, he called out, "Alexandra!" Closing the door quickly behind him, he crossed the room and stopped just short of the curtain that screened her from view. "You're coming with me. Do you hear?"

Alexandra wiped the tears hastily from her eyes, yet more rushed on, dampening her cheek. She turned toward the curtain, thrilled that he was here, with her. She watched as his hand pushed the curtain back slowly. He was so tall, he had to duck his head under just to look at her.

She thought she would never forget the expression on his face as long as she lived. It was full of love and determination all wrapped up into one. "I want you beside me until the day I die," he whispered. Dropping to his knees beside the tub, he took her face in his hands, gazing deeply into her eyes. With his thumbs, he brushed away the tears that drenched her cheeks. "Why are you crying?"

"I thought you wouldn't come to me," she whispered, her voice sounding hoarse and strained. "Did you hear me call to you?"

He nodded. "Yes, but I was torn about coming to you tonight until just now."

She touched his hands with her own, stroking them lightly. "I'm not just being horrible and stubborn. More than anything I want to be with you. I'm scared, that's all."

"I know," he said gently. And then his mouth was on hers in a full, deep kiss, his tongue moist as he plunged it hard into hers.

Alexandra sensed that something was different

about Ross tonight as she received his kiss. She felt his fine, fleshy hands slip lightly over her face, into her hair, as he continued to possess her mouth in a rich plundering movement, his lips warm, his tongue driving fully into her. There was an urgency in him she had not known before, an intensity that sent currents of fire streaming through her veins. He had never kissed her like this, she realized, a strange spark of fear and excitement igniting deep within her. Even if she wanted to end what had begun, she knew she couldn't, that nothing she could say from this moment on would persuade him to stop. Somehow, the knowledge of it only increased her desire for him.

She leaned her head back slowly on the makeshift pillow and he followed her, his mouth a constant pressure on hers, his hands working fitfully through her long red curls.

Alexandra.

He called her name and ravished her mouth, each movement of his tongue painfully sweet. She had not thought it possible to feel more pleasured than she was the last time they were together. But this! His touch, his hands, his lips, his kisses, were like sheets of water over parched land. She drank deeply, taking his tongue firmly within the pressure of her mouth. She thought he would ease back, but instead he kissed her harder still, rising up over her, his fingers splayed through her hair, pulling almost to the point of pain.

She reached a wet hand up to touch his neck, but he pushed it away, a movement that startled her. She tried again, but this time he took her hand in a hard grasp and pinned it under water in the tub.

When he released her hand, she didn't try to touch him again. The sleeve of his long johns had gotten wet in the tub, something she could feel as his hand drifted up her hip, to her stomach, to her breast, the wet fabric dragging against her skin. His fingers sought her nipple in a rolling motion, teasing her with a delicate stroke that almost wasn't there. For the first time since he'd come into the room, he stopped kissing her, running his lips slowly across her cheek. She caught her breath as his tongue began tracing the edges of her ear in a feathery sweep, matching the light strokes of his fingers on her breast. A chill rushed down her side, desire rushing to meet the shivery excitement that coursed through her. She wanted to touch him, but when she moved her hand out of the water and slipped her fingers over his back, he again caught her hand and held it tightly away from him as he plunged his tongue into her ear.

She moaned from the crisscrossing of pleasure and frustration he was giving her by touching her yet not letting her touch him. Tension built quickly within her as she strove with him, her fingernails digging into his hand in protest. But the more she struggled, the harder he held her hand and the more quick and seductive became the movements of his tongue as he ravaged her ear. Desire began cascading over her, her hips and body arching toward him, her body longing to be covered, to be touched, fulfilled.

Ross.

She spoke his name, or did she? Her mind cried out to him. She could hear her own breathing; how hard it was to breathe, to think. Her mind seemed full of lights that moved in circles. He breathed deeply into her ear, and spoke her name. Passion flowed in her, through her, as intense longing robbed her of words, of sense.

She didn't realize she had relaxed her hand, ending her brief fight against him, until he released her hand. He reached deep into the water, and caught her leg high, near her buttock, kneading the

278

flesh in a rough movement, close to pain, yet not.

Ross. Again her mind called to him, pleading silently to end the honeyed misery that he was bringing to her with the forceful plundering of his tongue, with his kisses, with his hands. Instead, he continued possessing her ear with ragged breaths that seemed to sprint needlelike the length of her side, impaling her nerves with a tight, unforgiving pleasure.

Ross felt as though every muscle in his body had become fitted with steel. He kissed and touched Alexandra unlike any other time before, handling her in a rough way that matched his inner determination to take her with him to Wyoming. Tonight he wanted her to feel his strength, to know him as a man, to respect him. And he wanted her to know pleasure like none before.

Alexandra felt his hand engulf her breast and caress it in a rolling movement. He slid away from her a little and touched her other breast in the same way, his tongue again reaching deep into her ear. His hands seemed stiff against her skin. She could feel that tension rode high on every stroke of his hand. His fingers dug into the fullness of her breast, curling around her nipples and pulling hard, hurting, but not hurting. His hands moved faster as his tongue plunged into her ear. Desire spiked deep within her, her hips growing restless. How much she wanted to touch him, but she was afraid to, afraid that if she did, he would stop what he was doing and she didn't want him to.

He shifted again, his tongue leaving her ear and seeking her mouth in another possessive kiss. She moaned, writhing with unfulfilled desire, wanting more from him. His hand moved from her breast in a long, smooth path across her stomach, into the water, easing down her abdomen. Alexandra held her breath as his fingers reached the soft down of her. His tongue played suddenly on her lips, teasing her as he gently began pleasuring the delicate folds of her womanhood.

Alexandra felt her sanity disappear to a hidden place in her mind. She drifted from one dark place to another as her body responded to Ross's touch, to his kisses. Nothing mattered but this moment, her hips moving in an ancient rhythm, covered in equal degrees of frustration and rising desire. He sought entrance, his hands exploring the soft, concealed part of her, and began a slow, easy thrust that seemed to reach all the way to her heart. She arched with this movement, her chest feeling weighted, so hard was it to breathe. A fog invaded her mind, everything was lost to her except his touch as his hand moved faster, driving into her. She felt herself holding him in response, rising to a peak, then falling back, only to climb again.

He slowed his movements, and easing back from her, caught her gaze. "I love you," he said, placing a gentle kiss on her lips.

Then he rose to his feet, leaned down to her and pulled her out of the small tub. He wouldn't let her do anything, but dried her off with the towel in long strokes. As before, if she tried to touch him, he would push her hands away. Then he spread the wool blanket, which she had used earlier, before the fireplace, shoving the tub aside, and quickly removed his clothes.

Alexandra had not seen him undressed before. Night had been his clothes, as well as her own embarrassment. But there was nothing hidden from her now as he stood across from her on the blanket, the fire washing him with light. Her gaze drifted over him — over his face, his strong shoulders, the black hairs on his chest, the scars on his arm and stomach, followed by the ridged strong muscles of his abdomen. As though mesmerized, her gaze moved on, taking in the rest of him. She felt her cheeks begin to burn, but right now she didn't care. The sight of his body was a pleasure to her.

He stepped toward her and fitted his hands about her waist, holding her so tight she could hardly take in a breath. "You're mine," he whispered. He kissed her hard, his thumbs digging down into her abdomen. Desire again began to flow through her as he slipped an arm behind her and forced her slowly down on the blanket.

He didn't wait but entered her right away, hurting her, but not hurting her. He took each of her hands in one of his, lacing his fingers through hers, imprisoning them in his strong clasp. And then he began to move into her, his chest pressed against hers, her arms bent at the elbow and her hands pinned next to her shoulders. He didn't kiss her, though, but looked straight into her eyes, his face solemn. She was overcome as much by the pressure of him moving deep within her as by the way he held her gaze. His eyes bored into her mind, taking possession of her soul, the way he possessed her body.

She was grateful that he held her hands, for at least now she could return his touch as he moved into her. She gripped his hands hard, and he thrust harder, her breath catching in her throat. Every thrust seemed to push her to the edge of madness, then the edge would slip away until he moved into her again, forcing her farther still. Passion began moving over her as Ross moved, an intense burning, rising with each thrust, only to fall and rise again. Was she breathing? She didn't know. She was lost in the thrill of being one with Ross, of having his body invade hers so completely. He was moving hard now, like he had never done before, connecting deeply within her, commanding her. She gripped his hands fiercely, moaning with each thrust, feeling ready to break. A sudden, intense swell of pleasure took hold deep within her and she cried out, her back arching as he plunged hard into her again and again. The feeling was perfect as it rolled over her in a wave of ecstasy, spreading like hot embers through her entire body. The heat remained, as Ross continued to drive into her.

Ross saw the pleasure that washed over her features and thrilled to what was happening between them. He didn't want the moment to end as he pressed into her, desire riding him hard. She surrounded him with a fire that burned through him.

"I love you," he whispered, catching her gaze and holding it fast. He felt ready to explode, yet holding back, waiting.

Alexandra felt a second rising within her that startled her. Ross was looking at her fiercely, passion possessing his eyes as desire climbed and fell within her again. She felt a wildness take over her mind, her body. She began moving with him in a fitful way. She tore her hands from his grasp and threw her arms about his neck, cleaving to him, as a second knifelike wave of pleasure ripped through. She sought his mouth and drove her tongue into his, moaning harshly, tears flowing from her eyes.

Ross felt caught up in her pleasure, carried with her as the seductive thrusts of her impassioned tongue invaded his mouth. He could hardly breathe as an intense rush of pleasure drove through him. He caught her deeply, forcing her hard against the blanket, his hips digging into her, letting the onward tide of ecstasy sweep him away.

Alexandra held Ross close, hugging him tight, tears still pouring from her eyes, her body satiated but her emotions raw. Ross sought her lips again and kissed her over and over, expressing his love for her, wiping her tears away with his lips. He remained joined to her for a long time, kissing her, touching her, loving her.

Only as the fire died down and the cabin grew cold did he finally separate from her and return to his tent. But before he left, he got what he had come for. She had promised, with all her heart, to go to Wyoming with him.

Chapter Thirty-three

The next several days seemed covered with a blanket of golden mist, lost in the perfection of love. Alexandra wasn't even sure her feet touched the ground. Ever since she had made the decision to accompany Ross to Wyoming, to stand with him whatever hardships came along, her heart had simply floated through each day. Her thoughts were full of him — where he was, what he doing, and she longed for the time when they would come together again. Until evening however, he wouldn't even so much as look at her if anyone else was around. She found his discretion almost funny; at the same time, it pleased her to know he cared so much about how others in camp thought of her.

Once in her cabin, however, with only a small fire in the fireplace to light the rooms, he would stay for hours. Most of the time was spent cuddling in bed, kissing, touching, and finally taking a long, slow climb to a place so exquisite, so satisfying that Alexandra frequently found herself crying with happiness afterward. Ross teased her about being worse than a leaky faucet, but since he always followed this up by holding her close and telling her he loved her, she didn't mind a bit.

One day, shortly after the noon hour, Alexandra stood in the doorway of the cabin, feeling an icy wind blow steadily off the mountain to the north. Clouds had begun piling up, obliterating the brilliant blue sky, and the feel of snow was in the air. It was time, of course. Winter was fast approaching the land.

Alexandra shivered suddenly as another sharp gust blew across the porch, tugging at the folds of her skirt, stinging her cheeks raw. If the snow fell deep, she meant to ask Ross to stay with her in the cabin. As she looked out at the tents, flapping with the growing wind, she wondered how the men would bear the cold. Each tent had a stove, but how warm could it keep the miners if the temperatures continued to drop as sharply as they had this morning alone?

She glanced up at the covered wagon and tent that housed Mr. Horn and his wife. She saw that he was hitching up his team of mules, and she breathed a sigh of relief. Ross had persuaded the young husband to take his wife to Mrs. McCormick's for her confinement, and though it had taken some talk, Mr. Horn had finally agreed to it, especially when he realized that neither Cecilia nor Alexandra had experience midwifing. Mrs. Horn's baby wasn't due for four more weeks, but as long as she remained in camp, Alexandra would not rest. So much could happen, and it would be far safer for mother and baby to be in a warm bedroom at Mrs. McCormick's ranch with a doctor in attendance than trapped out at the Alexandra with help so many hours away.

She watched Mr. Horn turn his head toward the tent and call out something indiscernible to his wife. He paused for a moment, then left off hitching up the team and went into the tent. His walk had seemed irritable, the way she would expect any young man to be with his wife in the last stage of her pregnancy. Alexandra couldn't keep from smiling. Poor John Horn had so much to learn.

But not more than any of us, she thought, letting her gaze again drift over the camp.

She noted with some amusement that the three Chinese, who had recently arrived to set up a laundering establishment for the miners, were arguing heatedly in their native tongues, the result of which was that one of them marched off into the forest, ostensibly in search of more firewood to heat their large cauldron.

Everything seemed to be moving along so well. The ribbon of gold, though giving the appearance of narrowing a bit, had more than paid for the stamp mill, besides paying the miners' wages. So far, the Alexandra had not realized a profit, but it wouldn't be long. More large beams for square-setting the tunnels had arrived only the day before, and in the distance Alexandra could hear the incessant pounding of the mill's five cast-iron stamps.

Just as Alexandra was about to turn back to the cabin, a flake of snow floated onto her blue shawl. She shivered again as another blast of snow-laden air whistled across the creek. Not knowing exactly why, she looked back at Mr. Horn's wagon and tent. He had not yet returned to finish hitching up the mules. It seemed odd that he would leave them standing in the cold, and suddenly Alexandra knew something was wrong. She saw movement from the corner of her eye, and noticed that Cecilia had come out of her tent and stood solemn-faced, staring toward Miriam's tent.

Alexandra felt a dark, cold feeling pass over her heart as she watched Cecilia. The woman had the strangest ways at times. If she helped Alexandra bake bread, she would be like any other woman, laughing,

286

talking, complaining about Crackshot. But at other times, like now, she took on the appearance of an angel of death, her demeanor prophesying doom, like the time Crackshot and Ross had almost been killed by the dynamite. Alexandra would never forget the look on Cecilia's face that night, her mouth open as though to speak, but no words passing her lips.

She watched Cecilia lift her hand slightly, and right afterward, Miriam screamed.

Alexandra was running, before the sound of the young woman's voice disappeared down the meadow. Snow was flying now, swirling about her as she raced to the tent. When she got there, the young bride was writhing hysterically on her cot, blood everywhere— on her hands, her face, in her hair, on her woolen nightgown, on the front of her husband's coat.

Mr. Horn stood on the other side of the tent, staring at his wife, his face deathly pale, his eyes blank. Alexandra rushed to Mrs. Horn's side and placed her hands hard on the girl's shoulders, forcing her to lie still.

"I'm dying," Miriam cried out, clutching at Alexandra's shawl. "What's happening to me! I want a doctor! Where's Mama? Why am I bleeding so?"

A minute later, Ross burst into the tent, his breath coming in gasps. "What's the matter?" he cried." We heard a scream—Oh, good Lord, good Lord in heaven! Alexandra, do what you can. I'll fetch a doctor right away."

Ross rode his mustang at a steady pace, knowing that it would do little good to wear his horse out. The ride into Prescott, though pleasant enough when the weather was fine, became treacherous as he wended his way out of the mountains, snow flurrying about him, covering the trail quickly in a layer of white. One thought kept him pinned in a state of painful anxiety. What if it had been Alexandra, instead of Mrs. Horn, with blood pouring out of her? He wouldn't think about it. Not now, as he gave his horse a kick, hurrying him up the hill.

Three hours later, when he reached Mrs. McCormick's ranch, he was exhausted from battling the storm. Mrs. McCormick refused to lend him a horse to complete his mission. Instead, she sent two of her hands after a doctor, ordering them to bring the closest one they could find. There were several who practiced in Prescott, but since they could be anywhere at this time of day, checking on bed-ridden patients, Mrs. McCormick's orders were understandable.

Ross sat at the dining table, drinking a hot cup of coffee as he watched the hands ride out the front yard heading toward Prescott. Within two hundred yards of the house, however, they disappeared into the snow of the storm. It was a bad one. How was he going to get the doctor back to the Alexandra?

An hour and a half later, the doctor came hurrying into the house, his black bag in hand, snowflakes melting on his face, clothes, and hat. "I understand we have a sick woman here," he said, his face white with alarm. "How long has she been bleeding? I presume I was called as soon as it started?"

Ross stepped forward, feeling panicky inside, "She's not here, Doctor. She's at my mine, at the Alexandra. I hope you're fit for a tough ride."

The doctor stared at him, horrified. What thoughts ripped through his mind were hard to guess at until he drew his brows sharply together and asked, "Where's the Alexandra?"

"Bee Mountain," Ross replied. He wanted to grab

the doctor's arm, turn him quickly around, and give him a shove toward the door, but something in the way the man's shoulders fell stopped him.

Setting his black bag on a narrow table by the door, the doctor shook his head. "My friend," he said hopelessly, "we can't go out there tonight. Why, we lost our way three times just driving out here to Mrs. McCormick's house. Do you really think, with the snow piling up faster every minute, we could make it all the way to your mine?"

"You've got to come," Ross said, his insides feeling tied up tighter than a calf at branding time. "She's bleeding to death."

"Your wife?" he asked, still standing by the door.

Ross shook his head. "No. Her name is Mrs. Horn. She's married to one of my miners. She's just a child, sixteen, seventeen, maybe. There was blood everywhere. She wasn't due to have her baby for a month or so. She and her husband were just preparing to come out to Mrs. McCormick's to wait out her confinement."

"I don't know how to say this, Mr. — "

"Halleck."

"Mr. Halleck. But I don't think there'll be any need for me now."

Ross couldn't bear hearing him talk like that, and without thinking, drew his Colt peacemaker and leveled it at the physician. "You're coming with me, do you hear? This lady is counting on me and I said I'd bring her a doctor."

Lifting his hands, clearly frightened by the sight of Ross's gun, the doctor said, "You don't understand, Mr. Halleck."

"Ross," Mrs. McCormick said, laying a gentle hand on his arm. "I don't permit anyone to use their guns in

289

my house. I insist you put it away or you'll have to leave my ranch for good."

Ross glared at Mrs. McCormick. "He's got to come with me," he cried. "Maybe if you'd seen Mrs. Horn, you'd understand. She was suffering badly, her clothes were all soaked with blood."

"Then why don't you give Dr. Adams a chance to explain. I think if you still aren't convinced by what he has to say, he will most likely agree to go out to the mine with you. But like him, I don't think it'll make a bit of difference."

It was the way Mrs. McCormick looked, the expression of compassion on her face, that reduced his hope to nothing. If she thought it would be useless to take the doctor out now, she must have a reason. He slipped his pistol back into his holster and followed her into the parlor. There, she instructed the doctor to explain the situation in detail to Ross, not to hold anything back. She then left, saying she meant to bring the doctor a strong cup of coffee.

Ross listened to the doctor, his heart failing him. In his opinion, Mrs. Horn had hemorrhaged, and badly. He'd seen several cases like hers, where spontaneous bleeding erupted late in the pregnancy. Without immediate surgery, the patient and baby died. With surgery, results were always poor. In the course of his practice, only one baby had survived, and the mothers usually died of infection a month or so later.

"You think she's dead, don't you?" Ross queried.

He nodded. "I do. I'm sorry. Even if I had been notified within an hour, it's my opinion that it still would have been too late. It's the Lord's will."

Ross dropped his head into his hands. "The Lord's will," he murmured.

"It seems to me," the doctor continued, "that you

did everything you could to keep that woman safe. It's likely she'd been experiencing trouble long before this. Maybe she didn't know better to say anything, I don't know. But I don't think you can blame yourself."

How could Ross explain the thoughts that pummeled his mind. The truth was, he hardly knew Mrs. Horn, and though he felt sorry for her and for her husband, the despair he was feeling had more to do with Alexandra than anyone else. She had tried several times to express to him the dread she experienced with the mere thought of living in an isolated region, where medical help was almost nonexistent. In his plans for their future, he had thought he could take Alexandra to the nearest town during the latter parts of her pregnancies. But what if a blizzard came up, like it did today, keeping them from setting out until it was too late. Wyoming would surely have its share of hard, natural calamity.

Oh, Lord, his mind cried. She had been so right to harbor such grave concerns. The question now was, would he be willing to risk her life like this? Maybe it was the Lord's will that Mrs. Horn and her baby leave the earth, but what if it was just because Mr. Horn had been careless in dragging his young bride so many miles across the frontier?

The doctor patted him on the shoulder and said, "If you like, when the storm breaks, I'll ride out with you to your mine. But I think it would be wise to take a preacher, too. Mr. Horn will have more need of him than myself, if my fears are confirmed."

"I can't return to face any of them without you along," he said. "I'll pay you for your time and trouble. We'll take a reverend, too, just like you suggest."

Chapter Thirty-four

Several days later, Alexandra watched Ross leave the tent where meals were served, her heart longing to call out to him. The miners were all heading into the mouth of the mine, and Ross was moving down the hill toward the stamp mill.

He's a different man, Alexandra thought as she began collecting the tin plates and scraping the remains into a bucket. Cecilia worked quietly beside her, taking the plates and washing them up in a small tin tub, stacking them on the table to drain afterward.

"Mr. Halleck not happy," Cecilia said, pushing back a graying strand of hair. "Miriam die and he mourn. He very sad."

Alexandra sighed. "I think he blames himself. But there was nothing he could have done. Even the doctor said so."

"Sometimes I think it no matter what anyone say," she said, pressing a hand to her chest. "Only what hurt inside."

Alexandra watched Ross disappear into the forested end of the meadow, skidding on the icy snow as he followed the trail to the stamp mill. "I think you may be right," she said at last, picking up another plate.

During the four days that had inched by after Mrs. Horn's death, Alexandra had found Ross growing more withdrawn daily. He hadn't touched her or kissed her since returning to camp; he had hardly even spoken to her. She suspected that the reason the death had hit him so hard was because he saw her in Mrs. Horn's place, a year or two down the road, and it was a vision he couldn't easily fit into his way of thinking about things.

But if Alexandra was perplexed by Ross's reaction to the tragedy, she was equally surprised by her own. She had cried, of course, off and on since the day Mrs. Horn had died. She hadn't gotten to know the young woman well, since she had stayed close to her tent, keeping to herself and to the business of caring for her husband, but Alexandra had held her hand, trying the best she could to console her during the final hour of her life. Mr. Horn had stood by, fixed in one spot, unwilling to believe his wife was dying. Mrs. Horn knew the truth and fought it, calling out hysterically to each of them in turn. She didn't want to die, she wasn't ready to give up all her dreams of holding her baby, of building a home, of helping her husband. Once the bleeding began, it simply didn't stop until her body started growing cold, her eyes lost their ability to see, and there was no longer a need to breathe. Alexandra watched the light disappear from Mrs. Horn's eyes thinking that death was a terrible thief, the greatest thief of all.

But for all the heartache of placing the young woman in the ground, and watching her husband stretch himself out full on her grave afterward, Alexandra had not once thought of herself in relationship to Mrs. Horn's death where Ross, and their future together, was concerned. She came to a startling realization that she had somehow passed completely beyond her fears to a knowledge that being with Ross for the rest of her days had become more important to her than anything.

It seemed terribly ironic to her, however, that Ross seemed to have drawn the opposite conclusion—that he would rather live without her than risk her life in an isolated portion of the frontier, as John Horn had risked, and lost, Miriam's.

Collecting the tin cups, Alexandra tossed any last dregs of coffee onto the snow outside the tent. The air was bitter cold, and her breath, even in conversation, came out in white puffs every time she opened her mouth. What concerned her now was the nagging thought that Ross, in his stubbornness, would be unable to relent to the promptings of his heart, that he would one day take his earnings from the mine, and disappear, heading northeast, toward the wilds of Wyoming, without saying a word to her. She had come to understand him well enough by now to know he was capable of doing just that. A different kind of fear rose in her heart suddenly, a fear that she was close to losing Ross forever.

Later that day, Alexandra searched around desperately for some way of getting Ross to speak his heart to her. She had tried to invite him to her cabin but he refused. After supper that evening, when she tried to talk to him harmlessly on the porch, asking what he was thinking about these days, and why he hadn't even kissed her lately, she was startled by the look of anger that flashed through his eyes.

"I can't believe you would even ask me such a question when the answer is plain as day. It's no good, Alexandra, just like you've been telling me for weeks. As soon as I can, I'm moving on to Wyoming—alone. I promised myself I'd never bury you like Mr. Horn buried—" He had gotten choked up, slapping his hat hard against his thigh and stomping off the porch.

"Ross!" she called to him, but he didn't even look back at her.

It was now a day later, and she again stood on the porch, but this time she was listening to the quiet of the snow-covered forest, her heart beating out a quick cadence of anxiety. For the second day in a row, the mill had stopped early in the afternoon.

She turned back into the cabin, where Cecilia was tasting a venison stew, and asked, "Has something happened to the machinery at the stamp mill? It's not like Ross to hold back milling the ore. Has Crackshot said anything to you?"

"He not like the ore as much. Ribbon gone."

"Gone?" Alexandra asked, closing the door behind her and feeling she had just had the wind knocked out of her. "Is it completely gone? All of it? Why didn't someone tell me?"

Cecilia covered the pot and turned back to face Alexandra. "Ross not tell you?" she asked, her face wrinkled with surprise. "After Miriam die, no more gold. I think she take it with her."

Alexandra dropped into a chair by the table, pressing her hands against her face. How was it possible, when they had had such a promising beginning? The gold was gone? She laughed to herself. No wonder Ross had already spoken of laying tracks for Wyoming. The promise of his future with her had disappeared along with his belief he could keep her safe.

Three days before Christmas, the miners packed up their gear and left the Alexandra. Desolation hung over the camp as heavily as the low clouds which laid another inch of snow on the meadow. John Horn was the last to leave, standing at the foot of his wife's grave for over an hour before he finally said his good-byes, hitched up his mules, and headed toward Prescott. He didn't smile once as he pulled out, calling to his mules and giving the reins a hard slap. Grief rode with him, but because he possessed the natural resilience of youth, Alexandra was sure he would quickly put the past behind him.

If only Ross could do as much.

Once Mr. Horn disappeared over the crest of the hill leading out of the camp, Alexandra turned to speak to Ross, but he had already started heading toward the stamp mill. Instinctively, she reached out a hand to him, in quiet supplication, but his back was to her by then. She wanted to call to him, but she knew he wouldn't respond.

She returned to the warm cabin and removed her shawl, draping it over the back of the rocking chair. What was she going to do about stubborn Ross Halleck? She began pacing from the front door to the kitchen stove and back, her thoughts rushing together, damming up in her mind until she was thoroughly frustrated. Why wouldn't he at least talk to her? Why was he being so closed up and mulish? He loved her, but was this the right way of showing it, even if he had made it clear that he intended to go to Wyoming without her?

After a few minutes, she came to a decision. Picking up her shawl, she threw it over her head, wrapped it tightly about her shoulders, and left the cabin at a brisk walk toward the stamp mill. She realized, as her boots crunched through the ice-capped snow, that all this time she had been waiting for him to come to her. Only now did it dawn on Alexandra that he wasn't going to. He'd made up his mind. He refused to discuss anything with her, and that was that!

Well, she wouldn't have it! After all they had been through the least she deserved was a little of his time and attention.

Chapter Thirty-five

Alexandra stood in the doorway of the high-ceilinged mill house, pulling her shawl tightly about her shoulders and fixing her heart with determination. She wasn't about to let Ross go without a fight, but how was she supposed to do battle with him when he wouldn't square off? Men could be such pig-headed, ornery creatures at times, she thought, and it would be no easy thing to persuade him to take her to Wyoming.

The mill was a narrow building, housing as it did the single five-stamp ore processing machine. Because Ross hadn't bothered to light any of the lanterns, the building was dark and uninviting. A grating near the ceiling was the only source of light otherwise, and because the day was cloudy, the mill appeared gloomy and abandoned.

She found Ross sitting on his haunches beside the trough, handling some of the last ore he had processed. The expression on his face was hidden from her, but she knew by the set of his shoulders and by the slight tilt of his head that he was very unhappy.

He didn't look up at her, but somehow Alexandra

could sense he was aware of her arrival. She wasn't surprised, therefore, when he addressed her. "I expect we rushed in too soon on this one, Alexandra," he said, hefting a lump of ore in his hand. "We don't have a penny of profit to show for that lovely line of gold we found." A sigh escaped him, a sad sound that rent Alexandra's heart. "At least we've paid our shot with the merchants, though I must say this mill is a pretty expensive house for rabbits and spiders. I'm afraid that's all these warped boards will amount to after a few years of standing empty."

"You're quitting, then," Alexandra stated. "I know you said you wanted to go to Wyoming, but I always supposed you didn't mean to leave until after you had worked this claim and were sure it had nothing left to give you—or us."

He rose to his feet, a bittersweet smile on his face. "I've learned a heap about myself since I've been here. One thing I know, this is not the life for me." He jerked his head toward the stamp machine. "I don't mind the work. But living day by day, not knowing whether you'll be rich or poor and relying on nothing but hopes and dreams to keep you going, has just about stripped me of any gold fever I might have had before I got here. And I surely do miss being on the back of my horse. I miss the land, too. I miss hearing the beeves when they bed down for the night, lowing at the stars, settling in." He paused, looking at the ore in the trough and shaking his head. "I can't believe it's gone. The vein just seemed to disappear. Well, tomorrow I aim to ride out. I've already told Crackshot, though he nearly bit my head off when he learned I was leavin' right away. Said I was a fool. Expect I am."

Alexandra stepped into the building and closed the

298

door behind her. Without the light from the doorway, the mill was darker than ever, and she could hardly make out Ross's features even though he stood but a few feet from her. She wasn't certain what she ought to say to him. But the moment he spoke of leaving so soon, desperation bolted through her. She wanted to cry out, to plead with him, to beg him to stay. At the same time, she knew she couldn't do anything of the kind, that she had to be careful about what she said. She had never seen Ross like this before, and she had little doubt he was feeling pretty torn up inside. He had made up his mind to leave, and her tears would do little to change his mind. What then?

She didn't know why thoughts of Mrs. Horn came to her at this moment. Instinctively, however, she felt it was time to talk to him about it. "I was with Mrs. Horn when she died," Alexandra said, her voice shaking a little from the knowledge that if she proceeded badly, Ross would be gone by daylight.

He looked at her, a concerned frown creasing his brow. "I thought you might have been," he said quietly. "I'm — I'm awful sorry I couldn't get back sooner. You know that, don't you?"

Alexandra nodded, lowering the shawl from her head to her shoulders. "It wasn't a peaceful death, as death goes. She wasn't ready to die, any more than I would have been in her situation, with life just ready to blossom for her."

Alexandra saw a coarse pain take hold of Ross's face, his gray eyes narrowing as though he was trying to fend off a harsh desert wind. "Why do you have to say this to me?" he asked, his voice a whisper. "Don't you understand how much this hurts? Why have you come here anyway? To make me feel worse than I do about what happened? To gloat that you were right about how terrible Wyoming would be for you and our children? That you'd be afraid every minute of your life that you'd perish like Mrs. Horn?" His voice broke as he shifted his gaze from her face, staring blindly at the stamp mill.

Alexandra felt his unhappiness blow through her in wave after wave. She didn't try to console him, instead she provoked him by adding, "We all know it was your fault."

He turned toward her, facing her fully, his eyes blazing as he cried, "My fault! Which part of it? That I hired that boy on? Or that I didn't make them leave a day earlier than they had intended? Or that I didn't get the doctor back here in time?"

"That's right, all of it," she said facetiously. "It's clear to me that you blame yourself, so I intend to do the same. The fact is, over the last several weeks I have come to rely on you to see into the future, to know exactly what will happen so that you can protect me, and everyone else around you, from disaster. Why else do you think I would finally have agreed to go to Wyoming with you? I was convinced you had powers no other man I know has, to take every event, every circumstance presented to you, and twist it so that I could be safe forever, and our children, too."

"Why are you taunting me like this!"

"Because Crackshot was right, you're acting like a fool!"

"And I'm about ready to wring your neck!" he responded.

"Well, if you did, it would certainly be a far sight better than what I've gotten from you over the last few days!" she retorted, standing very straight and feeling her eyes fill with unwanted tears. "At least then you'd be touching me, something I've missed more than

300

anything else in the world." She laughed slightly, feeling a little hysterical. "What is it? Have I grown a wart on my nose or something? Only tell me why you don't kiss me anymore?"

He looked away from her, sighing heavily. "I told you before. It's useless, that's all."

Alexandra wanted to go to him so badly, to slip her arms about his chest and hold him tight, to tell him all she cared about anymore was being with him, wherever he went. She didn't, though, knowing full well that he'd throw up his hackles farther and probably push her away.

"Ross," she said at last. "I won't try to argue with you. I can see you're determined to leave, but I think it's mighty unmannered of you to ride out before Mrs. McCormick's party."

He looked back at her, a faint expression of surprise on his face. It would seem he hadn't considered how his actions would affect anyone else around him.

Alexandra could see she had struck the right chord and pressed on. "She's been counting on both of us to attend, and if you think she wouldn't be offended, well, you're wrong. When a woman goes to that much trouble to prepare food and entertainment for her friends and relatives, she takes it mighty unkindly in anyone who doesn't show up—unless you're tied to a sickbed, of course. Besides, I've made the prettiest green party dress you'd ever want to see, and if you don't go, how am I supposed to get out to her ranch?"

He stood looking at her thoughtfully. She could see his mind working as his eyes narrowed slightly. "I hadn't been thinking about Mrs. McCormick or you," he admitted. "And I did promise her I would attend her party. Besides, I expect you'll want to break up housekeeping yourself pretty soon. I could arrange for a wagon to come gather up your things just before the party. I have to go into Prescott anyway a day or two early. I could make the arrangements for you then, if you like."

Alexandra felt so strongly against doing anything of the kind that it was all she could do to keep from telling him so then and there. He had made a huge assumption about what she would do if he left the Alexandra. Clearly he thought that since he was leaving, she would have no reason to stay, or perhaps lack the courage to stay on without him. Whatever the case, he was wrong, only she knew it would be a big mistake to tell him so.

"I'm not sure exactly when I'll want to leave," she responded, biting her tongue hard. "Don't hire a freighter just yet, until I know exactly what plans to make. When you go into town, though, would you please get me a room at the hotel for two nights? Mrs. McCormick wanted me to stay at her house, but when I realized how full it would be with her daughters, sons-in-law, and grandchildren all staying with her, I refused. She will have enough to keep her busy without me under foot."

He said he would be only too happy to do so, adding that if she set her mind to it, with a little careful planning she could board the stage the day after the party and return to Missouri where he knew she would have a chance at a good life.

"I'll give it some thought," she responded. She turned to leave, and as though she hadn't been planning the dinner for two weeks now, looked back at him with a smile and asked, "Would you share a Christmas dinner with me, Ross? I have a smoked ham and a few potatoes, and just enough apples left to make up a pie. We've gone through a lot together here, and it would make me very happy to have you with me on that day."

Alexandra could see that he was struggling within himself, that he had not wanted to spend any more time with her than he had to. "Please, Ross," she continued. "I don't know all that you're thinking and feeling right now, but try to understand what this is like for me. I had surrendered so completely to the idea of becoming your wife and going wherever you chose to go that the thought of not being by your side the rest of my life is hard to bear. And I won't pretend it will be easy shaping a new life for myself without you. You see, I had come to this funny place of knowing that with you the sun rose and set." She didn't cry, though her throat ached. She wanted him to hear her heart with no distractions. He watched her intently, an arrested expression on his face. And for a moment, just a moment, the guard dropped from his eyes and she saw his love for her reflected there.

It took every ounce of her strength to keep from running to him. "I guess what I'm asking is that you give me Christmas Day and Mrs. McCormick's party. After that, if you're still of a mind to be leaving, I'll wish you well."

Alexandra felt the distance between them disappear for a brief moment. Silent thoughts leapt through the air—of love, of desire, of need. Did he lift his hand toward her slightly? She wasn't sure. When he spoke, the rich timbre of his voice surrounded her heart, as it always did, "I suppose I owe you at least that much. I'm sorry for all of this, Alexandra. Christmas dinner and New Year's, if that's what you want."

Alexandra took a deep breath and nodded. "Thank you," she said in a whisper. She still knew a overpowering urge to cast herself on his chest, and to feel his

303

arms holding her tight as he had done so often before. She wanted to tease him and make him laugh, she wanted to feel his lips pressed against her own. But she couldn't. Not yet, anyway. Maybe never again.

Willing her feet to move, even though her heart commanded her to stay, Alexandra finally turned on her heel, covering her head with the warm shawl, and left the mill house.

She headed back up the hill toward the camp, and just as she topped the short rise, she stopped suddenly. Hitched to the porch railing was an unfamiliar horse and peering into the window of her house was a man she didn't recognize.

Chapter Thirty-six

Alexandra slid her way back down the icy hill toward the stamp mill, her heart racing. It had been several weeks since Crackshot and Ross were almost killed by the dynamite explosion, but the sight of a stranger in camp somehow brought the possibility rushing to the forefront of her mind that someone might still be after the Alexandra. Now that the miners were gone, they were truly a vulnerable outfit again.

"Ross," she cried, throwing the door wide and trying to catch her breath. "I know it's probably silly of me, but there's a man at my cabin who I don't recognize. I thought maybe you ought to come up and see who it is. I know that the vein played out, but do you suppose anyone would still be trying to claim-jump our mine?"

"I don't know," Ross responded, moving quickly. "Stay out of sight, though. After all, whoever tried to kill you, me, and Crackshot did it before we brought in the deep-rock miners. I suppose it's likely they've not given up yet, though I still can't imagine why."

He led the way back up the hill, crouching low.

But when the cabin came into view, he stood upright and breathed deeply. "You can relax," he said. "It's only Deputy Barnes."

Alexandra poured the deputy another cup of coffee, surprised at how much he perspired as he wiped his face for the third time with his red kerchief. She remembered him now, from having been introduced to him more than a month ago.

Sipping the coffee, he said, "I was sorry to hear that your mine played out. Seems awful funny after all the trouble you've had. Makes you wonder, doesn't it?"

"I felt real bad about having to let the miners go," Ross said. "They sure know their business. Did you ever see a pair of them double-jacking? Fast, accurate. And the strength of their arms! I wouldn't want to tangle with one of them in a beer-hall fight."

Barnes grunted. "Too clannish for my taste," he said, grimacing as he swirled his coffee around in his cup. He sat next to Ross at the table, chatting in a relaxed, friendly way. His kerchief, however, was not far from his hand, and he wiped his upper lip and took another sip of coffee.

Alexandra offered him a doughnut, but he refused, giving his stomach a pat and saying that if he didn't start being careful he'd be the size of grizzly pretty soon. He glanced about the cabin and complimented Alexandra on how nice everything looked, adding, "Mrs. McCormick told me she'd given you some of her things. She's sure a fine woman. You folks going out to her house for New Year's?" When Alexandra said she wouldn't miss it,

306

he said, "Well, that's just fine. I'll be playing my fiddle most of the night. I sure hope you like to dance."

Alexandra sat down at the table across from Ross. "I haven't danced in so long," she said wistfully. "I can hardly wait. How 'bout you, Ross?"

He smiled at her. "With both my left feet, I surely do! I'm not clever with my steps, but I'll be happy to swing you about the room a couple of times. Virginia reel's my favorite."

"It is fun, isn't? Sliding across the floor, whirling around. I'm excited just thinking about it."

"Better come hungry, too," Barnes said, setting his cup on the table and rising to his feet." Sarah McCormick is one of the finest cooks in the territory and she always provides food like she was baking for a regiment." He moved to the window and gazed out at the camp. "This is sure a lovely spot," he said. "Is this meadow fit for grazing in the spring and summer?"

"Into the fall right up until it snows," Ross responded.

The deputy sighed, "You know, if you folks are ever of a mind to sell this place, I'd be interested in buying you out. I'm getting too old for my job, and for the past few years I've been hankering to do a little prospecting myself." He turned back to the table and with a broad smile and said, "Except that I refuse to own a mule! There isn't a more infuriating animal on God's earth. I had one once, when I first came west. Every morning I'd wake up to find he'd wandered off. I'd try to get near him, and he'd look at me with one big eye, grazing away and just waiting for me to get within four feet of him, then he'd trot off a few feet more. It took me half a day to catch him the last time I went after him. I was so mad, why I just up and shot him."

"You what?" Alexandra cried, a little startled, wondering whether to believe him or not.

"He was going lame anyway," Barnes explained, wiping his forehead. "And I just wasn't going to put up with his antics anymore. Say, does Crackshot live in the tent yonder?" He jerked his hand backward, toward the camp.

Ross nodded, and when Barnes sat back down and took another sip of his coffee, he asked the deputy if Goodwin had made any progress on the Carver murders.

Barnes's eyes shifted away from Ross, letting his gaze rest on the snow-covered camp beyond the cabin. He shook his head in disbelief. "Justice is a strange thing," he murmured. "It comes at a man whether he's clever or not, I suppose." He fell silent for a moment, and Alexandra had the strangest feeling about Louis Barnes, that something was eating at him, but what? The deputy gave himself a shake and continued. "You see, the sheriff had it figured that a man by the name of Black, who took over the Widow Ferguson's store, had been behind the murders, that he'd bought her and her kids out, killing them all afterward to get his money back. It was never thought that he actually committed the crime, but that he hired some outlaws to do his work for him. Goodwin suspected that a band of Mexican desperadoes had done the killing. They're a mean bunch, and have a roost a few miles from Carver. But there wasn't any proof at all. Then a week ago, Black himself got killed and the rumor is that he took advantage of one of the Mexican's sisters—I beg your pardon, Mrs. Bradshaw, for speaking of in-delicate matters — and got his throat slit because of it. I don't think we'll ever know what happened, but when I was down there a few days ago, it seemed the general opinion of the few decent folks in town that justice had been served."

Alexandra felt her mind grow white and cloudy. She blinked several times at Barnes and finally said, "Did you say someone cut his throat?"

"I'm sorry, ma'am!" Barnes cried. "I can see that I've upset you. I oughtn't to be talkin' of such things anyway."

"It's all right," Alexandra said, staring into her coffee cup. Ordinarily, it didn't bother her much to have the hard truth spelled out for her, but in this case, she had been struck by the fact that Mr. Black had been murdered in the same way her father had.

"How could these men be so cruel?" Alexandra asked, looking up at Barnes. "To kill so easily, as though the lives they assaulted were worthless." She smoothed her hair and took a deep breath to clear her mind.

"Who's to figure," Barnes responded. His face looked pale, and he again had to mop his face with his red bandana. Alexandra had begun to wonder if he was ill and asked if he was suffering from a fever. He laughed nervously, saying that he hadn't been sick a day in the past five years, but that he thought maybe the cabin was a little warm for him. "I should be pushing on anyway," he added. "I want to get back to Prescott before sundown."

He stood up and settled his hat on his head. He was about to walk out when he seemed to recall himself. "I almost forgot," he cried. "I meant to ask if

309

you folks have had any more trouble. Nobody comin' in here with guns a-blazin'?"

Ross rose to open the door for him and shook his head. "We haven't had so much as a leaf stir."

"I never thought it made the least bit of sense," Barnes said. "I mean the attacks on you and Crackshot and Mrs. Bradshaw here. Why would anyone go to such lengths when the mine hasn't really proved itself? If anything, I would've expected trouble down at Powell's place. Why, he's been takin' more gold out of the streambed on his claim than I'm sure either you or Wingfield ever took out of the Alexandra. If he weren't a gambler, I expect he'd have a tidy sum in the bank by now." He shrugged, "Who's to figure."

Chapter Thirty-seven

"I don't think there's a worse smell than burnt potatoes!" Alexandra cried, staring at the cast-iron pot smoking miserably on the stove. "I've ruined them!"

Ross was seated by the potbellied stove in one of the dining chairs, a booted foot slung atop his knee and a cup of coffee in hand. "I never cared much for potatoes anyway," he said cheerfully.

Alexandra looked back at him over her shoulder and smiled. "I know you're just being nice! And if you'll remember, I've seen you gobble up my fried potatoes and even smack your lips afterward. Thanks anyway." She wondered if he had noticed she had worn her hair free and loose about her shoulders today. It wasn't so very long ago he had torn her braid apart and fluffed her hair about her face and then had kissed her! She hoped very much that the same memory would strike Ross now. In addition, underneath her pale-green gingham dress, she wore her corset cinched up so tight she could hardly breathe. But it would be worth it if Ross was again attracted to her small waist, like he had been when they had first met. For the past three hours, she had been hoping that when he saw her, he would feel inclined to see if his hands were still able to encircle her waist.

"Do you want some more coffee?" she asked, setting the pot of burnt potatoes on the back of the stove and covering it to keep the smell from permeating the small cabin. She wondered if any of her thoughts showed on her face.

"No, thank you," he said.

For the next few minutes, Alexandra concerned herself strictly with arranging her Christmas dinner on the dining table. Among the many things Mrs. McCormick had given her, there was a lovely white linen cloth that must have been an heirloom. She had already decided that no matter what happened, she would return the tablecloth to her. Surely one of her daughters ought to have it. But for now, she was thrilled to be serving Ross her dinner on the crisp, smooth fabric.

When all was ready, she asked Ross to come to the table. He politely helped her sit down and took his chair across from her, his back to the door. With great pleasure, she watched him take stock of the meal laid out before him, a smile of appreciation spreading over his features. Alexandra was pleased, as well. In the middle of winter, especially in so remote a frontier town as Prescott, a variety of foods were hard to come by. And even if you could find them, they were usually too expensive to buy. As it was, she thought she had done quite well. She might have burnt the potatoes, but she had sliced up a wonderfully smoky ham, prepared a heap of golden biscuits, and set out a bowl of Mrs. McCormick's delicious canned peaches.

She was about to pass the platter of ham to Ross

when he stopped her by saying, "One of the few memories I have of my father was of him sitting at a dinner like this and offering up a blessing. Would you mind if I did the same? You know I'm not a pious man, but right now I find myself immensely grateful—to be alive, to be here with you, to be enjoying such a nice Christmas when I had expected to be knee-deep in snow in the high country by now."

It wasn't that Alexandra was stunned by his request, it was more that she was deeply moved. "I'd be honored," she responded quietly. When he folded his hands over his plate and bowed his head, she did the same.

Alexandra scarcely heard what he said. Her throat had closed up tight and tears plopped on her lap. She loved Ross Halleck so much, and this moment made him all the more dear to her. He just couldn't leave her now, he just couldn't!

After a short time, she heard him call her name. She hadn't realized he had finished his blessing, but it hardly mattered, for she couldn't stop the tears from rolling down her cheeks.

"Alexandra!" he cried. "What's the matter? Did I say something wrong?"

She was on her feet quickly, pushing her chair backward and whirling away from the table. She grabbed her apron from off the long work table in the kitchen and pressed it to her face. "I'm sorry. I'm sorry," she mumbled, holding back a trail of sobs. Before she even realized he had risen from his seat, Alexandra felt Ross's hands on her arms. "Hush, now," he whispered, his breath warm on her hair. "Didn't I say a proper prayer? I know I'm not much in practice these days, but I spoke from my heart."

She knew he was just teasing and a chuckle escaped her, despite the fact that tears still flowed from her eyes. "I'm sure you did just fine," she responded. "The truth is, I didn't hear a word of it. All I could think about was all the special dinners you and I would never have together."

She felt his hands grip her arms as he leaned his head into hers, kissing her hair. Alexandra felt as if her heart was about to break. She couldn't keep her deepest thoughts to herself any longer. Turning around quickly, she slipped her arms about his back and leaned her head on his shoulder. "Please don't leave me," she whispered, holding him tight. "I can't bear the thought of living without you. I can't make sense of what I would do if you went off to Wyoming without me."

Ross buried his face in her sweet-smelling hair. Her words, the feel of her body in his arms, the desperation in her voice, all were like a knife cutting right through him. He held her fast, wishing that time would come to a halt so that they might remain together forever. A minute passed, and then another. He didn't say anything, but kept her close, his thoughts caught up in a whirlwind of divided feelings. He longed to tell her they'd never be apart again, as long as he lived. But then the memory of Mrs. Horn's white face, her eyes closed in death, would start haunting the edges of his mind. Panic would race through him, the way he had felt striving against the snowstorm and not being able to get the doctor back to his camp in time.

That was the whole of the trouble anyway. *His camp*. His responsibility. Alexandra might have taunted him about seeing into the future, but that was exactly what had happened to him. John and Miriam Horn had shown him the future, and he wouldn't have it, he couldn't live with it.

He felt Alexandra move in his arms. She lifted her face to his, and he made the awful mistake of looking into her clear blue eyes. They were red-rimmed and soaked with tears, but all he saw was her love for him, deep and resolved. He stroked her hair, his gaze locked into hers. Desire to possess her rose in a strong wave within him. Her lips were parted and waiting. Her eyes pleaded with him. Her hair felt wondrous between his fingers, her body warm and supple against his own. He wanted her.

Knowing he shouldn't, he leaned down to her slowly, his mind warning him it was mistake. He heard her breathe a sigh as his lips touched hers. They were soft and still wet from her tears, but tasted of heaven. She slipped her arm about his neck, lacing her fingers into his hair. Her touch burned him, begging something from him he could no longer give her. He kissed her hard, trying to warn her away, at the same time knowing she would be misled by his desire for her. Frustration overlapped his love for her and he drove his tongue deep into her mouth, as he had done so many times before. A moan escaped her throat. She tugged at his hair, returning his kiss fiercely. Someday she would understand how impossible it was.

"Take me to bed," she breathed, drifting her lips over his and touching her tongue gently to his mouth.

Ross felt like snow and fire had met in his mind, both hurting him. He pulled away from her, holding her back with his hands on her arms. "I can't," he

315

said, not daring to look at her. His gaze was fixed instead to the pattern of the green gingham checks on her gown. "I want to, you know that. But it would be a terrible thing to do."

Alexandra leaned toward him, struggling against the pressure of his arms as he held her at a distance. "Just once, before you leave?" she asked quietly. "Just once? Could there be any harm in that?"

He released her entirely. "Every harm, I'm afraid," he said.

Alexandra looked into quiet gray eyes and saw that his stubbornness had won the day. She hadn't meant to press the issue between them so hard. She thought it likely she'd made a mistake in pleading with him, in letting her heart be known to him so clearly. But what was done, was done.

At least her eyes were dry now, and though her chest felt heavy and burdened, she didn't hesitate to return to the table with him.

Conversation faltered at first, but Ross made a valiant effort to ease the tensions between them, speaking at length of his childhood, of the years spent droving alongside his pa when he was only a boy of ten. "Sometimes I think I was born on a horse," he said with a warm smile. "Pa used to say that when he was a kid he could remember only two weeks out of his life when he wasn't riding, and that was when he had the measles."

Alexandra watched the light in the cabin change, as the sun dipped behind the hills. She rose from the table, still listening to Ross, who was now describing the Texas Panhandle to her, and went to light a lamp. Every now and again she'd ask a question, but mostly he seemed inclined to ramble, and she let him. She had her own reasons. She wanted to memorize the sound of his voice and carry it with her wherever she went. He'd never know that, of course, and, to be quite honest, she didn't have all that much interest in exactly where the Charlie Goodnight Trail started and ended, but as far as she was concerned, he could talk all night if he wanted to.

When dinner was finally over, and Ross left the cabin to return to his tent, Alexandra washed up the dishes, thinking that never in her life had she felt so anxious. If she were to lose Ross now, she didn't know what she would do.

After she dried the last plate and put it away in the cupboard by the potbellied stove, she went into the bedroom. There, she opened the cupboard that housed her dresses and ran her hand the length of the green silk gown she would wear to Mrs. McCormick's party. It was almost finished and she was sure Ross would like it. But would it be enough to bring him around?

Chapter Thirty-eight

On the day before New Year's, Alexandra began the trek into Prescott on horseback, with Ross leading the way. Her emerald-green dress was tucked into a carpetbag slung over the pommel of her saddle and her spirits were lighter than they had been in over a week. She was looking forward to Mrs. McCormick's party, where she could pick up her skirts, dance for hours on end, and forget some of her troubles.

The air was clear, the sun bright, and the trail easier to travel than she had expected. A lot of the snow from the previous storm had melted throughout the warm days following Christmas.

Alexandra had hardly spoken to Ross since the special dinner they had shared together. She still served him meals, but as each day passed by, he seemed to grow more and more distant. He remained friendly, of course, but in every respect, he was a man bent on following his own path.

She had long since decided that whatever happened she would stay on at the mine, along with Cecilia and Crackshot, for a few more weeks — months if her funds held out. She wasn't as convinced as

Ross seemed to be that the Alexandra was a fool's dream. Even if it was, she wanted to stay and find out for herself whether or not the venture was hopeless. She was well provisioned with food, and still had a few dollars of her own left. Deputy Barnes's offer on the mine also made her think she could sell her interest in the Alexandra if she needed to.

As she thought about the mine, she remembered the conversation she and Ross had had with Barnes a few days before Christmas. She didn't have a high opinion of the deputy, for he appeared nervous and not real clever, but he had seemed sincerely interested in their welfare. Something that he had said, however, had given her an idea about her papa's mine and perhaps even a motive for those who had persisted over the past year in trying to take the Alexandra.

Just beyond the Dells, she broached the subject with Ross. "Do you remember when Deputy Barnes was here the other day and spoke of Lloyd Powell's claim?"

Ross glanced over at her and nodded, then shifted his gaze to the trail in front of him.

"I remember from Papa's letters, he said more than once that placer gold, especially if it's found in a stream, or a streambed, was often a run-off from the mother lode."

Ross nodded. "That's right, by all that I've heard. I think it's one reason a boom town springs up in the first place. A prospector finds a nugget or two in a likely stream, and the next minute the hills are crawling with hopeful argonauts all out to find a bonanza."

"I was surprised to hear that Powell had been so

successful at his digs. But it's all placer gold, isn't it?"

Ross nodded again. "Yes. He doesn't have any hard-rock mining going on there. He's just been tearing at the banks of the streambed for a long time."

"Well, Powell's camp is just downstream from the Alexandra. Isn't it possible that his gold has come from our mine, that we may be sitting on the mother lode?"

Ross looked at her, smiling this time. "Now you sound like Sam Wingfield's daughter."

"It's logical, though, isn't it?" Alexandra returned. "And doesn't it also seem possible that Powell, or someone in his camp, found a vein of gold worth killing for on our claim and has been trying to jump it ever since, say, beginning with my father's murder?" She found her heart beating fast. These thoughts had been safely rolling about in her mind for the past few days, so much so that she had become comfortable with them. But speaking her ideas aloud seemed to give them a shape they hadn't had before, a deadly shape.

For a long time Ross didn't speak, but Alexandra could see he was thinking about what she had said, as much by the slight drop of his head as by the tense frown on his face. When his horse began to slow down, she knew he was completely distracted. But what was he thinking?

When they were nearing the outskirts of Prescott and Ross still hadn't addressed her, she drew her horse closer to him and gave his jacket a tug. "So tell me what you think?" she asked.

Ross straightened his shoulders and resettled his black hat on his head. "You may be right," he said at last. "It's an awful lot of conjecture, but it makes sense. I hadn't given any thought to the size of Powell's earnings from his mining claim until you mentioned it just now — and he's right down the stream from us. I think while I'm in town, I'll have a talk with Goodwin. Something about Lloyd Powell has always troubled me."

A half hour later, Alexandra was standing in the lobby of the hotel and signing her name to the guest register. Ross had just left to speak with the sheriff when a voice across the room called to her.

"Alexandra?"

The pen froze in her hand as she turned around and met the critical brown eyes of William Bradshaw. She spoke the very first words that came to mind. "What are you doing in Arizona?" Not having had time to guard her tongue properly, she realized her words and her tone of voice must have sounded horribly impolite. "I mean, I never expected to see you here in Prescott," she amended. "How long have you been in town?"

"I arrived yesterday afternoon at four o'clock," he responded, his speech as clipped and precise as she remembered it. He was dressed in a brown suit with a cutaway jacket, his hair was slicked down and trimmed neatly, along with his muttonchop whiskers, and his fine leather shoes were spattered from the rutted, muddy streets. He was a tall man, though not quite as tall as Ross, and carried himself with pride. To most women, he was considered a handsome man. To Alexandra he was only her betrothed, a man who could hardly bear the thought of kissing her.

She felt defensive with him, and said, "I am in town only for a day or two myself. I'm living out at Papa's mine and I intend to stay there until I am satisfied one way or the other as to the worth of the claim. I don't know when I'll be leaving for good—if ever."

Already, she could see he disapproved of her. His lips seemed to thin as he watched her, and his eyes shifted about nervously. "You're living in a mining camp?" he asked, his brows snapping together.

She felt angry suddenly, that after traveling all this distance, ostensibly to see her and to speak with her, his reaction to their first exchange of conversation was to cast her in the wrong. Lifting her chin slightly, she said, "I don't know why you're here, William. In fact, I'm astonished you dared journey this far. I suppose you've come in response to my letter asking about Papa's death, but I want you to know something straight out, before we go any further. The main reason I left Independence when I did was because I didn't want to be married to your pretty constant disapproval of me." She was breathless by the time she finished speaking, her heart beating fast against her ribs, her knees trembling. She didn't realize how upset she had been about William's treatment of her until the words were out and hanging harshly between them.

She was stunned, however, by the effect this speech had on her betrothed. He seemed to crumple up a little, his face pinching into a frown of regret, his eyes looking almost sad. "I'm sorry," he said at once. "I didn't mean to make you feel uncomfortable. As a matter of fact, I've had a long time to think about

322

you, about us. I remember how you looked that time you—you kissed me and I rebuked you. I've never forgotten the horror in your eyes. I promised myself I would do better, but almost before I could begin, you were gone. Just now, though, thinking of you out at some dirty mining camp, without all the finer things you are used to, having to speak to strangers who have come from God knows where! Honestly, I couldn't bear the thought of it. Not for you, Alexandra. Not for the woman I—I love, and still hope to marry."

Alexandra felt as though a bracing wind had just blown off the mountains and nearly knocked her over. She was overwhelmed by the change in the man before her. "Why, William!" she cried, taking several steps toward him. "I've never seen you so—so humble. It becomes you."

He lifted his hand toward her and whispered her name. "Can you find it in your heart to forgive me?" he asked. "Will you let me try again? I can't promise that I'll always remember to be more accommodating and understanding. My upbringing was quite strict and I do have a serious philosophy about life."

Alexandra felt her heart soften toward him in a way it never had before. She came up to him, standing close and taking his hand in her own. "I know you're a good man, a man of honor with clear boundaries drawn all about you. But tell me truthfully, William, do you really think I'm the wife for you. I'd always be doing or saying something that sets your nerves on fire, like living in a mining camp, or kissing you when you didn't think it was proper."

"You don't believe me, do you?" he asked, his eyes filled with panic. "Doesn't my coming here tell you how sincere I am? Well, maybe this will!" And before Alexandra knew what he meant to do, she found herself caught up in an awkward embrace, William's lips pressed firmly against her own.

She had only one difficulty in the situation—to keep from laughing and hurting William's pride.

When Ross was unable to track down Sheriff Goodwin, he made his way back to the hotel. He was turning the matter of Lloyd Powell over and over in his mind. It all fit, but a little too neatly for his taste. There wasn't a thing he could do about it, though, until he could speak with the sheriff and see if he had learned anything new that might make better sense of everything.

His boots hit the boardwalk in front of the hotel and his thoughts drifted, as they always did, back to Alexandra. She would never know how difficult it was for him to be in her company and to know that in just a few days they would part forever. At least a dozen times during the morning alone, he had wanted to slip off his horse, pull her down from her saddle, and just kiss her, kiss her until she begged for more. At the same time, he was still convinced he could never take her, or any woman, with him to Wyoming. One thing he intended to do as soon as possible was to put her on a stage back to Missouri, before he left Prescott himself. He wouldn't be easy in his mind until he was sure she would be safe and cared for.

Ross opened the door of the hotel with all these intentions, feelings, and concerns spinning about in his brain. He thought this might be a good time to discuss with Alexandra the idea of her returning to Missouri immediately when he found her locked in a tight embrace with a man dressed like an eastern dude. He reacted instinctively, without one clear thought presenting itself in his head. He grabbed the stranger by the shoulder, pulled him quickly away from Alexandra, spun him around, and caught him square on the chin with his fist.

Chapter Thirty-nine

Several hours later, when the sun was making a steady descent over the tall ponderosa pines to the west of Prescott, Alexandra was busy tying up her stays. She was excited and nervous, and completely uncertain of what the evening would bring her. She was hoping Ross would somehow change his mind about leaving without her. In the depths of her womanly heart, she knew tonight would decide her fate. She cringed inwardly at the thought of a New Year's Eve party holding such power over her future happiness. And it was not as though she had some intricate, careful plan worked out. She didn't. But this was her last night with Ross before he catapulted them both, or at least tried to, into different parts of the country.

Her fingers were almost useless, as she unlaced the stays for the third time and tried again. She took deep breaths in hopes of calming her spirits, but with little success. She looked in the mirror, into anxious blue eyes, and began talking to herself in a quiet voice. She dwelled on all that she had learned since coming to Arizona, how she really couldn't count on each day or each hour to give her everything she wanted. And in the same way she surely couldn't persuade Ross Halleck to marry her and take her to Wyoming if he was dead set against it. Hard lessons, but true.

She closed her eyes and tried to get peaceful with her thoughts, but she couldn't repress her panicky excitement, not completely, anyway. Opening her eyes, she scrutinized her hair, hoping at least that Ross would be taken with her efforts. She had pulled her long red locks high atop her head, threading a green velvet ribbon through her curls and tying it in a bow behind her ear. She had been able to arrange her rebellious curls like she had wanted—they danced all over her head and trailed partway down her back. With her stays finally in place, she quickly donned her dress of emerald silk. It was a bold gown, cut low at the bodice and nipped tightly in at the waist, then drawn away from her hips and caught up in a bow behind her. Around her neck she wore her mother's cameo.

Finally, she was able to smile. She was very pleased with how she looked and she had only now to wait for Ross.

Because she was so nervous, she began pacing the hardwood floor, crossing the small room from door to window. On one of her rounds, she looked out over the street, and among a steady flow of men who had come to Prescott from all over the county in order to celebrate the New Year on Whiskey Row, she saw William standing on a corner, looking like a lost puppy. She sighed and turned away from the window.

After Ross had hit him, laying a dark bruise on his chin, Alexandra had immediately separated the two men. Once their identities were known to each other, they both stood before her, still bristling, the air alive with tension. If anything had given her hope that Ross might yet change his mind, however, it was the wild expression on his face after his fist nearly broke Wil-

327

liam's jaw.

Even so, she had gotten rid of him as fast as she could, since she wanted to settle her affairs with William. She took William into the restaurant of the hotel and there he argued bitterly with her over the choices she was making, about staying in Arizona, for the rest of her life, perhaps, about rejecting him as a husband and thereby forfeiting her rightful inheritance.

"It's not such a difficult thing to give up," she had said quietly. "It was never really mine anyway. Besides, it goes to an orphanage, doesn't it?" When he nodded, she said, "Then I won't think about it again. I feel like a lot of good will come of it, more than I'm sure my uncle ever expected."

After another half hour of strenuous arguments, William was finally worn out. "You're a strange girl, Alexandra," he said at last. He looked weary from his travels and from fighting her obstinacy about staying behind. He touched his jaw gingerly, shaking his head. "This is such a wild place. How can you live like this?"

Alexandra thought for a minute, wondering the same thing herself, especially because she had appreciated the comfort and security of her life in Missouri. "I think there was born in me a Western woman fit for life in the West. I didn't think so a year or two ago, but since I've been out here, I've seen a side to myself that I wouldn't have believed existed. I've even been able to forgive my father for carting us from one boom town to the next, mostly because I've come to understand that I'm his daughter, I'm very much like him. And you, William, why you look like someone I would meet in New York City, where everything has already been mapped out and planned carefully. That's why I can't marry you. We're just too different. After all, I was born in the West and I expect I'll die here."

He had been reconciled to her decision after that, and spent the remainder of his time with her, talking about his trip to Dodge City. "I spent two days interviewing as many storekeepers and bartenders as I could find who had seen your father just before he died. The sheriff didn't know very much and I think there's so much trouble of a similar nature in that lawless town that nobody pays much heed to a saddlebum or a prospector losing his life now and then. Anyway, what I learned was this: your father was murdered, as you have said, and his throat was cut. According to at least two sources, however, several Mexican bandidos had been drinking pretty heavily in the same saloon as your father. One of them was a half-breed, part Apache, and had a reputation for being skilled with a knife. They all disappeared from Dodge City the night Sam died, and have not been seen since."

Alexandra had listened to his recounting of her father's death with a mouth that grew as dry as the desert air. She still felt the horror of his murder whenever it was discussed, as though it had happened just the day before. She thanked him for taking so much trouble to find out what he could, then asked him to relay the same information to Sheriff Goodwin, if he had the time. He said he would be only too happy to. He did not stay chatting with her much longer, and in a few minutes rose to say good-bye. Alexandra had then startled him by rising to her feet, throwing her arms around him, and hugging him tight.

She smiled at the memory, since he had actually returned her embrace, before leaving the dining room on his familiar, brisk tread. She knew in her heart she'd never see him, or Missouri, again.

Ross stood outside Alexandra's room, preparing to knock, but holding back. He had already admitted to himself that this would be one of the toughest evenings of his life and that if he had a grain of sense, he would head out of town right this minute.

When he had found Alexandra in the arms of William Bradshaw, he had experienced a rage of jealousy so strong, so unexpected, that he was still astonished by it. For a long moment, he had wanted to kill Bradshaw. Even now, the thought of another man touching, kissing, loving Alexandra was almost more than he could bear! He wanted her, and he didn't want another man so much as looking cross-eyed at her.

And yet, he had to let her go. But how? Steeling himself to a night of misery, he knocked on the door. He waited, holding his breath, hoping she had grown that wart on her nose she had once spoken of, or something equally as unsightly. Unfortunately, as she opened the door, he could see right away that nothing of a helpfully disfiguring nature had sprung up to mar her features.

If a heart could stop beating, his surely did as his gaze drifted over the cloud of red hair framing her lovely face, to the creamy shoulders that led his eye to the swell of breasts visible just above the neckline of her gown, to the small waist that had from the first been his downfall, to the lovely folds of her skirts that were pulled back in a bustle behind her, enhancing the elegant lines of her hips and legs. He felt dizzy just looking at her, and knew an impulse to push her back into the room, close the door behind him, and take her in his arms.

Alexandra saw the hungry look in his eyes and the way his lips parted slightly as he took in every inch of her dress. She would have cried with exultation had his evident desire for her not struck a resonant chord in her own heart and set it to pounding hard. He was

330

dressed in a new black suit, with a starched white shirt and narrow black ribbon tie. His thick hair had been trimmed and brushed to a shine. He looked more handsome than she remembered, if that was possible. "How nice you look," she said. "So handsome and citified." She wanted to say more, but her thoughts seemed to jump all over each other, rushing together and choking her mind. She wanted him to kiss her so badly that her knees had started trembling. "Do you want to come in for a minute?" she whispered. "Just a minute or two?" She took a step backward and then another, his gaze following her. He appeared to lean forward, as if he meant to enter her room, then caught himself.

"No," he said abruptly, jerking his gaze from her and turning away. He didn't look at her as he said, "We should go now. I've—I've got the carriage out front waiting for us. I think you'll be comfortable, though you might want to bring a shawl. It's crisp outside."

Alexandra felt her breath shudder in her chest as she turned around to fetch a warm wool cape and a blanket for her legs. The moment had passed, but she knew Ross had come within an inch of entering her room and taking her in his arms. Her heart felt tight with excitement. Maybe something would happen tonight to move him from his stubbornness. He was vulnerable this evening, and regardless of whether he wished for it or not, she meant to take advantage of him. "Let's go, then," she said cheerfully, passing by him as she entered the hall.

The ride out to Mrs. McCormick's ranch was a delight. The sky was clear and stars sparkled in the moonless night sky. They were soon part of a caravan of travelers, a dozen or more couples or families, all heading out to the New Year's Eve party. Each had at least one lantern mounted on their wagon or carriage, and the winking of lights as the road dipped and rose in turns was almost as pretty as the starry sky.

As she slipped her arm through Ross's, Alexandra was deeply content and said so. He looked down at her in surprise, but didn't seem to mind her touch too much. The tension between them eased up after that and they were once again chatting like old friends, laughing and teasing each other as they had in the past.

When they were within a half mile of Mrs. McCormick's ranch, Alexandra gave Ross's arm a squeeze and, looking up into his face, said, "I'm going to miss you so much, Ross." She felt him stiffen slightly, and decided it was time she told him not only that she had no intention of returning to Missouri but that she meant to stay on at the mine. If he still planned to leave her by the time the party had played itself out, she wanted his mind to have a firm picture of her still living in the cabin, the place where he had first loved her.

"You can't," he cried, sounding insulted. "That's not what I want for you and it's not the place for you!"

"I don't see why not," she responded kindly. "I know you have other ideas for me, but . . ." She paused, a spark of pure deviltry entering her breast. Removing her arm from about his and folding her hands demurely on her lap, she responded primly, "I would only permit my *husband* to dictate where I can and cannot live."

When he uttered a grunt of disgust, she resumed her normal voice and demeanor. "I like this town so much," she said. "When I've had enough of our mine, I think I'll settle here. I'll find me a good man for a husband and I don't think I'll lack for suitors, do you, Ross? Why, the proportion of men to women here is

332

remarkable! Not that just any man will do—"

"Will you stop with your foolish prattle!" he cried. "I've never heard such nonsense. You're going back to Missouri like we discussed."

"So you think I should marry William?" she queried innocently, knowing that he was likely to fire up at the mention of her betrothed's name.

He was silent for a long, tense moment. Alexandra stole a glance at him, and could see by the dim glow of the lantern on his face that he was struggling within himself. She was very disappointed with his answer when he said, "I suppose it would be a wise and sensible marriage for you."

She slipped her arm back through his and leaned her head against his shoulder. Looking up at his profile, her hair still snuggled into his coat, she asked, "But do you think William could make me as happy as you have?"

She heard him release a troubled sigh. "I think in time he could. He seems to be a good man, forthright and honest."

"You may be right," she responded quietly. "Only I'd have to teach him how to kiss. Why, he's hardly a poorly lit oil lamp when it comes to kissing. But you—! Oh, Ross," she cooed, feeling mischievous all the way to her toes. "You're a prairie fire!"

Chapter Forty

By the time midnight arrived, Ross felt as if he had been battered enough to last him a year. Alexandra not only had been taunting him about staying on alone at the cabin, but she absolutely refused to listen to reason. As for marrying William Bradshaw, he realized by the time they reached the ranch that she had no intention of doing so. He knew her well enough to be convinced she had made up her mind and would not be surprised if William returned to Missouri alone within the next couple of days.

The worst of it was, there was a part of his heart that was so doggoned pleased about it, that in all honesty, his efforts to persuade her to head back to Missouri had been nothing short of paltry.

In addition, however, to steadfastly refusing to return to Independence, Alexandra had strolled up to him not less than a dozen times during the course of the evening thus far, and demanded to know his opinion about this gentleman or that. She would ask him, her blue eyes wide with false innocence, whether he thought the officer standing next to Mrs. McCormick's daughter would be a kind husband, or whether one of the local rancher's sons was old

334

enough to take on a wife. "I know he's young," she chirped happily, "but he's so strong. Look at the size of his chest and those arms! He's certainly fit enough to take care of a woman." He had about wrung her neck for that one, but she had tripped away so quickly that he had been unable to do more than glare at her retreating back. Of course, watching her walk had been a sore trial in itself, since the bustle swayed so interestingly and enhanced the narrow lines of her small, exquisite, seductive waist.

He had been doing his share of dancing, but Alexandra had outdone him completely. Her feet hadn't rested once, and anyone who asked for a dance was smiled upon and given a gracious *yes!* When he danced, though, his eyes always strayed toward whichever part of the room she was dominating, and when he stood back to support one of the walls, he had to watch her flying down the room, laughing, her red curls bouncing as fast as her feet.

He had only partnered her once himself, since she was in great demand, and had found himself whirling her about the room for the waltz. He had tried to use the time to reassert his arguments about why she ought to return to Missouri, but she had begged him not to spoil her one chance to have him in her arms again. How could he have pressed home his point after that, especially when she looked up at him with such a warm, affectionate smile on her face.

He was standing now on the far side of the dining table, a glass of whiskey in his hand. He could feel a fuzziness invading the edges of his mind, and he knew he'd already had a bit too much, to drink. Not that he cared right now, since Alexandra was standing close to one of the officers from Fort Whipple and smiling up into his face. The poor lieutenant was clearly besotted, his face flushed with admiration. Ross felt a knife of annoyance run straight through him and he took another hefty sip from his glass.

A minute or two later, he watched Alexandra excuse herself and saunter in his direction. Lord help him, he thought. She was as pretty and bright as the stars in the sky. Maybe the strong drink had had an effect on him, but right now he felt his love for her flow from the top of his head all the way to his feet, so much so that by the time she reached his side, he couldn't keep from whispering, "If we were alone, I'd kiss you, so help me I would."

Alexandra would have been overjoyed by this remark had she not already decided he'd seen the elephant, or at least its trunk and big ears! Looking up at him, she shook her head and clucked her tongue. "You're half drunk, Ross Halleck, so I don't take that as much of a compliment, thank you kindly!"

"Drunk or not," he said, leaning toward her slightly and gazing down into her eyes, "I want to kiss you again. I will, too, just before I put you on that stage to Missouri." He smiled crookedly, seeming pleased with himself.

She recommended he drink up a pot of coffee right away, and was about to return to watch the dancers when Mrs. McCormick joined them. "So how do you folks like our doings tonight?" she asked. "Have you had enough to eat and drink? Please don't be shy. By the way, Alexandra, I've been meaning to tell you what a lovely gown that is. I'll bet half the men in this room would gobble you up given a whisker of time alone with you! Let 'em suffer, I say." She then addressed Ross. "You keepin' an

336

eye on her?"

"Tryin' to, ma'am," he responded, his words thick. "But she's a hard filly to keep up with tonight."

Alexandra glanced at Mrs. McCormick with a grin on her face, and the older woman burst out laughing. The widow then took Ross's arm and pulled him down the hall to the kitchen, with Alexandra in tow. There she plunked him down in a chair, poured a cup of coffee for him, and told him to start drinking, fast!

Alexandra watched Ross as he put the cup to his lips and obeyed his hostess's command. She felt a sudden longing to walk over to him and smooth her hand across his shoulders. Maybe she would lean down and place a kiss on his cheek afterward. Lord, how she loved him. What if she couldn't give him enough cause to stay, to marry her, to take her to Wyoming? Her heart grew heavy with just the thinking of it. Giving herself a shake, she set aside her dismal thoughts and concentrated instead on how she was going to entice him into her room tonight.

She heard Mrs. McCormick call her name and, glancing over at the widow, was surprised to see her hazel eyes misted with tears.

"What is it?" Alexandra queried. Ross looked toward her as well, his expression equally startled.

"I—" Mrs. McCormick broke off, unable to quite say what was on her mind. Taking a deep breath, she turned to address Ross. "If you don't mind, Ross, there's something I've been meaning to show Alexandra and I think this would be a good time."

He nodded. "Of course. And if you don't mind I'll just sit here in the kitchen for a while and get some of this coffee in me. My head's spinning."

337

Mrs. McCormick nodded to him with a smile as she crossed the room and patted his shoulder in a kind, loving way.

The ranch house had been built on to over the years and rambled off in several different directions. Mrs. McCormick led Alexandra through a sitting room full of guests, into a hall that took a sudden turn to the left. As they moved down the newer part of the hall, Alexandra could hear the laughter and noisy chatter of the party slowly disappear. By the time they reached the end, the house was quiet except for the hushed, distant murmurings of the guests.

Pausing outside the last room, Mrs. McCormick tapped lightly on the door, before entering on tiptoe.

Hidden within the dark shadows of the room, Alexandra could see that Lupe was asleep in a rocking chair with an infant at her breast. Starlight shone through the window, bathing a second baby, in a faint glow.

"Samantha," the widow whispered, her voice a gentle chiding as she addressed the second baby. "What are you doing up so late. You're supposed to be asleep." Samantha was sitting up in a crib and squealed when she saw Mrs. McCormick. Even at that, Lupe still remained asleep.

The baby picked up her blanket with a wobbly hand and thrust it in her mouth.

Mrs. McCormick took Samantha in her arms, holding her close. The baby continued to suckle the blanket, but leaned her head against the widow's shoulder. Rocking back and forth on each foot, Mrs. McCormick addressed Alexandra. "Come here," she whispered. "I'd like you to meet my youngest daughter. I know you can't see much in the dark like this, but all this curly hair is a fine red color." Her face seemed to contract suddenly as she placed a kiss on Samantha's head. "She looks just like her pa and I think she looks an awful lot like you."

Alexandra was already crossing the room when Mrs. McCormick spoke these last words and comprehension dawned swiftly on her. "Samantha?" she queried, the name striking her hard. Her mind flew about in a fast circle. She remembered having seen the baby the first time outside Goldwater's and how strangely the widow had acted. She thought about all the things Mrs. McCormick had given her to make the cabin comfortable when surely she had others who had a greater claim to her property. She recalled her encouragement to not let Ross go — a mother's advice and wisdom.

Alexandra touched the baby's back, and saw the little face turn toward her. She couldn't discern the features well enough to know if Samantha looked like her father or not. Even if it had been bright as daylight in the room, she still couldn't have seen her clearly since her eyes were full of tears.

"She's my sister," she stated, awestruck. "You mean I have a sister? It's impossible!" She was reaching for her, taking her gently out of Mrs. McCormick's arms, at the same time asking if she could hold her. The widow gave up the child and went in search of a kerchief for each of them.

Alexandra tried to talk to the baby, but found it increasingly difficult what with the tears that choked her throat. Samantha, however, didn't seem to mind, having discovered the cameo at Alexandra's throat, and was busy touching it and trying to pull it off her neck. Alexandra laughed, and as Mrs. McCormick dabbed at her own tears, then Alexandra's, she asked her to please remove the cameo and give it to the baby.

"She'll chew it up but good. She's teething."

"Better set it aside then," Alexandra said, still whispering and holding the baby close to her. "Oh, Sammy," she cried, more tears pouring down her cheeks. She had lost them all—her mother and father, her brothers and sisters, even her aunt and uncle—but somehow she had made her way to Prescott and found Samantha all but waiting for her.

"I didn't know if you'd understand," Mrs. McCormick said, again wiping Alexandra's tears. "We weren't married, you see. Sam kept asking me, but I was afraid. He said he would settle in one place if I agreed to become his wife, but you know what he was. If ever there had been born an argonaut, it was that man. I finally did agree, though, just before he left, only he never came back." She turned away from Alexandra and moved to stand by the window, sobs shaking her body. "I was such a fool. By then I already had Samantha growing inside me."

It was several minutes before either of them stopped crying.

Alexandra took the baby to the window, and stood next to Mrs. McCormick. Samantha was a warm comfort in her arms, a kind of soothing balm that she had not felt in years. She had been given part of her life back, and drank it in with deep breaths. Holding the baby's hand, she watched her with a feeling of wonder in her heart. Life had come full circle for her at last, and in a way so astonishing she could hardly speak.

For a long time, she held the baby close, her eyes shut as she dreamed about days and weeks to come when she would hold Samantha, play with her, talk to her. She had so many things she could tell her about her papa. Her reveries seemed to loop around and around, her heart fairly singing with joy until she heard Mrs. McCormick giggle.

Alexandra opened her eyes, startled, only to find the widow staring out into the night, a wide smile on her face.

"He left the kitchen too soon!" she cried.

"Who?" Alexandra asked, inching close to the window and peering out. Against a starlit fence and corral, Ross ambled unsteadily down the path leading to the open grazing lands. He was singing, too, in full, resonant voice, even if the words tipped sideways now and then:

> " 'When I got up in Kansas, I had a pleas-
> ant dream;
> I dreamed I was down on Trinity, down on
> that pleasant stream;
> I dreamt my true love right beside me, she
> come to go my bail;
> I woke up broken-hearted with a yearling
> by the tail.' "

Then he let out a yell that made both women laugh and finally brought Lupe out of her slumbers. The exhausted woman let loose with a string of unintelligible Spanish words, staring at both ladies with a half-dazed expression.

Alexandra and Mrs. McCormick apologized to Lupe who, sleepy-eyed, said she thought Apaches had come to steal her baby. It was some time before she stopped rocking nervously, and then not until her own infant awoke and started to cry.

Through the window, Alexandra could still hear Ross singing and decided she ought at least go after him. "Once he starts walking," she whispered, "he's apt to forget where he is. I didn't realize he'd had so much to drink."

"Well, just don't let him drive back to the hotel or you'll end up in a ditch!"

Chapter Forty-one

By the time Ross had the team hitched to the buggy, he was completely sobered up. Alexandra had found him heading out into one of Mrs. McCormick's fine pastures, and had brought him back to the kitchen where he finished drinking the rest of his coffee. Once his mind cleared, he could see she was ready to return to her hotel and that she had something on her mind.

He remembered having told Alexandra he wanted to kiss her before he put her on the stage to Missouri. He had every reason to suspect she would hold him to it, and his only difficulty now was finding a way to keep from obliging her.

But when he set the team in motion, and they were a good mile from the ranch, he was surprised to find that Alexandra, far from trying to tease a kiss from him, was quiet, almost subdued. When he asked her if anything was wrong, she told him about Samantha.

"I still can't believe it!"she cried, pulling her cape around her neck and laughing. "I have a sister! It's such a miracle, such a—" She broke off, her voice catching slightly.

He slipped an arm about her shoulder, and gave her a hug.

"I have a sister," she murmured, then buried her face in his shoulder and wept, every once in a while wiping her eyes with her kerchief. Her arm made its way across his chest, and even when the last of her tears had dried on her cheeks, still her arm remained where it was and silence surrounded them, except the rattle of the wheels on the rutted road and the sound of the horses shuffling along.

Ross found it nothing less than comforting to hold Alexandra and to be held by her. If he could enumerate the times he had felt this way during the course of his life, he didn't think he could number them on both hands. The stars still shone on the mountain land, the air was nicely crisp but the buggy warm like summer where Alexandra rested against him. He didn't want the drive to come to an end. He knew he would never be this close to her again, and he kept the pace of the horses slow, giving them a gentle slap of the reins only when they threatened to come to a complete stop.

Looking deep into the future, Ross felt burdened with what he saw — a man growing into his middle years, riding the range alone, cooking alone, sleeping alone, building a ranch — *alone*. A sense of despair so great moved over him that his heart began to feel as though it was actually sinking in his chest. If he wasn't careful, he might give in to a powerful but selfish emotion and take Alexandra to Wyoming anyway.

"Ross," Alexandra said, disturbing the unhappy bent to his thoughts. "I could stay like this forever and ever. Does life get sweeter than this, I wonder?"

"No," he whispered. "It would be impossible, I think." He heard her sigh as she gave him a hug. For the first time that night, he thought seriously about taking her to bed. He didn't even try to give consideration to whether or not it would be wrong; he knew the

344

answer to that already. Nor did he try to figure out whether it would be harder or easier to leave her afterward. All he could think about was how sweet it would feel to be as close to her as he could. Maybe then the lonely nights ahead of him wouldn't be so hard to bear.

It was silly to even think about it. He couldn't take advantage of her, knowing he meant to leave her the next day. It would only hurt her more. Once again, his mind was set on the course he felt was right for him and a measure of peace finally lifted the pain that dominated his heart.

By the time Ross had walked her to her door, Alexandra knew that the task ahead of her was formidable, if not impossible. She had only to look up at Ross as he literally marched her down the hall to see that his usual stubbornness had taken root in his mind, and he would no more kiss her now than he would set the curtains in her room on fire. What was she going to do?

She felt a kind of panic come over her. Somehow she had supposed that by now, between teasing him at the party and the sweetness of their journey from the ranch back to the hotel, he would have relented. Instead, he seemed more distant than ever.

He fit the key into the lock and with a swift turn unlocked the door.

She had to think of something or he would be gone.

He pushed the door open and let her pass. How fast her heart beat, as she slipped the wool cape from her shoulders and laid it down on the bed. He followed her, entering the room for the sole purpose of placing the blanket next to her cape.

"Good-night, Alexandra," he said in a clipped way.

She stood beside the brass bedstead, the light from

345

the hallway pouring into the room and casting his profile in shadow. She could see it was hopeless and, with
a slight laugh, said, "You sounded just like William
when you spoke." She felt her shoulders droop as she
surrendered to the hopelessness of the situation.

Of everything Ross might have expected Alexandra
to say in this moment, he was thrown off his stride by
hearing, *you sounded just like William*.

"What do you mean?" he asked, offended.

She rounded the bed to light an oil lamp. "It was
nothing, I suppose," she said. "But William has this
way of talking like he's a soldier issuing orders to the
troops. The way you said good night just then, I felt
like a soldier rather than — than your friend."

She remained by the bedstand and folded her hands
in front of her. She seemed very resigned, even though
Ross knew she was upset by what was happening.
She'd made no secret of her love for him, and for the
first time that night, he gave some thought to how she
might be feeling. "I never meant for it to be like this, or
to say good-bye in a way that sounded harsh," he said.
He smiled faintly, and added, "I was just trying to get
through it, I guess. Alexandra, I know this is hard for
you and I didn't plan for it to be this way. It just — *is*."

Alexandra nodded. "I know," she said. "I also know
it's asking a lot of you, but I think I'd give my life right
now if besides saying good-bye, you'd kiss me. Just
once."

Ross knew it would be a mistake, but what could he
do? She had tears in her eyes and he could see that her
heart was breaking. Was it asking so much? Just a
kiss?

He didn't answer her. Instead, he closed the door behind him and joined her by the bed. He took her chin
in his hand and was about to kiss her when she said, "I

know this might seem silly of me, but anyone from the street could see our shadows on the curtains."

He looked into blue eyes still misty with tears and felt like he was drowning. He wanted her so much right now that he was startled by the strength of his desire for her from just looking into her eyes. He didn't hesitate to put out the lamp she had just lit. The room fell to darkness as he took her gently in his arms.

Ross.

She breathed his name, and the sound floated over his face as he pressed a kiss to her lips.

It was a mistake.

Ross felt like he had been put on the back of a horse who was ready to run for all he was worth. The horse plunged into a gallop and a hot wind blew against his face, stripping him of every good intention. Alexandra's lips were moist and sensual, and he felt like he was kissing her for the first time. Her lips parted easily beneath the steady pressure of his and with a groan, as the horse drove madly on, he tasted the sweetness of her mouth, sliding his tongue against hers, desire mounting quickly within him.

He should break from her now, he thought, but he could not command his body to obey his mind. The reins had slipped through his fingers and were now flying in the wind as the wild horse set his hooves pounding over the land.

Alexandra.

The sound of Ross speaking her name was like honey in Alexandra's mouth, tasting as sweet as the feel of Ross's tongue plundering her. Her mind drifted about in a strange way, first letting her feel only the softness of his tongue, then shifting suddenly to the sensation of his arms holding her fast, keeping her safe, preventing her from falling too hard into the well of his own passion, then to her feet, which no longer touched the floor—or did they? She arched her back, bringing her breasts tight against him as she eased away from his mouth. He followed quickly, possessing her lips again and catching her neck hard with his hand. He forced his tongue deep into her mouth this time, saying his good-bye's—this time, with force. How quickly the demand of his tongue lit a fire burning so deep within her that she felt close to fainting.

"Don't go, Ross," she whispered, throwing her arms wide and pushing his away. Just as quickly, she slipped both her arms about his neck, and returned the intensity of his kiss with one of her own. This time she took possession of his mouth, running her tongue the length of his. She heard him groan, his hands drifting down her sides, tracing the lines of her ribs, waist, and hips. Slipping his hands beneath the fullness of the bustle, he caught her buttocks hard in both hands. He pressed her hips against his. He released one hand, grabbing her about the waist, and with a wild motion, drove his body up against her so that she could feel the hardness of him.

She could hardly breathe, as the days of waiting and hoping came abruptly together. He thrust against her again, and she cried out with pleasure and relief, at the same time pulling away from his mouth. "You won't leave me tonight, Ross, will you?" she asked, her eyes cloaked with desire. She could hardly see him as she looked into his eyes.

"No," he whispered. "Not tonight."

She leaned her head against his chest, and sighed contentedly. "If this is our last night together," she whispered, the warmth from his chest a pleasure against her cheek, "this is the way I would want it, with you holding me and kissing me." She felt his hand pull

348

gently on her curls. She shifted her face so that she could look up into his eyes. Her vision was adjusting to the darkness of the room, and there was enough light from the street below, sneaking through the curtains, so that she could make out his features. She touched his cheek with the back of her hand and kissed his lips, then drew back to run her fingers over his brow, his nose, and across his lips, then kissed him again.

"I love you," he said.

She slipped her hand about his neck and let him possess her mouth again. Her body felt liquid and smooth as his tongue drifted over hers. She belonged to him, and she always would, no matter whether he left or not. She tried not to think about what her life would be without him; even so, a wrenching pain of loss coursed through her. She pressed his neck hard, kissing him boldly in return, trying to rid herself of some of the unhappiness that threatened to consume her heart.

His hands moved restlessly over her, first touching her hair then sliding quickly to caress her breast as though he wanted to do both at once but was unable. His hands gripped her waist until a cry formed in her throat only to die as he thrust his tongue into her mouth. A wildness accompanied his movements as his hands slid from her waist and dug deep into her buttocks. He forced his hips into hers, all the while ravaging her mouth until she felt bruised and full.

How much she loved him.

After a moment, he eased back, his breathing labored and uneven. "I've missed you so much, Alexandra," he whispered into her curls, his breath hot on her skin. "I don't know how many times it has taken every ounce of my strength to keep from grabbing you and holding you and kissing you. I only wish I could give

349

you more, take you with me—" He broke off, unable to continue.

"It's all right," she whispered back, her own hands clenched into his hair, letting the strands run through her fingers. "It doesn't matter right now. We're together tonight, that's all I care about. Truly." She felt tears burn her eyes as his mouth touched the sensitive ridge of her neck. He kissed her skin slowly, passionately, his breath sending shivers the length of her body. Down he moved, easing his lips across her shoulder. He pulled on the sleeve of her dress, slipping it over her shoulder, and drifted his mouth across her chest until he reached the swell of her breast. The lace edging of her camisole was exposed and he ran his tongue just beneath the thin white fabric, tracing seductive figures on her skin. She shivered with pleasure as each stroke of his tongue reached farther beneath the gown and the camisole. Her breathing grew shallow as his mouth began moving over the fullness of her breast. She felt his hand pull on the fabric, in an effort to release her from the confines of the gown. The green silk slid away, along with the white cotton of the camisole, his mouth seeking, hot, and whispery until he found the peak of her breast. She wanted to cry out for the pleasure of his moist tongue and warm breath as he licked and dug at her. She wanted more, her hands becoming fitful as she ran her hands again deep into his hair, and drew him against her. *Ross.* She called out his name, begging him to take more of her.

Ross took the breast full into his mouth, and sucked hard. He heard her cry out with pleasure and felt his own body spiraling into a knot of anxious desire. Every time he touched her, moved against her, into her, kissed her or suckled her breast, he felt the horse beneath him riding faster and faster. The hot wind still beat against his face, desire moving over him, in him, through him. He pulled hard on her breast, and felt her body begin to move in a restless struggle with him. Her hips sought his, but the awkward positioning of their bodies prevented it and she moaned in frustration. It would take so little, he thought, to be released from his own passion, but he didn't want it that way, especially not tonight, when the future was dark against their love.

Again he drew away from her, this time to turn her around and undo the buttons running down her back. When the gown slipped away from her, she undid the rest of her garments as he quickly began removing his clothes. The room was chilly, and the minute they disrobed, Alexandra all but jumped into bed. She squealed and shivered as the cold sheets touched her body, complaining the whole time that she was being bitten by icicles. Ross joined her quickly, stretching out beside her and gathering her body close to his.

"We'll have this bed warm in a minute!" he cried, holding her tight.

Alexandra couldn't decide which pleased her more, being held in an affectionate, comforting embrace by Ross or being loved, touched, and kissed by him. She closed her eyes, enjoying the feel of his body against hers, the hairs on his chest that tickled her back, the legs entwined with hers, the feel of the strong muscles of his arms beneath her fingers. She loved him and gloried in being so close to him.

As the bed sheets and blankets grew warm, Alexandra felt her body begin to relax. She stretched out her legs and Ross moved with her until she could feel his hips against her buttocks, his thighs pressed against hers and his feet curled beneath her own. She moved her head to see him better, and he shifted, lifting himself up slightly so that he could look down into her face. The room seemed well lit now that she was used to the darkness, and she met Ross's gaze, her heart calling to him. "I love you," she whispered as his lips met hers.

How quickly desire again rose within her. She was always startled by it, that one moment she could be shivering with cold and the next moment, with his mouth clinging to hers, she could be trembling with desire, passion streaking through her like lightning in the midst of a violent storm. How could just the touch of his lips do so much? She heard him speak her name several times, each time thrusting his tongue deep into her mouth. She turned her body into his as he slid over on top of her. She felt the hardness of him brush over her legs. His tongue plunged into her rhythmically. Her hips grew restless, moving as his tongue moved, wanting more from him. She rubbed her hands down his back, taking pleasure in the smoothness of his skin, the firmness of his body. Down her fingers slid, until she felt the muscular lines of his buttocks, his tongue plundering her mouth, a groan issuing from his throat.

Alexandra felt passion pulsing in a steady wave, from the heat of her lips into her throat, through her heart, deep into her body, burning painfully in the depths of her womanhood. She longed for Ross to take her. He was poised above her, barely touching his chest to her breasts.

She breathed his name, taking his tongue within the pressure of her mouth, holding it fast. She felt his knees push hers aside, and she released his tongue, her head falling backward as he sought entrance. He moved slowly, a hard pressure against her delicate skin. Each movement brought twists of pleasure run-

352

ning through her until finally he was inside.

Alexandra threw her arms about Ross's neck and pulled him close to her. Now they were one, as they had been before, his body joined to hers, possessing her. She felt tears trickle from her eyes into her hair. If only they could stay like this forever.

Ross felt complete in a way he could only dimly comprehend. He moved into Alexandra, the heat of her femininity sending painful shivers of pleasure the length of him. He moved again and felt her body shape itself to him, her arms still tight about his neck. She held him fast, as though afraid to let go, and yet he could sense the tension building in her. Even her arms were stiff with passion as her hips began moving with him. He sought her mouth, and let his tongue rest within hers as he eased his lips over hers. Her breathing came in shallow gasps with each thrust. Pleasure rolled over him, tied him in knots, then rolled back. The horse moved like the wind now, pounding, driving into the night, as desire rose, and fell, to rise again.

Alexandra took in deep breaths now with each thrust of his hips into hers. Her arms were wrapped securely about his neck as his tongue played within her mouth, a moist, sensual weaving of his love with hers. Each time he moved into her, tremors of pain and desire blended into a knife of pleasure that seemed to cut through her entire body. Ecstasy beckoned her forward, only to push her away, then draw her close. She felt teased, taunted, enticed, then cast aside, only to be caught up again. Her eyes were open, but she saw nothing, except the mirror of her pleasure in Ross's eyes. He stopped kissing her and looked deep within her mind, willing pleasure to sink its hooks firmly into her. She was caught now, tears blinding her as the knife sliced her apart and a brilliant fire moved up through

353

her with sharp, piercing flames, burning pleasure ever upward. Her back arched as Ross thrust into her, faster and faster, intensifying the flames, fanning them to a white heat that consumed her, flowing in waves over her body. She cried out.

Ross covered her mouth with his own, taking the sound deep within him. The waves of her pleasure surrounded him, stroked him, tortured him, until his own desire exploded into her, streaking through him, the horse bolting wildly out of control. He held on to Alexandra, still thrusting, his body writhing over hers, until finally he was spent. He felt her hand stroking the hair at the nape of his neck, her chest shaking. He knew then that she was crying almost uncontrollably.

Chapter Forty-two

Alexandra awoke the next morning feeling like a herd of buffalo had stampeded through her head. Her eyes still felt puffy from all the crying she had done — enough tears had dampened her pillow to wash it three times over. Ross had been very upset when he found her so distressed. As fast as she could, she brought herself under control, telling him that she wasn't feeling sad, but *overjoyed* at how wonderful their union had been. She had meant it, at least in part, and maybe it was because he needed to believe her that he didn't question her explanation. She had hugged him tightly after that, but not more than ten minutes later, she asked him to leave.

He didn't put up a fight, and maybe that's why she had then cried herself to sleep. He was going to Wyoming, and that was that.

Now, as she sat up in bed, the sunlight glowing on the curtains of her hotel room, she pressed her hands to her cheeks, wondering if she would ever feel well again. She scratched her head and realized that she hadn't even brushed out her hair. The green velvet ribbon hung off to the side, and she started pulling pins from her hair. She was about to swing her legs over the side of the bed when a sharp rapping sounded on her door.

It was Ross.

"Alexandra!" he cried, his voice sounding tense, almost panicky.

She leapt from the warm bed, the hardwood cold against her feet and quickly pulled her woolen nightgown over her head. "Just a minute!" she answered, struggling to get her hand through the sleeve, but catching it on the seam.

When at last she was covered, she unlocked the door and pulled it open. Peeking around the corner, she whispered, "What is it? Come in, come in! What's wrong? You look as though you've seen a ghost."

Ross entered the room quickly and closed the door behind him. His face was lined with fear and concern as he placed a hand on each of her arms. "I don't know which to say first," he said, swallowing hard. "Listen. I'm not leaving, and neither are you. We're staying here, in Prescott. I have no life that I want so badly that I would be willing to let go of you — and I can't take you to Wyoming, so I'll raise my cattle in one of the valleys hereabouts, but something's happened." Alexandra tried to interrupt him, her heart thrilling to his words, but he said, "No! Don't say anything yet. We'll work things out, Lord willing. Only, listen, the sheriff was just here and he's brought troubling news. The fact is, he is convinced Louis Barnes is behind the attempts to take the Alexandra."

"What?" she cried, astonished. "Louis Barnes? But he's a lawman. It doesn't make sense!" She stopped suddenly, thinking about the funny way he'd related the story about killing his mule. Maybe he wasn't all that he seemed to be.

"Do you remember when Barnes came out to the

mine a few days ago?" When she nodded, he continued rapidly. "As Goodwin and I have it figured, he was at the Alexandra to size up our outfit, like asking where Crackshot was and getting a lay of the land. He was also at Powell's camp the night of the dynamite explosion. Barnes could just as easily have met with the man who tried to kill Crackshot and myself as anyone else. Anyway, he left town an hour ago and according to another deputy, Fred Spangler, he's headed out to our camp. He's going after Crackshot."

"What do you mean?" Alexandra asked, fear rising in her. "Is he going to kill him?"

"That's what we think. Only he's not operating alone."

Alexandra didn't need him to explain anything to her. It all fit. "The outlaws from Carver," she stated. "It's them, isn't it, the ones who killed Black and probably my father. Barnes is working with them, isn't he?"

"As best as we can figure," Ross said, "he's hired them to do his dirty work."

"But what about Powell?" Alexandra asked. "Do you mean he's had nothing to do with it?"

"Looks that way. He's had plenty of reason to want to hurt your father. He was in love with Mrs. McCormick before Sam arrived, and lost not only his mine to your pa, but the woman he loved, as well. Goodwin has had a man watching him since your pa was killed. His nose is clean. But as for Barnes, he's been seen in Carver more than once and at times when he was supposed to be somewhere else. Barnes was a good friend of your father's, too. Sam could have entrusted him with information about his mine that no one else knew, believing a deputy of the law would be a safe ear. Who knows."

Trying to make sense of what Ross was saying, she

asked, "How does the sheriff know Barnes has gone out to the mine?"

"Spangler has had his eye on him for two months now, since I arrived in Prescott and was proven innocent of Sam's murder. He followed Barnes not half an hour ago out toward the Dells, where he met up with one of the outlaws from Carver. Backtracking the area, he found tracks of at least half a dozen horses, maybe more."

Alexandra felt overwhelmed by all that he had just told her, first that he meant to stay, and second that he was as like to get killed as not by chasing Barnes and a band of outlaws into the forest around the Alexandra. She shook her head, feeling frantic. "You can't go out there, Ross!"she cried. "Not now! Not when we're so close to—"

"Do you want Crackshot and Cecilia to die? They will if something isn't done fast! They're all alone at the camp and Powell and his crew, who might have been able to help, are here in town."

"I'll come with you!"she said, pulling away from him. "I've gotta come with you. I know how to handle a Winchester if you've got an extra one. It won't take me a minute to get dressed."

"No, darlin'," he said quietly, watching her rush from her bureau to her carpetbag and back again. "I'd be worried sick the entire time, knowing you might get shot in the crossfire. Go out to Mrs. McCormick's and wait there for me."

Alexandra knew what he said made sense, but as she stopped rummaging about in her drawers and retraced her steps to him, a dark feeling of foreboding came over her. Had they come this far only to separated by a gunfight at the Alexandra? She threw her arms about his neck and bid him a hasty good-bye, trying not to let him see the fear that rode her heart. As he turned to open the door, she smiled nervously and said, "Now don't you go getting killed on me, you hear?"

He smiled at her over his shoulder. "What? And miss dandling our grandchildren on my knees? Never!"

Alexandra breathed a sigh of relief, letting his optimism infect her. Of course he would be all right, of course he would. Ross Halleck had lived too many years on the frontier not to know how to handle trouble.

But after he had been gone a few minutes, and she was still brushing out the knots in her tangled hair, she became as restless as a rattlesnake on a hot desert rock. She had to do something, but what?

Goodwin had rounded up a posse of some seven men, including Fred Spangler and another man who stuttered. Ross looked all of the riders over and knew that there wasn't one among them who wasn't fit to ride the river with. The horses were all fresh and eager to run, so they were traveling at an easy lope. According to Spangler, who had ridden in only that morning from Carver, they weren't more than an hour behind the band of Mexican desperadoes who Goodwin was convinced had also killed the Widow Ferguson and her children.

Ross tried not to think of Crackshot and Cecilia alone at the camp. An hour! It might as well be a day. If Crackshot was caught unguarded, he'd be dead, and Cecilia, as well, if not worse.

Crackshot stood not twelve feet into the mouth of

the Alexandra, and spoke aloud. "Well, I'll be damned," he said. "Sam, if you wasn't the strangest man I ever knowed." He was staring up at the ceiling of the main shaft which was supported by square-set beams. All morning he had been hammering away at a section of the rock and had uncovered Wingfield's bonanza. It was a stope, all right, seven feet across, by his best reckoning, by four feet. It went straight up and looked about as pure as anything he'd ever seen in his life. It was a fortune.

It was only by accident he'd found it in the first place. He'd been working for two hours since breakfast, and had asked himself for the hundredth time why he stayed on. The answer was always the same: Sam had been so sure of his claim. And Crackshot sensed it had nothing to do with an argonaut's fancy, but rather with hard facts. He would have returned to his campfire and poured himself a cup of coffee as was his usual routine, but Cecilia was in one of her quirky moods, and he thought it wise to just let her be.

He had decided to sit in the main shaft, plopping down and leaning his head against the wall. That was when he'd seen it, just a sliver of gold catching his eye because he happened to be seated at the right angle. Something told him right away that this was it, this was what Sam had known about his mine, but hadn't told anyone, at least not Crackshot. Yet, someone knew about it, but who?

Now, as he stood staring at the uncoverd stope, he turned the mystery over and over in his mind. Did Lloyd Powell know? Powell had always been a slick one, but somehow he couldn't imagine Lloyd murdering anyone. Stealing from them, maybe, but murder? Not even for a fortune.

Who, then? And who would Sam have confided in?

Apparently, not even Mrs. McCormick knew of the stope. Well, he couldn't figure it out. Maybe when Ross and Alexandra returned they could come up with something.

Fear began working in his mind as he stared up at the rich shaft of gold. Men would kill for this, and a lot of men could be made rich by jumping the claim. He felt uneasy, his skin prickling, and when Cecilia started up with her wailing, he nearly dropped his britches. Confound that woman!

He moved quickly to the entrance to the mine, where he picked up his Winchester. Ever since he was a boy, he had been in the habit of keeping it close by. He sensed he would need it now.

He saw Cecilia rocking on the ground by the campfire, and was about to call to her when movement on the ridge across the meadow caught his eye. Instinctively, he stepped back into the shadows of the mine and scanned the hillside opposite the mine. He couldn't see anything, but he knew someone was out there.

Cecilia moaned loudly into the air, her sounds eerie and wild. He'd never heard her quite like this. Crackshot knew a deep sadness suddenly, and felt that his life had suddenly approached a narrow footbridge across a deep chasm. His feet felt stuck in one place, like a nightmare. He couldn't move. He knew he needed to call to Cecilia, to bring her into the mine to safety beside him, but he was having a hard time getting his mouth open. His heart began racing, his breath grew shallow and pulsed in his chest. He called to her, but his voice cracked with fear. He knew she was going to die if he didn't do something. He took in deep breaths and started speaking her name and finally let out with a wild cry. *"Cecilia!"*

At that moment it seemed the woods about the valley exploded with the thunder of gunfire. Bullets sang against the rocky hillside at the entrance to the mine and several made their way deep within. At the same time, the shouting of her name seemed to have broken the spell, keeping Cecilia locked to the ground by the campfire so that when the guns first sounded in the meadow, she had leaned into a sprint suddenly and was flying toward the mine.

Crackshot watched her graying hair fly behind her as she sped across the boards stretched over the creek, the buckskin dress dancing with the fast pumping of her knees. He couldn't hear anything, but saw only her face as she struggled to evade the bullets that flew around her. Her mouth was open, she was fighting for breath, her arms flailing in her flight. She was a woman who had known nothing but sidesteps in what should have been a good life but what had been filled with hardship and pain. It wasn't right somehow that trouble had snapped at her heels like a hungry coyote.

She cleared the opening and Crackshot called to her with relief. She looked toward him, smiling, and spoke his name just as a bullet slammed through the ribs of her back and came out her right breast. Her body was spun over once and once again as she crashed to the floor of the mine.

Crackshot threw himself at her, engulfing her head with his arms and holding her. His heart felt as if it was being torn from him. "Cecilia!" he cried over and over. Her eyes fluttered slightly, then opened. He couldn't believe she was still alive. "Darlin', darlin'," he cried, petting her face with his fingers.

"Mr. Peters," she whispered, her hand coming up to her breast. She hit herself once and said, "You make

362

me pretty." A long breath escaped her as she gave up her life and died in his arms.

Crackshot began rocking over her as he had seen her rock so many times before. He moaned in the way she had often moaned. Tears ran down his face, and he didn't bother to wipe them away. He didn't know how long he stayed like that, with the sound of gunplay and bullets brushing the air around him. Only when one clipped his arm, laying a burning track on his skin, did he gain a sense that he was still in a fight for his own life. He dove backward, pressing himself against the side wall, checking the rounds held within his Winchester, and, for his own benefit, firing once to make certain that his rifle was in working order.

How long could he last? he wondered. Maybe that depended on just how badly the men out there wanted the Alexandra. But as he looked up at the enormous block of gold, he knew he was a dead man.

Chapter Forty-three

By the time Alexandra had donned her blue serge skirt and white cotton blouse and had her hair secured tightly in a braid, she knew what to do. Within fifteen minutes, she had hired a horse for herself and found Dr. Adams, who had come out to the Alexandra previously in an effort to save Mrs. Horn. She explained the situation to him, expressing her conviction that he could be needed since the desparadoes from Carver were men with a vicious and cruel reputation.

For the space of a full ten seconds, the doctor had stared at her, appearing to weigh all she had told him. After that, he was a whirlwind of activity, gathering his equipment together, bringing his own sturdy Appaloosa up from the stables, and barking orders to his wife, who received his commands with an unruffled calm, bidding him only to be careful.

As they traveled at a steady clip, Alexandra explained to the doctor all that had happened over the past few weeks and months, in particular about her father's death. He listened politely to her, his own sense of urgency growing the longer she spoke.

"It would seem," he said after a time, "that you and Mr. Halleck are both lucky to still be with us. You did right coming to me."

"I'm just so scared," she said, setting her sights on the trail and spurring her horse on.

When they reached the McCormick ranch, Alexandra stopped to inform Mrs. McCormick about what had happened and was startled by her suggestion. "I'll gather my ranch hands and we will come out with you. Goodwin might need more firepower than he's allowed for. I'll bring the buckboard, too, in case anyone needs to be carted back to town."

Relief poured over Alexandra. For the last mile, she had begun to wonder if she wasn't taking a terrible risk with Dr. Adams's life. It had occurred to her that if the forces were in any way unequal, he might have to take up his rifle instead of his black medical bag.

"Thank you!" she cried, rejoining the doctor afterward and explaining the change in plans.

She didn't mistake the lightening of the good doctor's face as he responded with a nod of his head. "I won't pretend I'm not happy about this," he said. "If these are the same men who wouldn't hesitate to burn a woman to death, along with her children, I wasn't looking forward to the possibility of having to meet them myself. I don't like to admit it, but I'm not handy with a gun."

Within minutes, a large group of battle-ready men were mounted on fresh horses and loping toward Bee Mountain. Alexandra and the doctor rode behind, with Mrs. McCormick promising to follow along as soon as she could load her wagon with a few supplies.

Feeling better than she had in the past two hours, Alexandra trained her heart to a steady, careful beat. When fears for Ross rose up in her mind, as they did frequently, she set them aside. She would know soon enough, her heart warned her.

Ross led the way to the Alexandra as soon as the terrain grew rough and the trail began fading in and out. Snow still obscured shady stretches of the road where the sun didn't warm up the land behind outcroppings of rock and tall trees. They were within twenty minutes of the camp and Ross listened intently for the sounds of a gun battle. He strained to hear beyond the movement of the men and horses behind him and over the breeze that blew a steady humming in his ears. Only the sky and earth greeted him, though, and he wasn't sure whether to be glad about it or frightened out of his socks. When at last he heard the faint popping sound of a distant gun, he breathed a sigh of enormous relief and kicked his horse hard on the flanks. If there was still fighting going on, then Crackshot was alive.

The gelding picked up his stride and moved quickly along the winding trail. Never had Ross been more impatient to be at his destination than he was now, knowing that a good friend was in desperate need of his help.

When he finally rode within a quarter mile of the camp, he dismounted and tied his horse to a tree. He didn't need to motion for the others to do the same. It was understood. Ross had long since described the environs of the meadow and the mine to Goodwin and his men. Fred Spangler would take two men and head south to the riverbed and come up to the camp from the direction of the stamp mill. Three men would fan out and locate any of the outlaws positioned on the ridge overlooking the camp and disarm them if possible. Goodwin and Ross would head north, and come down through the forest behind the cabin. Each was prepared to kill if he had to.

Gun in hand, Ross headed north, cutting east in gradual stages. He crouched low, pausing every few feet to listen. In the meadow he could hear the exchange of several rounds as faint popping noises gave way to loud barks the closer they drew to the camp. The smell of gunsmoke was in the air. Where was Crackshot? he wondered. There could be only one answer, and he breathed easier because of it—his friend had to be in the mine. It was a perfect place to make a stand. He only hoped Cecilia was there, too.

Behind a thicket, Ross heard the familiar whinny of several nervous horses. He moved stealthily now, not knowing whether any of the bandits would have been left behind to tend the horses. He would have skirted the area, but he wanted to see how many mounts there were so that he could have an idea of the number of men they were facing. When he rounded the edge of the thicket, his Peacemaker held at gut-level, he glanced quickly around for a sign of one of the desperadoes, but saw no one. Then he counted the horses, and came up with a staggering dozen.

He glanced at Goodwin, whose face had grown grave. He ground his teeth together, his brows furrowed deeply. Ross could see he was angry, partly with himself for having underestimated the number of outlaws Barnes would bring with him to kill one man.

The deepening resolution Ross saw in his face, however, strengthened his own desire to confront the men who had robbed him of his ranch in Texas, who had murdered Alexandra's father and now threatened Crackshot's life. He moved faster now, feeling compelled to reach the camp before these men gained one more victory. He heard them whooping and jeering, calling to Crackshot in broken English. Where Barnes was, he couldn't imagine, though it wouldn't have surprised him if he was hiding until the fight was over.

Not twenty yards northeast, Ross and Goodwin stumbled suddenly upon three of the bandits lounging by a stream that cut in from the north. They were playing cards.

Somehow the sight of them at ease while their *compañeros* were attacking Crackshot set Ross's blood to boiling. He walked grimly forward, his gun at waist level, and told them to throw down their arms. The men were surprised, each of them heavily armed. They were a mean-looking lot, one of them scarred across the face from an old knife wound. Thick black hair hung heavily to the shoulders of each, and Ross saw the blend of Apache and Mexican in at least two of the bandits.

"Drop it!" he commanded again. He could hear Goodwin marching behind him and to the right. But the bandits merely smiled at each other, drew their weapons, and opened fire.

The small gorge screamed with gunfire for a short burst of seconds. The air reeked of smoke, and when silence again reigned, the bandits lay strewn on the rocky streambed, blood spattered onto the snow. Ross wasn't sure why he had escaped injury, but he thought maybe it was because he was too mad to get hit. The men were skilled with iron and he turned quickly to find Goodwin clutching his left arm and sinking down to sit on a rock. "You all right?" he queried.

Goodwin nodded, but then gestured toward the bandits. He was right, Ross thought, better make sure they're all dead or there might be the devil to pay. When he was certain none of them would see the light of day again, he helped Goodwin tie up his arm, then both men again circled northeast. The sounds of increased shooting suggested that more of Barnes's army had been confronted, but what the outcome was, neither men could guess.

By the time Ross and Goodwin came up behind the cabin, there had been at least a half dozen volleys. Goodwin's arm had taken a hit full into the muscle and the bullet was lodged there. He was in considerable pain. Ross told him to stay back and cover him as he edged forward along the side of the building to better see what was happening in the meadow below.

As he inched forward, his gun drawn and held close to his face, he listened carefully for the sounds of movement nearby. His eyes scanned the forest, leading southeast above the mine. Just as he was halfway down the length of the cabin, he saw movement on the ridge above the Alexandra, dropped to his knees, and fired. A bullet burnt across his cheek, becoming embedded into the cabin wall. His own shot hit home, and one of the outlaws rose up and toppled form the cliff to land at the opening of the mine.

"Spangler!" Ross called out across the meadow. He could get hit in a crossfire now and wanted to let the other men know his position.

"Here!" Fred called back. "Two of 'em dead by the mill. Another dropped by the tent. Don't know if he's dead or playing possum."

"What about Barnes?" he called.

"No sign of him."

Ross thought for a minute. "We've got four more left," he shouted back at Fred, "and that includes Barnes."

"Make it two!" one of the deputies called from the ridge.

Ross was startled. Could it really be this easy? But then they'd taken them all by surprise. Where was Barnes, though, and the last of the outlaws? He looked back at Goodwin, who was sweating and pale as he sat by a tree and held his arm close to his chest. "What do you think?" he asked the sheriff.

"In these woods? They could be anywhere. And we're still only guessing that twelve horses meant a dozen men. There could be more somewhere else."

Ross yelled back to the men asking if they had come across tethered horses. When everyone responded in the negative, both Ross and Goodwin thought it likely that twelve was the number with which they had to work. Two left, but where were they? Then he knew. The mine. The second entrance.

When Crackshot heard a volley of gunfire that wasn't directed against him, he had been at first stunned, remaining crouched behind a barrier of rocks he had built as fast as he could several feet into the mine. He was well fortified for defending himself, but with only one problem: he had run out of bullets fast and, for the past fifteen minutes, he had been waiting for the outlaws to discover his desperate situation.

The first exchange he had heard sounded distant, possibly well beyond the ridge. It had filled him with such relief that he actually dropped his head on his arm and wept. Still, he knew he was in trouble, a state made all the worse, almost intolerable, by the fact that Cecilia lay close by, her eyes half open, her white skin lifeless.

Gunplay had continued after the first volley, but always away from the opening of the mine, so that Crackshot knew for a certainty help had arrived. He didn't dare move, though, not until he was sure the outlaws had been beaten.

Now, as he heard Ross call out to Fred Spangler, he

really started breathing easier. Two men had left, but where?

Behind him, he heard the smallest sound, like the whisk of a shoe against rubble. Oh, Lord, no! Someone was in the mine. The other entrance! He had forgotten clean about it.

He sat up quickly, aiming his rifle into the depths of the shaft and cried out, "Hold it right there or I'll send you bleeding all the way to the judgment seat!"

His enemy moved into view, light from the opening of the mine glinting off the blade of the outlaw's knife. "You got no bullets, amigo," the bandido said, his accent thick. "And no one knows I'm in here." He laughed low as he walked forward.

Instinctively, Crackshot pulled the trigger, the empty chamber clicking miserably. Again the man laughed.

Crackshot watched him advance slowly forward, his black eyes alive with pleasure. "I kill you, then I leave. Very simple, very clean."

Rising to his feet, Crackshot held the rifle in hand and prepared for the killer to approach. Every muscle was readied and waiting. The outlaw was swift, running toward him as Crackshot swung the rifle at him. It seemed to glance off his shoulder, and Crackshot felt himself twist sideways at the same time the man caught him about the neck, holding the knife to his throat. "Not a bad day to die, señor. The sun shines and your woman is already dead. You may say a prayer if you like."

Ross left the safety of the cabin wall convinced that there was only one place the last bandit would be — in the mine itself. He had heard no gunfire coming from

371

the Alexandra and was convinced Crackshot was out of ammunition. He sprinted toward the mouth of the mine, the meadow silent behind him just as he expected it to be. He felt his heart pumping hard with fear for his friend. He ran up the ramp of tailings, the muscles of his legs painfully tight. He bolted into the mine, saw the loose black hair of the bandit as he held Crackshot tight in the crook of his arm. He didn't pause for a second, but took aim and fired.

Both men fell backward, Crackshot landing on top of the outlaw. But from deep within the mine, the sound of a rifle roared, blossoming orange. Ross took the slug in his stomach and fell sideways. He rolled over once, and with every ounce of strength pulled himself up on his elbows. Louis Barnes walked into view, his own face white with shock. Ross drew a bead on him, fired, fired again, and watched Barnes drop to the stone floor of the mine.

It's over, Ross thought, his mind drifting quickly away from him, as pain, immense pain, flooded his body. Then blackness engulfed him.

Chapter Forty-four

Ross saw Crackshot being torn apart by timber wolves. He felt his friend's pain as though it was his own. He wanted to save him, but Crackshot was pinned to a tree, his arms and legs tied down tight. He had to help him! He struggled to free himself of his bonds, but he couldn't. He called out to Crackshot, but the wolves snapped and snarled and started coming toward him. He screamed as one leaped onto his stomach, sinking his fangs deep. He was falling suddenly, back and back into a black, bottomless hole . . .

Alexandra stood by the doctor, watching him cut Ross open as several men held him down. She moved numbly, refusing to feel anything, but obeying the doctor's commands. He took forever to get the bullet out of Ross. It was buried deep, and there was so much blood and so much stitching up to do afterward. By the time he was done, Ross was unconscious. The doctor didn't think he would live through the night.

* * *

Ross watched his ranch burn and burn, the flames hot on his face. He saw horses racing madly around the corrals . . . everything was on fire! He tried to put the fire out, but he couldn't move. He'd gotten hurt somehow, and if he so much as lifted a hand, he screamed in pain. The dark of night moved in like a heavy fog . . .

Alexandra found the days blending together in a long nightmare of waiting, hoping, praying, begging God to spare Ross's life, of mopping his damp brow, changing soaked sheets, of forcing liquid down his throat, of not sleeping, of listening to him mumble and cry out in the night.

Mrs. McCormick helped the first two days, but after that, Alexandra was left alone with Ross, to follow the doctor's careful orders. All she could do was wait and see. He was still alive, but just barely.

Ross was so cold. He was in his tent, and a storm had come down off the mountain, tearing up the canvas and exposing him to the biting wind. Snow piled up on top of him and he couldn't seem to do anything about it. He shook with cold and called out for Katherine to help him, but she just smiled at him and drove away in her buggy. A white mist swirled around him. . . .

The chills seemed worse to Alexandra than the sweats. Ross's body convulsed with shivering and no amount of blankets seemed able to make him comfortable. She built up the fire so that the cabin became as warm as a summer's day, but still he huddled and shook and begged for help.

The field was pleasant, smelling so sweet of roses and violets. Ross had never seen so many colors in his life as he walked through the meadow alive with spring flowers. They were waist-high and he let his hands ripple across the top of the buds, the petals feathery soft against the palms of his hands. The sun was bright, almost brilliant. Even the sky was a pale yellow instead of blue. He closed his eyes, and walked and walked. He wanted to stay in this meadow forever. . . .

"Ross!" Alexandra shouted. He was lying still as death, his body quiet and peaceful. Too peaceful. She gripped his shoulders hard and shook him. "Don't you leave me! Do you hear me! *Ross!*"

He would stay in this meadow for the rest of his life, he decided. He couldn't remember knowing such peace before. All the pain was gone, and he felt whole and alive. He heard someone calling his name. He recognized the voice. How distant it was! Miles away. He heard his name again and turned around. He saw Alexandra's face, and just as he shaped the thought that he wanted to bring her to his meadow, pain surged over him like a wall of floodwaters. He writhed under the torture of the knife slicing through his stomach. He sucked air deep into his chest and cried out for someone to help him. Again he fell into a void of darkness . . .

"How much longer?" Alexandra wailed as she took hold of Ross's hand and pressed it to her cheek. Tears poured down her face. She wanted to let him go, but she couldn't. She needed him here. They had babies to raise and a ranch to build. Ross had grandchildren to dandle on his knee.

Ross tried to open his eyes, but the effort seemed beyond his ability. His mind was cloudy and gray; it swirled in and out, responding mechanically to the spoon at his mouth, then the glass. He wanted to speak, but his throat was thick and dry. It was hard to breathe. He felt a cool cloth on his forehead, then his neck, and down his arms. He heard a voice and a strange, distant thumping sound. Where was he?

The damp cloth reached his hand, and with a tremendous effort, he took hold of the hand and squeezed it, hoping that whoever was at the end of his grip would at least talk to him.

Alexandra felt the pressure of his fingers, and gasped. "Ross?" she whispered. She watched him nod, just barely, and her eyes filled with tears. "Oh, Ross, you're back."

He was confused by her words and forced himself to speak, "Where — have I — been?"

Alexandra laughed, stroking his hand and moving from her chair to kneel beside the bed. She pressed his fingers to her cheek and said, "You were shot up pretty bad, my love. You almost didn't make it."

Memories flooded Ross's mind. He saw Crackshot and the outlaw, he saw the flash of a blade, he remembered shooting, and, digging deep into his mind, he could see Louis Barnes toppling over on his face.

"Sleep," he murmured, his mind slipping away again.

"Yes, sleep."

Ross felt the cool pillow beneath his face. His eyes were open, just barely. He couldn't remember ever being this weak. His body felt as if it had been tied up in a knot, wrung real tight, then stomped on by a few hundred wild horses. Pain still rode him hard. Even taking deep breaths hurt his stomach like fire on an open wound.

He heard the same pounding noise as he had earlier. What was it? He struggled to open his eyes all the way, and when he did, he saw Alexandra standing by the window of the cabin, looking out at a blue sky. She was stretching her back as if she was very tired and he wondered what she had been doing to cause her to be so sore. She turned around, looked at him, and he received a shock. Her face was haggard with suffering, her brow lined with worry. What was wrong?

Then he remembered. He had almost died.

Alexandra smiled at him, and drew her chair close to the bed so that she could look at him. "How do you feel?" she whispered, taking her hand in his.

Ross wasn't even sure he could speak. "Sick," he returned hoarsely.

Alexandra nodded in sympathy. "It's been three weeks."

He was stunned. "Three? Are you sure?" He watched her nod again. *Three weeks*. He must've been hurt bad. He rolled his head and found himself staring at the ceiling. A thin cobweb hung from one of the rafters. He was suddenly grateful to be alive, to be *seeing* anything, to be feeling Alexandra's hand caressing his own, to be breathing, even though it hurt like hell, to be hearing the thump of the stamp mill. *The stamp mill?* He glanced at Alexandra. "Why is the mill running?" he asked.

For the first time, Alexandra's face lost some of its weariness as she laughed. "You won't believe this," she cried, "but Crackshot found my father's bonanza. It's a stope, Ross. A big one—seven or eight feet across, going straight up through the roof of the mountain. We'll have enough money to buy as many beeves as you want, as much land as you want, just about anything you've longed for all these years."

Ross's mind was not working perfectly. He had a hard time deciding whether he was just having another dream like the one where he had walked through a pretty meadow full of colorful flowers or whether Alexandra was in fact telling him he was rich, that *they* were rich. "I could buy my ranch in Wyoming," he murmured to himself.

His mind jumped backward and he asked about Louis Barnes. All he could remember was firing at him, then dropping into a pit so black he didn't think he would ever find his way out.

When Alexandra spoke, Ross could hear that the quality of her voice had changed. She sounded sad, but he wasn't sure exactly why. "Goodwin figures my father told Barnes about the stope before he left for Missouri," she said. "We'll never know now, since Barnes is dead."

A stope. Barnes dead. The mill running again. "Are the miners back?"

378

"A different crew this time, but Cornish all the same."

Even though he wanted to know more, especially why Alexandra sounded so different suddenly, Ross felt his mind growing misty. Closing his eyes, he drifted away, but not before he realized she was crying.

Alexandra watched Ross fall asleep. For a long time she sat looking at him, at the thin, drawn appearance of his face, the black hair tousled on the pillow, the cracked, dry lips. He had a long way to go before he was ready to ride up to Wyoming.

Knowing Ross had spoken from his heart when he mentioned buying a ranch in the wild northern territory, Alexandra could not help but wonder if he would decide in the end to purchase the homestead that had been a heartfelt longing of his for so many years. She thought it likely enough that tears plopped onto her blue skirt, and she didn't even bother to hold them back. She loved him so much, but their path together had been so rocky. Would they ever finally be of one mind?

Within two days, Ross was eating well and was able to talk easily. Alexandra had decided to say little until he actually asked about all that had happened. As for Wyoming, she had no real desire to discover what his intentions were.

When he finished a bowl of soup and a hefty slab of fresh-baked bread, Ross finally begged Alexandra to sit down beside him and tell him everything.

"First," he said, "did I get there—I mean, what about Crackshot? Is he dead?"

"No, no!" Alexandra cried. "He's very much alive. In fact he wasn't hurt at all. Not even a scratch except where a bullet singed his arm."

"That's good. I was so worried, so afraid we'd ride up too late. Cecilia's all right, isn't she?"

Alexandra found it hard to give shape to the words. She took several deep breaths before she could bring herself to give him the sad news. "She was killed trying to take cover in the mine," she said, her heart still burdened by the tragedy. Fairness had not ruled Cecilia's life, and the manner in which she had died seemed like one final miserable twist in a long string of hardships no person ought to endure. "We buried her alongside Miriam and the baby. Crackshot still has a funny look in his eyes. I expect he will for some time to come."

She then told him about Fred Spangler and his men, all of whom had survived, and how they had dug deep graves for the outlaws on the other side of the river. "They buried the men as fast as they could. The graves aren't even marked. No one wants these men to be remembered. Goodwin said he figured the good Lord would know best what to do with them anyway." She laughed slightly. "I know this is going to sound funny," she said. "but they didn't even keep the horses—they turned them loose in Mescal Gulch."

Ross didn't ask another question after that, but looked hard at Alexandra for a minute. "You look a little better today," he finally said. "Are you getting more sleep? I've only just started to realize what a tough time this has been for you." He smiled, as he continued. "Do you know this is the second time you've cared for me when I've been shot up?"

Alexandra nodded. "It seems such a long time ago."

"Only three months," he said, the smile fading from his lips. "So much has happened." He sighed and then patted the bed next to him. "I don't suppose you would come lie down beside me for a little while.

380

I'd like to put my arm around you and hold you."

Alexandra felt her heart grow tight in her chest. She didn't hesitate to ease herself onto the bed and stretch herself out next to him. She knew he was still in considerable pain and she did everything she could to keep from disturbing him. When he slipped his arm about her shoulder and gave her a squeeze, she placed her hand lightly on his chest. He was wearing a flannel nightshirt, and the fabric was warm beneath her fingers.

"So what do you think we should do with all our money?" he asked.

Alexandra felt her heart leap in her breast. She was afraid to ask the question, but she did anyway. "What would you like to do more than anything else?" Her heart tapped out a strong, frightened rhythm as she waited for his answer. When he didn't speak right away, her ears began pounding with fear.

Finally, he said, "You know, I'd like to head north."

Alexandra couldn't help releasing a heavy, mournful sigh. She hadn't meant to, but Wyoming had been hanging over her head, and now it just hit her with the force of a sledgehammer. "Wyoming," she stated flatly.

"Why do you say that?" he asked.

Alexandra twisted her head up and around so that she could see his face. "Well, Wyoming is north, isn't it? Isn't that what you meant."

"No," he responded, surprised. "I was thinking of Sions. I've been told there's a lot of good grazing land up there. It's just on the other side of Chino Valley."

Alexandra blinked her eyes several times. "You're talking about Prescott," she cried.

"Well, of course I am! I told you as much on New Year's Day. You and I are staying here, we're getting married as soon as I can get you to town, and then we'll buy a ranch, or some land, or some of both. Besides, Samantha's here! You couldn't leave your only sister!" He paused for a moment, then continued. "There's just one thing I want to know, though if you still feel like you can't tell me, I suppose I'll have to forget all about it, but — " He broke off, apparently reluctant to pose the question.

Alexandra was surprised, wondering what he meant to ask her. "What is it?" she queried softly. "I can't think of anything I *couldn't* say to you now."

"Well," he drawled. "just what was the condition to your uncle's will?"

Alexandra chuckled. "You won't believe it for a minute," she responded. "If I wanted to inherit his money, I had to marry William."

"What?" he cried. "Why, I've never heard of such a thing. Marry William?" He drew in his breath, as a second, more profound thought struck him. "You gave up a fortune for me?"

Alexandra couldn't keep from teasing him a little. "Not for you!" she responded. "I would've married just about anybody before I walked down the aisle with William Bradshaw. You had nothing to do with it!"

His mind seemed stuck on his original notion, however, as he hugged her to him and repeated, "You gave up a fortune for me." He was silent for a moment. "We'll have a good life together, you and me," he said at last. "We'll have maybe ten or twenty kids, all of 'em born with a rope in one hand and a branding iron in the other. I wonder how long it would take to get some

382

of that eastern stock out here. You know, I think the future's in fattening up the beef you have, then selling it to local markets . . ."

Alexandra let him talk as she snuggled her head against his shoulder and took his hand in her own as it rested on her arm. Her gaze drifted about the room. Her father had built this cabin and worked this mine and unwittingly had given Ross to her. She felt full of gratitude as she intertwined her fingers through Ross's. She would need a milk cow and some chickens for their new home. She wanted some ducks, too, but just to sit in a pond out in front of her house and make noises every time a horse rode through. She'd drive over to see Samantha every week, maybe on Sundays after church services. And every night, no matter how tired either of them was, she would make Ross hold her like this and he could tell her anything he wanted to while she would dream of the future.